ZANE PRESENTS

Bad AS IN GOOD

A NOVEL

Dear Reader:

It's always a pleasure to introduce new authors in the Strebor Books family. J. Lovelace has penned a debut novel that is sure to tantalize readers. It is complete with drama, relationships and challenging decisions as we follow lovers Tariq and Erin.

While the two experience the ups and downs in their adventures, they explore past romances that are eye-opening. Sit back and relax as you travel along this journey in search of truth and trust, with roadblocks of temptation.

As always, thanks for supporting the authors of Strebor Books. We strive to bring you the future in prolific literature today by publishing cutting-edge, inspiring, thought-provoking titles.

Blessings,

Zane

Publisher
Strebor Books
www.simonandschuster.com

ZANE PRESENTS

Bad

AS IN

GOOD

A NOVEL

J. LOVELACE

SBI

STREBOR BOOKS

NEW YORK LONDON TORONTO SYDNEY

Strebor Books
P.O. Box 6505
Largo, MD 20792
http://www.streborbooks.com

ISBN 978-1-59309-570-3
ISBN 978-1-4767-5880-0 (ebook)
LCCN 2014931191

First Strebor Books trade paperback edition July 2014

Cover design: www.mariondesigns.com
Cover photograph: © Keith Saunders Photos

10 9 8 7 6 5 4 3 2 1

Manufactured in the United States of America

For information regarding special discounts for bulk purchases,
please contact Simon & Schuster Special Sales at 1-866-506-1949
or business@simonandschuster.com

The Simon & Schuster Speakers Bureau can bring authors to your live event.
For more information or to book an event, contact the Simon & Schuster Speakers
Bureau at 1-866-248-3049 or visit our website at www.simonspeakers.com.

To a family that loves me and a husband that supports me.

CHAPTER 1

Tariq

Four years ago...

There she was. My boo. My wifey. My ace boon-coon. Whatever people or I was willing to call her, minus the official title of *wife*, she was. And there *she* was tonguing some other poor soul down in the middle of the Japanese steakhouse she'd been fighting to get me to take her to. I wasn't down for all that teppanyaki and sushi. I always passed, but that ain't stop her from going out and finding her another dude to take her there while she used the guise of "shopping with the girls" to keep me from being on to her games. I eventually realized that when she kept coming home glowing with no shopping bags, she wasn't really shopping.

She ain't know I followed her this time. Well, technically, I wasn't *really* following her. Ain't like I waited ten minutes after she left to hop into my car, turn off my headlights, and tail her from streetlight to streetlight while I stayed two cars behind. I was smart and less crazy about all this. Outside of her credit cards *not* being maxed out on Prada bags and Gucci shoes, I had no real proof that she was stepping out on me. I couldn't justify, to my mama or myself, that I had a reason to stalk my own woman. However, I had to consider the asinine possibility that my congeniality may have forced her into the arms of *Mr. Convenience*. I thought up the least likely place she'd expect me to spot her, grabbed the darkest table I could find, and posted up.

The first hour there, I was amped. I sat there with the menu covering my face, dodging waiters and customers who ain't feel comfortable with a black man hiding out in a dimly lit booth of a Japanese steakhouse. Every time a woman walked in, I hid my face and gorged on saké. The second and third hour, I couldn't dodge the waiters anymore. I had to order something or risk being thrown out for looking plain weird. After filling up on Kobe beef, rice and broccoli, I lost the initial zeal I had. I started to settle into the notion that I was paranoid and my woman really was out there watching her money and enjoying the comforts of window-shopping.

The fourth hour, I asked for the check. To my server's delight, he dropped my dinner bill on my table and skipped away. As I pulled a few bills from my wallet, I noticed a tall, statuesque woman stroll in. Large bumblebee shades covered her eyes and rested on top of her high, taupe cheekbones. She wore a tight black dress that pushed her breasts together and cupped her ass in all the right places. Her brown, curly hair bounced on top of her shoulders as she glided to an empty table. I stared her down and watched her remove her glasses. Bright, almond-shaped chestnut eyes, shaded by long overlapping eyelashes, almost took my breath away.

My waiter returned asking for his money, but I shooed him away to watch as my woman sat alone and waited. I was hoping she was waiting for her girls to roll through. *Maybe they needed to eat before heading home*, I thought. After a quick glance at my cell, I ignored the fact that she didn't call me to let me know she'd be home late while I focused on how that wasn't the dress she was wearing when she left the house. When the waiter handed her a drink without even taking an order, it was clear that she'd been here long enough to have a usual.

Suddenly, some dude walked in with a bouquet of flowers and a big-ass smile. He was a tall linebacker-lookin' dude with a thick neck and a wide frame. His skin was dark as night with eyes that were beady and mischievous. His long, oblong face reminded me of a walking horse, yet, as he held a bouquet of flowers, my woman stared up at him as if he was a modern-day marvel. Although according to her, she hated flowers, but her face lit up as she jumped up and down in her seat when he placed the bouquet in her arms. I wanted to believe that this was their first time meeting. I could forgive an innocent slip-up. But the way he kissed her hello, the way he wrapped his arm around her waist as if to proclaim that she was *his* boo, wifey, or ace boon-coon only solidified the telling fact that they were more than first-time acquaintances. I noticed the way she giggled and blushed as he brushed her hair behind her ears. The way he rested the palm of his hand on her lap irked me. But what really did me in was how he squeezed the back of her neck, my woman's neck, to exude his dominance, then pulled her in close to devour her lips to prove his ownership of who I *thought* was my woman. From the outside looking in, she was *his* woman and I was another poor sap that couldn't help but stare.

I glared at them. Even as my waiter rudely tapped his foot, my eyes stayed glued on the show they put on before me. She ain't care who saw. I contemplated walking out and dealing with her when she got home, but that wouldn't be the type of guy I was. I slapped the money for my meal on the table and bumped my server as I walked in their direction.

"Deja," I said when I reached their table. "How you been?" I spread my lips to show off all my teeth and continue the charade she put on.

I wanted her to jump when she saw me and stutter her words as she scrambled to determine how to recover. When she looked up at me, she dropped her shoulders and took a sip of her drink. Her date asked her, "Do you know this guy?"

I tensed my jaw and squeezed my fists. "This guy?" I asked. "Yeah, Deja, *do* you know *this guy?*"

My woman avoided eye contact but refused to move away from his hold. He kept his arm around her waist and she kept her hand between his thighs. Luckily, for them, a table separated my anger and my fists. "What are you doing here, Tariq?"

"I finally decided to try this place out like you been begging me to. It ain't half-bad. What the fuck are you doing here?"

She took a deep breath and exchanged glances with her date. Staring at the dude, I realized that he had pulled his lips in while he squeezed his fists as if *he* were uncomfortable with me standing there. "I'm Traevon. How you two know each other, bruh?"

"Well, she used to be the woman I was fuckin'. The same girl I pay all the bills for. The bitch who come home to me every night. How the fuck do you know her, *bruh?*"

"Don't cause a scene, Tariq."

I was more pissed at how they still stayed so close together. The longer she touched him only introduced the blatant disrespect she had for me to my face. When her waiter came by, he only added fuel to the fire. "Is everything all right? Do I need to escort this gentleman to his table?"

I hated the role I was forced in. Deja and *fucking* Traevon were together while I stood back and watched—as if I was wrong for questioning the whereabouts of who I thought was my woman. I took a deep breath and refrained from doing anything that would get me arrested. "I'm gone." Without saying another word, I walked away. I didn't punch the dude's eye socket in—even though my fists were itching for the feel of blood. I simply gathered the strength I needed to go home and contemplate how I handled being the man to play the fool in a relationship I had considered taking to the next level.

Deja snuck into my life and set up shop, but there she was dating another man in my face as if I didn't matter. I'll take blame in the matter and say that I ignored the signs, but who was I to think that my woman had it in her to lie and cheat? I drove back to the apartment we shared and gripped the steering wheel as if I was gripping Traevon's neck. I wish he would've met me outside. I wished I had the opportunity to avenge my broken heart by tearing the fool apart. Then again, I wished I hadn't caught my woman claiming another man right in front of me with no remorse. Even though my eyes watered, I wouldn't allow myself to bitch and moan over a woman who obviously had no respect for me. I wiped my face and drove in silence. I patiently awaited the unraveling of the life I thought I knew.

CHAPTER 2

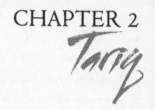

Now that she had been found out, she ain't have to put up the charade. She could stay out late and come in the next morning without coming up with some bullshit lie about how she and the girls lost track of time. Now, she strolled her ass in with the same clothes from last night, hair pulled back, and no regard for the man she left waiting at home.

I couldn't even go into work that morning. I needed to process the events that occurred last night. I had questions that needed answers, and I wouldn't be able to think straight 'til she gave 'em to me. I sat on the couch watching a blank TV screen as she walked past me and headed for our bathroom.

Every thought ran through my mind. She used *our* key to walk into our home, but she waited until the sun came up to leave the embrace of a dude who I *knew* couldn't do her body like I could. She was my woman; yet, she was Traevon's date, lover, and his friend that he met up for drinks while she seduced him with tight dresses and sweet perfume. Perfume that I bought her for Valentine's Day. As the sound of the shower drowned out my thoughts, I realized that it did nothing for my pain.

The woman who I shopped for engagement rings with had another man on the side that she let tap the inner folds that rested between her thighs. And now, she was in our shower, cleaning off the stink his nut left on her skin. I squeezed my fists and followed her into the bathroom.

When I swung the door open, I noticed her back on the shower wall as she stood with her arms folded over her chest. Through the shower door, she watched me enter. On any other day, my entrance met my boyish desire to disrobe and meet her for a replay of the shower scene in *How Stella Got Her Groove Back*. Now, the very thought of us reliving any movie scene or me slipping my penis into the same slot the other chump had his dick in less than six hours ago made me sick to my stomach.

I couldn't stare at her any longer. Her naked presence couldn't make my knees weak like it used to. I asked, "You really getting home *now?*" She stood quiet. The deafening noise of the shower drove me insane. I took a deep breath. Luckily, for her, my mama taught me that hitting a woman was the move of a coward. Problem with that theory was my mama never told me a woman could hurt me like this. "When you plan on moving out?"

Even though the fog blurred the shower door, I could tell she finally stared me down as if she had a real interest in carrying on a conversation with me. "I dunno. We have a lot of things to talk about."

Her suggestion that we had more to talk about beyond how soon I could help her move her things out of the apartment I paid all the bills for was amusing. I smiled. "No, I can call yo' family and find out the soonest time they can help you move yo' shit out my place."

Under her breath she mumbled, "*Your* apartment? You're talking all hurt as if you didn't see any of this coming, Riq. What did you expect me to do?"

My smile dropped. She knew what comments to say to get a response. At first, I tensed my jaw to hold back what I wanted to come out, but I then decided to give her what she wanted. "If I fucked every bitch that came my way and lied to you about it, then had the audacity to come in your face and tell you, 'You should've seen this coming,' how quick would you have your brothers over here to try and kick my ass? How soon would all your girls have my picture up on 'He-a-dog.com'? But because you felt a lil' neglected since I'm out there working to be a good man for you and be the man you been dying to make me into, you decide to go out and fuck some other dude, and I'm supposed to have *seen this coming?*"

I rarely ever cursed at her. If I ever slipped up, she'd turn her nose up and lock the coochie down for a week as my punishment. But seeing as I had no desire to gain entry between her legs anymore, I had free reign to curse all I wanted. Before I knew it, she pulled out the heavy artillery. At first, I was strong. I went in there with my shoulders back and legs spread, ready to come in and shut things down. How could I ever underestimate her?

With a crack in her voice, she said, "I'm sorry, Riq-ee. I know I was wrong." She sniffled and dropped her head in her palms. She stood in the shower crying, letting the water beat down on her head and seep through the satin cap she pulled over her hair. She was vulnerable. "You're never home. I got lonely. I didn't know things would lead to this, baby. But I never meant to hurt you."

When she started crying, the love I had for her resurfaced. I wanted to run inside and hold her like she was begging me to do. I wanted to be the man I've always been for her. My shoulders dropped and my anger shifted toward concern, but as quickly as it shifted, it shifted back. "You never meant to hurt me? Then what were your intentions when you laid up with the dude? Did you think I'd cheer you on? Throw you a mothafuckin' parade?"

She paused. She realized that it would be best to keep her apology to a minimum. She was losing the grip she had on me, and it was heartbreaking for her. Still, I couldn't ignore the pain and embarrassment she put me through. "How can we fix this?"

It was evident that I cared. It was obvious that she wasn't some chick I kept on the sidelines 'til the right woman came along. She was supposed to be *it*. She could tell by the fact that I practically stalked her the night before that I wasn't in this as a hit-it-and-quit-it relationship. Somehow, the fire was gone. I couldn't fight for a woman who couldn't fight for me in the face of her lover. I couldn't fix a relationship that had clearly ran its course. My mama was gonna have to put the grandkids on hold for a while.

"We can't." I hoped this didn't change me. I liked being the nice guy who cared for his woman. But how far did that get me when my woman can't even care for me. I opened the door to the bathroom and said, "You might wanna get yo' shit out by Thursday, 'cause the trash get picked up on Friday."

Even though half of the work day had already passed, I still decided to go in to work late. I couldn't deal with Deja's crying in the shower. I needed to remind myself of the coldness I developed toward her. If I allowed myself to become victim to her tears, then I'd never leave. And soon, I'd become the typical, cheating black man who couldn't stay faithful to his girl because he was too afraid to commit to a woman he could barely trust in the first place.

I tried to keep my work life separate from home, but when I saw my coworker, Damien, I couldn't help but show the stress at home on my face. We sat in my cubicle shaking our heads at the audacity of women.

"You caught her with the guy?" he asked me.

"Tonguing him down and everything. She ain't even come home 'til this morning."

"Damn." Damien shook his head. "What did you do?"

"Kicked her ass out. What else could I do?"

"Where she at now?"

"Hell if I know. I ain't really kick her ass out yet. I told her she goin' to have to find another place to stay by Friday before the trashman comes."

"You see, I tol' you shit like this is what happens."

"Tol' me? Man, when did you tell me all this? If I woulda known my woman would be out doin' dirt, I wouldn't have contemplated waiting fo' her new man outside in the parkin' lot fo' 'bout twenty minutes."

Laughing, Damien said, "I tol' you that females can't be trusted."

At first, when Damien would stroll by, peekin' his bobblehead over my cubicle wall and shiftin' his bug eyes my way spouting that nonsense about how women couldn't be trusted and how all of them would ho themselves out for a cheeseburger and a fifty-dollar shot at fame, I'd roll my eyes and humor him. At the end of the day, he was still alone, secretly wishing he had a chick to come home to. But now, I was actually sittin' there listenin' to him. In the midst of my pain, he was making perfect sense. "I hear you."

"Are you really hearin' me?" He rubbed the bottom of his chin and stared up at the ceiling. "Bitches nowadays are always on to the next—bigga an' betta' things. So when a bitch try you like this, ain't no surprises. It's in her nature to do men wrong." Damien stopped rubbin' his chin and stared at me with bright eyes and a stern jaw. "Fall of man has always been at the fault of women. Shit, I ain't goin' to fight nature. You see me comin' into work cryin' 'bout some random broad who can't keep her legs closed to get attention?"

"Deja wasn't some random broad, but..." I took a deep breath. "I do hear you." I must've been sleepin' through life. Everyone else saw this comin' but me. "Fo' real, Damien, you ain't neva fall for a female before?"

Damien smiled and went back to rubbin' the scraggly hairs under his chin. My question made him revisit a past that he liked to keep in his back pocket. Rather than use bad experiences as learning lessons, he used them as looking glasses for what life had planned for him. "There was this one chick, bad bitch, too. Dark, chocolate skin. Hazel eyes, long, thick hair, thick thighs, small waist, and big ol' titties." He chuckled and slapped his hands together. His face lit up as his memories poured back into his present. "I was seventeen and had a scholarship to play ball. She tol' me she loved me." His smile dropped and the light in his face turned to darkness. "I let the good schools go and decided to go to college at one of the two-year schools around the way. Long story short, I ain't play ball after high school no mo', and I found out on *Maury* that she was pregnant wit' some fool's baby an' couldn't find out who the daddy was. Bitch had twelve mothafuckas who weren't the daddy. *Twelve*, man. I went berserk. I called her every dirty name in the book. One week later, she had a restraining order filed against me and I'm dropping out of junior college. At the end of the day, she was hopin' my ball playin' could take her hoeing to the big leagues." He rolled his eyes. "Eight years later and I'm adjusting insurance claims, tryin' not to blow my damn brains out in my ten-by-ten cubicle. I'm tellin' you, man, females ain't shit."

"You mean to tell me that one shiesty female turned you cold for life?"

Damien stood up and shrugged his shoulders. "It only takes one." Before walking back to his desk, he said, "I mean it is what it is, though. All I know, I ain't the nigga 'bout to change the locks on a bitch."

Any other day, I would've felt disrespected. You talk about my woman, and it was time to get down. Today, the first time in ever, I was indifferent. I pursed my lips at his comment as if his blatant disrespect for the deficiency in my relationship was called for. However, as I replayed the recent events in my head, I realized that it really was. It was completely called for to disregard a relationship I spent four years creating, 'cause there was nothing left of it to defend.

My mama raised me to be a good man to women, treat them right, and not hurt their feelings. But where were all their mothers? Where were the mothers that were supposed to encourage their daughters to be good to their men, treat them right, and not sleep around? I had to come to grips with the reality that my mama must've lived in a world where that advice rang truer. Nowadays, bitches ain't shit.

CHAPTER 3:

Erin

Present day...

Damn. I was standing in this storm, strolling down the dark streets of Lake Underhill in wet socks holding on to a pair of five-inch boots, one with a broken heel, the other one scuffed up beyond recognition. My cell phone battery was dead. I couldn't call my girl Loraine, and I stupidly left my wallet in Tariq's front seat. I couldn't even use a payphone to call a cab. My freshly relaxed hair was ruined, my makeup was running, and I'd be sniffling come morning. "I hate men," I whispered to myself. All I wanted to do was get home, pop open a bottle of Johnny Walker Black Label, and throw back a good, hard drink. Usually after a first date, I'd go home and sip on a tall glass of Riesling while Sade played in the background. Tonight was different; tonight, I needed to yank Tariq's picture from the top drawer of my nightstand, stick it in a trashcan, and set it on fire—not before I gave Loraine a good tongue-lashing for thinking that Tariq and I would actually be a *good match*. I wiped the snot that slowly dripped from my nose. Throwing my hands in the air, I kicked the big puddle of water in front of my feet. Tonight was the last damn straw. I freaking hated men.

When I got home, I had to ignore the awkward glances I got from my neighbors who couldn't understand why a pretty girl like me would actually be walking home in the rain. When they tried not to stare at me, I wanted to say, "What the hell's your problem? You never saw a black girl come out the damn rain before? Mind your damn business!" Instead, I ended up faking a smile while I kept my head down and searched for my keys.

Before I could unlock my door, Alonzo, the wiry banker from down the hall, shot me a smirk and waved. I tried to ignore him, but my wet hands couldn't find my keys quick enough.

He yelled out, "You all right?"

I utilized the overly expensive therapy technique I had learned in my sessions and breathed deeply. "I'm good. Trying to get to bed."

"Did you need any help with anything? You look like hell."

I couldn't take it after that. I shot him an evil glance and flared my nostrils. Realizing that he'd crossed the line, he stopped walking closer to me and dropped his goofy smile. But before I gave him the chance to tuck tail and run, my neck started rolling, my finger went to wagging, and my lips started snarling. "I said I was all right, damn. Can't a girl walk into her damn home without everybody in this got-damn apartment building trying to figure out what's wrong? I had a bad night. It's not like I came here with a wounded Siberian tiger under my skirt, rocking a shaved head and bright-orange nail polish. Can I walk into my apartment, Alonzo? Can you give me that courtesy, please? Shoot!"

Alonzo opened his mouth to speak, then snapped it shut quickly. Without another word, he nodded and turned on his heel. Walking back into his apartment, he yelled back, "Have a good night." He then slammed the door shut behind him.

Confident in my victory of finally getting to tell *some* man off, I found the key to my apartment and walked inside. Dropping my keys, purse, and shoes to the floor, I grabbed my Johnny Walker bottle and headed for my bathroom. I stared at myself in the mirror.

I tried to wipe what was left of my running eyeliner. I looked like Tariq had given me two black eyes instead of kicking me out of a moving vehicle. I brushed the few strands of hair stuck to my face behind my ear and wiped the smeared foundation from my dimpled cheeks. I took a deep breath and tried not to remind myself of the hundred and fifty hard-earned dollars I had spent on my not-so-fresh relaxer two days prior to my date. My wet hair sat on top of my head, limp and dead, like the rain had a vendetta against me. I couldn't understand how an almond-eyed, full-lipped, earth-yellow complexioned bombshell like myself would find herself walking home in pouring rain as my overly expensive MAC makeup melted off my face.

I stripped naked and examined how my round breasts, slim, waist and wide hips would scare a man off. Halle Berry ain't have nothing on me, but I was being treated like Ron Berry. Dang, I hated men. After stripping naked and dunking myself into a warm bubble bath, my fingers got to dialing. When Loraine's groggy voice scratched through my phone's receiver, she got the tongue-lashing that had been waiting on her.

"Girl, I am so damn mad at you."

"What happened?"

"*What happened?* That fool put me out his car."

Loraine's pause only revealed how she was trying to contain her laughter. "No, he didn't."

"Girl, I am not playing. While we are actually driving down the 408, we get into a fight over his presets. Girl, he got mad at me for changing the dang station, and then he puts me out the car…in the rain."

"I can't believe he'd actually do that. You must've done something else to set him off."

I stared at the phone for a minute. "Do you hear yourself? He put me out of his car in the middle of the night, no phone, no money, no nothing. I don't care if I cursed his mama out; it doesn't give him the right to put me out his car in the rain."

"Tariq's not a bad person, Erin. This sounds so unlike him."

"Well, it *was* him. Tariq Johnson, right? The mixed claims adjuster with Chico DeBarge hair, rich brown eyes, and drives a black Lincoln? That Tariq, right?"

"Yea, girl, that's him."

"I thought so." I swallowed the rest of my half-empty bottle, tilted my head back, and rested on my plush bath pillow. I whispered, "I'm so tired of dealing with this nonsense."

"It was one bad date, Erin…"

"One among hundreds, Loraine."

"I really think you got a bad dose of Tariq. He's a great guy at work. Everybody at the office loves him."

"You sound like the dozens of women who still stand behind an abusive man claiming it's the woman's fault. Provoked or not, no man has the right to attack another woman for the hell of it, like it didn't give Tariq the right to throw me out of his car in the middle of a thunderstorm." I tried to take a deep breath, but breathing wasn't calming me down. "And besides, if he's so great, why has he been single all this time?"

Loraine finally shut up at the fact that she couldn't locate an answer to my brilliantly asked question. She sighed and paused. I tapped on my empty scotch bottle, awaiting her response. Finally, she responded, "Maybe he's been waiting on the right girl."

"Or maybe he's too busy throwing the right ones out of moving vehicles."

"Okay, fine. I was merely trying to help. You asked me if I knew anyone; my boss is single and cute. He seemed nice enough to me."

"Girl, Tariq is many things; nice is not one of them." After getting out the last of my frustrations, I rubbed the skin between my eyes and licked my lips. I shouldn't be blaming my friend for a service she didn't have to provide me. I couldn't deny that I had gotten on my knees and prayed that the brown-eyed cutie wasn't taken. I tithed extra on Sunday when I prayed that he'd be willing to take me out on a date, too. Now when I attended church, I'd be praying to God that Tariq lost my number. The only problem with that theory was that I still needed to see him one last time to get my wallet back, assuming he didn't steal from me, too. Then, I got an idea. "I know how you can make it up to me."

"How's that?"

"I left my wallet in his car. You think you could get it from him when you get to work in the morning?"

"I guess." Loraine's hesitation bothered me. Two seconds ago, she was singing this man's praises, and now she was too apprehensive to pick up my dang wallet. "Hopefully he doesn't try to dodge me in the parking lot when I see him."

"He better hope I don't see him walking down the street when I'm driving. I'll probably run him over."

Loraine laughed. "Girl, you are a trip."

"Whatever, girl. Do me the favor of getting my wallet so I don't ever have to see his stupid face and be charged with vehicular manslaughter, or better yet, homicide."

"Okay, I'll see what I can do."

When I got to work, I was counting down the hours until lunch. As soon as the clock hit twelve, I made sure Loraine remembered my wallet. Part of me felt comfortable with the lie that all I cared about was my wallet while a bigger part of me knew that I was anxious to hear how things went with Tariq. Would he apologize for being a jerk and ask to literally kiss the ground I walked on to get back in my good graces? Or would he tell her that he threw my wallet out in the rain, too— three miles after he kicked me out? My good sense was leaning more toward the latter, but a small part of me was itching to be hopeful.

When I finally got Loraine on the phone, I contained my composure. "Did you get my wallet?" My tone was relaxed while I nibbled on my fingernails.

She paused for a second as if she had no clue what I was talking about. Before I got to cursing her out, she said, "Oh, yeah. I spoke to him today, and he was surprisingly nonchalant."

Was he nonchalant about throwing my belongings out the window or indifferent about the girl he kicked out of his car? Or did he keep my wallet in his front seat because he didn't even remember my name two seconds after he drove away? "What does that mean? What did he say?"

"I thought he was going to bite my head off when I saw him, but he was still the same nice, sweet Tariq from the office. He even bought me, and the rest of the office, coffee and donuts." I could hear her smiling through the receiver. I pressed my ear to the phone as I patiently waited for the point in the conversation where she talked about me. "But anyway, he told me he left your wallet at his place and would bring it to you tonight after he gets off work."

My mouth dropped. My wonderfully executed plan to avoid Lucifer's spawn had backfired. Aside from the fact that he showed no emotion to kicking a beautiful woman like myself out of his car in a storm, he invited himself back to my home without my consent. "Why didn't he leave my wallet in his car? Did he go through it or something?"

"I don't think he did anything like that. Maybe he saw it in his car and brought it inside his place."

"I guess that makes sense. Did he say anything else?"

"Nope, that was it."

I went to breathing deeply again while I squeezed my fingers around my cell phone. I should have been upset that I wasted most of my lunch hour talking about how little Tariq talked about me. I knew more about the damn donuts than I did about his sentiments toward me. And now, I was unwillingly prepping myself for an impromptu date with a man I hoped I would never see again. Of course, it wasn't a real date, but I'd be lying if I said I wasn't planning to fix my hair, throw on some rouge, and order some takeout to make the house smell like I knew how to cook. I hated feeling pissed and nervous at the same time. Rarely did I ever know which emotion to go from. I sighed as I glanced at my watch. "Okay, Loraine. I'll get to my lunch and talk to you later. Thanks for asking."

"No problem. Tell me how it goes with Tariq tonight."

Tariq didn't show that night, but he did have the audacity to show two nights later. No call, no warning. He popped up at my doorstep with my wallet in tote and an obnoxious smile plastered across his face. If he weren't such an asshole, I would've stood there and stared at his hard jawline, straight teeth, and chiseled cheekbones all night. I pictured myself resting on his sculpted chest while he wrapped his toned arms around my waist. In my fantasy, I crept my hand to the top of his head and ran my fingertips along his tidal waves. He stood there looking good enough to make me wanna get over whatever it was I was angry about. My hair was barely combed. I definitely didn't have on any makeup, and the house smelled more like leftover frozen pizza as opposed to "home-cooked" Italian food. By that point, I was more interested in getting my wallet than being nervous about a fake date.

"Weren't you supposed to drop this off like three days ago?"

He shrugged his shoulders. "I forgot."

I put out my hand. Days of worrying about my credit cards being stolen and having to carpool because I had no license, and all this fool had to say for himself was, "I forgot."

"Gimme my wallet, please."

"You're not gonna let me in?" Although he asked a question, it sounded more like an accusation. Either that or he was implicitly demanding an invitation into my apartment.

I folded my arms over my chest, shook my head, and rolled my neck. "You have some nerve. You're lucky I didn't call the police and claim that you *stole* my belongings. I had to call and cancel my credit cards so I wouldn't have to worry about you racking up a fortune at my expense."

His smiled dropped and his easygoing demeanor changed to that of annoyance. Like that, the Tariq from our date showed up.

"You think I'm a thief? Girl, you are crazy. I wasn't planning to steal yo' raggedy credit cards."

"You've had my wallet for almost a week and made no attempts to give it back. I don't know you. I called you. You never called back. Next thing I know, you're here. You ain't have to come see me. You could've given my wallet to Loraine."

Tariq dropped his shoulders and flashed his Colgate smile. "Well, maybe I wanted to see yo' pretty face again. You ever thought about that?"

"I ain't know what to think wit' you. I ain't think I'd be walking home in the middle of a thunderstorm on our first date. For all I know, you could be goin' 'round stealin' people's wallets."

"That's my fault—"

"Dang right, it's yo' fault! Why the hell should I let you in after the mess you put me through? I ain't deserve that, Tariq."

He hesitated for a moment before taking a deep breath. "You're right. No woman deserves that. I can respect that. A woman who looks out for herself, you gotta respect that. And despite what my actions may have shown, I respect you, Erin."

I dropped my arms. I didn't want to admit that I was flattered by the compliment, but when a man as fine as Tariq flashed his million-dollar Colgates and the moonlight reflected off his brown eyes, I couldn't help but get flushed. "Are you going to hand me my wallet or not?"

"I was still hoping you'd let me in."

"That's not gonna happen, Tariq."

He looked me up and down. I watched him lick his lips as a lion did before attacking his prey. Even though *sexy* didn't ooze from me in my gravy-stained gray sweats and ripped tank top, his glare made me feel as if I was being hunted.

He whispered, "You look good, even in your house clothes. You ain't need to impress me with caked-on makeup, tight dresses, and…" He stopped and glanced at my hair that was tied up in a loose ponytail. "I thought you had on a weave, but I guess that's all you."

Sliding my hand down the end of my ponytail, I asked, "And even if it was a weave?"

"You still look good, *Erin*." The way he said my name. Each syllable dripped off his tongue like melting ice cream. We stared at each other and let the awkward pause dance a jig between us. I didn't want to give in, but when he licked his lips again, I imagined him licking mine. "I ain't tryna start any trouble. I know you're not tryna see me, especially after how I treated you. I was going through a lot at work. I got people quitting and calling off work all at the same time. I was stressed, and my car was acting up earlier. I flipped. You're right. A woman as beautiful as you didn't deserve that. I'm here, with your wallet, hopin' you'll accept my apology and let a brotha inside."

Even though there technically was no apology, I was partly comforted by the halfway attempt at pacifying my emotions. The other part of me was disgusted by how quickly I wanted to forgive him, but there wasn't much I could do. He hovered over me and stared into my eyes. I was putty in his hands and couldn't do much to stop it. I whispered, "Fine, but only for a minute."

"Of course."

CHAPTER 5

"He finally dropped off my wallet last night."

"Finally. I was beginning to get a little worried."

"So was I."

"So, how'd it go?"

"Good, I guess." I ran my fingers through my mid-length tresses. "He dropped it off. I took it. That's it."

"That's it, huh?"

"That's what I said." I hated lying to Loraine; I always felt worse when she caught me in my web of lies with nothing to say for myself. "What else did you think would happen?"

"Tariq was late for work this morning."

"What does that have to do with me?"

Loraine sipped on her white zinfandel while we sat at a local bar during happy hour. I nibbled on my curly fries trying to avoid eye contact. Noticing my uneasiness, she said, "He was probably late because your apartment is a half-hour away from our office."

I was forced to look up at her then. She stared back at me with her piercing gray eyes accentuated by her fire-engine-red dreads. Her gaze was like a truth serum. Whenever I tried to lie to her, I always avoided her eyes since I couldn't stay dishonest for long. She used that to her advantage. That's how she caught her cheating ex-husband. I often told Loraine the police could use her as their own personal polygraph.

"What does my apartment have to do—"

"Cut the crap, Erin. I know he slept over."

"And how do you know that?"

"Weren't we supposed to meet for drinks last night?" She searched my face for an answer. I stirred the straw in my Long Island Iced Tea and kept my eyes down. She continued, "You stand me up, and Tariq shows up late. I'm putting two and two together."

As the bar light illuminated her rosy-brown cheekbones, she tapped her clear-polished fingernails on her full, soup-cooling lips and waited for my response.

I sighed, brushed a few flyaways behind my ear, and pushed my half-eaten curly fry basket to the side. "Okay, so we slept together. He came over, told me how beautiful I looked, apologized, and then invited himself in. Next thing you know, my feet were on his chest with my panties around my ankles." I closed my eyes and imagined his smile. "He snuck out of my apartment early this morning."

Loraine giggled and nodded, satisfied with her mystery solved. "Was it good?"

My legs trembled with the thought of Tariq inside of me. I licked my lips. "Girl—"

Loraine laughed and slapped my shoulder. "I ain't mad at you. You plan on seeing him again tonight?"

"I'm here with you, aren't I?"

"Wait…so what's the deal with you two? Are you two together now or what?"

"If I knew, I'd tell you. He flattered me, spanked me, made my knees buckle, and kissed my forehead before he left. Wham, bam, thank you, ma'am."

"Don't say that. He's probably going to call you later."

"I'm not keeping my hopes up. I'll be thankful for a night well spent."

Loraine shrugged her shoulders and took another sip of her wine. "He'll call. I know it."

When I got home that night, Alonzo was going through his mail at his front door. He glanced up and caught me walking up the stairs. He tried not to make eye contact. Feeling guilty, I made sure to catch him before he rushed back inside his apartment. "Hey, Alonzo."

He met my greeting with a smile and shoved his letters into his back pocket. "Hey, Erin. Glad to speak to you again." I nodded and pulled out my keys. "I'm sorry if I offended you the other night. I wanted to make sure you were doing okay."

"It's okay. It's not your fault. You caught me after a bad night. I'm sorry for biting your head off."

Alonzo grinned and stared at me as the uncomfortable silence between us grew. Finding my door key, I stuck it in and waved goodbye. Before shutting the door behind me, he said, "I saw that ad campaign you did for Sunrise Lemonade. The copy was real impressive. Made me wanna drink more lemonade."

I smiled. "Thanks. I appreciate the compliment." Not feeling up to prolonging the conversation, I waved goodbye again and shut the door. It was clear that Alonzo wanted more playful banter, but I wanted to continue to pretend that I wasn't waiting for Tariq's phone call in seclusion. I thought about pouring myself another drink, but my next workday started early in the morning. I disrobed and headed for bed, disappointed at the empty bed I planned to lie in once again.

Underneath my comforter, I noticed my cell phone light up. I looked over at the clock. "Midnight. Who's calling me this late?" I reluctantly grabbed my phone after reading the name across the screen. "Hello."

"You 'sleep?"

I rolled over in bed and stared at my bedroom wall. Hearing Tariq's voice late at night sent shivers up my thigh. I tried to deny the feeling and stick to my principles for the night, at least until the weekend. "I was about to be."

"Want some company?"

"No, I can handle sleep on my own."

"We don't have to do too much sleeping."

I contemplated pressing the End button. "Well, at this hour, that's all I got time for."

Tariq was quiet for a while. I had a feeling he was racking his brain trying to figure out a way into my pajama pants at twelve in the morning on a work night. Five more seconds of his thinking, and I was pressing the end button for sure. "I miss you, Erin. I wanna make up for a bad first date."

"You can make it up by giving me a better first date, not a booty call."

"Booty call? Erin, you are more than some booty call."

"When you call me at midnight asking to sleep over, you could've fooled me."

"I been busy all day. Now is the first time I've had to call you. I been thinkin' 'bout you all day, and I was hoping to end my night with you."

For a dick, Tariq knew the right things to say to get me moist, no matter how corny it sounded. It also might've been my inner thighs thinking on my behalf. My better judgment should've been enough to get me off the phone and head to bed, but the weakness within me craved to be held at night. As more time went by, I found myself rationalizing his previous actions. *Maybe I did disrespect him for messing with his presets. Being mad over it is petty.* Thinking that it was okay on some level for him to kick me out of his car should have been a sign that this man wasn't the right man for me, but his deep voice sounded so sexy over the phone. "I gotta get up in the morning."

"Then why spend the time talking over the phone when I could be on my way."

Ugh, why was he able to do me like this? "Fine." I slapped my forehead and frowned. "Don't keep me waiting."

CHAPTER 6

Tariq

Three years ago…

I was tired of hearing females play the victim. A year's worth of talks with a man like Damien can have a funny way of warping perception. Not too long ago, I was ducking female-bashing chats with Damien. Ultimately, I welcomed his skewed view on women because it gave me new insight on what was really goin' on. I was raised never to call a woman out of her name, but Damien had me noticing the type of bitches I surrounded myself with.

I was playin' myself to think that Deja would be the type of bitch that I'd marry. I was disgusted with myself for bringing her home to meet my mama. Still, I couldn't let the past dictate my future and with a new frame of mind, shit was going to change. One day when I happened to meet a woman with *Poetic Justice* braids who was struggling to get her briefcase into her truck at the supermarket, I went in for the kill. Ordinarily, I would smooth talk a woman into her phone number. Eventually, that led to a date that would turn into three more dates and ultimately into meaningful sex. On that day, I was more interested in seeing how quickly I could help her put something else in her trunk. I asked her, "Need help?"

She smirked and dropped her shoulders in relief. "Please."

I grabbed her briefcase and eased it into her car. We smiled at each other. "Need help wit' anything else?"

She shook her head and stared at me as she waited for me to close the deal. Closing her trunk, I stepped away from her and turned as if I planned to walk off. "All right then."

She held my elbow and then let go once she realized what she had done. "Wait...thank you."

She ended her gratitude as if she had more to say. "Don't mention it." Folding my arms across my chest, I licked my lips and eyed her up and down. She had long slender legs, the type of legs I saw walking down runways. When she opened her mouth to speak, I could catch the glint from the metal ball of her tongue ring. I loved how chocolaty smooth her skin complexion looked in the sunlight. With her, all I saw was sex. Long legs that I could wrap around my waist. Chocolate skin melting on my skin. Long thick braids I pictured swaying back and forth. A juicy tongue that wrapped completely around my penis. I needed her body more than she knew.

"Can I thank you over dinner?"

I grinned and dropped my arms to my waist. "Yeah, that sounds cool." We exchanged numbers and planned for a date I knew would end at my place or hers.

"What did you say your name was again?" I asked the question but I didn't listen for the response. I got distracted by how she scraped the plate with her fork. I sat across from a dark-eyed woman with full lips and thunder thighs, and all I could focus on was how she couldn't pick her utensils up when she ate her food.

When I called Poetic Justice for a date, my dwindling bank account prompted me to request a date at the local bar and grill up the street. The Chili's booth was dark, but I noticed the tension in her face. It bothered me how she tapped her fingernails along the wood table and avoided eye contact. She played with the skin on the back of her neck. From my distance, I could hear her loudly scratching between her naps while chewing on her lips, sucking off her cheap lipstick. "Mayra."

"You nervous or something?"

She stared up into my eyes. I couldn't deny how sexy she looked when her dark brown eyes pierced into mine. When her lips spread to speak and I remembered that metal ball hiding in her mouth, I smirked. "I'm fine," she said. She licked her lips, cleared her throat and then stared down at her plate. "So, what do you do, again?"

"Claims manager. An' you're a cashier, right?"

"Pharmaceutical rep."

My lack of interest in her life should have struck a chord with her. I expected her to respond to my error with an eye roll, a neck twist, or at least a finger wag, but nothing. She corrected me as if she didn't tell me her occupation three times before we sat down for dinner and one more time after we got our appetizers. I dropped my eyebrows and my shoulders in disappointment. A small part of me wanted my dinner with a side of sass, something to entertain my buildin' thirst for a woman to put a stop to my silent rebellion against all womankind. Instead, she let me forget her name and her occupation, and she smiled when I used sexual innuendos to describe how I planned to finish our first date. "What made you get into that?"

She glanced up at me, then back at her half-eaten steak. "I could never finish pharmacy school."

"You ever plan on goin' back?"

She shook her head and giggled. "Probably not. I want to, though."

Even though I could not have cared less about what she did and who she was, it intrigued me that I found myself sittin' across a chick who couldn't complete the goals she set forth. By the time I got off my train of thoughts, I made up in my mind that I couldn't wife a chick who couldn't complete simple tasks. Although I never made any intention to, I found peace in the truth that she only had the potential to be a sometime chick that I could call when I didn't feel up to going after the more unattainable game that came my way. "You wanna get out of here now?"

"I'm not done with my food."

I laughed. "You may *want* to finish it, but you know you're not."

She smiled and stared at me with those pretty brown eyes. "You're right." She pushed her plate away and rubbed her stomach. "It's almost like you know me already."

I sipped on my iced tea to keep myself from chuckling. To avoid any more unnecessary conversation, I waved the waiter down to get the check. After I paid for our meal, I put pleasantries aside and asked the question that was on both of our minds. "Your place or mine?"

CHAPTER 7

Erin

Present day...

Nights with Tariq were something I couldn't describe. I say *nights* because we rarely ever spent our days together. He was gradually turning me into his late-night fix, and I didn't know how to break free from the spell he had over me. He'd call. I'd resist at first, but by the end of our conversation, we were already making plans to see each other's privates before the sun came up.

When he finally invited me over to his place, I actually thought we had made some progress. I had to lie about my place being fumigated for bedbugs to finally get the invitation, but still, I headed over there in my sexiest "freak-me" pumps, accented by my tightest mid-thigh dress. Tariq made the smallest effort to profess his limited feelings toward me, but I felt compelled to gain his deepest affections. I lay awake in bed praying that he was thinking of me too. I soothed myself with the notion that him blowing up my phone at three in the morning was his way of showing me that I truly was on his mind.

When he buzzed me up to his condo, I finger-combed my hair and checked my breath. Confident in how good I looked, I knocked on his door and waited for an answer.

"Hey, beautiful," he said.

I smirked and walked past him, sure that I did look good. When he shut the door, he left no room for small talk. He grabbed my waist and pulled me close. Pressing his lips against mine, he lifted me off the ground and straddled my legs around his waist. Though I craved the opportunity for a brief convo where he gushed about how good I looked, my legs trembled as he slipped his tongue between my lips and squeezed my ass cheeks. I felt a warm surge creep up my thigh as we stumbled through his living room and into his bedroom.

When he dropped me onto his plush sheets, I spread my legs and stared into his eyes, hoping he'd stare back. When he did, my lips curled up into a grin as I licked my lips. We must've shared a connection. However, instead of allowing us the time to marinate in the moment, he dropped his jeans and slid off my panties. After grabbing a rubber from his top drawer, he bit his bottom lip and whispered, "You look so good tonight." We really *did* share a connection. He was feeling me as much as I was feeling him and soon, our late-night visits would turn into daytime lunches and weekend strolls along the shoreline. I got wet thinking about the potential.

When Tariq rolled off me after a bout of marathon lovemaking, I wiped the sweat from my forehead and staggered to the bathroom to wipe myself clean. Tariq lay panting on the bed, trying to catch his breath after the hurting I put on him. After cleaning myself up, I walked back into the bedroom to find Tariq checking his phone. His look of satisfaction and relief had turned to frustration and concern.

I asked, "You okay?"

He didn't respond at first. Before I had the chance to ask him again, he blinked a few times and stared up at me. "You have to go."

"What? Why?"

"I got a few things to take care of."

"At four-thirty in the morning?"

He glanced back at his phone, then up at me. Without saying anything else, he grabbed the used condom and ran into the bathroom. Once I heard him flush, I realized that it would be best to start getting dressed. Even though I was curious to know what phone call or message he got to make him start acting so jumpy, I wasn't too naive to think we could finish round three.

I walked into the bathroom to find Tariq searching through his phone and biting his nails. When he realized that I was standing in the doorway watching him, he sneered. "Are you still here?"

"You never told me what your problem is."

He rushed out of his bathroom and pushed me toward the living room. "You have to go, Erin. I'll call you in the mornin'. I ain't got time to explain anything right now. But—"

His sentence was cut short by a knock at the door. He watched the door, questioning what to do, then glanced back at me. He whispered to himself, "How'd she get in without me buzzin' her up?"

"Who are you talkin' about? You kicking me out to be wit' another woman, Tariq?" At that moment, I snatched my arm from his grasp and refused to keep my voice down.

"No, it's not really like that but…" He searched his apartment for an exit plan and locked eyes on his bedroom. "I gotta get you outta here."

"Why, Tariq? Let the bitch in. Apparently, you too scared to face her, so let me." I was pissed at the idea of Tariq stringing me along. He had a girlfriend whose opinion he obviously cared about and now was standing outside his condo door requesting to be let in. It was clear that I was his sideline ho, and I wasn't about to agree to the role easily.

Nevertheless, he pushed me back into his bedroom and pointed at his fire escape. "You have to go—now," he said in demanding voice as his palms sweated and his voice shook. "I'll call you later."

I didn't want his damn call in the morning, I wanted an explanation. I couldn't let him push me away while I scurried down his fire escape like I was some burglar. He was the one in the wrong, not me. Why was I fleeing as if I were the guilty culprit? It was Tariq who made me play the fool by toying with my emotions while he pretended to be a man he wasn't. "I'm not going anywhere until you tell me what's going on." I folded my arms over my chest and rolled my neck.

Tariq grinded his teeth and cut his eyes back at the door as her knocks persisted. "Can you go, please? Stop playing games."

"Games? You called me over here at two in the morning, and now you want me to climb down some rickety fire escape so yo' girlfriend doesn't catch me. You got some nerve, Tariq."

"She's not my girlfriend, Erin. I'm sorry, but I can't have you go out the front door, not now. I need you to leave. I'll call you later. I promise."

"Who is she if she's not your girlfriend, then?" I stood my ground and pretended as if her knocks didn't irk my nerves like they did. When his phone started going off, I knew it was her. But she wasn't getting in unless I opened the door for her.

Tariq huffed and squeezed his fists. Shaking his head, he stared at his blinking phone and then sighed. "She's my wife."

I felt a rush of anger flow through my body like a river. My arms dropped and my heartbeat sped up. Now, when she banged on his door, it did more than irk my nerves. Each knock felt like a blow to the stomach, and it took everything in me not to storm through his living room and put us both out of our misery. However, for some reason, I stood there shaking my head and holding my breath.

"She's your what?" I didn't need him to repeat it, but something inside of me needed him to retract his statement.

He stepped back. He must've felt my growing urge to slap him. "It's not all what you think. We're separated, and I know it sounds bad, but I can't let her see you in my place."

"Tariq, I can't believe you—"

"Look, I'll explain it all to you later. I promise I'll call you in the morning before you head to work. Can you please leave, now?" That time, he didn't wait for me to respond. He turned on his heel and closed the bedroom door behind him.

I contemplated going against my better judgment, cursing him out, and walking out the front door like a lady. Then I heard her voice. "Why the fuck weren't you answering the door, Riq?" she screamed.

Her sultry voice hinted at the possibility that she was a six-foot Amazon with long flowing hair, curvy hips, long legs, and piercing eyes. I felt threatened without even seeing her face. However, the pain in her voice was authentic. She was another hurt woman, victim to the power Tariq had in his hurricane tongue and kissable lips.

"I was busy," Tariq, or *Riq*, assured her. "I was taking a shower and ain't even hear you knockin'."

"I texted you and told you I was coming over. I need to talk and…you've been ignoring my calls and messages. You haven't been by to pick up your son. What's been up with you, Riq?"

With the mention of a son, I realized that it really was time for me to go. I wanted to go out the front door, but I couldn't think straight after hearing all that. Two minutes ago, Tariq was an asshole with a solid gift at making my eyes roll back. Now, *Riq* was a husband and a father. Even though Tariq was an asshole, I'd prefer him over *Riq*. So, I didn't cause anymore stir. It wasn't her fault she married a dick. I didn't want to be the woman responsible for her failed marriage, even though it was really his fault. I grabbed my purse and slid out his bedroom window, still kind of hoping that he'd call in the morning.

"Bad case of the Mondays?"

I popped my head up off my keyboard and cleared my computer screen of the serious line of *b*'s my forehead let scurry across my screen. I glanced up at my supervisor and smiled. I only hoped that my pearly whites were enough to get him to forget that he caught me sleeping at my desk at ten in the morning. "Morning, Eric."

"Good morning, Erin. I see you're off to a slow start this morning."

I chugged down a gulp of my black coffee and concealed the burp that was tempted to creep through my lips. "I had a long weekend, but I'm fine."

"Fine enough to get to work, I hope."

"Of course, Eric. I'm getting to that as soon as you leave. Did you need me for anything?"

My tall and husky superior eyed me up and down while rubbing the dry skin on the back of his neck. Whenever I had a bad day, I hated looking at him. His tall stature towered over me, judging me. His dark eyes were murky pools of resentment and superiority. The deep, rugged lines that cluttered his face looked like subway routes that couldn't find one destination. He had large hands that would engulf his coffee mug and tap the carpeted walls of my cubicle. He'd tap and tap while I cringed inside. His judgmental demeanor and his curly peppered hair stalked my frustration as I faked a smile and hoped he'd walk away as silently as he walked in. I could try to not blame him for his piss-poor supervisory behavior and be understanding of his three failed divorces, but I didn't. He was a man betrayed by a woman, and like every other poor sap like him, he had to take it out on every undeserving soul that got in his way. After taking a small sip of his French roast, he shook his head and faked a smirk as he walked off. The look in his eyes was him warning me that he didn't want to catch me asleep at my desk again. I heeded his warning and got back to the stack of files cluttering my desk. I pushed aside my fresh new stack of business cards that read my brand-new job title: "Sr. Copy Editor" and sighed. I hoped my promotion would get Eric off my back, but with more responsibility, came more visits from the bitter Hispanic man with a score to settle with his black female counterpart.

I wanted to get to work. I wanted to tackle today's copy with zeal and vivacity, but after a weekend like mine, I was more interested in cuddling up in bed with a bottle of Moscato and goldfish crackers. Of course, Tariq never called. I'm sure he was too busy being *Riq* to his wife and son. It shouldn't have really mattered anyway. I left any chance of a future between us in the bedroom that I hid in while a woman came home looking for her husband. When I woke up in the morning, I dressed, wiped the tears I shed for another man not worth them, and headed in to work. As I stared at my computer screen, I felt myself drifting off again. I didn't want it to happen, but I was unsuccessful. Fortunately, the ringing of my desk phone caught me before my forehead hit the keyboard. "Iaras Advertising. This is Erin."

"Why'd you stand me up again?"

"Loraine?"

"Yes, girl. Why did you stand me up this morning?

"What are you talking about?"

"We were supposed to go jogging this morning before we went to work. I was almost late to work, waiting on you. What happened?"

I breathed deeply and rubbed the skin between my eyes. "Tariq happened."

"What do you mean? Did you two sleep together again? Are you two together or what?"

"Girl, no. That man had me up 'til about six in the morning."

"Damn, girl, I didn't know he had it like that."

"No, Loraine, it wasn't even like that. We were done by four somethin', but I had to climb out of his window, shimmy down his fire escape and then hike half a mile back to my car in five-inch heels since I couldn't find a dang parking spot in front of his place." I shook my head as I replayed the night before in my head. I felt like kicking myself for actually putting up with this mess. "When I finally got to my car, I realized that I locked my keys inside. It took almost an hour to find a locksmith who was willing to actually drive into that shady neighborhood. I was lucky I didn't get robbed."

"Why did you have to climb out his window? Why didn't you call Tariq? Why didn't you call me?"

"'Cause his damn wife came home."

"What?" Loraine yelled through my phone. "He is *not* married!"

"According to him, they're separated. But he is still very much a married man."

"He has never mentioned his wife at work. He doesn't wear a ring or have any pictures up."

"Why would he? Apparently, *they're going through some things*." I rolled my eyes at the memory of him saying that. "She came over to work things out."

"How do you know that's why she went over there?"

"Because I could hear them talking right before I snuck out his bedroom window. According to her, he needs to be there for his son."

"Oh my goodness, girl. I don't believe you."

"Girl, I couldn't make this mess up if I tried." I took a deep breath and shook my head. "You know I'm blaming you for this one, right?"

"Erin, how was I supposed to know he was married?"

"You talk about him all the time. Talkin' 'bout how great of a boss he is. I would hope you wouldn't hook me up with a married father."

"If I knew anything like that, I would've never let you talk me into giving him your number."

"Whatever, Loraine. You have to make this tragedy up to me before I end up cutting off all my hair and burning his condo down."

Loraine giggled. "I'm sorry, girl. Well, now I know you're free to come jogging with me after work." Since Loraine divorced her husband of two years after finding out he was screwin' his boss, she's been on this mission to get back in shape so she could find her next Mr. Right. If she asked me, she was really tryna shed the pounds and strut her new figure in her ex's face. "Exercising will help clear your mind, too."

I wanted a better solution to my problems than jogging, but there wasn't much I could do. I'd either spend the night gaining five extra pounds burying my face in liquor and ice cream, or I'd burn the depression off jogging five extra miles around the block. I breathed deeply and agreed. "Fine, girl. I might as well. I gotta look good when the next cheating husband comes knocking on my door."

Loraine chuckled. "Whatever. I'll see you after work. Try not to break up any more happy homes today."

"Home must've not been too happy if he's screwin' me."

t had been a month, and I hadn't heard a peep from Tariq. I didn't want to pressure Loraine into getting any information out of him, but I would be lying if I wasn't itching to find out what was up. I deserved some sort of explanation. *Right?* I understood that I didn't share his last name or bear his child, but I did let him lie up in me every other night while I gave him the leeway to make me believe we'd actually share a future. I deserved something.

As I sat on my couch watching *Girlfriends* reruns, the quick tap at the door incited hopefulness. I hoped it was Tariq with divorce papers in his hand. I even hoped it was Tariq, on bended knee, telling me how bad he screwed up and wanted to spend the next thirty minutes groveling for making me climb down a fire escape. So, when my hopeful self opened the door to find an overly excited Alonzo greeting me on the other side, I hoped that I hadn't opened the door.

"Hey, Erin. What have you been up to?"

"Watching TV."

He paused and peeked into my apartment. "Want some company?"

"It's ten o'clock at night, Alonzo."

"Do you have a curfew?" He smirked.

"Alonzo, what made you knock on my door this late hoping for an invite into my apartment?"

"I'm not tryna get into your bed or anything. I noticed how depressed you've been lookin' lately and felt like I should offer my company."

When I first moved in, Alonzo was the first person I met. He was kind, generous, and always willing to drop what he was doing to come to my rescue. Whether it was a leaky pipe or a broken AC unit that maintenance neglected to tend to, Alonzo was there. I wasn't born yesterday. He wanted more than to be my friendly neighbor, but that's all I cared for him to be. Unfortunately, he was a relentless little bugger. "I appreciate that, Alonzo, but I'm tired and ready for bed."

"Well, I'm not gonna push my luck. I wanted you to know that you're not completely alone."

I cringed at Alonzo's halfway offensive reference to my absent social life. I was a lil' pissed that he noticed how frequent and infrequent my doorbell rang, but I *was* getting older. I didn't have the luxury of partying up 'til the break of dawn when I had a nine-to-five. I didn't have to make excuses for myself, but Alonzo's insinuation made me uneasy. "I never thought I was completely alone, Alonzo." I faked a toothless smile and pushed my door forward.

Before I slammed my door shut without a goodbye, Alonzo stretched out his neck and yelled out, "Have a good night," before my door slammed shut in his face.

Alonzo always got the short end of my bad days and agitated nights, but my guilt remained lacking, along with his ability to understand when I didn't want to be bothered. I didn't feel bad for cursing him out a few times or slamming a couple doors in his face as long as he butted his nosey head in my business. I wondered what happened to the days where apartment neighbors gave a simple nod in the hallway and quickly escaped into the confines of their apartment walls while remaining none the wiser to the body they may have stuffed under their floorboards. I'm not saying Alonzo had a dead body in his apartment, but I wouldn't expect him to keep a secret like that, or any of his business from me. If anything, Alonzo was the one who felt completely alone and wanted me to be the one to alleviate his loneliness. Too bad for him.

When my phone rang, I hadn't completely realized that I sat on the couch staring off into space and not watching TV while Joan and her friends went about their business on my TV screen. My hope of expecting Tariq's number to flash across my screen had disappeared. I emphasize number instead of name because I sho' 'nuff erased his number from my phone after I had to leave his damn condo out the fire escape like a criminal. Even though I had his number committed to memory, I felt empowered to clear his name from my call log and contact list. When I noticed Loraine's name flash across the screen, I reluctantly answered. "Hello."

"Eww. Why do you sound like that?"

"I am having a rough night."

"Why?"

"Girl, why not?"

Loraine snickered one of those fake laughs as if to tell me she didn't really care. "Well, whatever you're going through, shake it off. We're going out tonight."

"Says who?"

"Says me…and my little sister who came in for summer break."

"How old is your sister again?"

"Twenty. She'll be twenty-one next month, though."

"Was that last lil' tidbit s'posed to ease my discomfort with the fact that she can't get in to any twenty-one-and-up clubs?"

I could see Loraine rolling her eyes through the phone. "We can sneak her into a twenty-one-and-up club. She has a fake ID." Now, I was the one rolling my eyes. "And don't roll your eyes either, Erin. You need to get out the house and stop stuffing your face with junk food and watching *Girlfriends* reruns."

I glanced over at the empty bag of Cheetos lying on my end table and winced at how well Loraine knew me. It was disgusting how open my life and mannerisms were to this woman. "I'm happy living my life this way, Loraine."

"Please. I bet you broke Alonzo's heart again tonight. It's sick how in love with you that man is."

"Okay, I've got to get new friends. Ones who don't know so much about me."

Loraine laughed. "Whatever, girl. You love me. Now get dressed. We'll be there in thirty minutes." The quick click and the homepage on my BlackBerry revealed that I had no real say in the matter. Loraine decided for me that I was going out tonight, and I'd be wise to take heed.

I let out an annoyed sigh and headed for my closet. Tonight was gonna be one of those nights.

When we got to the club that night, I tried to conceal my disinterest in the event with a suitable coating of concealer, dark eyeshadow and red lip gloss. Loraine saw through my makeup, skinny jeans, and oversized halter top, though; I was dressed like a sexy mom lookin' for a night away from the kiddies. Didn't matter much. With Loraine's red locs pulled up and her donkey booty squeezed into her little black strapless dress, we still looked dressed to kill, and my poor attitude wasn't about to stop every Tom, Dick, and Raheem from stepping our way.

When I saw Loraine's sister, I expected to see an underage, overly accessorized, underdressed college student who was too excited to get into her first *adult* club. But when I saw Teona with breasts bigger than mine and thighs thicker than peanut butter, wearing natural makeup that accented her sienna complexion, I couldn't help but envy how confident she was to wear her hair cut into a Mohawk. Her all-white bodycon dress barely covered her booty, but as she strolled up with her broad shoulders back and her glitter body butter gleamin' in the moonlight, she almost fooled me into believing that she was an older woman looking for a night out with her girls.

"The club is thick tonight," Teona said as we walked toward the entrance. She spread her lips slowly and locked eyes with the bouncer guarding the door. With a lick of her lips, he stopped focusing on the crowd of people that swarmed the outside wall and focused all of his attention on us, or mainly her. I would be lying if I said I ain't strut a little harder, poke my chest out, and smack my lips a bit more to catch up with her. I was almost ashamed to be intimidated by her but impressed with how well she carried herself. She was a pro at the art of seduction, and she knew how to use it to her advantage.

When we reached the entrance, the doorman kept his eyes on her cleavage as his hand pulled back the ropes. No words were exchanged. Teona gave him a wink as she twisted her hips inside the club as we followed. I barely even noticed the pissed-off patrons standing outside in the humid Orlando weather.

When we hit the bar, Teona rested her breasts atop the counter and smiled at the helpless bartender. Within seconds, he ignored the customers that waved him down across the bar and damn near stumbled his way over to us. "Whatchu three PYTs drinking tonight?" As he flashed his hollowed-out gold tooth and finger-combed his balding Jheri curl, I was surprised that men still used the term *PYT*.

Teona batted her long eyelashes as she primped her short tresses. "What's the special?"

The bartender smiled back and pulled out three wineglasses. Filling it with White Zin, he shrugged his shoulders and said, "It's on the house."

Upon grabbing our drinks, Teona gave him a wink and walked away. At that point, I couldn't hold back. "How old are you again?"

"Twenty."

"I thought this was your first time in a twenty-one-and-up club."

Teona pursed her lips and then smirked. "My first in Orlando, maybe."

We settled into a well-lit corner across from the bar and sipped our drinks. "How long have you been at this?"

"At what?"

"Playing with men's hearts like this."

She chuckled. After slurping the rest of her drink, she set her glass down on the table behind us and licked her lips. "I don't play. I never insist or suggest. I'm my normal self. If men wanna buy me things, pay my way, or forget to check ID, that's on them."

Although she was good at her game and made sure to look good doing it, her immaturity was still apparent. She played a dangerous game that would end badly if she played her cards wrong. Still, I had to give the girl her props. When I was twenty, I wasn't using my feminine wiles to get free drinks and skip lines.

"Teona's been this way since she turned sixteen," Loraine chimed in. "She even had a man beg her to let him buy her a car. All he asked in return was the chance to get her name."

"Did you give it to him?" I asked.

Teona smiled. "Not my real name. The car wasn't all that anyway."

I cut my eyes at Loraine and gulped down the rest of my wine. "You let your little sister drive a car that some man gave her when she was sixteen?"

"No one *lets* me do anything," Teona interjected. "Loraine is not my mother. I could do what I damn well please. Besides, I gave it back."

Loraine gave me a look that said, *"See."* I shook my head and smiled.

When Loraine finished sipping her drink, two men from the bar made their way in our direction. They were both well-groomed and prepped to pounce. They weren't the finest men to look at, but they still served as a healthy distraction from Tariq.

"Hey, beautifuls," one man said. He had on denim jeans, a white T-shirt, and a gray sports jacket, very simple but pretty well put together. He had an air of unwarranted arrogance as his lightning bolt of gray hair pierced through his structured fade. He folded his arms across his chest and smirked while the incandescent lights illuminated his tree bark complexion. He had a square head and fade cut like Morris Chestnut from *The Best Man*. He definitely wasn't as fine as Morris Chestnut, but he was still someone I'd entertain for the night.

"Hello," Loraine said. Teona avoided eye contact, and I smiled back.

"I'm Vince, and this is my man, Brad," said the sports jacket.

"Hello, Brad and Vince," Loraine responded.

"Only one of you talks," said Brad. Brad's dark skin reminded me of the mahogany brown furniture that accented my living room. That was his good quality. His pimply face and narrow eyes chipped away at the one good quality he had. And the other bad part of him consisted of the fact that he couldn't keep his eyes off of our breasts. If he let his tongue fall out his mouth, I'd have to complete his look with a leash and a collar. He was short and stocky like a buff teddy bear. I usually didn't like bald guys, especially since the look of dried sweat leading from the back of his neck to the center of his skull disgusted me. But on this crooked-tooth loser, his bald head and skin color were all he had going for him.

Teona pursed her lips.

I said, "I'm Erin."

"And I'm Loraine."

"Can we buy you three ladies a drink?"

"If that's okay with you, miss." Brad reached for Teona's arm. When she politely snatched it back, Brad's smile dropped from a bruised ego.

"My name is Dana," said Teona. "…not Miss. And yes, you can buy me a drink."

A smarter man would've taken Teona's attitude as his cue to move on to the next, but it was pathetic how easily men went for the chase. Teona's flip sense of self was enough incentive for Brad to grin widely in an attempt to make Teona his prey. Unluckily for him, he was already Teona's.

The night was was over. Teona was already halfway drunk from the slew of drinks Brad showered upon her seemingly insurmountable thirst. Eventually, Vince and Brad realized the game Teona was playing and decided to spend the little money they had left on women they could actually get into bed that night. As we left the club and entered the parking lot, we all stopped in our tracks as a tall, caramel brotha with eyes the color of a sunset stepped in front of us. His honey-blond dreads rested between his shoulder blades as he sucked on his bottom lip and kept his eyes on Teona. Usually, I didn't hate on any female when another man was checking her out, but when he flashed a set of perfect white teeth, and the club lights changed his eye color from sunset to Pacific Ocean blue, I couldn't help but clear my throat and step up a little to get noticed.

"Te—" The letters dripped off his heart-shaped lips. Then he ran his tongue across his lips and made my panties more moist than the color of his eyes. "Where you been?"

Teona fronted as if the depth in his voice didn't make her knees weak like it did me. I had to hold on to Loraine's shoulder to keep my balance. "C'mon, let's go." Teona grabbed Loraine's hand and attempted to drag her past the Mandingo warrior dressed in a black V-neck sweater and jeans that cupped his butt and crotch in all the perfect places.

I hadn't even realized I was holding Loraine back until Teona swirled around to see why Loraine wasn't moving as fast as she wanted. The gentleman wrapped his arm around Teona's waist and held her back. "Where you goin'?"

Teona rolled her eyes so hard I thought she lost them in the back of her head. "Get your hands off me, Dre."

Dre threw his hands up and then finally gave Loraine and me some attention. "I'm sorry. My name is Andre. To whom do I owe the pleasure?"

Andre put his hand out for Loraine and me to shake. Loraine hesitated but I gladly took the opportunity to feel his hands. My fantasies wanted a better understanding of how his hands would feel wrapped around my waist. "Erin."

Andre licked his lips and winked before turning his attention to Loraine.

"Loraine." Loraine shook his hand like she was doing him a favor.

Teona yanked Loraine's hand from Andre's grasp and then yanked her away.

"Can you please leave?" Teona demanded.

"I've been callin' you." Andre's smooth demeanor slightly shifted as his intrigue turned to irritation. "Where have you been?"

"Mindin' my damn business."

Teona kept walking as Andre followed. Loraine and I followed after them as we watched the spectacle. Tired of chasing after Teona, Andre circled around her and turned his heavenly smile into a menacing frown. "Where's my watch, Te?"

"I dunno what you're talkin' 'bout."

"Don't play stupid wit' me, Te."

Teona turned around. Loraine sensed trouble and put some pep in her step as we headed in the opposite direction. "Who is that man, Teona?" Loraine asked.

Teona huffed an annoyed breath. "Some lil' boy who's apparently following me."

Andre grabbed Teona's arm and swung her around. Putting his finger in her face, he clenched his jaw and squeezed her wrist. "I'm not playin', Te. My granddaddy gave me that watch. You think I'ma let you take it?"

Teona wrenched her arm back and twirled her neck. "Don't you put yo' hands on me."

Loraine got in between them and pushed Teona back. "Excuse you. Don't put your hands on my lil' sister."

"Well, your lil' sis is goin' 'round stealin' my shit. She lucky she suck dick good o' I woulda came for her a long time ago."

Andre was quickly transforming into a menace as opposed to a Mandingo. "Teona, what's goin' on here?" Loraine asked.

Teona sucked the enamel off her teeth as she folded her arms over her chest. "Dre, you need to go."

Andre brushed past Loraine and grabbed Teona's forearms. "You think shit is funny, Te?" Andre's Pacific Ocean eyes slowly turned blood-red as the fluorescent streetlights showed off the black, weed-smoke residue on his heart-shaped lips. He squeezed Teona's arms as he pulled her close. "Gimme my shit."

Loraine smacked Andre's shoulder and then pulled out her stun gun. When Andre noticed what Loraine had in her purse, he let Teona go and put up his hands. "Leave my sister alone."

Afraid of where this night would lead, I turned Teona around. "If you have something that belongs to this man, please give it to him. We don't wanna end up on the news tonight."

Teona stomped her foot. After going through her purse, she pulled out a gold watch with a diamond-encrusted rotating bezel. Andre swiped the watch from Teona's hand and examined it. Pleased with its condition, Andre blew Teona a kiss and then disappeared into the night.

"What the hell was that about, Teona?" Loraine asked as she put away her stun gun.

Teona shrugged her shoulders. "Same shit, different night." With that, she walked toward the car. Loraine and I exchanged looks as my heartbeat steadied.

"Is she serious?"

Loraine shook her head. "Same Teona, different dang night. Let's go."

When I got home, I kicked my shoes off and headed for the wine bottle waiting on me. As I stood barefoot in my kitchen, I thought about gettin' nice and liquored up by making Amaretto ice cream floats and sippin' on Pink Moscato. Unfortunately, my plans were interrupted by a gentle knock at my door. I took a deep breath and glanced at the clock on my microwave. Taking a deep breath, I untied my hair and scratched between my tender roots.

When I opened my door and noticed Tariq's tall frame taking up most of the space in my doorway, it took my breath away. I literally held my breath as my eyes scanned the fine specimen before me. The last thing I expected was his haughtiness knocking on my door at four in the morning, especially after how we ended things. Still, my breath found it hard to come back as my eyes gazed over the way his nicely fitted button-down caressed his chest and his slacks gripped his body in ways that I only wanted to. I cursed myself for being jealous of men's pants. "What are you doing here?"

He licked his soft lips and gazed over my body. "I wanted to talk." His deep voice danced off my eardrums and slid between my inner thighs. I squeezed the door and tried not to squeeze him.

"We have nothing to discuss. You're married, and I don't date married men."

"That's what I want to talk to you about."

"Save it for the next chick you try to screw over."

"If I was tryna screw you over, I wouldn't be at your door tryna talk."

"Talk? You're probably horny." He sucked on his bottom lip and smiled. Yes, my knees quivered, but I folded my arms over my chest like his lip suckin' didn't do me any favors. "Like I said, save it for the next chick you try to screw over."

"C'mon, Erin. It's not even like that. I can't lie and say I'm not thinkin' 'bout that when you standin' here lookin' sexy in skinny jeans, breasts all out, hair down—man's goin' be a man. But I did come here to talk to you."

"About what?"

"'Bout what happened. I ain't wanna leave things like they've been."

"It's been a month, Tariq. It's been left. There's nothing more to discuss. And as my outfit points out, I've moved on to other things."

"Is that right?" Within seconds, his words were on my neck and his arms around my waist. I tried to push him away but his lips met my skin and I was lost in translation. His previous actions showed me we were over, but as his lips spoke dirty little nothings on my neck, all I could understand was how sweet his lips tasted when they touched mine. Before I realized it, we were in my apartment, trying to make it to the bedroom as quickly as our clothes hit the floor.

I felt so stupid for letting him do me like he did, but as soon as my panties hit the floor, I was his. I was his to lay himself inside of and my emotions were his to toy with. Nonetheless, in that moment, I needed him. I needed to feel a man as strong and as sexy as Tariq freak me right and assure me that the woman that stared back at me in the mirror deserved to be pleased the way she needed to be pleased. And Tariq was the man who knew how to please.

"You can't stay here, Tariq." I wrapped my legs around his waist so he couldn't leave. "We can't do this," I assured him as I tilted my head back and let him suck the spaces below my chin that always sent shivers up my spine.

"You know you missed me," he whispered in my ear as he pinned my wrists back and stroked his body on top of mine, He slowly satisfied me and forced me to reach my climax. "I came to make you come."

A task he knew all too well. As if his dick was meant for my satisfaction, I needed it to do to me what I lay in bed alone hoping he'd come back and do. I was fooling myself if I thought I had any say over what was going to happen the moment he knocked on my door. As soon as he knocked on my door, our fates were sealed and we were destined to lie in my bed soiling my sheets with me begging for more—and he knew it.

"That little girl brought home some random man." Loraine stomped through my apartment pacing back and forth as she huffed and puffed. Loraine caught Teona sneaking some guy she met at the club that night into her home. Instead of being remorseful, Teona couldn't understand why Loraine couldn't accept her hustle. Two nights after my sexcapade with Tariq, I got a call at one-thirty in the morning that Teona dropped the bomb that Loraine was jealous. I didn't even have to ask. Teona would be out the door and Loraine would be two seconds away from knocking down mine.

I sat on the couch watching her, trying not to reveal the glorious night I had with Tariq. Tariq and I never really talked. I didn't get the answers I truly needed from him. Questions like, *Where's your wife?, Where's your son?, Why didn't you ever feel the need to tell me?* were left hanging in the same spot where I asked myself, *"Why do you always let him in?"* Either way, I came four ways 'til Sunday and damn sho' wasn't complaining. "You knew your sister wasn't an angel."

Loraine placed her hands on her hips. "That does not excuse the fact that she met some man and had the nerve to invite this strange man to *my* house at one o'clock in the damn morning. I almost kicked him *and* her out my house *tonight*. That ho has two days before she's out."

"Why didn't you?"

Loraine cut her eyes in my direction and stopped pacing. With her finger in my face, she clenched her jaw and said, "I sound like I'm playing, Erin. I'm pissed the fuck off. You think I ain't wanna kick the ho out my house? That man is definitely gone, but she's my damn sister, no matter how many strange men she lets lounge inside her."

"You're taking it too far. I'm sure she's not a ho and—"

"How would you know? You saw how she was at the club. Flashing her tits around for free VIP and drinks. And then there was that mess wit' Andre. I dunno what that ho would do for jewelry, cars, and clothes. I don't wanna know." Loraine ran her hands through her locs, and went back to pacing a hole into my floor.

When my phone vibrated, I couldn't help but smile at the text Tariq sent me. *"Miss u."* Albeit short and sweet, it was a message that had me lit up for the rest of the night.

"What the fuck you smiling about? Did Teona text you?"

I tried to hide my glee by sucking my teeth and changing the subject. "Why would Teona be texting me? She's prolly at your place setting a blaze to all your things before she packs her things and leave."

"Girl, please. That girl ain't crazy."

"After you cursed her out and told her she had two days to find another place to stay, I wouldn't be surprised if she did."

Loraine brushed that notion off and refused to let my text go. "Who's texting you at three in the morning then?"

"That's my business."

For the first time since she stomped into my apartment, Loraine calmed down. She took a deep breath and relaxed her shoulders. "Look, my head's real out of it right now. I realized my lil' sister was…different, but I tried to ignore the possibility that she might be this active to get the perks she's been receiving. You wanna know the reason why she felt justified to bring home some man she met at a club? Because he promised to pay off her student loan debt. This bitch is fucking for loan money." Loraine plopped down on the couch next to me, shaking her head. "I'm not her mother, but why would she feel the need to bring this type of shit to *my* doorstep? I ain't that easygoing."

"Ain't that the truth," I joked.

Loraine slapped my thigh and rested her head on my couch pillows. She sighed and rubbed her forehead. "Forgive me if I've been difficult for the past hour but—"

"You ain't gotta explain nothing to me, girl."

"I don't wanna get a call in the middle of the night about her, y'know?"

"I understand. I guess it's 'bout that time you two have a real sister-to-sister talk."

"We do. I don't want her to blame her behavior on our dad not being around. I'm tired of hearing the excuses. I need her to be a woman and stop playing these reckless games. I had to give her an ultimatum, for the sake of our relationship. But, I guess I'll sit down and talk to her before she leaves."

We sat there quietly. Loraine's head had to be filled with thoughts of her fast-tailed sister. My head was full of thoughts of Tariq. My phone vibrated again. It was Tariq; this time it was a call. To avoid the scolding, I tried to quickly silence it before Loraine caught wind. I would've gotten away with it if he didn't feel the need to follow up his missed call with another text that read, *"I need 2 c u."*

"Who is blowing up your phone, girl?"

"No one important."

"Must be important enough. The first time you got a text, you were lit up like a Christmas tree. Now the calls are coming."

I waved it off and shrugged my shoulders. "It's nothing, girl. I'm here to focus on you."

Loraine sat up. "Listen, the last thing I wanna be doing right now is focusing on my problems. You got a new man or something? Who's blowing you up like this?"

I took a deep breath and stared at the wall. "Tariq."

"What?" Loraine jumped up and put her finger back in my face. "Tariq, who?"

"You know who I'm talkin' about."

"*Married* Tariq? What's he saying?"

"Yes, *married* Tariq. He's not saying much."

"Well, he must be sayin' enough 'cause you couldn't stop smiling when he first texted you. What's up, girl? You holdin' out? You and Tariq messin' around again."

"He showed up the other night. I tried to resist him but…" I rubbed the throbbing skin between my eyes and then sighed. "It's nothing, though."

"Is he still married?"

"We never had the chance to discuss that."

Loraine stood quiet. I expected her to go through this entire spiel about how irresponsible I was being and how bad this was going to end. Instead, she quietly sat back down and shrugged her shoulders. "It is what it is then, I guess."

"That's it? You ain't got nothing else to say?"

"Girl, I got my own problems to deal with. If this makes you happy, then do you."

CHAPTER 11

Tariq

Three years ago...

I reached a turning point in my life. By the time I graduated from college, I had a plan for myself: find a job, develop a career, find a woman, and get married—all by age thirty. At twenty-eight, I was well on my way to marrying my woman with my career in tote. By twenty-nine, shit changed and my only goals were to make money and make moves. I lost interest in finding a suitable mate for myself; I was only interested in my next fix. I denied the pain that Deja had caused me by using easy women to cure the hurt; but easy women were only Band-Aids—nothing to heal me of my ailment truly. Still, I used them and abused them, and left no excuses.

When I met Simoné, I was impressed by her drive. Initially I was solely impressed with how tight her jeans fit and how intently the sun highlighted the small crevices of her mocha skin—the small of her back, below the calves of her long legs, and the folds of her eyelids that overlapped round eyes sitting on top of her taut cheek bones while peeking through her long, black bangs. When she spread her soft lips and said her name, "Simoné, pronounced *See-Mo-Nay* but spelled like Simone with an accent mark," I smirked.

"I'm Riq," I whispered in her ear as she touched my thigh in the back of a crowded soul food restaurant. Although the room was packed with hungry ol' fools looking to pack their faces wit' collard greens and cornbread, I was only lookin' to pack my face with the moistness that sat between the thighs of the pretty mocha chick that sat in the back booth.

"How 'bout we get out of here? It's too packed in here." She knew what she wanted and went after it. I recognized I was in trouble when I realized that I remembered her name. I was blinded by her bright smile and plump breasts that sat on top of her table. I should've seen that I was falling victim to the same characteristics she shared with Deja. Her sultry voice, beautiful eyes, and soft lips all reminded me of a love I tried to forget. Although I had yet to taste those lips, I could tell they'd be trouble once my lips got a hold of 'em.

I stood up and grabbed her hand and led her to my car. Claiming her before I was given her last name—still shocked that I remembered her first name. *Simoné.* With her palm resting on my chest, she whispered in my ear, "Nice car." She eyed my chocolate brown 2012 Infiniti G and slid her finger along the body. Resting her plum booty on my door, she folded her arms and licked her lips. "You're so cute."

I laughed. "Whatchu got planned fo' me?"

She laughed, too. She moved in closer and pressed her breasts against my chest. She confirmed my permission to slide my hands down her waist to her ass. She grinned and moved her face closer to mine. "What do you want me to do?"

I pulled her head closer and took over her lips like a savage. She was mine for the taking in the middle of the parking lot in broad daylight. We had met ten minutes ago and already my tongue was down her throat. I could feel her wet pussy on my thigh. Any other day, I would have taken this as another win, but her boldness enticed me. *Who was this chick to let me do this to her for everyone to see?* When we pulled ourselves apart from each other, I licked my lips and sucked the taste of bubble gum lip gloss from my lips. "Where'd you park?"

"I rode with my girls so I can ride home with you."

"You goin' to invite yo' self to my house?"

She smiled. "You can come home wit' me instead."

Why is this so easy? More importantly, why do I like it so much? I tested the waters. I needed to see what lines she'd let me cross and determine if she was worth the crossing. "We could hit the backseat instead."

Her smile faded as quickly as it came and her head tilted to the side. When her hands went to her hips and her eyes started rolling, I chuckled. "We could not, " she said.

I threw my hands up in surrender. I tested the waters and didn't like what I got. I pulled out my keys and agreed to take her home. I couldn't pass up the chance to feel something different than what I'd been feeling. When she hopped in my car and I cranked up the ignition, I continued to stake claim on my possession. I slid her panties to the side and was delighted in the fact that she didn't ask me to stop—and at the rate we were going, I didn't know how.

Simoné. I couldn't stop saying her name. Simoné. My usual routine was to love 'em and leave 'em. With her, she had me checkin' in every other day. She easily allowed me to slide in between and gut her like a fish, and I foolishly gorged on that. It wasn't long before I found myself sleeping over after sex, having meaningful conversations, and meetin' her girls. I was breaking every rule in the player handbook and I didn't care. It wasn't like I had any real plans of marrying her. I still fucked around when I could, but Simoné was my main. She was down fo' whateva, and I was always down wit' it. However, wit' all good things, the end will surface.

"Who's this bitch callin' you?"

I grabbed my phone from my bedroom dresser and tucked it in my back pocket. I stood up and continued zippin' my pants. "Ain't nobody important."

With her breath on my neck, she said, "Must be important enough if the bitch got the nerve to keep blowin' up yo' phone."

I took a deep breath and stood up. I didn't love Simoné, but I respected her emotions—to an extent. Usually, when she expressed emotion, it was anger or lust. This was the first time I experienced jealousy. "Why are you trippin'?"

She put her hands on her hips and twisted her neck. "Fuck you, Riq. I'm asking you to tell me who the fuck you got blowin' up yo' phone like she the fuckin' police. Tell me who she is!"

I cocked my head back and laughed at the audacity of this woman. Although I cared about her enough to listen when she spoke, she ventured into dangerous territory—the type of territory that involved her feelin' as if she had pull in the business I handled outside of our relationship. Yea, I called her back when I couldn't answer. I paid a few bills. I even rubbed her feet a few times. However, if I ever gave her any inclination that she was more than an unhealthy convenience, the change had to start today.

"Lemme leave now 'cause you must be on somethin'." I grabbed my keys off her dresser and headed for her bedroom door.

Before I had the chance to pass through the doorway, she grabbed my arm and yanked me backward. "Did I say I was done talkin' to you?"

I stepped back and glared at her. "Who the fuck you think you talkin' to? I ain't one of these weak-ass lil' boys you be fuckin' wit'. I'm a grown-ass man."

"Well, a grown-ass man knows how to respect his woman."

"How the fuck am I disrespecting you?"

"By havin' some random ho callin' yo' number an' not having the respect to tell me who the fuck she is."

I yanked my arm from her grasp and headed for her front door. I hoped she'd let me leave and handle my business, but like a four-year-old, she beat me to the door and blocked my exit. "Aye, man, go on wit' that bullshit. I ain't got time to be dealin' wit' all this."

"Oh, so you got time to lie down and fuck me, but when I need you to be real, you quick to pussy out."

"Man, apparently you been smokin' on some shit 'cause I dunno where none of this is even comin' from. You need to move."

She folded her arms across her chest. "Or what?"

I laughed. Her show was amusing. When I met her, she made it seem like she wasn't with all this petty nonsense. But like every woman, she was showing her colors.

"For real, girl. Go on somewhere wit' that. Get out the way, Simoné."

She licked her lips and stood her ground. She didn't have any plans of moving from her spot any time soon, and I wasn't the man to put my hands on her to make her move. I had two options. I could either tell her that the woman on the phone was one of my many sideline hoes I had on speed dial who was lookin' to ride a dick worth straddling—or I could do what her lips were asking me to.

I walked up to her, firmly pushing her back against the door, and sucked on the side of her neck. She tried to push me off, but I pinned her wrists to the wall. "Get the fuck off me, Riq." She moaned. When I grabbed her thighs and wrapped them around my waist, she nibbled on her bottom lip. "I hate when you do this."

I chuckled and licked the bottom of her chin. "Yea, I know," I whispered as I sucked on her lips while I unbuckled my belt. With my pants on the floor, I slid my tongue between her lips and found the wetness she tried to hide behind her protests.

When I dug inside her, she freed herself from my hold and grabbed the back of my neck. "Oh, Riq," she groaned as she gritted her teeth and squeezed her thighs around my waist. "Yes, don't stop."

I kissed a trail of kisses down her neck and chest while I beckoned for her arrival. Yet, instead of allowing her to continue to barricade my only way out, I grabbed her ass and led her quivering body to her plush living room couch. "You want me to stop?" I jokingly asked as I stroked deep inside of her.

She squeezed her hips tighter around my dick to warn me not to. I smiled as I kissed her lips some more. "You better not." Between kisses, she moaned while gripping my head and clutching her couch cushion. When her body started shaking and her breaths became shorter, I listened to her body and matched my movements with hers. Quickly, yet thoughtfully, I caressed her skin while pushing inside of her. I slightly trembled at the melody her *oohs* and *ahs* made as she came. She fell limp to her peak. I slowly slid out of her and pulled up my pants.

"I'ma call you later," I said as I ran for the door.

"I love you," she whispered.

Before I had a real opportunity to answer, I let the door close behind me as I proceeded to my car.

I was wrong, but I had to do what I had to do. I did feel guilty. Even though I never confirmed my exclusivity to her, she had the right to assume that she was my only woman. And expressing her true emotions in the midst of my haste was her prerogative. However, her sense of the title of "Tariq's woman" spanned way beyond what I was willing and ready to give her. Unfortunately, in my refusal to give her the treatment she deserved, she was forced to fill in the blanks that I left with my avoidance, denial, and missed phone calls. Nevertheless, I couldn't ignore the fact that my original intentions with her hadn't changed; rather, I didn't want them to change. By now I would have been on to the next; yet, I was still there. Our consistency allowed her the option to sneak into my subconscious at night and get me daydreamin' 'bout her. I often fantasized about her lips, her voice, and her presence. She had me breakin' all the rules, and I was doing everything in my power to refuse it. Nevertheless, Simoné was nothing if not persistent, and it was a turn-on that I couldn't deny. My original intentions were not to settle down but keep her in the rotation. Hence, I've achieved my goal. Still, she wanted more, and I tried not to give it to her. According to her, she loved me; unfortunately for her, I didn't want to reciprocate.

CHAPTER 12

Erin

Present...

The thing between Tariq and me was complicated. We became each other's drug, and damn if it ain't feel good to get high off him. However, I couldn't keep playin' the fool, especially with a man I had no business playin' with.

"Are we ever goin' to talk about your wife, Tariq?"

He dropped his boyish smile. At first, he was playfully tickling my stomach, trying to go for round two, as we lay naked in my bed at two in the morning. Then, he rested his back on my headboard and chewed on his bottom lip. "You had to kill the mood, huh?"

I sat up and put on my robe. "Tariq, we have to discuss your marriage at some point."

"Does it have to be right now?"

"If not now, then when?"

He shrugged his shoulders. "Is it even important? I ain't even tryna get into all that right now."

I yanked off my covers. "Then you need to leave."

I stood up and pointed at my front door. I ran the risk of ending a very beneficial sexual relationship, but I had to do what was best for me emotionally. It felt good to feel him inside of me, but it felt worse to watch him leave. I was left with sticky thighs and a head full of questions. I was tired of crying over a man that didn't belong to me. I would miss his company, but I had to respect the woman that stared back at me in the mirror.

"It's like that?"

"You're not gonna play me like I'm the fool in all this. You had me jump out yo' damn window, Tariq, while your wife stood in your living room. Then, I don't hear from you in a month. So, yes, it's like that."

He was lying there staring at me. I wanted badly to hear what had been going through his mind. Was he secretly laughing at my *Waiting to Exhale* moment? Here I was thinkin' we might have had something going when all he wanted was a quick nut. I wondered if he was he truly hurt by my dismissal. Could he have actually fallen for me after countless nights of dry kisses and sweaty embraces?

He turned his head and got out of bed. "All right, then."

We didn't exchange any more words. He put on his clothes and walked toward my front door. I wanted to be done with him. I didn't want to cry when he shut the door behind him, but I couldn't deny my feelings. I was fallin' for him. He disrespected me, mistreated me, and lied to me, but I thought about him at work. I let him enter my bed night after night while he left his wife questioning his whereabouts. I was the other woman. I was mad at him but more mad at myself for lettin' him do me like he did and actually enjoying it. It was time to move on to someone who was willin' to treat me right.

When he walked out my door without even a goodbye, I wiped the tear that crept down my cheek and meandered back into my bedroom. This time, when I lay naked in my bed, it wouldn't be next to a man who would rather lie to me than love me.

"Did you speak to your sister?"

Loraine and I sat across from each other at a coffee shop during our lunch break. We both hung our heads low as we contemplated our lives. "I decided to let her stay."

"That's nice. How'd that work out?"

"I couldn't kick my little sister out. Besides, she's going back to her dorm in a few weeks anyway." Loraine sipped on her tea and twirled one of her loose locs.

"What's the vibe between you two now?"

"It's definitely different. I don't see her as my innocent lil' sis. I realized she was no saint but…" She sighed and took another sip of her tea. "I don't know what that girl does while she's in college. I hope she's not that girl who fucks her professors for all As."

I swirled my spoon in the cold coffee I spent six dollars to waste. "Don't say that. You two should spend the next few weeks tryna get over this hump."

"How are things with you and Tariq?"

I wanted to redirect the conversation back to Loraine and her sister, but it would only have us going around in circles. I pursed my lips and shrugged my shoulders. "It is what it is."

"What's that supposed to mean?"

"I kicked him out of my apartment the other night."

Loraine raised her eyebrows in disbelief. "I'm surprised you had the balls to actually do that. I expected you to actually keep the charade going."

"*Charade?*"

"How long did you expect an affair with a man who barely cares about you to last? You should've never let him back in the first time."

"The same could've been said when you foolishly let your ex-husband back in your life after he cheated on and mistreated you only to do it to you all over again." I took offense to her blatant disregard for my bruised emotions and paid no regard to her ego. "Every woman plays the fool at least once in her life, but what can you do?"

Loraine sucked in her lips and sipped on her tea. She wanted to snap back, but she had it coming. Even though I was the friend whose shoulder she cried on when her ex-husband of two years revealed his year-and-a-half-long affair, I callously reminded her of the pain it brought when after lettin' him back in, she let him do the same damn things for another year. The heavens opened up when she finally broke free from that prison sentence. "Let's get back to work."

The Christian in me wanted to apologize. She was obviously still hurt by her past, and I had no right to flaunt her mistakes in her face. But the crying little girl in me felt it was best to end the lunch date early. We parted ways without any more words. Usually, we'd end with a hug and a promise to call each other later. This time, we gathered our belongings and walked away in separate directions. Once I got back to work, my guilt would overpower me and I'd apologize for my rudeness. However, as I walked away from my real friend, all I could selfishly think about was how good it felt to be the one causing the pain instead of feeling it.

I went the entire day without calling Loraine back and apologizing. I kinda wanted her to call me first and have my apology be a response to hers. But as I walked into my big empty apartment, I was compelled to pick up my phone and face the problem I had caused. However, as always, a knock at the door interrupted my plans.

When I opened my door, my initial hope that I'd see Loraine

on the other side holding a bottle of wine and a *Waiting to Exhale* DVD in her hand was cast aside by the appearance of Tariq's face.

I rubbed the skin between my eyes and placed my phone back in its holder. "What are you doing here?"

For the first time, I wasn't dizzy from his fragrance. When I stared in his eyes, my knees didn't go weak. My stance was firm and un-wavering.

"Can I come in?" He looked good, too. He never spared me the opportunity to see him in a shirt that caressed his skin in ways that revealed his muscles or pants that gripped a butt I could imagine myself grabbing between my thighs. Still, I was steady.

"No. I have plans." I pushed the door to shut it in his face, but he held it before I got the chance.

"I'm not tryna spend the night. I wanna talk about the other night."

"Why? You had your chance to talk and you walked out."

"You kicked me out."

I looked down at his hand that held on to my doorknob. "You need to leave, Tariq. I have better things to do."

"You not gonna give me the chance to explain?"

"You had ample time to explain yourself. All of a sudden I'm supposed to stand here and let you tell me some bullshit story you came up with because *you* decided to?"

He licked his lips and scratched the back of his head. "You're right. I should've talked to you 'bout all this but...I dunno. I... I've been real out of it lately."

I shook my head. "Tariq, I can't do this tonight. Like I said, I have plans."

When he didn't say anything in response, I could tell he didn't expect to hear me deny him. I wasn't quietly beggin' for him to rip off my clothes or suck on my lips. I honestly wanted the chance not to cave in to a man who didn't deserve it. He let go of the doorknob and nodded his head. "All right. I can respect that."

"Good." I tried to close the door but he held it. I breathed deeply and twisted my hip to the side. "What, Tariq?"

"Call me when you get free, though." I nodded my head. "I'm serious, Erin. Call me."

"Okay." I closed the door and abandoned all plans to call Loraine. Her apology could wait. Tonight, I reveled in my win over a man who I used to let win every time before.

I called Loraine the next morning but got her voicemail. I assumed she went in to work early, but by the time five o'clock hit, I realized that she wasn't tryna speak to me. I was hurt but not hurt enough to beg her for her a phone call—not yet at least. When I walked up the stairs to my apartment, I noticed a half-dressed woman lying on the floor in front of my door. I pulled out my cell phone and prepared to call the authorities if necessary. By the time I reached her, I realized that it was Teona passed out at my doorstep. I ran my fingers through my hair and took a deep breath.

I called Loraine again. This time, it rang twice before going straight to voicemail. Certain that she was ignoring my calls, I opted to send her a text informing her of her little sister's whereabouts. Once my text was sent, I nudged Teona awake and unlocked the door. "What are you doin' here, Teona?"

She looked up at me as if she didn't recognize me. We stared at each other for a second. She looked around to verify her surroundings. "Erin?" she asked.

"Get inside, Teona." I helped her to her feet and led her to my living room sofa. Whatever led her to my doorstep had to be something serious, but I didn't wanna risk my neighbors findin' out about it as we discussed it in my hallway.

When she swiped the few flyaways from her forehead, she scanned my apartment and smirked. "You have a really nice place. Damn! How much does a copy editor make?"

"Teona, what are you doing here?"

Teona opened her mouth to say something before she drunkenly scurried to my kitchen sink to throw up. "Fuck!" was the last thing she yelled before filling up my sink with yesterday's stink. She kicked off her heels and hugged my counter as she let the water pour over her head.

"Does your sister know you're here?"

After coughing up her own spit, she wiped her face, smeared her makeup, and washed her hands. "My sister doesn't give a fuck where I am."

"You know that's not true. How did you even get here?"

"I'm surprised I remembered how to get here." Teona turned around and slid down to the floor with her elbows on her knees and her head sunk in her lap. "I have someone waitin' on me."

"You do? Where?" I took out a washcloth and ran it under some warm water.

"Downstairs." She struggled to stand back up but fell atop my kitchen counter. I grabbed her arms and led her back to my sofa. As she laid her head on the back of my sofa, she wiped her eyes with the sweaty palms of her hands. "I was supposed to come up and see if you were home so we could come inside."

After handing her the washcloth, I snapped. "Who's *we?*"

"Timothy…or Travis…or Rick or maybe it was Alfred o' somethin'. Whoever he is, he's downstairs."

"Teona, you have some random man downstairs waiting to come inside *my* apartment? What the hell is wrong with you? Don't come bringin' some man you don't even know to my home."

"Calm down, Erin. You sound like Loraine right now."

I walked into my kitchen and grabbed a cup from my cupboard. I filled it with tap water and shoved it in Teona's face. "Drink this, lil' girl."

"I'm not a fuckin' lil' girl, old woman. Calm down. Todd or Mike is harmless; he wanted to have some innocent fun."

"How long have you been here?"

"Since like ten o'clock, I think."

"Ten in the morning?"

"Yea, what time is it now?"

"It's almost six at night!"

"Oh!" She burst into a hysterical laugh that caused her to slide off the sofa trying to hold her balance. When her bottom hit the floor, she yelped. "I guess Alfred or Jonathan ain't outside no mo' then, huh?"

"You been here since ten in the a.m. and no one called the police?"

She shrugged her shoulders and mumbled. "Some nigga named Toronto…Rudolpho…Reynaldo or somethin' said he'd check up on me 'til you got home. He tried to invite me in but I wasn't tryna be alone in that weirdo's apartment."

"Alonzo." I corrected her. I grabbed my cup from her hand. Trying to help her up, I jumped when I heard someone banging at my door. Hopefully, it wasn't Tariq, Alonzo, or the random man she had waiting downstairs for half the day. When I opened my door, Loraine brushed past me, going straight for Teona. "Girl, what the hell are you doing here?"

Teona rolled her eyes at Loraine. Then she glanced over at me and snarled. "You called her?"

Loraine turned her around to face her. "Lil' girl, what the hell is wrong with you?"

Teona pulled on my sofa cushion to pull herself up to a standing position. "I thought I tol' you not to call me *lil' girl.*"

Loraine grabbed her arm. "Let's go."

Teona yanked her arm away and pushed Loraine. "Don't touch me, bitch! I ain't ask you to come here an' do me no favors."

Loraine glanced back at me, then back at Teona. "Fine, *lil' girl.* I'm done." Loraine turned on her heel and stomped toward my door.

"Loraine, don't walk away from your sister."

"Leave me the fuck alone, Erin. I'm done—with both of you." I pulled on her arm to stop her from leaving. She tried to pull herself free but my grip was strong. "What do you want from me? Let me go."

When I noticed the tears in her eyes, I realized that my words may have cut deeper than I thought they would. On the heels of her sibling turmoil, the last thing she needed to hear was her only friend bringin' up nonsense from her past. "I'm sorry. I was wrong for bringin' up mess about your ex-husband. That wasn't meant for me to bring up; especially at the time I did."

"It's not that, Erin. I may not cry and whine about every little problem in my life, but I am going through a lot. And then I gotta deal with this fast-ass lil' girl fuckin' strangers fo' gas money. I'm really tired and the last thing I need to hear is bullshit from someone who I *thought* was my best friend."

"I know, and I'm sorry. I was feelin' a lil' heartbroken."

Loraine wiped her face and took a deep breath. "I was wrong for coming down on you, but you needed to hear that. I don't need any of this shit I'm going through. I'm sorry if I hurt you, but you didn't have the right to bring that shit up. You know what he put me through."

"You're right. But I'm still here and…" I looked over at Teona who had collapsed on my sofa. "Teona will be back in school in a few weeks."

Loraine squeezed her fists and bit her lip. "No, she won't. She got her ass kicked out of school."

"When did that happen?"

"It happened when her dean found out she was fuckin' her professors. I told you that girl was fuckin' for As."

"Hey, I can fuckin' hear you talkin' 'bout me!" Teona yelled.

Loraine leaned up against my refrigerator door and wiped her face again. "I don't know what to do wit' that girl."

"Well, like I said, I'm here and we'll figure this mess out together."

Loraine took another deep breath and held the back of her neck. "Thanks. I appreciate that." She looked over at Teona. "I dunno how I'm gonna explain all this to our parents. She got kicked out wit' only a year left. My mama is goin' put all this on me." Loraine sighed. "What would you do?"

"Thank my mama for not givin' me any lil' sisters."

CHAPTER 13

Erin

"My mama set me up on a blind date." After an uncomfortable visit with my mama leaving me frustrated and more aware of my loneliness, I had to hang out with Loraine and make up for the time we missed while being mad at each other.

Loraine tried to hold in her giggles but was unsuccessful. "Really?" We sat on my sofa watching *Carrie*. On any other day, Loraine would be at her house while we played phone tag. But ever since her lil' sister set up shop in her guest bedroom, she jumped at any chance to make her way over to my apartment. "What's wrong with him?"

"Girl, I don't even know. I tol' my mama about Tariq, an' next thing you know we're discussing Deacon Benson over fish and grits."

"Yo' mama cooked fish and grits and you didn't invite me?"

"Well, I tol' her you're the one who hooked Tariq and me up, so she wasn't ready to see yo' face."

"How was I supposed to know Tariq was *that* guy? It's not my fault. I can't believe you blamed me!"

"I didn't blame you. I told her the facts. Come to church with me on Sunday and we can meet Deacon Benson there while you find the time to kiss up to Mama. Hopefully, this one at least has all his teeth."

"I have to go to yo' mama's barely air-conditioned church to say sorry? I can't send her a gift basket or something?"

"The only place Mama forgives is in the house of the Lord. Any other day, you better pray."

"Fine. I'll go, but I better be invited to dinner next time."

When my phone vibrated, I put it on silent. "You wanna open a bottle of wine?"

"Who are you ignoring?"

"Tariq. He's been blowing me up the past few days."

"Wow! And you've been ignoring him all this time?"

"I told you. I'm done."

"I'm impressed. I can't lie. I thought you would cave."

I smacked her shoulder. "That's not even right. I'm a grown woman; I don't need to be chasin' after no married man."

"I know that, but I see Tariq at work all the time and he is too fine. If I were you, I'd be tempted too. Hell, if I were me, I'd be tempted."

"Please, girl. Being fine only made him stay one day longer. When a woman's fed up..." When my phone lit up again, I placed it on my end table. "I will say the sex was on point. My insides quiver every time I send that fool to voicemail."

Loraine nodded and grinned. "Really? I can only imagine." Her tone was calm and unsurprised. I thought about dismissing it, but she left me vexed. Usually when I brought up the possibility of talkin' sex, Loraine readily chimed in. With her not-so-active sex life butting its head in our lives every so often, Loraine would some-times live her sex life vicariously through me. Tonight, she was eerily unresponsive.

"Why'd you say it like that?"

"Like what? What do you want me to say?"

"I was expecting you to ask for some details. You never ask me for details when it comes to Tariq. To be honest, I need some sex therapy. Talkin' 'bout it might relieve some stress."

"Then talk." Her nostrils flared as she fidgeted in her seat and played with a loose dreadlock. "Are you gonna open that bottle or what?"

I walked into the kitchen and pulled out a bottle of Moscato d'Asti. After pouring a full glass, I sat back and waited for the alcohol to take effect. A tipsy Loraine was a lot easier to manipulate than a sober one.

Once she was two full glasses in, I gave my questions another go. "Is there something I don't know about Tariq that you do? Have you heard stories?"

"Like what?"

"I dunno. Anything I would need to know. The fact that you *don't* wanna know makes me think that you already know."

Her eyes glazed over and she tapped the wine bottle for a refill. Upon another sip, her face went cold and body tight. After a long pause, she sat her drink down and took a deep breath. "Girl, I'ma come out and say it. Tariq and...well, Tariq and I had sex."

As quickly as she released her next breath, my breaths had stopped short. My emotions were scattered, and I didn't understand which ones to pick up first. I sucked in my bottom lip and nodded. I didn't know what else to do but nod in agreement even though there had been nothing to agree to. Now, when my phone lit up, I paid attention. I could have ignored it, but I was forced to regard every detail of that moment. "When?"

"It was a long time ago. Way before Tariq and I even worked together. It was a one-time thing. Nothing serious; a friendly passing." Loraine left out any pauses. She answered my questions hurriedly, while apologetically dismissing any wrongdoing on her part.

"Last I checked, friends ain't fuckin' in passing."

She stopped before she said anything else to set me off. Not long

before, I was professing my freedom from a sap-sucking relationship. Now, I was back in imprisonment by the same woman who
gave me my initial sentencing. She picked her glass back up and
sucked down the rest of her drink. At that time, we both glanced
at the clock. Twelve-thirty. We planned to stay up late watching a
movie centered around a girl gettin' even, but her happenstance
confession ruined all plans for late-night gab sessions. "Erin, I
didn't—"

"Why would you introduce me to a man you fucked? Why would
I want your leftovers?"

"He's not my leftovers. We weren't datin'. He took me out on
two dates. The second date he closed the deal and I never really
heard from him again. At the time, I was engaged to my ex-husband
and wasn't lookin' for a relationship wit' Riq." *Riq*. Now, Tariq was
Riq to her. I was sick. "It was somethin' that happened. When I
got hired at his office, we talked but we both knew nothing was
there. I thought he'd be a good guy for you."

"Why wouldn't you tell me this when you hooked us up? Why
wait 'til now? Don't you think that's a detail you shouldn't leave
out? Loraine, you told me about the car he drove, the diamond
earring in his left ear, and even the type of shoes he wore. Whether
you fucked him or not is something I'd like to know way more
than the type of shoes he wears."

"I dunno. I didn't think it was that important."

"If I'm supposed to be your friend, I would think you would
know what type of person I am. Wouldn't you want to know if I
fucked your ex-husband, Lorenz?"

She lowered her eyes and hunched her shoulders forward. "You're
right."

I breathed in deeply and sighed. I looked over at my blinkin' phone. When I stood up and stopped the DVD, she understood that our night was over. "It's late. I have to get to bed."

Gathering her things, she said, "I figured you'd freak out if you knew we had sex, but I didn't want that to get in the way of you meetin' a nice guy. Well, I thought he was a nice guy."

"We don't have to discuss this anymore. You said your peace and I'm done. Let's get some sleep."

"I'm sorry, Erin."

I ignored her apology as I scrolled through the slew of text messages sent over by Tariq. "Lemme walk you out."

Loraine dropped her eyebrows and cracked her knuckles. She stood up, stretched, and headed toward my door. "Don't be mad at me."

I didn't want to be mad but wondered why I shouldn't be. Even though Tariq was not worth my time, my best friend's sexual past shouldn't intersect with mine, especially when it came to a man like Tariq. I gave Loraine a fake smile and closed the door behind her while I determined which emotion was a suitable fit.

CHAPTER 14

Tariq

Two years ago…

I tried to get away from Simoné. At first it worked. Initially, my relationship wit' Simoné had slowly dissolved. Eventually, the emotion she thought was love shed its coating and revealed itself as mere lust. My refusal to return to the same monogamous lifestyle I abandoned for a woman I barely trusted gradually became a pill too big for Simoné to swallow. Soon, my calls stopped coming. Then, I stopped answering hers. For a while, I thought I was rid of her.

I kept datin' when I could. There was this one chick. Loraine. She had red, shoulder-length dreads and beautiful, cool gray eyes. It turned me on to find a woman with all of her own hair on her head. Wit' all the weaves, relaxers, and press and curls, natural hair intrigued me. When I saw her smile at me through the bulletproof glass at the bank, I couldn't help but smile back.

"Is there anything else I could help you with today?" She twirled her hair in her fingers and blushed when I slowly licked my lips.

"I'm diggin' yo' whole natural thing." Her face went red as she bowed her head and ran her fingers through her locs. Soon, our conversation went from her hairstyle to her structured rose-colored cheeks that accentuated her chestnut skin and petite frame, all leading to her giving me her number. I ignored the impatient customers tappin' their feet and clearin' their throats behind me in the teller line. She was mine, and I'd have her panties on my wall by the end of the week.

"What do you do?"

"I work in insurance." I chugged down my Bud Light Lime and looked into her eyes when she spoke. We sat across from each other at dinner as she nervously snickered and twirled her hair like a teenage girl. I hated the initial "gettin' to know you convo" that all first dates were accustomed to. With Simoné, we skipped all that and got down to the nitty-gritty. With Loraine, I was back to fake smiles, corny jokes and empty discussions about our future.

"That seems boring. What made you get into that?"

"It's not that borin'. You got good and bad days." With my steak halfway done and my second beer runnin' through me, I was ready to end the night at her place. I'll admit she was difficult to read. We'd end up with her legs on my shoulders, but her shyness made me question how long it'd take. I liked good girls for two reasons: they were good at pretending they were too wholesome to fuck too early, and they were even better when they did. "Whatchu got planned for tonight?"

"After dinner?" She looked down at her empty plate and realized that the night was coming to a close. "I dunno. Did you have plans?"

"I'm leaving that up to you."

She smiled and swallowed the rest of her Shirley Temple. "I guess we can get out of here and go from there."

I asked for the check and led her to my car. With a full stomach and a tipsy mind, I was all but aching to see what treasure she hid beneath her pencil skirt. It took all my strength not to reach over and feel between her thighs as we drove home. She was feelin' me, but I couldn't risk movin' too fast an' leavin' wit' nothing.

When we stopped outside her apartment building, I turned off the ignition and waited for her to make the invitation. We sat in my car quietly as our breaths surrounded our silence. After glancing at her phone, her nervous smile slightly faded as she looked up at her building. "I would invite you in, but I have to get up in the morning."

Damn. I realized our night would go one of two ways. I mentally calmed the beast in my pants and nodded. "Okay, I understand."

I pulled her face close to mine and then slid my tongue between her lips. She pulled back initially and surrendered her lips to me. She moaned as I gripped the back of her neck and slipped my lips over hers. I let my other hand creep up her thigh as she tickled my tongue with hers. As my hand moved closer to her panties, I sucked and nibbled on her lips to distract her from my mission. She kept moaning as our kiss goodnight turned into more than she bargained for. I kept her close to me and licked her lips to my satisfaction. Then I let my fingers tickle her drippin' wet pussy folds while my tongue ventured for the back of her throat. She innocently spread her thighs to let my hand go in further. I expected her to move away but was surprised when she guided my hand to her g-spot. We sucked each other's lips as I finger-fucked her in her parking lot. She hadn't expected to let me get this far, but wit' magic fingers like mine, I wouldn't have to stop 'til she came. However, until my penis felt what it grew hard for, I couldn't allow her to come before me.

When her body vibrated and she squeezed my shirt with her tongue atop mine, I pulled away against her demands and smiled. "You sure you don't want me to come in?"

She caught her breath and stared at me with confusion and frustration. She looked back up at her apartment and shook her head. "You can't. I can't let you in tonight." She fixed her panties and wiped the sweat from her forehead. After pullin' down my visor, she pulled up her locs and retouched her lipstick.

As I watched her prep herself to walk into her own apartment, I laughed at my sudden realization. "Is there a specific reason why I can't come up?"

"N-no," she stuttered. "I'm…" She calmed down and caught her breath. "I'm not that type of girl. Maybe next time." She smiled and unlocked the door. "Call me later?"

I nodded and watched as she scurried away. There was no doubt in my mind that she was runnin' to meet the man she left at home. I assumed that she expected he'd be home later, but her timin' was off. I'm sure this wasn't the first time a woman used me to satisfy the void her man left in her sex life; however, this was the first time I was made aware. I didn't enjoy being the same type of man that took my woman from me, but I couldn't deny the role I played. I was the man who paid no regard to the lives my lovers lived outside of my bedroom. Plus, I couldn't lose out on the chance to lie up with a woman whose pussy was tighter than I had felt in a long time. I drove away, ignoring the guilt I felt for knowingly planning to lie with another man's woman.

When I saw Loraine two weeks later, I assumed the secluded diner where she asked me to meet her was a location her man rarely frequented. I asked no questions; I went with the flow and gave her the fuel she needed to eventually drop her panties at the time of my choosing.

"You come here often?"

She shrugged her shoulders and sipped on her lukewarm coffee. "As often as I can."

With little desire to force small talk, I got right to it. "Let's get out of here."

"You don't wanna order anything first?"

"I ate a few hours ago and I'm still full."

"You sure? The pancakes here are really good. And where would we go?"

"Anywhere but here."

"I dunno, Riq."

"I missed you. I haven't seen those eyes in too long." I leaned in closer to her and deviously smirked. "I don't wanna share you with anyone."

She turned her head to hide her wide grin. Checking her watch, she nodded. "Okay, let's get out of here."

We left her jeep at the diner and I drove her to my place to avoid any possible run-ins with her man. When I walked her inside, I led her over to my couch and turned on the TV. I dunno what was playing, but I needed her distracted long enough to let me kiss down her neck. Like always, she coyly pretended as if she didn't want it and moved away from me.

"You have a really nice townhouse."

I smiled and pulled her closer. "I told you. I want you all to myself."

She licked her lips and invited me to kiss them. I leaned in and gently kissed her plump lips while grippin' the back of her neck. This time, I wasn't takin' it slow. I couldn't risk her getting a call from her man demanding to know her whereabouts while she lied her way out of my embrace. I held on to her waist and laid her back on my couch. When I spread her legs and began pullin' down her panties, she resisted. I compromised by putting my fingers to work while I sucked in her lips. She moaned as her arms wrapped around my neck and she willingly spread her thighs for my fingers to get through. She whispered, "Ooh...yes."

With my approval for entry, I pulled the condom out from my back pocket, unbuckled my pants, and sucked and nibbled on the side of her neck. With her panties to the side, I slid myself inside of her and trembled as her lips gripped my dick. It felt like I was in something brand new as she clenched her jaw to hold in her shrieks of satisfaction. "Do you want me to stop?" I whispered into her ear as her hips gyrated beneath me.

"Don't stop." Her legs spread wider to give me room to dig deeper. I pulled down her dreads so I could watch them bounce off her shoulders as I thrust inside her.

Unprepared for how good she felt, I moaned, too. "Shit." I gripped the couch cushions. I was closer to a come than I thought I would be.

I pulled up her shirt and unhooked her bra to reveal perfectly round breasts. With a body like hers, my initial guilt resurfaced. I didn't want her to myself because she'd only remind me of unnecessary pain. She damn sho' wasn't no saint, but wit' lips that supple and a body that stacked, some man had to be missin' her.

"I'm about to come," she revealed as her body shook. As she screamed in satisfaction, her legs wobbled and the veins in her throat surfaced. I watched as her eyes rolled to the back of her neck and her pussy lips held on to my dick and vibrated. I wanted to come too, but I held back and slid out before her grip forced me to change course.

I sat back on the couch and watched the seven o'clock news on my TV screen. There was a report runnin' about how neighbors found the body of a local businessman shot in the head. Apparently, a cheatin' wife's husband found her lover sneakin' out the back door. Husband got him before he hit the lawn. Immediately, I was cold. I remembered this Bible verse my mama once told me. "A jealous husband shows no mercy." I ain't wanna be the man that stood between a woman and her jealous man. Loraine sat back and caught her breath.

As we avoided each other's eye contact, I checked the time. "Did you want me to take you back to the diner?"

She didn't look at me. She nodded and fixed her crooked panties. "I need to use your bathroom for a quick sec."

I pointed toward my half bath and watched her hips rock from side to side as she strutted inside. While the bathroom sink kept flowing, she was tryin' to wash my scent from her skin and conceal her cheatin' ways wit' cheap perfume and warm water. When she walked back out, her hair was up, lipstick back on and low-cut shirt tucked back in her skirt.

"You ready to go?"

She nodded her head and headed toward my door. We didn't have any more words to exchange. We got what we wanted from each other although our guilt continued to tap us on our shoulders, callously reminding us of the experience we shared. While it wasn't all my fault for breaking up a happy home, but not long ago, I wouldn't even think to screw another man's woman. I changed my ways to keep up with the times. No one was faithful anymore. For all I knew, her man was prolly between the legs of another woman while he checked *his* watch and made sure *she* wasn't home. I was playing the game all men were tryna win.

Two years ago...

Life isn't meant to be lived alone. At night, everyone gets lonely. I start craving the opportunity to hold someone. I begin wanting to caress the soft skin of a woman who wants nothing but to lie close to me. Eventually, I yearn for the whisper of her voice in my ear, professing her love for me. The random women that I picked up at banks, soul food restaurants, or park benches weren't enough to feed my hunger for companionship. My sex drive seemed quenched, but I stayed hungry.

Damien was the man who pushed me into my path of hedonism and recklessness. With a slew of women under my belt, I could thank him for giving me the courage to stop playing the sucker and play women instead—get them before they got me. My gratitude, however, was mysteriously absent when I saw him at the gym.

"What have you been up to since you left the job?"

He wiped the sweat off his face and shrugged his shoulders. "You know, same ol' same. I got a job workin' in collections. Doing me, y'know?"

I rested my back against the wall and waited for my turn to use the set of weights I'd been eyeing. "How's everything else? You finally settled down yet?"

He cut his eyes at me and chuckled. "Who me? Why the hell would I do something stupid like that?"

"You been single longer than I have. You almost forty now, right? Ain't it time to give it up?"

"I ain't never givin' it up. Bitches ain't shit." Damien grabbed one of the heavier free weights and started doing reps. "Why you askin'? You been pussy whipped all yo' life. I hope you ain't plannin' on settlin' down again."

"I'm thirty. Of course, I'm thinkin' 'bout it."

"What does that mean? Hoes are hoes at any age. You had yo' fill already?"

"I mean, it's cool, but you don't get tired of a different woman every other night? Playin' games, not havin' anyone to hold you down. Deja definitely pulled one ova on me, but I liked believing that she was down fo' me. I don't have that living like this."

"Fuck it. Get married then. Don't let me stop you. I'm happy. If it wasn't fo' bitches, I'd be living off my millions after goin' pro straight from college. Instead, I'm workin', callin' mothafuckas, an' askin' *them* for money. You wanna wife one of these hoes, cool. Don't get mad when they pull another one ova on you, like they always do."

When my weights were free to use, I walked over to them to start my reps. I was conflicted. Damien made sense, but I couldn't help but not feel right. It didn't feel normal going through women like objects. I wanted to slow down and recharge my batteries. I wasn't lookin' for a wife, but I did want something more than this. Whether Damien saw it or not, good women gave men balance. The men focused less on sleepin' around and focused more on their goals. My mama was living proof good women were out there. I ain't wanna be the forty-year-old player makin' a livin' workin' collections and fuckin' bitches.

When I left the gym, I called Simoné. She didn't answer. When I called the second time, I hung up after the third ring. I wanted to hear the sound of her voice. When her automated voicemail robbed me of that opportunity, I sat at a green light, confused. Staring at my phone, I didn't notice the three cars behind me honking. I stepped on the gas and pulled into the corner store parking lot. I somberly walked through the entrance and trekked down the aisles in search of bubble gum and hot fries.

"Flamin' Hot Cheetos are the best." The sultry voice tickled my eardrums and excited me in more ways than I thought it would. When Simoné's thick black bangs and glossed supple lips greeted me, I smiled mischievously as my eyes slid down to her red pumps, up her long legs, and stopped at the sight of her breasts squeezed unmercifully in her push-up bra. It looked like she threw on her nude, skintight dress to come see me.

"Hey, beautiful," I said.

She looked me up and down and grinned. "Whatchu doin'?"

"On my way home so I can head to work late." We stood there in the snack aisle, staring each other down, waiting for the other to say something. "Whatchu doin'? You going' somewhere?"

"I'm mindin' my business." She gazed at me a lil' while longer and turned on her heel. Before I let her walk away, I held her elbow and blocked her way. She pulled back and folded her arms across her chest. "What, Riq?"

"Where you goin' so fast? You ain't got shit to say to me?"

Simoné twirled her neck. "What would I have to say to you?"

"I called you. You ain't answer."

"And?" She stood there silently and dared me to question her avoidance.

I licked my lips and chuckled. "So you avoiding me now?"

"What the fuck do you want, Riq? You ignored my calls, so why can't I ignore yours?"

"I can't wanna talk to you?"

"If you wanted to talk to me, you wouldn't have pushed me away like you did." She turned around to walk away, and I skirted around her to stop her from leaving again.

She stomped her foot on the ground and grunted. "Riq, would you leave me alone? I blew you up like some groupie while you acted like I wasn't shit. Now you wanna stand in my way like you care about my feelings. If you genuinely cared, you wouldn't have tried me like you did. I'm tired of you trifling niggas coming in my face like I'm supposed to run back to you when you decide you're ready to make this work. Fuck you, Riq. Get out of my way."

I wasn't about to beg Simoné for a chance. I respected her frustrations, and although I wanted a chance at making things work, I wasn't about to make an ass out of myself at a raggedy corner store.

I nodded and stepped to the side. "All right. Do you."

She clowned me, but I wasn't about to let her gain the satisfaction of watching me beg for her. As I walked away, she was still standing behind me with her arms folded. I didn't even get what I went in there to get. I got in my car and headed home to get ready for work.

For the past three weeks, I was preparing to interview for a promotion to Compliance Manager. The last thing I needed was to worry about was a bad meeting wit' Simoné. I ain't even answer when her name came up on my cell phone.

When I got home from work, it was late. I sat on my couch drinking a beer. I cleared Simoné's missed calls from my screen and deleted her unread text messages. I considered callin' it a night when I got a call from Damien. "What's up?"

"I heard you got the promotion!"

I was smiling but held my composure. "It's not set in stone yet, but I'm pretty sure I did."

"Nigga, please. You know you did. Who else were they goin' hire, Big Luke from accounting? That job was yours before you even walked in to the interview."

"How you know all this? You talkin' like you still work there."

He chuckled. "Just 'cause I don't work there don't mean I don't know people that still do. An' I got good news, too. I left collections. One of my boys got me on this personal trainer gig. I'm making more and setting my own hours."

"That's what's up!" Lookin' at the time, I asked, "What were yo' plans for tonight?"

"There's this new club off OBT that we should roll through. I heard the ratio of women to men is like twelve to one. Plus, they got bottles goin' fo' forty. It's goin' be on point. And wit' this promotion, we gotta celebrate."

My phone beeped. Simoné was callin' again. I sighed and smacked my lips. "All right, let's go."

When we got to the club, Damien wasn't lying. For a second, I woulda thought we broke into a harem. Damien had the connections. We didn't even stand in the line that wrapped around the block. He slipped the bouncer a hundred and we walked right through. It was packed. Usually, with so many women in one place, the amount of ugly ones always outnumbered the fine ones, and the amount of cheap, stank ones outnumbered them all. Tonight, it was a sea full of sirens with bright smiles, fat asses, tight dresses, and loose morals. When we got to the bar, Damien ordered a couple of bottles and headed for the VIP corner. Like superstars, we sat down and watched as the women swarmed. In minutes, my head swooned from vodka and Hen shots while my lap overflowed with vibrating bottoms of drunken bad girls.

I had never partied wit' Damien before, but he was sure to please. Eventually, he disappeared into the sea of women and left me with three gyrating women. They placed my hands on their hips and bumped and grinded off beat while loading up on shots of Patrón. Lil' John was their master as they let his beat move their bodies in ways their parents wouldn't approve. I happily accepted their debauchery while the intoxication took control. It was time for a breather when I caught a girl suckin' up Damien in a dark corner. I shook my head and refused another shot. I wasn't tryna get my dick wet like that tonight.

I squeezed out of VIP and headed toward the bar. A few women gave me a wink as they silently called me over with a sway of their hips. I ignored them. Only an hour had passed, and already I was worn out. Suddenly, I felt a woman's touch on my stomach. I shook my head and moved her hand away. "Lemme order a drink and catch my breath," I said without looking back.

"I see you went back to ignoring my calls." When her warm voice met my ears, I turned around. Simoné looked finer than she did when she was in the corner store. She wore coochie-cutting sequin shorts and a see-through blouse. Her hair was blown out and curly, but her shadowy eyes still poked through thick, jet-black bangs like they always did.

I sucked in my bottom lip and tried not to stare at how juicy her lips were tonight. With all the fine-ass women in this club, she still looked the finest. "What's up, Simoné? You came to cuss me out again?"

She stared down at her open-toe shoes and back up at me. She innocently smirked and squeezed my arm. "I'm sorry." She moved in closer and rubbed her hand back and forth on my chest. "It felt good to be the one to make you look like a fool, though."

I moved away and glanced back at Damien in VIP. He was smackin' a girl's ass while she jiggled her bare booty all over his lap. I dunno why I thought Damien planned to take me to an upscale club. This was the type of mess ol' playas was in to. When I turned to face Simoné, I could smell the liquor on her breath. It was then that I noticed her droopy eyes and flushed skin. She was drunk and horny, and saw me as the man to release her from herself.

"I gotta get back to my boy."

"I saw you as soon as you walked in here. You had hoes all over you tonight. I had to say somethin' when you finally got away from all that."

"Well, you said somethin', an' now I'm out."

"Why are you trippin', Riq?" She pushed my shoulder, rested her arm on the bar and then propped her other hand on her waist. "You can dish it out but can't take it? Why are you treatin' me like this?"

"How am I treatin' you? You tol' me how you felt. I'm givin' you what you want."

She folded her arms. "I'm so tired of yo' bullshit, Riq."

Damien grabbed my shoulder from behind and laughed. "Tariq, man. What the fuck are you doin'? You gotta get back to VIP." He turned me around and pointed at the light-skinned chick with long straight hair and slanted eyes. "She's half-Asian, bruh. You gotta come back. She's been askin' fo' you."

Damien yanked me away from Simoné with a big grin on his face. I turned back to look at Simoné, who had her eyes down, but I could tell she was boilin' inside. Before I got too far, I yelled, "Have a good night," before disappearing into the crowd.

When I got to VIP, the Asian girl licked her lips slowly and twisted her hips to the sound of Usher. I got behind her and let her work her body on me like she was my private dancer.

She leaned back and whispered, "You gotta take me home tonight."

She bent over and rested her booty on my belt buckle. The way she backed it up on me, I had to catch my balance before I fell over.

"Shit!" I yelled out as she slid up her dress to show off her thong. I felt like I was in a "Tip Drill" video. When I looked up, I saw Simoné. I tried to look away and focus on the woman dancing and winding in front of me, but I couldn't help but notice her. She was grippin' the bar with one hand while the other hand wagged in some man's face. I watched the spectacle go on as the man she cursed out stared her down but kept his hands in his pockets. I was about to look away, but he backhanded her across her face and pushed her to the ground.

I stopped moving. Simoné held her face and yelped. I saw a look in her eyes that I wasn't used to seeing. She was scared. At that moment, I didn't notice the fat-assed Asian woman bouncing on my dick. I pushed my way out of VIP and rushed to her aid. The punk-ass dude stood over her berating her like she was his child while she sat on the floor afraid of gettin' back up.

When I met face-to-face with the tall, scrawny nigga wit' the receding hairline and lazy eye, I puffed my chest out, forcin' him to back down. He couldn't weigh more than a buck thirty, and there he stood like he was six feet seven weighing 200 pounds.

He got in my face. "What the fuck you want?"

I didn't see or hear anything else but my mind tellin' me to fuck this nigga up. Next thing I knew, my fist was ramming its way into his walnut-shaped head. I punched twice before he hit the ground. After knocking him to the ground, I pounded my Timberland boot into his birdcage chest as he heaved forward and blocked his face for protection.

"Aye, man! Chill!" he cried out as he crawled away in panic. The music stopped as two muscle-bound security guards rushed over and held me back. By that time, the damage was done. The nigga's pride was gone as he limped his way out of my face.

Damien ran up behind me and got the security guards to let me go. "Calm down, man. Let him go. He's good. Let him go."

The guards reluctantly let me go as they signaled the DJ to get the music back on. "He tries this shit again, and he's out on the streets," one guard said as they walked off. Damien nodded and held me back.

I knelt down and helped Simoné up. When she noticed the guy was gone, she snatched away from me and ran out of the club. I thanked Damien for an interesting night before I ran after her.

When I got outside, I saw Simoné stumbling down the road toward the parking lot. Once I caught up with her, I said, "You all right?"

She rubbed her bruised face. "Do I look all right?"

"Who the fuck was that?"

"Some fool who doesn't like being turned down for a dance. Why the fuck do you care? What happened to the *half-Asian* chick?"

I completely forgot about her. At one point, I was actually looking forward to takin' her home. But, as Simoné stood there needing me, my plans had changed.

I licked my lips and pulled Simoné closer to me so I could inspect her face. I muttered, "If I wanted her, I'd be with her and not fighting random niggas in the club for you."

"I didn't ask you to."

"What type of man would I be if I didn't?" She stood there rubbing her face and holding back the tears that welled up in her eyes. "Where'd you park?"

"My girls drove."

"Then how were you gettin' home?"

"I was gonna wait in the parkin' lot 'til they got out."

I held her hand and pointed at my car. "Lemme take you home. Where your girls at anyway? They weren't goin' help o' say somethin'?"

"So they can get beat down like me?"

We walked toward my car and I sat her down in the passenger side. When I got in and closed the door, she rubbed my thigh and stared out the window. "I don't wanna be alone tonight, Riq."

I started the ignition and drove to my townhouse. We didn't say anything else; we drove in silence as I played back the night's events repeatedly in my head. When we pulled up to my place, I led her in. She kicked off her shoes and walked into my bathroom. When I heard the shower runnin', I sat on the edge of my bed and rubbed my fists. As soft as that dude from the club looked, I ain't expect his jaw to feel that hard. I sat there listening to the running water while I took off my shoes and pulled off my shirt. When the shower stopped runnin', I unbuckled my pants and reclined back. The door opened and five seconds later, a moist Simoné climbed on top of me and leaned forward. She pressed her soft, unglossed lips on top of mine and curled her tongue around mine. While she kissed me, she slid her bare pussy back and forth on my stomach while I squeezed her thighs. She then slid off my pants and rested her face between my upper thighs.

When she grabbed my dick, I tried to pull it away; I didn't want Simoné suckin' on the same sweaty dick that half the club grinded on. "Lemme take a shower first."

Simoné moved my hand away and glided it between her wet

lips. She stuffed it into her mouth while working her tongue like a snake. She sucked it up and down and gently grazed her teeth around my skin while flappin' her tongue around it, sucking it clean of any indiscretions from before. I moaned as she held it firmly and sucked the head. I almost forgot how good she sucked. My toes curled as she swallowed my penis and let it nudge the back of her throat. She moaned and let her esophagus vibrate around my dick, allowing her tongue to tease the shaft. On the brink of coming, I pulled away and sat up. She climbed back on top and licked my neck.

"I gotta get in the shower."

I could feel her getting wet and I almost caved. I didn't want to be with her sweaty and sticky, but she tugged on my body, making it hard for me to get away.

"I love you, Riq."

I stared at her silently. She stared back at me with vulnerability.

"I'm not expecting you to say it back; I want you to know how I feel. I missed you and…thank you…for tonight."

"It's cool. I missed you, too."

"You don't have to tell me you love me, but I do need you to respect me. If you goin' be in this, then you can't be fuckin' around wit' other women. I can't find out about you an' half-Asian girls fuckin' when I'm not around. Don't disrespect me, Riq."

I smiled. "You think you can handle me all by yourself?"

She giggled. "I'm serious, Riq. Tell me that. When I call, don't ignore me, and I won't ignore you. I'm through playin'. I wanna be wit' you, Riq. I'm being real."

"All right. It's you and me."

She wrapped her arms around my neck and sighed a sigh of relief. "Good. Now let's go take a shower together."

CHAPTER 16

Erin

Present...

I haven't spoken to Loraine in two weeks. Time apart like that was unheard of with us. However, I didn't appreciate my close friend withholding the essential detail of us sharing one of the most intimate experiences I assumed I kept to myself. Although she called and texted, to avoid me cursing her out, I made sure she only heard my voicemail.

After receiving another call from Tariq, I decided it was time to see him tonight. Aside from the fact that it gave me the opportunity to watch him fawn all over me, it also gave me the chance to find out more about his fling with Loraine. I made no effort to pretty myself up as I answered the door in boxers and a T-shirt with my hair pulled up. When I opened the door, his eyes scrolled down to my bare feet, then back up to my high ponytail.

He smiled and stepped inside. "I'm glad you finally called me back."

I pursed my lips and closed the door behind him. As we strolled toward the couch, I couldn't help but twist my hips and give him a glimpse of what he'd been missing. "What did you wanna discuss?"

We sat on the couch as he gazed at me—watching my movements, studying my mannerisms. He slowly licked his lips and moved closer to me. "How much I missed you."

I moved back and sighed. "Please, Tariq. Talk to me. Where's your wife in all this?"

His eyes dropped to his shoes as he took a deep breath and pressed his hands together. "You always jump straight to that."

"I have to. I don't like being a home-wrecker, Tariq."

"There ain't no home to wreck."

"What about the child you neglected to mention? You keep me out there like I'm some groupie or somethin'. I've never been one to chase any man, dang sho' not a married man at that. If you don't want to give me what I want, then you don't have to be here."

He moved away from me and shook his head. "You comin' at me wit' all this. I ain't tryna be…" He clamped his jawbone and sighed heavily. "I dunno whatchu want me to say."

"Tell me what your intentions were when you decided to take me out, get in my pants, and tell me mess like *you miss me?* Were you tryna play with me?"

"I do miss you. I dunno. I thought…" Tariq dropped his shoulder and then stood up. Rubbin' the back of his head, he pulled in his lips and shook his head. "You looked good, and I wanted to see what was up wit' you."

"What does that even mean?"

"I dunno. You tryna make this out to be more than what it is."

I stood up. "And what is it? An overrated booty call?"

He chuckled. I didn't appreciate his rude amusement at my frustration. I was more than some married man's booty call, and I'd be damned if I let him stand there and laugh at me.

I turned on my heel and headed for the front door. He chased after me and grabbed my arm. "Wait! I never said that's what you were."

I snatched my arm away and opened the door. "You didn't have to."

With the invitation back into the world outside my front door, Tariq asked, "You kickin' me out again?"

"You talk a good game, but when it comes down to it, you can't give me what I want."

"And what's that?"

"A relationship. A real relationship where I call and you answer. One where I don't fear if your wife's around."

We stared at each other. I contemplated how soon I could get him out of my space before the neighbors noticed me kicking the fine, light-skinned dude out of my apartment in the middle of the night again. I hoped he contemplated givin' me what I wanted because he knew that I was worth it—but hopes never went far with Tariq.

He put his hand on my door and sighed. "I can't give you all that right now, but if every time shit get tough you ready to put me out, how am I supposed to trust in your ability to hold me down? I'm here, right? Obviously, I'm tryna be wit' you even after you keep puttin' my ass out on the street. I'm married, but trust me when I say that my marriage don't mean shit. I dunno why I keep fuckin' wit' you. If you want me out, then cool. I ain't goin' beg you to stay, but don't come askin' fo' somethin' you can't handle."

"Can't handle? You're married! If yo' marriage don't mean shit, then get a divorce. Why stay in it? Why have me climb down the damn fire escape if you don't care about it?"

"Shit ain't that easy when you got a kid. If I get a divorce, I might never see my son again. She sees you and then next thing you know, I'm in court while she beggin' the judge to raise my child support payments, even though I take care of my son. If you want a relationship o' whatever, you gotta be able to deal wit' this 'til I figure shit out."

"I dunno if I even want to."

He stood there staring at me as if he wanted to say something. I watched him turn his head and wipe his face. "Whatchu want me to do, Erin? You got me blowin' up yo' phone like *I'm* a fuckin' scrub. I keep comin' back. I'm here now. Let's work this shit out now. But if I leave, I'm gone."

I let my doorknob go and folded my arms. I wanted to be with Riq although all the reasons to justify my desire made no sense. He made my mind go crazy, but I liked hearing him say that he wanted me, too. Nevertheless, I wasn't naive. I could recognize game when I heard it. When Tariq spoke, however, my emotions were blind to the bullshit. I happily accepted his games and lambasted him when he tried to win. Tariq was somehow becoming my kryptonite, and I knowingly injected his poison into my bloodstream while allowing him to be the pain my heart could barely endure. I took a deep breath and gave in. "Fine." I nodded my head and closed the door. "You *are* here,—right now." I turned around, walked back to my couch, and sat down.

Tariq stood at the door for a moment and followed me chortling. "It's hard to get a good read on you, Erin." I smiled. He sat down next to me, and as if his dick never missed a step, he rested his hand on my inner thigh. His touch sent shivers up my body. When he looked into my eyes, I held my breath. "Erin, my situation at home ain't ideal. She's my wife and I have a son. I…I ain't happy. I can't be with her."

"Then why did you marry her?"

He dropped his head again to stare at his feet. He then sat back and shrugged his shoulders. "Why is it always so damn hot in here?"

"Answer the question, Tariq. No one put a gun to your head. Why marry a woman you can't stand to be with? Do you even know what you want?"

He paused and looked back up at me. "Yeah...you."

Of course, I blushed. I didn't want to, but his compliment, however shallow, made my face red. I wanted to smile and marinate in our gushy moment, but I had more questions. We were on a path, maybe not the right one, but a path nonetheless. Either way, we were far from anything concrete. "What about Loraine?"

He cocked his head and scrunched his brow. "What about her?"

"You tell me."

"There's nothing to tell."

"Not even anything about you two having sex?"

He paused for a moment and laughed. "Oh yeah. That did happen, huh?"

"Don't act like you didn't remember."

"I didn't...seriously. But that was nothing—at all."

I moved his hand from my thigh and sighed. "Then why didn't you tell me anything about it?"

"'Cause I forgot. And besides, that's something she should've told you."

He moved closer to me and returned his palm to my inner thigh. I pushed his hand away. "Did you enjoy it?"

He jerked his head back and turned away. "What kind of question is that? It was what it was."

"I wanna know how makin' love to my best friend was for you. Sex ain't sex, especially not with you."

"The last thing we did was make love. An' I dunno if it was more for her, but it damn sure was nothing for me. She had a man anyway. You ain't got nothin' to feel threatened about. You're the only woman I met in a while to get me to keep comin' back. Honestly."

Although he meant that statement as a compliment, it didn't put him in a positive light for me. "How many girls have you been with since you've been married?"

Tariq dropped his shoulders and played with the hairs on his chin. "I tol' you, my situation at home ain't been good. I ain't proud of it, but...I was out lookin'. We've been separated longer than we've been married."

"Then why not get a divorce?"

"We have a son. Shit changes when there's a baby."

"How old is he?"

"Almost two."

Things do change when there's a baby. While I imagined us throwing caution to the wind and allowing ourselves to fall into each other, I almost forgot about the young life mixed up in the middle of all this. So fresh into this world, the last thing he needed was to be reminded of the pain of a broken home. I couldn't contribute to a young boy's heartbreak. "You probably need to go back to your wife."

"Why? I'd rather stay with you."

"Because you need to focus on makin' a home for your family, and not messin' around wit' women like me."

"If I met more women like you, I wouldn't be in my situation."

"Your marriage is not a situation...it's a commitment you made before God."

"Trust me, it's nothing more than a situation. I wanna divorce her, but shit's kinda complicated. I keep comin' back to you 'cause things aren't complicated wit' you."

With the back and forth that went on between us, I was never too sure if Tariq was playin' me or genuinely into me. "I'm not kickin' you out, but you really do need to go."

Tariq rubbed his hand up and down my thigh and licked his lips. He stared into my eyes and gently squeezed my skin as we silently inched closer to each other. I hadn't had sex in a while, and the thought of wakin' up to Tariq after a long night of him lying inside me made me weak.

I reluctantly brushed his hand from my thigh and stood up. "You really want me to go?"

"No, but you still have to. I need time to think."

"I'm not going back to my wife. I don't even like callin' her that. I'm here wit' you 'cause I wanna be, not because I'm runnin' from her."

"Still, Tariq."

He waited it out at first, expecting me to change my mind. If he waited a second longer, he would have gotten his wish.

"All right."

When he stood up, I moved away from him to keep from fallin' victim to his embrace. I walked to the door and ignored the wet panties huggin' my skin.

With the door open and Tariq one minute away from leavin' me high and moist, he whispered, "Come here."

He pulled me into his arms and pressed his lips against mine. I struggled to catch my breath as I wrapped my arms around his neck. Usually, he'd make my knees weak by slowly sliding his tongue between my lips. This time, he held no punches as he slid his hands up my boxers and gripped my booty. Moaning as he pulled my body near his, he wagged his tongue in my mouth like a beast. He ravaged my body in my doorway as I pretended as if I wanted him to stop. If we didn't stop soon, we'd end the night with the top of my head banging against my headboard.

"Hey, Erin."

We stopped with Alonzo's interruption. I dropped my arms and moved away from the sexual trap Tariq set for me.

Tariq cut his eyes at Alonzo and back at me. "Who are you?"

"He's my neighbor." Tariq didn't care to hear who he was. He tried to pull me back, but I moved back further. "I'll talk to you later, Tariq."

Tariq grimaced, obviously frustrated by what he lost—a night of him having me right where he wanted me once again. For the first time, I was grateful to see Alonzo in my hallway. Tariq stood there towering over me, quietly begging me to reconsider. We both knew that the moment was gone, but apparently Tariq hadn't planned to give up that easily.

With my arms at my side and Alonzo still standing behind us, Tariq took a deep breath and then walked away. When he turned the corner, I finally opened my mouth and breathed. Alonzo said, "I'm sorry to interrupt. I dunno what I was thinkin'."

I shrugged my shoulders and smirked. "Lucky for you, it's all good."

"It looks like your friend didn't appreciate it."

"He prolly didn't, but what can you do?" Uncomfortable with standing at my door in a shirt and a pair of twisted boxers, I grabbed my door to close it. "Well, I'll see you around."

Alonzo opened his mouth as if he wanted to say something else, but he smiled and nodded instead. I shut the door without another word and then pressed my back against the wall. If it weren't for Alonzo's awkward greeting, Tariq would be inside me right now, with no question.

I grabbed the bottle of red wine peeking out of my wine rack. As I walked toward my bedroom, I realized I'd be making a detour for my bathroom in search of my vibrating companion. With Tariq heavy on my mind, I'd be satisfied one way or another. I could call Tariq a headache, but I loved the pain.

CHAPTER 17

L ouis was the manager at my local grocery. With Tariq not callin' and me trying ever so desperately to keep him off my mind, I did a lot of experimenting in the kitchen. I used my local grocer and my steel pots and pans to release my frustrations. I may have not been sexually satisfied, but I knew how to make a mean lasagna. Eventually, Louis couldn't resist the urge to chat me up at the checkout line. And with his chiseled jaw, milk chocolate skin and shoulder-length dreads, I couldn't resist the urge to chat back. His game was safe and I liked it. One second we were exchanging numbers in the parking lot. Next, I was cookin' him dinner in my apartment.

"I love a woman who can cook."

"I like a man who can appreciate it."

Louis and I had been on our fifth date since we exchanged numbers. When I finally invited him over, I slipped into my little black, V-neck dress and let my hair down—so did he. Our dates never went past simple kisses and long hugs goodnight. Tonight, with his hand on top of mine and our mouths full of meat sauce, I was yearning for a little more than hugs and kisses.

We watched each other chew as we sat at my dinner table. There was an awkward silence that sat at the table with us. He wanted to end our night together in bed as bad as I did. However, we couldn't get past go *and collect.*

When we finished our dinner, I cleared the table and led him to my couch. "Dinner was real good."

I kicked off my heels and leaned back. "I dunno why I thought about wearing pumps to dinner at my own home. My feet are killing me."

"Want me to rub them?"

I didn't remember the last time Tariq offered to rub my pretty little feet—if he had ever offered at all. I happily accepted his offer and placed my feet in his lap.

When he put his hands on the arches of my feet, I melted. He carefully massaged my feet and rubbed my toes while gazing into my eyes. I bit my bottom lip and moaned. "That feels so good, Louis."

Licking his lips, his hands felt softer, rubs were a little gentler, and strokes a bit slower. "I like makin' you happy."

I never knew my toes had a G-spot. I squeezed my thighs together and grabbed my couch cushions as he massaged my ankles and toyed with the fine hairs of my skin. Not before long, his hands had trailed up my legs and between my thighs. To green light his entry, I spread my thighs and permitted him to rub in between. When he touched the outside of my wet panties, he grinned mischievously. I tilted my head back, then jumped when I heard my phone vibrating. I looked over at my screen and sighed when I noticed Tariq's name scrolled across the top. I pressed ignore and went back to the man who had made it his mission to make me happy.

Louis asked, "Who was that?"

I waved it off and tilted my head back. "No one important." As I closed my eyes, I lifted my booty to give Louis permission to slide off my panties. I whispered, "Did you wanna take this to the bedroom?"

His grin widened like a Cheshire cat as he held my hand and stood us up. "I thought you'd never ask."

I poked my head out of my cubicle and searched for my supervisor's face. With Louis and I having a late night, any possibility of me making it in on time for work had come and gone with the arrival of my second orgasm. It felt good waking up to the sound of his heartbeat as I rested atop his chest. Even after I saw the time, I pressed the snooze button a few more times before finally giving in. After Louis said things like, "We can make this our snow day, boo," I almost called in sick for the whole week. However, my mama raised me to never miss work for a man who wasn't my husband—then I'd be left without a man or a job.

When I didn't notice my supervisor, I relaxed my shoulders and breathed. I started my computer and tapped on the mouse while I waited for it to load. "Good morning, Erin."

I jumped and turned to face my supervisor. "Eric, good morning."

Eric glanced at his watch and back at my clock. "It doesn't look like our times are off."

I sarcastically grinned and turned to face my computer. "Yes, I was a little late. I'm sorry."

"Was there a reason why you decided to come in almost an hour late?"

"I had a very personal issue that I tended to. I wanted to make it to work on time, but my personal issue impeded my opportunity to do so. For that, I apologize."

To avoid any calls from HR, Eric avoided any further questioning in an attempt to pry into my personal life. Eric maintained a very impersonal yet uncomfortably personal relationship with his other employees. To avoid those awkward stares or judgmental accusations, I made sure to keep our relationship strictly professional. He would always try to get more out of me, but I knew better. With no more questions to ask and my unrelenting stance on keeping our personal lives separate, he nodded and walked away, saying, "Don't make it a habit."

I logged into my computer. When I checked my email, my irritation quickly subsided when I opened the email Louis recently sent me. *"At work wishin' we had our snow day, boo. Hope to see you soon."* I quivered. I was in such a daze that I almost kissed the computer screen. After reading and rereading his message, I leaned back in my chair confident that this day would turn into a good one.

By the time lunch came, Louis and I had already exchanged a few dozen cute little notes professing our emotions for one another and reeling about how great our night had been. I didn't want to leave my computer, but my stomach was growling, and his email would be there when I got back. I quickly headed to the sub shop down the street from my job and pre-ordered my favorite meatball sub.

I was on such a high that I almost didn't react when I bumped into Loraine. She nervously smiled at me, staying quiet until I made the first move. "Hey." I was in a good mood; I could take the first step.

Her smile widened as she breathed and relaxed her shoulders. "Hey, Erin."

"How have you been?"

"You know, same ol' same."

I checked the time. We stood there awkwardly waiting for someone to say something, unaware of how this conversation would turn out. I certainly hadn't planned to jump down her throat in the middle of a sub shop, but all I needed was a reason. "How have things been going with your sis?"

She shrugged her shoulders. "Girl, you know nothing ever changes with her."

I was upset that our conversation evolved into forced dialogue in a crowded sub shop. I missed my friend. However, I couldn't let her think that lying by omission was a good way to carry what I thought was a great friendship. "Well, I need to grab my sub and get back to work."

"Still eating those meatball subs, huh?"

"Loraine, it's been a month since we talked. I'm not switching subs that quick."

"I know. I...I missed you, Erin."

And there it was—my opportunity to address our issues by either dismissing them or breathing life back into them. If I admitted to missing her, too, I'd give up all leverage and have to forgive her right then and there. If I ignored her comment, I'd be the bitch who was taking things a little too seriously for a man who never treated me right in the first place. *Should I continue to punish my dearest friend for keeping a secret of that nature from me?* She definitely deserved to feel the wrath of her betrayal, but it got fuzzy when I tried to determine the proper time limit for my "coolin'-off period." We stood there, both of us waiting to hear what I had to say. My lunch hour was almost up, and I had to make a decision before I walked out of that shop. I took a deep breath. "Because I miss you too doesn't excuse what happened. I'm still upset with you."

Loraine lowered her eyes like a bad little girl and responded carefully. "I understand. I don't even know why I would keep that from you. I dunno what was going through my mind."

"I dunno either."

Loraine shifted her weight to her left leg and sighed. "I wasn't even single when I had sex with Tariq. My ex-husband and I recently had moved in together after he proposed. I was having second thoughts about everything, and I saw Tariq. After it all happened, we both regretted it. It didn't even bother me that he never called afterward; I really didn't want him to." Loraine was never the cheating type, so her guilt was understandable. "I wanted to tell you, but I didn't wanna talk about it. I recognized that I was wrong as soon as I left that info out. I'm sorry, Erin."

I headed for the counter to pick up my order. "I'll get over it... eventually. I didn't expect you of all people to keep secrets."

Loraine turned her head to avoid another apology. With an attempt to change the subject and get our friendship going again she asked, "How are you two doing, anyway?"

"I'm seeing someone else. The one good plus is I'm pretty sure this one isn't married."

"That's great, Erin. I'm happy for you." Her bright smile and wide eyes confirmed her excitement.

"Thanks." The awkwardness had returned, and it was time for one of us to end the conversation and make it back to work before our lunch was over. "Well, I gotta get going."

Loraine wanted the opportunity to sit down and dish about Louis, but I couldn't force it. What we had going was good enough. "I'll call you later?"

With my sub in tote, I walked to the door and realized that it would be best to respond with a nod and a smile. I was happy that our friendship was getting back on track, but was I wasn't foolish enough to think it was back to normal. One day it would, but it wasn't goin' be today.

"I love spending time with you."

I looked away from Louis and smiled. We cuddled up on my couch as we played with each other's fingers and discussed stories about our pasts. I talked about how hard it was growin' up without a father, and he discussed how difficult it was knowing that he was adopted. He struggled heavily from abandonment issues, and it was new for him to be in a relationship and actually trust again. After spending intimate time with one another, I relaxed my fitted jeans and form-fitting tops to slowly introduce my tank tops and sweatpants into the routine. Eventually, we evolved into a relationship and our guards were down. I said, "I love you spending it with me."

"What we have almost doesn't feel natural, unreal. I feel like I can tell you anything, do anything with you. I feel safe with you."

"I feel the same way." I moved in close to him and kissed him. His lips were soft as pillows, and I couldn't deny my addiction to his kisses. When he held the small of my back, I loosened my nerves and fell into his hold. I found myself imagining our lives beyond mere *boyfriend and girlfriend.* When his phone vibrated, I kind of snapped back into reality. When he peeped the screen, he ignored the call and immediately went back to kissing me. I pulled away and asked, "Who was that?"

He paused and then responded, "Nobody as important as you, boo."

I shrugged my shoulders and fell mesmerized by the silkiness of his lips. "I hope not." I said between kisses. I slid out of my sweatpants and panties before climbing on top of him.

He unbuckled his pants and grabbed onto my waist. With his pants dropped to his ankles and his dick peeking through the slit in his boxers, I saddled up and began to ride. With my hips bouncing off his lap, he trembled as he sucked in his lips and squeezed his hands around me. As I grinded up and down, he looked into my eyes and whispered, "I'm fallin' for you, Erin."

I put my head back as his words sent chills up my spine. I wrapped my arms around his neck while I sucked in my bottom lip. "I'm fallin' too." It felt too early for the L word but right in time for the belief that this could be more than a *simply kissing on the couch* relationship. I wanted him daily and craved him nightly.

I gritted my teeth as I pulled on his shirtsleeve and gyrated on top of him. He gripped my cheeks and kissed trails down my chest. Pulling off my shirt, he unhooked my bra and devoured my breasts. I shook in his arms as I tried not to come so quick. "You always feel so good," he moaned.

Before I got the opportunity to respond, there was a knock at my door. If it was Alonzo, he'd better hope he boarded up his windows because Hurricane Erin was going to blow him off his Nikes. I tried to ignore it, hoping it would go away. Suddenly, my phone vibrated. I didn't want to lose my concentration. I closed my eyes and focused on arriving to our desired destinations. However, the knocks only persisted. "Shit," I murmured.

Louis looked over at my phone and back at my door. "Who's at your door?"

I looked over at my phone and noticed a missed call from Tariq. I froze. For a moment, I almost forgot what position I was in. I grabbed my phone and read his texts. *"Why haven't you been respondin?" "You can't answer your phone?" "Are you ignoring me? We need to talk!"* I cleared my missed calls and messages and contemplated waiting him out. If he was at my door, the last thing I wanted to do was answer it. Although the mood was certainly gone, I didn't wanna move. I sat atop Louis straddling him as I chewed on my fingernails and prayed for the knocks to stop. For a second they did. I took a deep breath as I thanked God for gettin' rid of my intruder. However, sooner than later, the knocks started up again. "Damn," I mumbled.

"You need me to answer it?"

I frowned and shook my head. My heart pounded through my chest. If Tariq stood on the other side of my door, this night would not end well. I didn't lie when I told Louis I was fallin' for him, but I would be lying if I claimed I was over Tariq. Even though I was practically starting a new life with Louis, I was still reluctant to surrender the made-up one I had with Tariq. I forced myself off Louis and dressed myself; Louis did the same. When I reached the peephole, I held my breath as I peeped through. Realizing who it was, I understood there would be no going back now. I opened the door and accepted that the night was over.

"What are you doing here, Teona?"

"Are you busy?"

I turn to look at Louis and then back at the barely dressed, hardly alert Teona that stood before me. I was grateful that it wasn't Tariq; nevertheless, I was annoyed with Teona's intrusion. She had wandered over to my apartment after a hard night of partying. "Did you bring some man over here again?"

She giggled and leaned on the doorframe. "I thought about it." She cleared her throat and peeked inside my apartment. "But he wouldn't come home with me." She waved at Louis and looked back at me. "Am I interrupting something?"

"Yes, you definitely are."

She hesitated initially, but she knew as much as I did that she couldn't make it anywhere else in her condition. "Can I come in?"

I moved to the side and let her stumble inside. "Louis, this is Teona, my girlfriend's little sister."

Louis waved a halfhearted wave and stood up. His frustration with being cheated out of an orgasm showed all over his face. Teona hunched over my kitchen sink and ran the water over her head. Also realizing that the night was over, Louis kissed my forehead and headed for my door. "I'm gonna let you care for your friend. I'll call you later."

I wanted him to stay and hold me tonight. I was pissed that even though Loraine and I weren't exactly speaking on the best terms, her problems still landed on my doorstep. I sighed and walked him to the door. "I wish you could stay."

"I do too. Don't worry. I'm not going anywhere. We'll have time alone again." He kissed me quickly and sweetly before he disappeared. After I shut the door, I watched Teona drench herself in water to revive herself from a bender she obviously wasn't prepared for. She was *drunk* and couldn't even lure a man over to sex her like she wanted him to.

I led Teona to my couch and gave her a towel. "Did you call your sister?"

"Please, don't. Not tonight." She plopped her head down on the arm of my couch and passed out. I thought about tending to her to make her night asleep on my couch more comfortable, but after she robbed me of my orgasm, I decided to shut the lights, lock my bedroom door, and whip out my old and faithful vibrating companion. Tonight was gonna end my way—one way or another.

CHAPTER 18

Erin

B y the time I woke up the next morning, Teona vanished. She wasn't on my couch and nowhere in my apartment. I was partly glad that I didn't have to deal with her hungover condition, bitter attitude, and snippy comebacks. However, I was partly upset that she didn't give me the chance to scold her about how disappointed I was with her. Still, I looked forward to heading into work and reading the sweet notes I'm sure Louis left in my inbox.

"She's dragging her trifling ass in here now," Loraine said. I had called Loraine on my way to work to make sure Teona hadn't stumbled off into the arms of the wrong type of strange man. "Thanks for looking after her."

"I did my best—even though she interrupted my date with Louis."

"I'll apologize on her behalf. I'm gettin' so sick and tired of this heifer. I'm hoping our parents find a way to get her out of my place and back to only visiting me during the summer breaks."

"With her acting like this, you might need to consider doing an intervention. This type of behavior doesn't seem healthy or safe. She's gonna end up bringin' the wrong man home, and she might end up bringin' him home to my place." The thought of her bringin' a serial rapist home scared me, mainly because with her, it was likely to happen. "I might have to start turning her away. I don't want her to end up sleepin' in my hallway, though."

"Girl, do what you have to do. Call the cops if you need to. A night on a cold park bench might snap some sense into her."

"I dunno about all that."

"Listen, the chance of Teona actually bringin' some crazy man right to your doorstep is likelier than you think. The only reason why she keeps coming to you is because I turn her away and you don't. Like you, I don't like strangers showing up at my door. You'll start singing a different tune when you find a drunken girl and five big, horny perverts knocking at your door at three in the morning."

I didn't want to turn Teona away, but Loraine made a valid and creepy point. I wasn't looking to call the police on her, but I also wasn't looking to tolerate her clearly violating my privacy by inviting random men to my apartment. The thought alone was infuriating. I took a deep breath and said it. "I miss talking to you."

I could hear her smile through the phone. "I miss talking to you too, girl. Let's skip work and have a spa day."

"Sounds tempting, but I've been getting a little too lax at work and need to catch up. Louis has my mind all over the place sometimes."

"I'm happy you found someone who you can actually enjoy being with."

"I am too. I can't let him interfere with my money, though."

"Well, we have to catch up soon."

"We will."

Loraine and I ended our phone call as I reached my desk. Before I settled in, I logged into my computer and checked my emails. Twelve new emails. I scrolled past the few emails from my supervisor and looked for Louis's name. Two new ones from him. The first one read, "Is it wrong for me to miss you so much when I saw you the other night?" I blushed. I let that email simmer as I put away my purse and hooked up my phone charger. I got nice and settled in to read the next email. It read, "I love you, boo."

Everything kind of stopped. I read the words eight times in an effort to make sense of them Although the words were nice to read, it would've been nicer for me to hear them. My feelings for Louis were growing; it had already been three months. However, I wasn't sure if I would describe my feelings as *love*. Nevertheless, I couldn't stop blushing. I enjoyed being loved by someone I could imagine myself loving back. I enjoyed the excitement of coming into work to read the words of affirmation that he left in my inbox. But I couldn't help but feel conflicted. For three months, it felt as if Louis and I were living out a fantasy. Addressing the topic of love introduced a new reality. Unfortunately, I was still enjoying the fantasy.

I couldn't respond. I wasn't comfortable responding to an email like that unless we were face-to-face. I wanted to read his face when he said it. Would his eyes sparkle? Would he place the palm of his hand in the arch in my back, slowly moving his moist lips while the words oozed off his tongue like sweet red wine? Would we end the night making a new form of love as our bodies moved to the rhythm our heartbeats made? Would I literally melt in his arms every moment he spoke? Or would his reality destroy my fantasy and have me questioning my sanity? Suddenly, I wished that I ventured off to that spa day. I was so wound up I couldn't finish my workday without a billion thoughts and questions permeating my cerebrum. The hands on the clock couldn't possibly move fast enough.

"Are you sure?"

I stared at the blank screen of my television as I pressed my phone to my face. "Yep. It was right there in print."

"Do you love him too?"

"It's only been a few months. I dunno. Is that even enough time?"

"Apparently, it is."

"What would you do?"

Loraine took a deep breath. "I wouldn't know what to say. I wouldn't put too much on it, though. Talk to him."

With a knock on my door, I snapped out of the thoughts going through my head and walked to the door. When I looked through the peephole to see who it was, I said, "Lemme call you back." I hung up the phone, checked my breath, and opened the door. "Hey."

Tariq stood in my doorway with his hands stuffed in his pockets. "You can't answer your phone?"

I held back my smirk. "What do we have to talk about?"

"If you picked up yo' phone, maybe you'd know."

"Are you still married?"

Tariq threw his hands in the air. "Here we go."

I said, "No, we ain't got to go nowhere. We talked about this, Tariq."

"You tol' me you was goin' call me later. What happened to that?"

"What is there left to discuss?"

Tariq scanned my hallway and looked into my apartment. "Can I come in? I ain't tryna be interrupted by yo' nosey-ass neighbors."

"You still haven't told me what you want to talk about."

Tariq took a deep breath and rubbed the back of his neck. "I miss you."

"Sounds like you're horny."

Tariq licked his lips and laughed. "Damn! I can't miss you?"

"I'm not playing, Tariq. You have a family to be missing..." I paused as I decided to tell him what he needed to hear. "And I have a man now."

He stared at me with a puckered brow. Deliberately, he rubbed his ear as if to make sure he heard right. "All right, so it's like that?"

"Was I supposed to wait on you? I ain't yo' fuck buddy. I ain't your sideline ho, and I dang sho' ain't the woman you're gonna keep stringin' along 'til you feel ready to make a decision about the status of your life. Therefore, I made a decision for myself. I gotta man now."

"What does that mean? Last time I was here, you were cool. Now, you comin' at me all sideways. What does your man have to do wit' me?"

"It means you need to go."

Tariq moved in closer to me. I could feel his breath on my neck. My pussy throbbed. It was as if my private parts were aware of his presence while silently welcoming him home. I moved back and reminded my lower regions that they belonged to Louis. Tariq held my waist and sucked in his bottom lip. "Why you playing these games, Erin?"

I moved his hand from my waist. "What games? I tol' you I needed time to think. You're the one playing cat and mouse. I'm through playin' wit' you, Tariq. I found a man willing to rub my feet, take me out, call me back, and treat me right. I'm done, Tariq."

Tariq moved in to whisper in my ear, "I'm not ready to let you go." Without enough time to react, he pulled me in and pressed his lips against mine. I could hear my pussy lips screamin' about how *Daddy was finally home*, but my heart knew better.

Before I let him slide his tongue in between my lips, I pushed him off and caught my breath. "You have to go."

Tariq stared at me with his lip poked out and his head skewed to the side, obviously offended by my rejection. Even though my body had ached for him to keep going, I wasn't going to be the cheater sucked into Tariq's empty diversions. Tariq threw his hands up and stepped back. "That's fucked up. You prolly had the nigga around all this time. You're the one playin' fuckin' games!"

"Because I don't wanna screw a married man, *I'm* playin' games."

"Ain't shit change! I been here tryna be wit' you. You knew my situation."

"Don't mean I like it. Why should I wait around for you an' yo' problems when I don't have to?"

"I'm a fuckin' problem now? You the one that can't be real and tell me this shit over the fuckin' phone."

"I don't have to answer to you."

"Whateva. You're about that bullshit."

The Tariq from our first date was back with the vengeance. The egotistical jackass with no respect for women was at my doorstep, and I wanted nothing more from him but to get out of my life. "Whateva, Tariq. You can think whateva you want about me. Don't call me anymore."

"'Cause you got new dick, all the shit we been doin' doesn't mean nothin'. Now my *fuckin' wife* is the reason why you through? Not too long ago, you was callin' me for my dick. What's up? Yo' new man can tame that pussy betta than I can?"

I stood there almost dumbfounded by his audacity. "Goodbye, Tariq." I slammed the door shut without another word. I dunno why I actually thought a man like Tariq was worth me dealin' with. I washed my hands of it all knowing I hadn't seen the last of him. Since I was used to his games, I was confident that his departure wasn't forever. His ego pushed him back into the arms of his wife, and it wouldn't be long until his horniness sent him back to my doorstep.

A half hour after Tariq left, I was still sitting on my couch staring at the wall. I would be insane to go back to Tariq again and expect a different result. There was a time where the mere thought of him inside of me excited me more than the thought of Louis confessing his love for me. Now, the idea of Tariq five feet away from me disgusted me. I couldn't love Tariq, but Tariq's presence always raised my adrenaline. He made my heart beat fast, and often times, it wasn't in a good way. Regardless, he would be back. His weakness for strength forced me to find more clever ways to reject him. But I felt sick in knowing that Louis's role in my life meant more to me when pissing Tariq off rather than satisfying me.

I was silently fuming when another knock returned to my door. I was slightly relieved that it wasn't Tariq looking for round two. Louis smiled and lifted a bag of takeout in one hand and a bottle of wine in the other. "Dinner's on me tonight."

I let him in and followed him to the dinner table. "Whatchu bring?"

"There's this new Chinese food place down the street from my place. I had to share it with you." As I watched him set up, I imagined our lives together like this; Louis was safe. He made sense in my life, and I needed to make a point to embrace that. And as he stood there, I expected him to bring up the email he sent me. My skin was covered in goose bumps as I predicted the outcome of our discussion. "How was your day?"

I said, "I got pretty busy." He plated our food and sat down across from me. He didn't say anything afterward. He chowed down as if not long ago he hadn't confessed his love for me. "How was yours?"

He shrugged his shoulders. "Nothin' exciting." He stuffed a spoonful of fried rice in his mouth and scratched his chin. "Well, we caught one of our employees stealin' from the register. It's a shame. He said he was tryna feed his family, and I believe him. He shoulda talked to me, though, not stole from me." He went back to consuming his food.

I expected him to question me. When he told me he loved me, I didn't respond. I accepted it as if we always ended our daily emails that way. I didn't want to discuss it, but his avoidance made me feel like I had to. "Are we gonna talk about your email?"

He stopped chewing and stared at me is if he were as confused as I was. "My email?"

"Yeah, Louis. You told me you loved me."

He swallowed his food and popped the cork of the Riesling. Grabbing another spoonful of rice, he shrugged his shoulders and said, "Yeah... I did." He stuffed his face and grinned. "You not gonna eat?"

I sat down, grabbed a fork, and played with my shrimp fried rice. "I wasn't expecting you to say that, especially not through email."

"Well, that's how I felt at the time, I guess."

"You guess? Are you sayin' you shouldn't have said that?"

"No, I'm saying..." He let his words trail off. I wanted answers, and he gave me nothing.

"Louis, I don't understand."

"Erin, I love you. I meant it then and I mean it now. What else did you want me to say? I love you, boo."

"I'm not asking you to say it simply to *say it*; I want to understand the meaning behind it."

"What other meaning would you expect to be behind it? I care about you. Maybe I shouldn't have said it through an email, but, I'm tellin' you now. I love you." He chugged down his wine and wiped his lips. "I mean...I'm not expecting you to say it back. I know it's fast. Sometimes I can be a lil' fast. We spend so much time together. I love it. I love talkin' to you. I love...you. And I said it."

I wasn't expecting our conversation to go as it did. I expected more emotion, more of something. I leaned over the table and kissed him gently. He ran his fingers up my neck and pulled my face closer to his. As we kissed, I tried to ignore the feelings I had. After reading his email, I wanted to hear him say the words. I hoped hearing the words would make me feel at ease, ready to tell him how much I loved him too. However, after hearing him say it, I felt nothing. If anything, I was turned off. His feelings felt premature and almost happenstance. Oddly enough, I wanted more of a chase. Nonetheless, I slipped my tongue in his mouth and held his cheek while he caressed my lips with his. Usually, my panties would be wet by this time, and I'd be pushing to skip dinner and get right to the bedroom. Tonight, I was ready to eat and go to sleep. Pulling away, I said, "Let's finish eating."

He smiled and dug in. As I watched him eat, I tried not to stare at the way his jaw snatched back while he stuffed globs of food down his throat. It was as if I was watching a snake devour its prey. I even noticed the way his shoulders slouched forward like a Neanderthal, awkwardly cowering over his meal as if he hadn't fully evolved from the primal being he once was. I quickly ate my food before I lost my appetite. I hated what I was going through. Not too long ago, I saw us being the perfect couple. Now, I imagined how long before he I'd give in to Tariq's nonsense right on my living room floor. I felt guilty knowing that I was turned off by a man who was willing to give me the things I wanted while I secretly craved a married man. A married asshole that wasn't worth the thought.

When he finished his food, gulped down the rest of his glass of wine. "Can we take this to the bedroom?"

Ugh, I thought. "I'm still eating, though."

"The food's not going anywhere. Erin, you have no idea how much I missed you."

"We saw each other the other night."

"Am I wrong for missin' you?"

To keep up the appearance of unwavering interest, I said, "Of course not."

He grinned and held my hand as he dragged me into the bedroom. Sex with Louis certainly wasn't the marathon love-making session I had with Tariq, but it was tolerable. At the end of the day, I still climaxed—sometimes even multiple times. He focused all of his attention on pleasing me, which was good, but sometimes I liked being flung onto the bed while my man took charge. I was disgusted with myself for being so hard to please, but I couldn't fight the feelings, no matter how hard I tried. The chase was over.

CHAPTER 19

Tariq

Two years ago…

Simoné moved in. I was through being that old dude in the club chasin' after half-naked women with Damien. Simoné gave me stability and eventually, the rumors were confirmed; I got the promotion I interviewed for. I settled back into my cushy life of having a woman who was down for me and a career that mattered. My life was good and I enjoyed the company. That was…until one fuckin' afternoon.

I came home from work early. I anticipated surprising my woman and makin' love to her on the kitchen counter. When I got home, I heard her on the phone. Once she saw me poke my head in the bedroom, she quickly ended her call and smiled. "You're home early, boo."

"Who were you talkin' too?"

"My girl Yolanda."

"You ain't have to hang up the phone on my part."

"I didn't. We were already done talkin'. Whatchu doin' home so early?"

"Shit was slow, and I wanted to come see you. After my promotion, I can do things like that."

"That's great, baby." She grabbed her purse and car keys as she headed for the living room.

"You goin' somewhere?"

"Oh…um, Yolanda and I planned to meet up and grab lunch right before you walked in. I'ma meet her, and then we can chill."

"You can't cancel wit' her? I took off work to see you."

"I know, but…her husband left her. Took the kids too. She needs a shoulder to cry on. I can't leave her hangin'. She needs me—more than you."

I loosened my tie and slid out of my shoes. "Where y'all going to eat?"

"I dunno. Prolly something quick and cheap like Chili's." When Simoné got to the door, she scrolled through her phone and dropped it in her bag. "But I gotta go, baby."

As I watched my woman dressed up in a mini skirt and a low-cut top, bright-red lips, and hair weave flipped and spritzed, my curiosity got the best of me. I said, "You look too good to be goin' to Chili's. You sure that's all you doin'?"

She shook her head in dismissal. "Boo, I don't have time for this. She's already on her way, Riq."

I walked up to her and pulled her close. Inhalin' the fragrance on her neck, I whispered, "You smell real good, too." I sucked on her neck as she squeezed the doorknob. "Stay home with me."

She sighed and pulled away. "Riq, I can't do my girl like that."

I pulled her to me, placing her hand on the crotch of my pants. "Then be a lil' late." I moved my hands up her skirt and pulled down her lace panties. Unbuckling my pants, I lifted her up and let her slide down on my dick. With her legs wrapped around my waist and arms grippin' my shoulders, I yanked up her shirt and unhooked her bra to let free her plump and bouncy breasts, accented by erect nipples. "I missed you all day, boo."

"I missed you too, Riq." I sucked on her breasts while springing her up and down my joystick. She licked off her lipstick while she whispered my name, "Ooh…Riq." Her pussy throbbed as she held on to my neck and arched her back. I could feel her phone vibrating on my back through the purse she still ain't drop.

"I want you to stay home with me. Tell yo' girl that you made other plans."

"I can't, Riq."

I spread her thighs apart and pushed her back against the door. She sucked on her lips, almost sucking off the skin, as she screamed in satisfaction. "Tell her you'll see her tomorrow."

She nodded as her body shook. "Fine." I could feel her pelvic muscles tense as her bodily fluids poured out like a waterfall. "I'll stay, Riq."

I supported her thighs as I led her to our bedroom. She dropped her purse to the floor as I let her collapse on top of our sheets. I passionately reentered her body. She craved more, and her body was openly receptive. I fed her like a starving nation and revitalized our bodies in more ways than one. She cried out in ecstasy while she held me close with her feet and dug her nails into my skin. "You better stay." I joked as I kissed her repeatedly, ruthlessly commanding her body onto mine.

She gleamed, and when she came again, her body trembled beneath me. I pulled out not, wanting to come yet. I felt the need to punish her body like a criminal. Catching her breath, she said, "I have to run and take a shower. You made me come too much." Without another word, she grabbed her purse from the floor and ran into the bathroom. When she turned on the shower, I sat up and stared at the bathroom door. Remembering that I hadn't come yet, I walked to the bathroom door. Locked. I jiggled the handle and then banged on the door.

"Simoné, open this door." Three seconds later, she opened the door naked. Her phone resting on the bathroom sink. I asked, "Why would you lock the door?"

She shrugged her shoulders, "I dunno. I'm sorry. Let's get in the shower so I can make you come. I'll let you get my hair wet this time."

I wanted more answers, but my throbbing dick needed to come. We got into the shower, and I pinned her underneath the shower-head while thrusting myself inside her from behind. She let the water soak her head while she pushed against the shower walls for support. I held her hips for guidance. When I came, the feelin' was bittersweet. I couldn't shake the sound of her phone vibrating on the bathroom counter. I also couldn't shake the fact that her girl, Yolanda, was usually at work the same time I was at work. I wanted to say something, but Simoné distracted me with her wet breasts and tight pussy. She kept throwing it at me as if to buy herself time. I didn't like it, but my penis fell for her traps every time.

From that day, my mind was buggin'. Simoné would talk, and all I'd hear was her phone vibrating. She'd lie next to me asleep, and I'd ignore the fact that she'd turn it off to make sure it wouldn't ring in the middle of the night. Simoné never really gave me a reason not to trust her, but shit was different. One day when Simoné forgot her phone at home, I contemplated my next move. I thought about how I should approach the circumstance she had put me in. I ain't wanna be that type of dude who went through his girl's phone, but I couldn't go through this again. I wondered what other opportunity would I have. I sat in the living room pretending to watch ESPN, but all I could think about was how her phone vibrated on our dresser. I took a deep breath and decided to capitalize on my opportunity.

Simoné had a password, but having spent enough time with her, it wasn't hard to crack her code. I typed in "Maxwell," the name of her favorite singer, and the name of her dog that passed twelve years ago. I was in.

"IS HE HOME?" That was the beginning of their chat log. Her and some nigga named Jamar, *fuckin'* Jamar.

"YEA. HE'S HOME," she responded.

"FUCK. Y U WIT THAT BITCH NIGGA? U COMIN OVA OR NOT?"

"I NEED AN EXCUSE TO GET OUT." The way she disregarded his blatant disrespect toward me brought back old memories. According to whoever Simoné was texting, I was a bitch nigga, and she was okay with that.

"FUCK HIM. GET YO ASS OVA HERE. IM TRYNA GET IN THAT PUSSY TONIGHT." I put the phone down and stared at the front door. I wanted Simoné to come home and answer for this. Luckily, I wasn't in a public place, which meant if I needed to get loud, I had that right.

"I KNOW, BOO. I'M COMIN." The texts came through today around four in the afternoon. Around that time, Simoné had to run and grab some ice cream from the corner store. Little did I know she was gettin' a different type of dessert.

"HURRY UP," was the nigga's last text. The nigga that was bold enough to talk shit about me through a damn text message. At the same time, he was the one fuckin' my girl without me knowing. Maybe I *was* the bitch nigga. For some reason, I kept attracting women who felt the need to lie up with some other man behind my back.

When I heard the front door slam shut, I met Simoné in the living room and waved her phone in her direction. When she saw her unlocked phone in my hand, she froze. I expected her to almost shrug it off, accept her defeat, and try to weasel out of it by blaming me. She placed the bag of ice cream on the coffee table and smiled nervously. "What are you doin' wit' my phone?"

"Who the fuck is Jamar?"

All the color in her skin melted. She wiped her bangs from her eyes and sighed heavily. I should've known something was up when she walked out the house to buy ice cream wit' no panties and a sundress, easy and quick access for *fuckin'* Jamar. She spread her lips and sat on our couch. "I'm so sorry, Riq." Her voice cracked.

I threw her phone at her feet. I wasn't tryna hear it. I gave Simoné the benefit of the doubt and stayed faithful to her against my better judgment. Damien's warnings reverberated in my head as I heard my heart beating through my chest. "I ain't tryna hear yo' fuckin' apologies."

"I didn't go, Riq." She stood up and ran up to me, clutching my clothes, trying to force me to notice her and her tearful confessions. "I know what you read, but I didn't go. Nothing happened."

I pulled away from her and shook my head. "I ain't tryna hear none of this. I need some time to myself."

"Riq, please. Listen to me."

"Ain't shit to listen to." I walked to the front door, but she beat me to it. She wiped the tears from her face and tugged at my belt loops. She gazed into my eyes and pleaded for the chance to speak. I smacked her hands away and stepped back. "What the fuck do you have to say?"

"I know things look bad—I know. But I didn't fuck him. We've been talkin' for a while and—"

"Who's *we?* Who the fuck is Jamar? You still ain't tell me that."

"He's a friend. I knew him before I even met you. We've always flirted and shit, but we never fucked, at least not while we were together."

"So you have fucked him?"

"Not when I was wit' you, though, Riq. We've been talkin' and… I should've shut it down, but I didn't. I'm sorry. I dunno what I was thinkin'."

"Simoné, I ain't no pie-ass nigga, regardless of what yo' man think."

"He's not my man, Tariq."

"Whateva. I ain't tryna be that bitch nigga going through my woman's phone, but I ain't got the time to be dealin' wit' bullshit like this. You wanna be with that dude, then cool. You ain't gotta lie to me."

"But I don't, Riq! I don't wanna be with anyone but you. That's why I didn't fuck him. He was there for me when you weren't and… sometimes I wasn't sure if I could trust you and…"

"You telling me that you fucked some other nigga because you can't trust me? Does that make sense to you?" I jingled my car keys and reached for the door handle.

She pulled my hand away and got in my face. "We never fucked when we were together, Riq. We talked."

"Simoné…" I took a deep breath to calm my nerves. I needed air, and with her in my face, I was suffocating. I stepped away from her and grabbed the back of my head. "I gotta go. I can't think straight, and ain't shit that you can say right now to calm me down."

"I want you to believe me, Riq."

"Simoné, you ain't listening. Ain't shit registering right now. Lemme take a ride somewhere. But I can't stand here and keep listenin' to this shit. How the fuck you goin' tell me how this nigga was there for you when I'm not? Where the fuck am I that you need to be cryin' on some other man's shoulder? I've been right here, workin' an' doin' shit for us. We've been good; yet, all that I do for you ain't enough. I ain't tryna hear it. I gotta go before I say some real shit that I regret."

She stood there wanting us to kiss and make up. I wasn't for it. She finally nodded her head and sat down on the couch. I stormed out my front door without looking back. I got in my car and drove. I tried to wipe away any emotion I felt from going through the same type of heartbreak Deja put me through. At least Simoné showed remorse, but in the end, she still blamed her infidelity on me. I wanted things to work out. I hoped that I could stay out the game and prove Damien wrong. But what could I expect? Bitches weren't shit before, an' they ain't shit now. If I'm the nigga makin' these hoes cheat, then I couldn't bother being wit' 'em.

CHAPTER 20

Present…

"Something's wrong with me."

Loraine stared down at her phone and back up at me. "Why do you say that?"

"I'm not into Louis anymore."

Loraine squeezed her phone in her palm and twirled her dreads. "Why not?" It was two in the morning on a Friday night, and Loraine and I sat at my kitchen table in our sweats trying to play cards. She spent most of the night checking her phone, playing with her hair, and tapping her foot.

I didn't appreciate the split attention I received from her. "What's on your mind?"

Realizing that I caught on to her distraction, she smiled and put her phone down. "I'm sorry, girl. I haven't heard from Teona, and I'm a lil' worried."

"Usually, you'd be happy not to hear from her."

Loraine picked her phone back up and scrolled through it. "You know that was all talk. I won't tolerate her nonsense, but I'm always concerned for her safety."

"You said she needs to spend the night on a cold park bench."

"That doesn't mean I want her to go missing." Loraine looked at my phone. "She hasn't contacted you, right?"

"You know if she did, I'd tell you." I shuffled the cards and dealt them, even though neither one of us was in the mood to play. Accepting the fact that my topic of conversation wasn't as important as hers, I asked, "When's the last time you heard from her?"

"Yesterday afternoon. I dunno what this girl does with her days. She doesn't have a job, and doesn't go to school, but she's gone all day until she drags her drunken ass in from partying on a Tuesday. It's going on two nights I haven't seen her—no one has." All the random thoughts that ran through my mind had to be going through Loraine's.

I dialed her number, hoping it would be easy enough to get her to answer. Strangely, someone did. "Hello," I said.

Silence.

Loraine stared between me and the phone. "Is that Teona? Put it on speaker."

Following her demands, I put the phone on speaker and set it on the coffee table, but there was still white noise. We stared at each other and back down at the phone. "Teona?"

Nothing.

"Is someone there?" Loraine asked. She grabbed my phone and held it close to her as if it were Teona. "Teona, where are you?"

"Who is—" The phone cut off before we could say anything else. Loraine and I stared at the phone as if it were going to grow a mouth and start talking.

"What the fuck was that?" Loraine quickly redialed the number. When it went straight to voicemail after seven more attempts, panic spread. "We need to go." She gathered her things and headed for my door.

"Where?" I stood up and looked for my purse.

"I dunno, but I'm not staying here. She could be in trouble."

"You sure your mom hasn't seen her?" When I found my purse, I followed Loraine, who was already down the hallway dialing and redialing Teona's phone.

When we reached my car, we both jumped when the phone rang. We paused, nearly forgetting how modern technology worked. "Hello," Loraine said. She put the phone on speaker and held her breath.

"Hello…who's this?" the voice asked.

Looking at my caller ID and realizing that it wasn't Teona's number, I quickly asked, "Who's this?"

"Loraine, is that you?"

Loraine grabbed the phone. "Mom?"

"Loraine, where are you?"

"Have you heard back from Teona?"

Loraine's mother sighed loudly. "Yeah…I have. She's here."

"Here where?"

"Here wit' me. I picked her up from the police station. I'm gonna meet you at your house."

"The police station? What was she doing there?"

"I'll talk to you when we get there." *Click*. I could hear the irritation in Loraine's mother's voice, and I could see the aggravation written across Loraine's face. The lines in her forehead had already anticipated a story far worse than we had imagined, only to be side struck by a short call from her distraught mother. She twirled her dreads furiously, switching her loc from one finger to the next in a fast tango while she chewed on her bottom lip.

I would've let her drive home on her own, but she was too beside herself to drive without possibly causing a ten-car pileup. I unlocked my door and waited for her to get in. "Let's get you home."

She hesitated at first, but she hopped in my car and stared out my windshield as she continued to play with her hair and bite her lip.

When we reached her home, we were both surprised to see her ex-husband sitting on the doorstep. The sun glared on his bald head as he hid his ashy brown face in his hands. Long, lanky fingers swallowed his elongated face while he sat his bony elbows on his high knees. Loraine's confusion flew into a rage as she jumped out of my car before I even had the chance to come to a complete stop. "What the hell are you doing here?"

He stood up and scratched his head with his fraternity letters keychain. His eyes were sunken in as if he hadn't slept all night. As he towered over her in his pinstriped suit and crooked smile, she wagged her finger in his face with her other hand on her hip. His con artist demeanor only angered her more as he refused to speak; instead, he moved out of her way as Hurricane Loraine blew his way.

Before Loraine could spew out any more words, a blue sedan pulled into Loraine's driveway. Two seconds later, Loraine's petite mother was making her way up to Loraine and her ex while a makeup-smeared Teona wobbled in their direction with her heels hanging off her fingers and her mini bodycon dress barely covering her butt. I considered getting out of the car, but I felt as if I'd be infringing on a family situation. But when Loraine stared at me as if she were all alone in a world full of pinstriped cheaters and drunken jailbait, I realized that I was the only one on her lawn that was on her side.

"What are you doing here, Lorenz? As you can see, I'm going through a lot."

"I called him." Teona brushed a few loose strands of hair from her face and squirmed past Loraine as she headed toward her front door. Even when Loraine grabbed Teona's arm to stop her from walking in, Teona ripped her arm from Loraine's grasp and unlocked Loraine's door. "I can call whoever the fuck I wanna call." Without another word, she disappeared into Loraine's home and slammed the door shut behind her.

"Give her some time, Loraine," Loraine's mother said as she held Loraine back from chasing after Teona. We all stood outside quietly, trying not to address the elephant on the lawn.

Loraine avoided eye contact with her ex-husband by staring at her front door and twirling her hair between her fingers. Lorenz, who at first kept his eyes glued on the pavement, glanced over at Loraine and chuckled. "You love playin' in yo' hair."

Loraine cut her eyes at Lorenz and stared into him as if she were trying to burn fiery coals on the pores of his skin. "What are you doing here, Lorenz? You have yet to answer that question."

"Teona called him and then he called me," interjected Loraine's mom. She may have only stood five feet three with salt-and-pepper dreads that almost reached her ankles, but her deep and booming voice was powerful enough to bring their bickering to an immediate halt. "If he hadn't called, we would have never heard from your sister."

Loraine scowled at Lorenz and gritted her teeth. "What was she doing at the police station?"

"Police picked her up on some street corner," Lorenz answered. "She told me it's not what it sounds like, though."

"It's never what it sounds like when you're dealin' with that girl." Disgusted with the situation Teona had placed them all in, Loraine grunted and walked inside. I followed and watched as Teona, with her hair wrapped in a silk scarf and dressed down in men's boxers and a white tank top, ate a bowl of cereal over Loraine's kitchen sink.

Teona avoided eye contact with all of us as she stared at Loraine's walls. Loraine's mother and ex-husband walked in a few seconds later. "Did you take a shower and wash the stench of the police station off you?" Loraine's mother questioned. Teona ignored her mother's question and stuffed spoonfuls of Fruit Loops into her mouth. "Little girl, I picked yo' butt up from a police station after not hearing from you in almost two days. You better answer me."

Teona slammed her spoon down and rolled her eyes to the ceiling. "Yes, ma'am." With that, she flipped her leftover cereal bowl into the sink and stormed into Loraine's guest room.

"She's going home with you, Mama." Loraine shook her head and walked into the kitchen to clean up Teona's mess. Lorenz walked into the kitchen as well. With his presence less than two feet away from her, Loraine stopped and folded her arms across her chest. "You couldn't call me and tell me where she was?"

Lorenz squeezed his fists. "Why are you trippin' so hard? You don't even answer my phone calls. I had to call someone who would answer."

"Bullshit. You like the fact that Teona came to you instead of me."

"No, I'm genuinely concerned for her."

"And I'm not?"

"You're not acting like it."

"Why are you even still here? Teona's here. You can go now. You ain't have to show up here."

"I wanted to make sure everything was all good."

"It is—bye."

"Loraine, stop talking to him like that." Loraine's mother stepped in with her unwanted motherly advice and quickly realized how un-wanted it was when Loraine cut her eyes at her and twisted her neck.

"Mama, this does not concern you. If I wanna kick some random man out of my house, that's my choice, not yours." Loraine's mom scratched her scalp loudly as she pursed her lips.

"I'm random now?" Lorenz interjected.

"You're still here?"

Lorenz stared at Loraine, then at me. I was nothing more than an innocent bystander unfortunate enough to be forced into being a witness to the events of a woman scorned belittling the man who scorned her. I averted eye contact and decided to look through my phone and read Louis's text messages and emails.

Lorenz asked, "Why can't we talk like two adults, Loraine?"

"I would if there was another adult in front of me. Bye, Lorenz."

Lorenz flicked his tongue. After a deep sigh, he said, "Bye." He walked past Loraine and stomped out her front door. Loraine's mother and I both kept our eyes out of their business as they sorted through their own affairs. Nevertheless, we silently wished that Teona would walk back in so we'd have other issues that we could actually poke our noses in.

Loraine dropped her arms to her side and took a deep breath. "Mama, can you call your other daughter out here, please?"

Loraine's mother did as she was told, and we all waited for Teona to step out of the room. Five agonizingly long minutes later, Teona crept out and greeted our curiosity with an attitude. "What, Mama?"

"Come sit yo' butt down here."

Teona stared at her mother, initially testing her authority. She walked over to Loraine's couch after losing her mother's stare-down. "I'm really not in the mood to talk right now."

"Teona, I'm 'bout sick and tired—

"Be sick and tired!" Teona cut Loraine's sentence short with an intense eye roll and a serious smack of her lips. "I'm sick and tired of you tryna act like my mama."

"Well, I *am* your mama, and I've *been* sick and tired of your mess."

Teona looked up at her mama as if she wanted to talk back, but she knew better. "What do you want me to say, Mama?"

"We want you to explain. I've been patient with you for a long time, Teona. But the day I pick you up at a police station because the police suspected you of streetwalking, my patience has all but run out."

"I wasn't streetwalking."

"Then what were you doing?" Loraine asked.

Teona scratched the top of her head in attempt to avoid answering her sister, but her mother looked down at her, waiting for an answer. "I was…I left the club early to meet up with some guy. I must've been real drunk 'cause I forgot where I was supposed to meet him. I walked down the street looking for him, and some guy pulled up—I thought it was the guy. Turned out to be an undercover."

"What was the guy's name, Teona?" Loraine asked.

"Does it matter?"

"You darn right it matters," Loraine's mother answered. "Teona, you keep playing these games thinkin' these men are playing, too. Sooner or later, you goin' realize that these men aren't playing. This time, I picked you up at the police station; tomorrow, I might have to come identify your body. I'm tired of this. I thought you spending time with your sister would've helped, but this has gone far enough."

Before Teona had the opportunity to say something, we all stopped when we heard someone banging at the front door. We all glanced at each other before looking back at the door.

Loraine walked to the front door and peeked through the peephole. "Who is it?"

Loraine shrugged her shoulders and opened the door slightly. "Can I help you?"

"Is Teona there?" a man's voice asked.

"Who are you?"

He stood quiet for a while. I noticed the man's feet fidgeting as Loraine waited for an answer. "Look, I'm sorry to be banging on your door like this. Teona's been blowin' my phone up since last night, and I wanted to talk to her, if that's okay."

"You still haven't tol' me who you are, bangin' on my door like that. How do you even know to find her here?"

"She invited me here once. You must be her sister, Loraine. I apologize for my rudeness; I'm a little distraught. I wanted to make sure she was okay."

The man's voice had calmed down, but I could tell he was irritated. Loraine swung the door open, which allowed Teona to see him. The man stepped inside and searched for Teona's face. Teona glanced over at him for a second, but I was the one staring. His voice sounded familiar, but I couldn't keep my eyes off his shoulder-length dreads, chocolate skin, and chiseled jaw.

"Louis."

Initially, in his search for Teona, he hadn't noticed me standing there wondering *why* he was searching for Teona. He ran his fingers through his dreads. He slapped his hands together and stepped back outside.

Loraine asked, "You know him, Erin?"

Teona refused to meet my glare.

I walked over to Louis, who nervously rubbed his hands together. "What are you doing here, Louis?"

"Erin...what are you doin' here?"

"I asked you first."

Teona walked up behind me and poked her head in my business. "He's here to see me." Squeezing in between us, she addressed Louis. "As you can see, I'm fine. Maybe you should've returned my calls."

As Teona stood between us, I cocked my head back and sneered at Louis. He walked backward and realized the mess he had entered.

Loraine tried to pull me back, but I yanked myself free. "Louis, what the fuck is goin' on?"

"Nothin'…it's not what you think it is."

"Then tell me what is goin' on."

Teona put her hand up. "Erin, he's here to see me. Can you give us a minute?"

"Excuse me—"

When I smacked Teona's hand out of my face, Loraine pulled me away before things got worse.

"Erin, calm down."

I pulled myself loose and closed the front door behind me so Loraine could stop interfering. "Louis, you better start talkin'."

"I gotta go. Can we talk about this later?"

"Louis, if you leave without giving me an explanation, don't worry about ever callin' me again."

Loraine's mother opened the door. Teona got in Louis's face. "Can we talk somewhere else?"

I couldn't breathe. I heard my pulse racing. Beads of sweat formed on my forehead. No one was giving me answers, but everyone was tryna push me away. "You know what, Louis? Goodbye."

As I brushed past him, Louis followed me and held me back. Teona grabbed onto Louis, forcing Loraine's mom to intervene. "Teona, get out of grown folks' business and get in this house."

Teona ignored her mother's warning as she pulled Louis backward. I took his hands off me and tried to rid myself of this entire situation. "Erin, wait. Let me explain."

I flung around and snarled. "I've been waiting for an explanation for the past five minutes, Louis. Talk!"

"It's not what you think. I'm not messin' around with Teona. I'm not cheatin' on you. Things are real crazy right now."

I folded my arms and slowed things down. "Louis...what...*the fuck*...are you doing here?"

"I told him I want him back, and he's here to come get me." Teona yelled out before Louis could respond. My blood was literally boiling, and I couldn't stand there and hear Teona talk.

"I'm leaving." I stormed past everyone, shooing away grabs that tried to hold me back. I was done hearing anyone else speak, and if I heard Teona's voice again, Loraine would have to pry my hands off her neck with a crowbar.

Louis blew my phone up for three days straight. He would pop up at my house, and I'd pretend I wasn't home. Sometimes, I'd let him know I was home and still not answer. Loraine called me, too. I wasn't mad at her, but if I heard Teona's voice, I wouldn't be able to stop myself from driving over there. I lied in my bed in the dark, thinkin'. I was knockin' on thirty, and I was the woman feening for a married man while I dated a man who knocked down doors to chase after a harlot. Eventually, I would need answers.

When I saw Louis after work, I skipped the small talk and led straight into the hard stuff. "What the fuck was that, Louis?"

Louis and I stood in my kitchen. I stood in baggy sweats and a tank top, hair pulled back like I was ready to fight. Louis came in with his dreads down. I loved when he wore his hair down, and he knew it. He also knew how much I loved it when he wore V-neck shirts that hugged his skin and slacks that gripped his ass. He looked good and wanted to show it. He said, "I'm sorry about all that. I'm happy you finally agreed to talk to me. I was dying not being able to talk to you."

"You're not answering my damn question, Louis. I *will* kick you out."

He took a deep breath. "I was datin' Teona at one point." I opened my top cupboard in search of my unopened wine bottle. "It's not what you think, though. I didn't know she was so young. I also didn't know she was sleepin' around with other guys; some of 'em were guys I knew. I backed off at that point."

"So you were fuckin' her."

He licked his lips and averted eye contact. I poured myself a tall drink of wine and gulped it down. "Erin, it didn't mean anything then, and it doesn't mean anything now."

"What were you doing there, Louis?"

"She was texting me."

"And?"

He took another deep breath and tied his dreads up. We were both hot, and I wasn't letting up. "Ever since I left, she's been texting me, callin' me. Talkin' 'bout how she wants me back. I've been ignoring her. A few nights ago, she started talkin' 'bout committing suicide. I called her back, but she never responded. I got a lil' worried."

"Well, aren't you a good boyfriend, huh?"

"I was never really her boyfriend, Erin. C'mon, I'm sorry you had to be in the middle of all that. I didn't know if she was serious. I had to be sure."

"Why didn't you tell me you knew her? You were here when she drug her triflin' ass in here one night."

"I didn't know what to say. I didn't know what you'd think." I shook my head and poured another glass of wine. "I know you don't believe me, but I'm being honest."

I took a deep breath and then sipped my wine. Louis pulled out his phone and handed it to me. "What am I supposed to do with this?"

"I can show you the texts she sent me; I can prove to you that things were over with us before we started dating. I didn't wanna go into all that at the house. As you can see, Teona knows how to put up a big front. I ain't want you in the middle of all that. But I can prove to you what's been goin' on. I can show you the emails, text messages, whatever you need to see so you can trust me. I love you, Erin. I'm not tryna let a girl like Teona stand between you and me. If you wanna call her over, I can prove it to you that way, too."

"Why didn't you say anything while we were there? If you're willing to confront her now, why weren't you willin' to confront her then?"

"I was blindsided. I wasn't expectin' you there. And then you stopped talkin' to me, avoiding me. Babe, I've been dying without you. You gotta let me prove it to you."

I stared at Louis and questioned his motives. The last person I expected any of this from was Louis. I hated it. I wanted him to prove it to me. I wanted to believe in the man I considered loving back. I didn't appreciate a little girl claiming my man in front of me while my man did nothing. "I didn't expect this from you, Louis."

There was a knock at my door. I wasn't mentally prepared to deal with anyone's nonsense. I walked past Louis and opened the door. When Teona's overly made-up face stared back at me, I wanted to the slam the door shut in her face. But I realized that this was my chance to get real answers. She wore a sheer blouse that was tied above her navel and liquid tights. Her hair was gelled back, and she wore more makeup than a clown college.

She said, "We need to talk, Erin."

I let her in. When Teona saw Louis, she chuckled and dropped her purse on my kitchen table.

I closed the door behind me and stared at Louis. "Here's your chance."

Louis wiped his face and rubbed the back of his neck. "You need to stop following me, Teona."

Teona rolled her eyes. "Boy, ain't nobody followin' you. I came here to talk to Erin, and here you are."

"You know what you're doin', Teona. Stop."

"Why are you talkin' to me like this, Louis? You're actin' like you haven't been contactin' me, too."

"Are you serious? You know we're not together. Stop blowin' me up and puttin' me through this high school nonsense."

"You told me you loved me. What happened to all that?"

Louis looked at me and back at Teona. "Teona, you fucked like four dudes when we were together. I left. You gotta let that shit go."

"Why? For *her?*" She pointed at me without looking at me. "You wanna let what we had go for *her?* It wasn't that long ago you were singin' a whole different tune. You're the one playin' games."

"Teona, I'm a grown-ass man. You lied about your age; you lied about how many men you slept wit'; you've been lying since I met you. I love Erin. I don't love you. I need you to let me go, so I can move on wit' my life."

"Grown-ass man? Louis, you were chasin' after me for months, actin' like a sad puppy when I ain't return yo' calls. All of a sudden, you're a grown-ass man in love with Erin?" She scoffed and put her hands on her hips. "You pick up a rebound, an' I'm supposed to believe you really have somethin' special? Puh-lease, Louis. I bet yo' top lip still smells like my pussy."

"Teona!" Louis snapped. I pulled in my lips and shook my head. Louis, sensing my frustration, took in a hard breath. "I'm done. You need to go with all this bull."

Teona stood there. She looked down at her platform pumps and up at Louis. "Fine." She turned around and glowered at me. "You can have him."

She grabbed her purse and walked out my door, slammin' it shut behind her. Louis sighed and smiled. "See."

"See what?" I scratched the back of my neck. The relationship between Teona and Louis was unfolding, and I didn't like what I saw. She was more than a fling. She was someone he had possession of. At one point, he was her man. I realized that I didn't know the man he was. I was the rebound for one of *Teona's* men; I didn't like the feeling. Licking my lips, I said, "You need to go, Louis."

"Erin, what else do you want me to do?"

"Did you love her?"

Louis swallowed the lump of air in his throat. He took a step back and quickly answered. "Why would you ask me somethin' like that? I'm tryna be wit' you, but you keep bringin' her up like she's a factor in our relationship. I love you, not her."

"I want you to leave."

"Why? I did what you asked!"

"I ask you questions about her, and you dance around them like you're hiding things. I'm through asking unanswered questions. I didn't ask you to resolve your relationship between you and your ex-girlfriend in my apartment. You even talk different when you're around her. You're another person, and…I don't wanna be your rebound."

"You're not my rebound. What I feel for you is genuine. Teona was…nothin'."

"She must have been somethin' if you're banging on Loraine's door worried about her. Louis, you need to go home and resolve some unfinished business. The way you looked at her…" I shook my head as I remembered the passion they shared in my kitchen. I felt like a dirty voyeur watching them have it out in front of me in the raw. "You need to go home, right now."

"Erin, what else do you want me to do to prove to you that what

I had wit' Teona was a thing to do, nothin' special? What we have is special, Erin. Can we—?"

"Louis, I'm not gettin' into this. Can you respect my feelings enough to leave and let me sort things out?"

He moved closer to me, but I moved back. I pointed at my door and waited for him to leave. Realizing that I wasn't letting up, he nodded and walked to the door. "Call me later?"

"Go, Louis."

He walked out quietly, his silence begging me for a second chance. I disregarded his plea and locked the door behind him. Standing at the door for a while, I pulled out my vibrating phone. When Tariq's name flashed across, I sent him to voicemail and headed for bed.

I finally called Loraine. When she told me that Teona went back to their mother's house, I realized it was safe for me to see Loraine and get some things off my chest. Tomorrow was her off day, and she'd be willing to spend the night dishing. When I got there, twenty minutes after she cursed me out for ignoring her for the past few days, she was more than willing to dish.

"I can't believe she came over. What was she thinkin'?"

"She was thinkin' she had my man."

We both chuckled at the idea of an immature girl taking any man from me. I left the wine at home and brought over a bottle of Ciroc for our late-night gab session. "I thought you were gonna whoop her butt at my house the other day."

"I was. You kept holdin' me back."

Loraine laughed. "I'm glad I did then." We traded shots of vodka as I tried not to think about Louis. Loraine wasn't having that, though. "You need to give Louis a chance."

I wrenched Loraine's glass from her hand and slammed it down on her coffee table. "You must've had too much to drink."

Loraine picked her glass back up and shook her head. "I'm serious. I know how bad it looked, but he cursed Teona out after you left."

"Is that right? What did he say?"

"It was obvious he was tryna get rid of her. He cursed her out for blowin' his phone up, and she begged him to take her back. Girl, it was a sight."

"I dunno if I can be with a man who had sex wit' your sister. How would you feel if she had sex with Lorenz?"

Loraine cringed. "Don't even get that image in my head. Listen, I know how bad it sounds, but he was agitated over it all. You could tell he was torn up after you left. He wanted to run after you, but Teona kept gettin' in his face."

"Why couldn't he shut her down when it was happenin'?"

"Did you see how that girl was actin'? He was probably embarrassed. I would be. I can understand you being mad, but Louis genuinely cares for you. Whateva he and my sister had, it wasn't anything."

"You didn't see how he acted when they were together. When he's with me, he's a gentleman, sweet and earnest. With her, he's passionate, gritty and raw. She brings something else out of him, and I don't think I like what I saw. I already get gritty and raw from Tariq."

"However he acts, I'm sure he's no Tariq."

"What do you think I should do?"

"You can let Louis suffer for like another day or two, but let it go. He really cares about you."

I took another shot and reluctantly agreed. "Okay."

"Look on the bright side."

"And what side is that?"

"At least you get some awesome make-up sex out of this."

"I better." We laughed as I fantasized about the make-up sex Louis would have planned for me. Once the liquor began to kick in, I decided to switch gears. "How have you been since that day?"

Loraine shrugged her shoulders. "I've been fine, I guess."

"Have you spoken to her?"

"Nope. She's with who she needs to be with right now, my mama. There's nothing for us to discuss right now."

"Have you spoken to Lorenz since?"

Loraine screwed the top off the Ciroc and quickly poured another glass. "Why would I speak to him?" She gulped down her glass and continued. "I mean, he came by the next day to check on the status of Teona."

"How was that? Teona was gone at that point, right?"

"Yep. I still let him in, although my better judgment told me to let his bastard ass stay outside."

"You didn't kill him and bury the body somewhere, did you?"

Loraine's initial hesitation worried me. Her eyes were vacant and disturbed, but then she smiled. "No, but I'd be lying if I said I didn't contemplate that before."

"What did you guys discuss? The tension between you two was crazy. I can only imagine how crazy you two get when your mother isn't there to mediate."

"It can get pretty crazy, but that's how it goes with us. He gets under my skin. Every time I see him, all that anger resurfaces, and I have to hold myself back from putting my hands on him." Loraine sipped on her vodka. "We didn't discuss anything new. I cursed him out for being an asshole, and he defended himself. Eventually, we couldn't stand to be around each other for much longer."

"When did he leave?"

"You're sure asking a lot of questions," she barked.

I paused in confusion. "What do you mean? I'm tryna keep the conversation going. I can't ask questions?"

"He left when he left. It's not that serious."

Loraine's defensiveness clued me into the reality that she wasn't telling me everything about her and Lorenz's encounter the other day. I opened my mouth to say something and stopped. When I noticed the gold condom wrapper hiding underneath her loveseat, I chuckled. "What happened with you two, Loraine? Be honest."

Loraine poured another glass and sighed. It looked like she wanted to lie again, but she caught a glimpse of her poorly hidden condom wrapper as well. "You're right. We do have a lot of tension between us. And without my mother to mediate, we go all in. There we were, having it out. I seriously wanted to punch that fool in his face. One minute I hated him, and the next minute I was on my back remembering all the reasons why I loved him." Loraine gulped down her vodka again and took a deep breath. "It was so good, too."

I wanted to be angry with her for backsliding, but I didn't see the point. She'd been lonely and yearning for a man's attention. With all that was happening in her life, she was owed a little *ex-sex.* "I can't even be mad at you."

Loraine cocked her head back. "I'm surprised. I was afraid I'd get it worse from you."

"Who am I to judge? I was sleepin' around wit' a married man. All you did was have sex with a single man."

"A single man that put me through hell."

"Do you miss him?"

Loraine paused and stared at her wall. She twirled her dreads as she breathed steadily. She opened her mouth to speak and shook her head. "I miss what we had. I sometimes wonder if it was my fault. I cheated on him before we got married. I didn't appreciate him. When we got married, things changed. He wasn't as sweet as he once was. He stopped opening doors for me, taking me out, and buying me flowers. Soon, I felt underappreciated. Instead of fighting to fix things, I nagged him. The more I nagged, the less he did. Then one day, I woke up and the roles were reversed. I tried my hardest to give my all to a relationship that seemed to have run its course." She took a sip of her alcohol. "I was working on us while he worked on other women. He lied, cheated, and abused the love I gave him. And a part of me didn't try to fix things because I felt like I deserved it for doing it to him first. I could've said something, but I felt that he'd know I cheated or worse. It turned out he already knew and was waiting on me to tell him only for him to finally get up and leave."

"If he wasn't treating you right, what made you endure? What made you take him back even after you found out about the baby who turned out not to be his?"

"Guilt and fear. I was guilty for hurting him the same way he was hurting me. I never apologized for it, and I didn't expect him to. Plus, I feared that if he left, I would have to face the reality that it was my fault a good man walked out on me. I am the reason that a good one turned out to be a *Tariq.*"

I giggled. "Girl, nobody can be a *Tariq*. But it wasn't your fault. It was all Lorenz's doing—"

"It was those type of lies that I told myself, Erin. *He's the one with the problem. He'll change eventually. What he did isn't that bad. Things will get better. If he leaves, you'll never find anyone better.* And then he left, and I still haven't found anyone better. When he comes by looking sexy and we're yelling at each other, I keep picturing him kissing me and holding me. The next thing I know, I'm on top of him, riding him like he's a black stallion. I dunno if it felt so good 'cause I haven't had sex in so long or if I forgot what it used to be like." She ran her fingers through her locs and sighed. "I miss being able to miss a good man. It's a luxury that not many women have the pleasure of having."

"Do you want him back?"

Loraine trembled. She poured another glass and twirled her tresses between her index and middle fingers. After a long slurp of vodka, she caught her breath and contemplated taking back a man that she had tried to shun from her life many times before. "I dunno anymore. He's been trying to change. I know I don't want a man who's gonna mistreat me. But I don't know if that man is Lorenz."

"What if he does it again? What if all you're seeing is the effort he's puttin' into gettin' you back and *not* the work he hasn't put into doing you right? You think it's time to start dating?"

Loraine shook her head as she tucked her foot under her butt. "I don't know anymore." Gulping down the last of the vodka, she asked with dazed eyes, "You think I'd be missing out if I stay away from Lorenz?"

"That's a question only you can answer. However, if sleepin' wit' him while you sort things out makes you feel better, don't let me stop you. Make sure you don't get hurt in the process."

Loraine exhaled. "Lorenz was always damn good in bed. I actually wouldn't mind sex with him. But you don't know Lorenz. He has a way of makin' you stick around. I dunno if I wanna risk it."

"Well, don't. All I know is that you haven't glowed like this in forever. Your skin looks fresh, your shoulders relaxed, and your eyes bright. Good dick did something right, and there's no reason to stop it now."

"It all depends on the one who's giving it to me."

"Whoever it is, make sure he's giving it to you right."

Forgiveness was a curious symptom. It was attached to a disease that had the potential to cripple me, enter my bloodstream, and corrupt my judgment. Nevertheless, as I considered forgiveness, curiosity introduced itself as a new symptom. I was curious about the man Louis really was, and ultimately, without Tariq to scratch my urges, I was horny. When I saw Louis again, he was a like a hungry seal. He couldn't stop bouncing and grinning as I forgave him for his misdeed and allowed him back into my life.

"I'm gonna make it up to you," he whispered as we embraced.

"You definitely will." I hadn't had sex in weeks, and I was ready to make up. I led him straight to my bedroom. He followed me like a trained puppy and bounced on the edge of my bed, anticipating what I planned to do next. Biting my lip and batting my eyelashes, I slowly disrobed before him, leaving on my panties and bra. He put his hands on my waist and pulled me closer to him. While he rubbed my skin, I straddled him and put my arms around his neck.

When I leaned in to kiss him, he pulled back and smiled. "I was beginning to think that you didn't wanna see me anymore."

"You're lucky Loraine pleaded your case." Finally pressing my lips against his, he gently slid off my panties and unhooked my bra. Unhooking my bra, I could feel him growing between my thighs. I whispered in his ear, "I missed you."

He stood us up and laid me down atop my bed sheets. After dropping his trousers, taking off his shirt, and slippin' into a condom, he climbed on top of me and whispered back, "I missed you, too."

When I felt him inside me, I tilted my head back and dug my nails into his skin. I told myself to imagine how good he'd feel loving me until morning. I smiled. When I felt his lips over mine, I slid my tongue inside his mouth to taste how sweet his tongue was. I trembled when he sucked on my bottom lip and pushed in deeper.

"I love you," he said, assuring me as he grabbed my thigh and pressed it up against my left breast.

He went deeper as I arched my back and pictured him kissing me again. I fantasized about how deep he could push inside me while I sucked on his lips and rubbed his back.

I moaned in satisfaction when he pulled out and went in deeper than before. "*Ooh*," was all that I could let slip through my lips as I struggled to catch my breath. Louis definitely didn't feel this good the last time he was inside me. When he pulled out again, he yanked me toward his chest and assertively stuck his tongue between my lips in search for mine. Victim to his touch, I welcomed his advances as I tugged at him to finish what we started. "Put it back in," I said between kisses.

He turned me over and let my ass find his lap. Finding his way back inside me from behind while propped up on all fours, he held my waist and rhythmically pulled in and out. I squeezed my sheets and gritted my teeth, silently begging for more. "I really missed you." It had been almost two weeks since I saw Louis, and we had barely spoken. As my orgasm tapped on the wet inner folds that hid between my thighs, I questioned what made me take so long to come to my senses. Why wouldn't I want a man who enjoys being with me? What stupid world did I live in where it would be okay to let a man like Louis slip between my fingers or slip out the lips that held him inside me? I really missed the opportunity to cuddle on my couch and watch TV with a man whose warm embrace made me fall asleep to the sound of his heartbeat. I certainly missed the chance to spread my legs and beckon his entry while I soiled my 1,000 thread-count sheets with orgasmic nectars.

"I really missed you, too," I blurted out between coos of elation. And with that, my knees buckled and my body was set on fire. Burying my face in my pillows, I yelled out in pleasure.

Louis wrapped his arm over my chest and pulled me forward. While sucking on my earlobe, he whispered, "Don't hide your satisfaction in the pillows. I wanna hear you scream my name." Leisurely stroking inside me, he played with my breasts as I rested the back of my head on his shoulder.

"Louis," I moaned as I shook in his arms holding his wrists to support myself up. When he tried to pull away, I had held him closer to me and quivered in his embrace. "Don't stop," I commanded.

"I won't," he whispered to me as I collapsed atop my pillows. He sped up a little, squeezed my cheeks, and pushed in deeper. When he throbbed inside of me, I responded by clasping my lips around him. I could feel him about to come, but I wasn't ready for him to stop. I pulled away and turned over on my back. Moving with the flow, he wrapped my legs around him and pulled my thighs close to him. I tried to get more out of him. I curved my back and screamed in ecstasy. He pulsated within me and groaned while his pleasure overflowed. Catching his breath, he rested on top of me. I felt guilty for greedily wanting to come again, but I hadn't felt what we experienced in so long, and I couldn't risk getting any less than I could handle. "Damn, Erin."

"Did you wanna take a shower together?"

Having caught his breath, he smirked. "You're tryna go again?"

I shrugged my shoulders and smirked back. "Why not?"

Louis stared into my eyes for a while and kissed me. The kiss was short, but his lips were sweet and pillowy. I didn't want to move. I wanted to stay there with him on top of me, kissing me. "Okay, let's go take a shower."

CHAPTER 22

Tariq was back at my door. He sent me a text apologizing for being so disrespectful, and he had to come explain himself. More confident in my attraction to Louis, I was stronger in my stance against him. I couldn't deny how good he looked in a dress shirt and slacks—or how his low haircut and his face cleanly shaven didn't weaken me. I made no effort to look good. I wore my hair in a head scarf and dressed down in a sweatshirt and athletic shorts. I considered gettin' dolled up for Tariq in hopes that he could see what he had been missin', but I chose not to. Louis was comin' over soon, and I wanted Tariq's visit to be brief. Admittedly, I realized that Tariq would want more time than I was willin' to give him. Either way, Louis was my man and Tariq had to respect those boundaries. "Still got a man?"

"Yes, I do."

He licked his lips and nodded. "Is it disrespectful if I ask if we can talk?"

I cut my eyes at him. "Nothin' can be more disrespectful than you cursing me out 'cause I hurt yo' feelings."

"That's my fault."

"I know it's yo' fault. It dang sho' ain't my fault."

"C'mon, Erin. I came ova to talk to you."

"About?"

"Some things I need to get off my chest."

I folded my arms and rested my shoulder on my doorframe. "Start talkin'."

Tariq stared at me and shook his head. "Can I come in?"

"Why can't you talk out here?"

"Erin, I'm trying to be respectful. But if you can't respect my desire to have a normal conversation with you like two adults, let me know."

"I'm being disrespectful by not letting you in my apartment? The last time you were here, you threw a tantrum. I am trying to respect my relationship with my man. If you take that as disrespect, that's on you."

"I'm not here to do anything. I honestly wanna have a conversation with you. I'm sorry for goin' off on you like that. Gimme the opportunity to explain myself. You wanted us to talk about what's been up wit' me and my situation. I'm here to talk."

"I'm not sure that's any of my concern anymore."

"You want me to leave?"

"If you come in here, you need to respect me, my household, and my man."

"All right, Erin. You goin' let me in?"

I didn't want him to leave, but I didn't fully trust myself alone with him in my apartment. And I definitely didn't fully trust Tariq. We fooled around on my couch to the extent that I feared the possibility of old emotions resurfacing. My feelings for Louis were strong, but whatever it was that I felt for Tariq always enticed me. I wanted answers, though. I deserved to know. I took a deep breath and moved out of his way. When he walked in, the scent of his cologne made my palms sweat. I sighed and stopped him at my kitchen table.

"We can talk right here." I closed the door and sat across from him. I felt safe knowing there was a solid wood table between us.

He sat down and slowly licked his lips as his eyes slid up and down my body. I rubbed my hands nervously as I waited for him to start talking. "How you been?"

"Fine." I stood strong. I wasn't lookin' for small talk, only answers. Tariq sat there quietly, though, as if he needed me to ask about him. "And you?"

"Been good." He stared at my wood table and said nothing else.

I breathed heavily and annoyed. "Talk to me, Tariq. Tell me what's up."

He scratched under his chin and laid his hands flat on the table. I felt like a detective, and he was my criminal. He had committed the crime, and I was lookin' for details. No games. The real deal. "You wanted to know about my situation."

"Your *marriage?* Yes, Tariq. I'm done chasing you down."

"As much as I been blowin' you up, I been the one doin' the chasin'."

"Why should I answer when you never have anything to say?"

He took a deep breath. "All right, Erin. My wife…" He paused. "I'm in a weird situation. She's the mother of my child. We thought gettin' married was the right thing to do at the time, but shit ain't work out. We went through hell before we got married. I should've known it was goin' end the way it did. I love my son. I'm there for my son, but…I'm not happy. I've asked for an annulment, a divorce, all that. She ain't havin' it. She swears we can work it out."

"You expect me to be okay with you havin' a wife? Especially one who is committed to workin' things out wit' you."

"There ain't shit to work out, not wit' us at least. Don't get me wrong. I ain't coming here tryna confess my love to you o' nothin', but I'd be lying if I ain't say you don't cross my mind—more often than most women do." He picked at his fingers and breathed deeply. "I'm feelin' you. It fucked wit' me when you tol' me you had a man. Shit came out of nowhere; I snapped. I ain't mean to disrespect you. I liked what we'd been doing, and I wanted to keep doing it."

"I don't. I don't like sneakin' around and climbing down fire escapes. I like being in a real relationship with a man who cares about me."

"I care about you."

"You care about yourself. The only reason why you're finally discussin' your wife wit' me is because you're jealous of Louis, not because you care about me."

"That's his name? Louis." He chuckled. "I ain't jealous of no nigga named Louis. I don't like—"

"You don't like it when other men play wit' your toys. Let's be honest. That's all I was to you, a toy. You played with me when you were bored and discarded me when you wanted something else to play wit'. When you saw someone else playin' wit' me, you realized that you had some more playin' to do. Well, I'm done playin'. I want something real, Tariq. Not these games."

Tariq sat quietly for a while. Finally, he sighed loudly and sat back in his chair. "I ain't mean to make you feel that way. I mean, I like you. But, I'm in a fucked-up predicament." He stood up and shrugged his shoulders. "Really, I wanted to apologize for disrespecting you. You got a man to give you what you need, and that's what's up. I can't give that to you."

"You keep calling your marriage a *situation* or a predicament. It's not a situation, at least not to me it isn't. I was stupid for lettin' myself get pulled into it, but I can't let it go further. It's not right. I can't be the type of woman I am and continue dealing with a man like you. 'Cause you're right, you can't give me what I need. Damn sho' not in your *predicament*."

"Call it what you will, but at the end of the day, it's a problem. I like being with you, but this is something I've been dealing with before you and probably will after you. She's a problem I can't get rid of, a poison I can't eliminate. I know it's not easy for you, but it is what it is."

"What do you even like about me, Tariq? Most of the time when we're together, we're not talkin'. Do you only like havin' sex with me?"

"I can respect you. There's not a lot of women I can respect. I mean, you actually care that I have a wife. Most women are down for the cause. And yeah, the sex with you is good too…real good."

I hid my blush with an eye roll. "What type of women do you go after that would be okay being with a married man?"

He laughed hard. "Not women like you, I guess."

I nodded and stood up. "Well, thanks. I appreciate you apologizing and bein' honest." I expected an asshole with slick lines and a high libido. Instead, I got a Tariq who was apologetic and awkward.

"I guess I'll leave then. Ain't nothin' left for me to say."

When we walked to the door, I couldn't allow myself to move away from him. He moved closer to me and breathed in my breaths. He reached behind me to open the door and my brain kept tellin' me to move out of his way, but he stared at my lips as if he were using mind control to pull me in. Like a lamb called to slaughter, I moved in closer to him as my body warmed. My skin felt flushed, and somehow I found my hand on his belt buckle.

Tariq sucked in his bottom lip as he stared down at mine. "I can't be the only one that feels what I feel every time I'm around you." His voice was low, and I could feel its depth in the pit of my chest.

I kept tellin' myself to move away before we did something I'd regret later, but my mind went blank, and all I could see were his lips moving closer and closer to mine. We both jumped when there was a knock at my door. I wanted to ignore it. We were both turn on, and I couldn't let something as stupid as a knock at my door stop us from fulfilling what my body ached for. Like a flood, memories of the plans I made with Louis came rushing back. I moved back and tried not to shiver when his palm grazed the small of my back.

"I have to answer that."

He stepped back. I reluctantly pulled away and opened my door. When Louis's smile greeted me, I pulled him with a kiss that I almost gave to a man who wasn't worthy of it.

When we pulled apart, his smiled widened. "Hey, baby."

After he walked in, he looked Tariq up and down and waved hello. "Who are you?"

"I'm a friend. I was about to leave, though." As Tariq walked toward the doorway, I tried to avoid eye contact with Louis to hide my guilt.

Louis asked me, "This friend got a name?"

"I'm Riq. I came by to catch up wit' Erin, but I'm all caught up." Tariq looked Louis over and disappeared down the hallway.

Once I shut the door, Louis met me with confusion and curiosity. "What was he doing here?"

"He stopped by. We haven't talked in a while."

"You never mentioned a Riq before. Where do you know him from?" I wondered if he felt the heat that resonated in my apartment. I had to slip out of my sweatshirt to keep from gettin' faint.

"He, Loraine, and I were once mutual friends. Nothing serious. He's married, has a family. He was trying to catch up."

The mention of Tariq's wife and kid seemed to calm Louis's suspicions. It didn't do much for the lump in my throat. There was definitely a side of me that wanted that kiss to happen, but there was that other side that was grateful for Louis's timing. Either way, I spent most of my night with Louis in bed staring up at the ceiling, contemplating Tariq's hands touching me. The more I stared, the angrier I became as I reluctantly accepted Louis's warm embrace. I hated the effect Tariq had on me, even when I acted my role at showing how much it didn't. He was a married man, and dating him would violate the morals I spent all my young-hearted mistakes developing. Maybe the lack of discussions regarding his personal life made it easier to believe that there was a chance. When he walked into my apartment looking good enough to eat, lick, and suck, and told me the history of his marriage, he brought forth a reality that I secretly tried to avoid. Yeah, I told him I wanted to know, but no woman wants to know about the woman the man she thinks she loves is married to. Who would want to know about the family her *kinda* man has obligations to? It almost felt as if he were throwing his family in my face. Even though I asked him to and gave him the ultimatum And when he finally did, internally, I hated him for it.

When I exhaled, Louis squeezed my forearm as if to ask what was wrong. I lay silently for a while hoping he'd let it go. I kept my eyes closed and imagined sunlight. The sooner the sun rose, the easier it would be for me to get up and escape the conflicting emotions I imprisoned myself in. If this were a contest, Louis would win easily. But with one awkward moment, I was questioning the authenticity of a relationship that had been nothing but good to me.

"You okay?" I remained quiet and tried not to let the flurry of emotions running through my mind show on my face. I attempted to hush my thoughts; they were so loud it was surprising he hadn't said anything earlier. It was quiet for a while, and I felt him press his soft lips atop mine. I opened my eyes and smiled. "I knew you weren't 'sleep."

I licked my lips and turned over to face him. "I was sleep."

"Then why were you breathing so hard?"

I paused and sucked on my lips. "I didn't even know I was."

Louis leaned in for another kiss. My first reaction was to turn my head; instead, I let it happen. I allowed his lips to find solace in mine, and I unsuccessfully shooed away ideas of Louis's lips being Tariq's instead. Secretly, I relived that brief moment between Tariq and me, and instead of Louis interrupting, our lips touched. With my back pressed up against the wall, Tariq slid his tongue between my lips and sucked on my tongue. In my mind, I wrapped my arms around Tariq's neck. I moaned while Tariq's palms gripped the cusp of my ass and released the juices that flowed between my inner thighs. Dizzy from my fantasies, I spread my legs and let Louis come in closer—I wanted to feel Louis's body pressed up against mine while I imagined that Tariq was mine alone. I sucked on the tip of Louis's tongue while my lips caressed his, and I arched my back silently begging him to enter. When Louis pinned my wrists back and slid out of his boxers, I envisioned Tariq's smile peering back at me. I smiled back and beckoned him to come hither, continue his mission, and to make me climax like only he could.

"Shit, I missed you," I whispered.

"I did too," Louis responded. In my imagination, I was still in that moment with Tariq with my back up against my wall and my legs straddled around Tariq's waist. When Louis pushed my panties to the side and then very slowly slid inside me, I dropped my head back and pictured Tariq kissing down my neck.

"I needed this," I moaned as I cupped the back of his head, forcing him to dig into my skin as if he were searching for nourishment. "Don't stop."

My body rocked back and forth, as he held my thighs apart and pulled them closer to him. As wet as I was, I slid off him with glorious ease. Back and forth as I held on to my sheets. I was on a rollercoaster. I kept my eyes closed, threw my hands up, and tried to picture the location where I'd rather be—naked atop Tariq's sheets while he gave me more reasons to soil his mattress. "You never been this wet before…damn." When he pulled out, I opened my eyes, delirious and infuriated at the same time. Yanking off my panties, Louis went back in and gave me another reason to moan. "I guess you really did need this."

When my body trembled, I inched away from him, incapable of taking it all at once. He held on to my waist and pulled me closer to him. "Don't run from me." When he pulled out again, I sat up on my elbows and watched him gradually make his way down to my pelvic bone. He kissed trails down my chest and stomach as if he were leaving breadcrumbs. With his face planted deep between my thighs, he worked his tongue around my lips like a serpent, gently kissing and sucking my labia as I clutched his dreads. My moans evolved as they went from silent coos to exasperated shrieks. When he sucked on my clitoris and twirled his tongue around, my eyes literally rolled to the back of my head. Three minutes later, like little tremors tickling every inch of me, I felt a rush of heat rip through my body as I dug my top row of teeth into the skin beneath my bottom lip and screamed in satisfaction. Still weak and vulnerable, he spread my legs wide and pushed in deeper than before. While I could barely move, and my voice was hoarse, I dug my nails into his back and groaned. It was a bittersweet emotion that I couldn't articulate, but I whispered his name, "Louis," being sure not to slip and say *Tariq* like my subconscious tried to so many times before.

When he came, he grinned widely as we both collapsed and caught our breaths. "I wish you missed me like that more often."

I faked a smirk as I continued my thoughts of a man that didn't belong to me. I'd never cheated before, and didn't plan to cheat, but the emotional fantasy I shared with my man made me feel guilty. I wanted to call someone and discuss the misdeed that transpired. Loraine should understand, especially after she had been sexing a man who emotionally abused her for so long. Then again, her man was single. I was sexing a man who pledged his relationship before God. I was breaking up a family; Loraine was revisiting an old one. It was best to keep it to myself. I held Louis's hand in mine and led him to the bathroom to cleanse ourselves of each other. I kept a fake smile to continue the charade. When he wrapped his arms around my waist and rested his chin on my shoulder, I cringed—internally. Louis was good to me, and I hoped that our shower would refresh my memory and clear my head of the nonsense I imagined.

CHAPTER 23

Tariq

Two years ago…

I grew soft. When I caught Deja wit' another dude, I was strong. I was able to kick her out and change the locks without a glance back. She'd fill up my missed call log, and I'd clear my history with no remorse. With Simoné, I felt pity. I accepted her apologies and looked past her discretions. In the back of my mind, I realized there was more she hadn't told me, but somehow, I was drawn to her like moths to a flame. She burned me, and I couldn't help but get burned again. Things did get better, though. I stopped questioning her whereabouts and her shady behavior dissipated. My confidence in our relationship was unrelenting, and lucky for her, it blinded me.

I worked late a lot. Today, I needed to come home early. Thursday was my late day but I was tired. Employees were fuckin' up, and the last guy who had my job ain't know what he was doin'. I needed peace of mind, and I could find it at home wit' Simoné. Since I was never home early on a Thursday, I wasn't used to the afternoon air. It was thick and sat on my skin like a hand-knit sweater.

"Hey, Riq." My neighbor walked out his front door wit' his toolbox. He popped the hood of his car and sat the toolbox down on the ground. "It's so hot out, ain't it?" He wiped his forehead and turned to his car without my response.

I nodded and stood at my front door, sure that I would be walking into a home I was used to coming home to. My day was fucked, and I needed my woman to rejuvenate me. As sure as I was, I couldn't shake the muggy feeling left on my skin. The humidity sat on me as if it were tryna keep me away, warn me about what lay ahead. I ignored it. I unlocked the door and walked into an empty living room. Then, I heard the shower running.

I sat on my couch and slid off my shoes. As I loosened my tie, I pictured my neighbor working on his car. I could hear him bang out the dents in his car and grunt as the weight of the heat and hard labor bore down on his shoulders. At the same time, I winced when I heard the sound of the pipes rattling as the shower ran. I had to call a plumber, but Simoné didn't want to spend the money. With the sound of my neighbor's labor and the rattling pipes banging, my senses felt numb. Still, I was used to hearing it, so I paid it no mind. I stood up and walked to the bedroom. *Bang. Bang. Bang.* As hectic a day I had, my neighbor's car troubles and my rattling pipes were the least of my worries.

When I walked into the bedroom, I fixed the tussled covers on my bed and unbuttoned my shirt. *Bang. Bang. Bang.* Whenever my neighbor got frustrated, he'd bang on his car in frustration and grunt in a booming fury. It often sounded like it was coming from inside my house. I took a deep breath and rubbed my temples. Unbuckling my pants, I opened the bathroom door to greet my woman.

Bang! Bang! Bang! I had never heard my pipes rattle like that before. I dropped my pants to my ankles and wiped my face. The steam from the hot water hit my face like a slap. I looked into the shower. *Bang! Bang! Bang! Bang!* "Ooh, that feels good." Simoné screamed out wit' her eyes closed and her hands banging into the shower wall. The nigga behind her stared down at the ass she threw back at him. His back bumped into the other side of the cramped shower with each time she threw it back. He grunted loudly as he smacked her ass, held her hips, and pulled her to him. *Bang! Bang! Bang! Bang!* I pulled my pants back up and buckled them. The water was on full blast, and they couldn't hear me as I breathed through my mouth and squeezed my fists so tight my fingernails dug into my palms.

Bang! This time, I was the one to bang my fist into the shower door. They both stopped. The banging stopped. They looked at me and at each other. Simoné stood up straight and covered herself like it would make a difference. It didn't. I already swung the shower door open and yanked the wet, naked dude out of my shower. I grabbed him by his neck and flung him to the ground like I was spiking a football. When I noticed the terrified expression on the dude's face, I instantly recognized him from the club. The same dude with a lazy eye that thought it was okay to slap Simoné upside the head in the middle of a crowded club was the same mothafucka giving it to her from the back in my damn shower. I was done reminiscing. I stomped my foot into his chest. Wanting to hear his rib cage crack, I stomped him into my tile floor and hoped my desire would be fulfilled.

When Simoné grabbed my elbow, I snatched her hand off me and stomped into him again, wishin' I hadn't taken off my shoes when I walked in the door. "*Fuck!*" was the first word that came out my mouth.

"Riq, stop! You're killin' him," Simoné said.

"Aye, chill!" he cried.

He scrambled up off the floor, causing me to stomp my foot into the tile floor. The pain of stomping into hard ceramic tile shot through my calf like a lightning bolt. I didn't let it show. I threw a jab as quickly as he opened his mouth to say something. He threw his arms up and blocked his face. My fist caught the side of his jaw and he flew to the bathroom sink and held on for support. Simoné ran in between us and threw her hands up. "Baby, wait. Please!"

She was caught up in the moment. She forgot she was still wet and naked. Too wet and naked mothafuckas in my damn bathroom, and Simoné had the nerve to protect this nigga like I was really tryna hear it. I walked out. I didn't hear the crack in his chest, but I realized I knocked a tooth loose when I caught his jaw. I found peace in that. I put on my shoes and grabbed my car keys. Simoné ran out of the bedroom in a robe. I wasn't goin' to hear it. I walked out the front door and headed for my car. My neighbor tried not to hold eye contact.

He knew what was goin' on. He knew what I was about to walk in on. He hadn't even really started workin' on his car yet. He stood over the front of his car in the hot sun trying not to stare at Simoné as she ran out the house after me. "Tariq, wait! Don't leave. Not yet!"

I didn't speak. I got in my car and started the ignition. Simoné ran behind the car to keep me from leaving. I put the car in reverse and drove. I wasn't thinkin' straight. I didn't care if I hit her. I pressed the gas and eased out of my driveway. Simoné stood her ground at first, but she ran out the way when the trunk of my car nudged her stomach. Our eyes met when I put my car in drive. Her eyes were apologetic. Big round eyes that peeked through soggy, jet-black bangs. I squeezed my steering wheel and drove off. I didn't know where I was going, but this good-guy shit was for the birds.

When Simoné called, I ignored it; and she called a lot. She got one text from me after I left. "Get yo' shit out and go." She wouldn't go without a fight. I decided to sleep on Damien's couch until I could think straight. She'd blow my phone up, and she heard my voicemail every single time. Eventually, Damien got tired of seein' my ass print on his couch, and it was time to go back. "I need you to roll wit' me. If I go alone, I can't be responsible for my actions."

Damien shook his head and grabbed his keys. "Let's go, man."

When we got to my townhome, I took a long breath. If I saw another naked dude in my place, God couldn't stop me from the damage I would do. I opened the door, and there Simoné sat wit' her bags packed by the door. I told Damien, "Take her shit to her car."

Damien gazed at her demeanor. Simoné looked up at us wit' swollen eyes and tear-drenched cheeks. She wore my University of Miami T-shirt and a pair of her old jogging pants. She pinned her bangs back and then braided the rest of her hair down. I was used to seeing a bombshell when I got home; all I saw right then was a shell of a woman. "Riq…" Her voice cracked.

Damien grabbed her bags and walked out my front door. Simoné stood up and walked toward me. I threw my hands up and sucked in my lips. "Simoné, I told you to go."

"I couldn't leave without talkin' to you first." Two inches away from me, she raised her hands as if she were asking for a hug. I stepped back and turned my head away from her. "Riq, can we talk about this? You won't gimme the chance to say anything."

"There ain't shit to say. Simoné, I can't have you in my face right now. I'm not goin' stand here and talk about the bullshit you put me through."

"Baby, that wasn't supposed to happen. I dunno what I was thinkin'."

"You were thinkin' I'd be home late, allowing you to fuck another nigga in my crib while I sat stupid at work."

She shook her head and wiped her nose. "No, Riq. That's not what I was thinkin'. I called him over to tell him he needed to stop textin' me and—"

"You ain't fuckin' listening, Simoné." I smacked my hands together and moved away from her. In that moment, I saw myself smackin' her. That's when Damien walked back in. "You got to go, right now. I called yo' mama before I got here. You might wanna call her."

She looked up at me and rubbed her forehead. "Whatchu mean you called my mama?"

"I knew you would still be here." I moved out of her way and pointed at the door. "She's expectin' you."

"You really weren't goin' talk to me? You goin' kick me out to my mama house?"

"Simoné, I don't give a fuck where you stay. If you ain't tryna move into yo' mama house, that's cool, but yo' ass ain't stayin' here."

Simoné slid her tongue over her teeth and shifted her weight. Suckin' her teeth she said, "Baby…"

"Simoné, I dunno what else to tell you. I dunno why you think I'ma sit here and listen to any more bullshit. I'll call the cops and have them put you out if you keep fuckin' around. I ain't tryna be another nigga to put his hands on you. I'm givin' you the chance to *woman up* and walk the fuck out my place on yo' own will."

"Oh, it's like that?"

I nodded and walked past her. Damien opened the door and showed her the way out. She cut her eyes at him and at me. Damien said, "I left yo' shit by the trunk."

Simoné rolled her neck. "Fine, Tariq." She bumped past Damien and walked out, slammin' the door behind her.

Damien chuckled. "Damn, Riq. I ain't know you were cold like that."

"Damien, I caught the girl fuckin' in my bathroom. Wit' my own eyes, I see this girl throwin' her ass back to some chump in my mothafuckin' shower. What would you have done?"

"I'd be in prison for double homicide."

I laughed. Inside, I was hurting, but on the outside, I was a strong man who took out the trash. I laughed and thanked God I didn't buy a gun like I planned two years ago.

Shit was different. I was moving fast and couldn't tell which way was right. I tried to bury myself in my work and avoid women at all costs. I dunno if my broken heart was a magnet for desperate women because I couldn't fight 'em off. Not even at work. As I sat in the new office I got after being promoted, I'd watch the new intern wink at me and blow me kisses. She was young, a bright-eyed college graduate with high expectations and hormones.

I disregarded her advances. I let it go when she purposely brushed her ass up against my dick in the workroom. Her ass was abnormally fat, and she wore skintight dresses to show it off. I gave her the eye when she made my hand touch her left breast and pretended as if it was a mistake. Her breasts weren't bigger than B cups, but they were full and sat up straight when I walked into a room. I even told her to calm down when she *accidentally* let it slip that she forgot her panties on her bed at home. I looked at her skin, dark chocolate with caramel undertone, and tried not to stare at her wide lips and platinum tongue rings—she had two, 'cause apparently she liked double penetration.

After she started staying late with me, I began noticing things. I noticed how her Coke bottle shape popped through her pencil skirts and low-cut, see-through blouses. I studied how perky her breasts looked when she squeezed them into push-up bras. I watched her slender legs walk past my office door. When she said my name, I couldn't take me eyes off her shiny red lips. I loved how she chewed the end of her pencil and constantly tucked her curly weave behind her ears. There were days when she would let her hair down and let it sway while she skipped through the office. One night she said, "You need to relax. I can help with that, y'know?"

I dropped my pen as I tried to peel my gaze off her five feet two presence. "Oh yeah?" I responded. "How you plan to do that?"

"You really wanna know?"

I shouldn't have wanted to know. If anything, I should've ended the conversation and gotten back to my work. It was late, and I had reports that needed to be out by mornin'. Instead, I was in my office alone with a bouncy, horny twenty-year-old who wanted to make me relax. I still said, "Yeah, tell me."

"Well, I got this trick."

"What kinda trick is that?"

She walked inside. She leaned on my desk and made her breasts meet me at eye level. I couldn't look away; they were callin' my name. "I start off with my hands."

"What can your hands do?" My eyes still glued on her cleavage. I wanted to look away, but her voice was soft like clouds, and my dick was hard like a semi-automatic.

"From there, I use my tongue." She ran her tongue across her lips slowly. She dug inside my candy jar and pulled out a tootsie pop. Pulling off the wrapper, she wrapped her tongue around the sucker in a serpentine motion. First, she licked it up to get it wet, then she licked it down slowly to get it juicy. Next, she sucked it hard, sliding it down her throat and slurping the extracts that leaked. She kept her eyes on me the whole time, sucking the tootsie pop like it was her last meal. She barely used her lips as she sucked in the sides of her mouth to take hold of the sucker while she worked her tongue all around it. I grabbed my dick and looked away. I had to catch my breath. When she put the lollipop down, she sashayed toward me and straddled me. My hands wanted to throw her off; instead, they caressed her waist and pulled her closer. She pulled up her skirt and leaned forward. In my ear she sang, "I forgot my panties again."

I was stiff. I wanted her off me, but my body acted differently. I felt a feeling I hadn't felt in a long while, horniness. I asked myself what had been takin' me so long to get her calves on my shoulders. Tugging on her blouse, she slid out the gold condom wrapper from her bra and grinned.

"Can you fit one of these?" She simpered as she licked her lips and ripped the package open with her teeth.

When I tried to stand up and take control of the situation, she yanked my belt buckle and unzipped my pants. My dick had been poking her pussy since she sat on top of me, and there was no way she was letting up without a fight. Before I had any say in the matter, she held on to the back of my neck and lowered herself on top of me. Her pussy felt so tight and wet, I almost came instantly. I couldn't think straight. All I wanted from that point was more. I grabbed her thighs and made her bounce. She pushed down on her calves and rode my dick like I was a thoroughbred. "Fuck," I muttered in disbelief. I couldn't believe how good her pussy felt. I wondered if all pussy that didn't belong to Simoné feel this damn good. I squeezed her waist while she bounced and bounced, twisted and twisted, and churned and churned some more. I dropped my jaw as she held my arms for support while she worked me over.

Feeling myself pulsating too quickly, I picked her up and turned her around to face my table. I spread her legs and pounded her pussy, making the table move with us. She pushed papers around and off my desk while she cocked her leg up so I could get in deeper, and I did. I drove deeper inside of her until I couldn't reach any further. She screamed, "God, yes!" Praising the heavens, thanking Him for sex like mine. "Don't stop! Please, please…don't ever stop," she shouted as she begged for more.

When her leg buckled and she tussled around like a wet fish, she tensed her pelvic muscles and shrieked in excitement. Feeling her coming, I pulled out and came in the trashcan under my desk. Even though the latex engulfed the skin of my penis, I didn't trust her intentions. I'd always heard of condoms with needle holes in them so I wasn't ready to experience it firsthand. When I sat back down in my chair and rubbed my face, I kept shaking my head as I watched her catch her last breath. Once recovered, she pulled down her skirt and fixed her shirt. She gazed at herself in the mirror as she fluffed her hair with her fingers. The slick smirk on her face and raised eyebrow revealed how she was proud of what she'd done. Fucking her boss—a job well done.

Once put together, she faced me and said, "I told you I could make you relax." She winked and walked out of my office without another word. I was tired and upset, but damn if I wasn't relaxed. When I checked the time, I got up and shut my office door. I still had work to do, and I couldn't risk her coming back for seconds. As I sorted through papers, I grew frustrated. I was mad at how easily it was to nut for a woman I didn't respect. But what made me so furious was how good it felt afterward. It was a bitter feeling that felt tender to the touch. My dick was soft, and I used a moist toilette to wipe the dried sweat from my face and neck. The brighteyed intern fucked me to where I was sick to my stomach, but it was a pain I gladly endured.

CHAPTER 24

Tariq

A year and a half ago...

After the night with the intern, I tried to avoid the little traps she would set to get me back inside of her. At the end of the day, I was still her boss, and I couldn't let my pecker get me into trouble. I worked hard to get out the office by six and avoid being left alone wit' her. Eventually, she moved on to Hector from the fourth floor. Hector was the assistant VP, and it was common knowledge that he cheated on his wife relentlessly. What was also common knowledge was that Hector spoiled his mistresses like princesses; and with' pockets as fat as Hector's, the intern put her pussy into overdrive for his wallet.

I moved out of my place. With the bigger salary, I was able to afford a two-bedroom condo with a doorman. I couldn't stay in the same house my woman fucked other niggas in, and when Simoné kept findin' ways to show up at my place, I realized that I needed out. I moved past the pain and got used to being on my own, worryin' about my own shit. Any dreams of me findin' a wife were put on hold almost indefinitely, and I enjoyed the freedom of doing me.

I sat on my couch in my pajama pants wacthin' ESPN when there was a knock at my door. I stared at the door like it had done something wrong. Scratchin' my head, I walked to the door and sighed. It was my day off, I hadn't heard from Simoné in three months, and I was hopin' for a day wit' no distractions. When I opened my door, I couldn't really move. I surveyed the woman that stood before me and wiped my sweaty palms on my bare chest. I was nervous as I stared at the brown-skinned woman wearing large bumblebee shades covering eyes that sat atop high cheek-bones. Her curly hair flowed down to the small of her back.

"How'd you—"

"Your mom told me where you lived."

"Deja, what are you doing here?"

"I had to see you."

"No, you didn't. You can't show up at my place unannounced." In my head, I cursed my mama for giving out my personal business. I stood there standing in front of the only other woman I considered spendin' my life wit', the only other woman who I gave the power to hurt me. I stood in front of her hoping she would've gained a hundred pounds and lost all her hair by the time I saw her again. Instead, her body was tight like hard knocks, and she had an ass that stood out further than she did. Even with all the pain she caused me, I wanted to feel her. With all of the anger I harbored toward her, I craved to release that anger sexually. I wanted to watch her love faces and listen to her scream my name while I made her come over and over…and over and over. Shit, my dick was weak. "What do you want?"

"I wanted to talk to you."

"About?"

"So much…everything. Us…me, you." She removed her shades, held my wrist, and looked into my eyes. I could sense she was praying I didn't turn her away. "Please, hear me out, *Riq-ee*."

Riq-ee. Two years ago, I was her Riq-ee. I used to love hearin' her call me that as soft as it sounded. In fact, I still loved hearing it. I moved aside and let her voice do what she knew it could. She smiled and walked in. I closed the door behind us.

When she noticed ESPN playin' on my TV, she pointed and smiled. "No matter what time of day, I can always count on you watchin' ESPN." I used the remote to shut my TV off and stood three feet away from her. I stuffed my fists in my pajama pockets and stood there. I didn't have anything to say. She had the floor. After two minutes of stillness, she moved a foot closer. "Your mama tol' me about your promotion."

I shrugged my shoulders. On the inside, I was heated. I hated the relationship she shared with my mama. Though I made sure to keep her out of my life by ignoring her calls and texts begging for forgiveness, my mama had been prepping her for the opportunity to come back in my life and fuck things up.

She smiled nervously. Her eyes darted from corner to corner as she stood there in khaki shorts, a skintight white tank, and black stripper pumps. She dressed in an outfit she knew I'd imagine undressing. Something to remind me of the loving we had. Her caramel-covered thighs glistened in the appearance of sunlight. Her lips were covered in pink lipstick, and her eyes shadowed with black shimmer. We stood in my living room trying not to stare at each other, taking one another in. Watching her turned me on. She never let herself go. Before she cheated, a woman like Simoné would have never had the chance to sneak into my bedroom and hurt me like she did. I reminded myself Deja was the reason why I was in that situation. I stopped watching her and refused to let that anger resurface. "Your mama also tol' me that you're not datin' anyone...anymore."

"Damn, you and mama talked about me all day." I stared down at my bare feet. "You still haven't told me why you're here, Deja."

"I miss you, Riq-ee. I miss you all the time. When I heard you moved in wit' someone else, I went crazy. I lost ten pounds, and my hair was fallin' out. I miss you so much." She moved a foot closer. "Then when I heard things weren't going, well…I know it sounds bad, but…I was happy. I was happy to know that there was a chance that we could make it."

"We can't make it. All the shit did was sour me toward you even more."

"Riq, you never gave me a chance. You never even tried to work things out. You saw me with someone else and that was it. How do I know that you even loved me when it was so easy for you to walk out on me? Your mama told me how you gave her a second chance, and look what she did to you. I was pissed. If you gave me another chance, I wouldn't have messed up again, Riq."

I moved a foot closer. The anger resurfaced. My muscles tightened in the worst way. My blood temperature rose, and I wanted that same opportunity I had to punch her lover in the face when I saw him in that restaurant. "Excuse me?" I rubbed the top of my head and chuckled. Pissed that I couldn't speak, all I could do was laugh. "Because I didn't fight for a chick who lied to me, fucked around on me, and embarrassed me, *I'm* fuckin' wrong?"

"I never fucked around on you, Riq. He…he was the only one."

"That shit makes it better?"

"No…you could've given me the chance to talk to you. Shit, you fought for her. You shut me out like I wasn't shit, Riq."

"You weren't!" I was in her face. My eyes stared deep into her almond-shaped chestnut eyes—hurt, longing eyes that needed me to hold her. I stared into her light-brown eyes and refused to give in to that feeling of wanting to hold her. I moved a foot backward. "I loved you, Deja. I was so crazy in love with you, and you still chose to make a fool out of me. Why would I fight for you? You wasn't tryna fight for me."

"Did you love her?"

I smacked my lips and turned my head. "Hell no."

"Then why did she get a second chance, Tariq? Why wasn't our love worth it?" She licked her pink lips and took a deep breath. She moved a foot away from me. Folding her arms beneath her breasts, she shook her head and pushed up her lips. "Besides, it wasn't my fuckin' fault I cheated on you, Riq."

"What?"

"You heard me. I'm tired of you goin' 'round blamin' me like I fucked our lives up. You never appreciated me, never talked to me, and never took me out. Hell, you never did anything but work and sleep. What the fuck was I supposed to do, Riq? You come in my face talkin' like you're the victim. He was there for me and you weren't. You did this to yourself, and you need to stop blaming' me. I'm tired of it."

I jolted my head back and dropped my jaw. I turned around when all I saw was her lover's face. On her shoulders, he stared back at me, taunting me. I pictured him making love to her, holding her, caressing her, listening to her call him *babe*, and kissing her pink lips. I was through reliving that pain. I rammed my fist into my kitchen wall and walked to the front door. I didn't look back; I opened the door and gestured for her to leave. "You gotta go, Deja."

She stood there. I realized she would stand there for a couple seconds before she agreed to leave, and I was cool with that as long as she left. Instead, she shook her head and walked to my couch. "No, Riq." She sat down and crossed her legs as she stared at my blank TV screen. Avoiding eye contact. "We're gonna talk. I'm not giving up this time. You're angry, and I can understand that, but we can move past this."

I slammed my door shut and didn't move. I wasn't going to physically throw her out, but if I moved too fast, I'd see his face on her shoulders again. I'd see his face laughing at me, and all I'd want to do is black his eye like I wanted to the first time. I stood at my door not moving.

"I know you missed me, Riq." She bounced her knee as she wrapped her hands around her knees. She looked over at me. "That's why shit hasn't worked out with you. You're not over me. I know it because I know I'm not over you. And we won't be rid of each other that easily. I love you, and you love me."

"According to you…" I paused and sucked in my lips forcefully. I squeezed my door handle and took deep breaths. "Accordin' to you, I didn't love you. Not like yo' man could. I had what was coming to me."

"I didn't mean to say it like that. Can you come sit down and talk to me? Can we get past this?"

"No! I dunno if you got stupid o' something, but shit ain't that easy. You've always been so fuckin' spoiled. You think I'm supposed to get over this shit 'cause *you* say so? Is that why you decided to fuck that dude? Is it because he let you run over his punk ass? Say whatever the fuck you wanna say, but I wasn't sleepin' around. I didn't fuck other hoes, which is what I would've done had I stayed around. You were feelin' neglected and wanted me home more? You should've told me something. You cheatin' on me ain't my fault. That's all on you."

"I told you, Riq. I told you how I wanted to spend more time with you. I told you how lonely I felt. I never hid that from you."

"I never knew you were *that* unhappy, Deja, at least not to that extent. Not to the extent to which you would be with another man and humiliate me like I ain't mean shit. I never thought you of all people would do some shit like that."

"I'm sorry, Riq. I'm sorry a million times over." She stood up and walked toward me. I didn't want her near me, but she didn't pick up on it. She drifted in my direction with a devious look in her eyes. "I need you to forgive me. I need us to get past this. I made a mistake, and I paid for it but, please forgive me, Riq-ee." By the time she was through with her plea, she was damn near on top of me. My back was against the wall, and I felt trapped like a prisoner. We were standing there, centimeters apart. Feeling her breath on my neck was a familiar feeling that I actually missed. She was so close I felt her heart beating through her chest like a drumbeat. *Boom...boom...thump...thump...thump.*

When she moved in closer, I tried to move away, but I was paralyzed. She moved in and kissed me like she used to. Her kisses were always warm and gentle. Her kisses were reminiscent to summer breezes, kindly flowing through and around my lips, makin' my knees weak. She was an unhealthy weakness that I missed—emphatically. I craved her like a narcotic. I held her close to me and reluctantly kissed her back. We kissed like we used to, slowly and passionately. We'd tug at each other's tongues and let our lips fall over each other's like parachutes. When she slipped her arms around my neck, I was through with the tenderness. I was angry and needed to release it on the person who deserved it most.

I unzipped her shorts and led her to my kitchen counter. She wiggled out of her shirt and slid it off her shoulders. We stepped over it as I pushed her into my kitchen and pulled down her shorts, taking her panties down, too. When they hit the floor, I pulled away from our kiss and gazed at her. Her body was beautiful. I rubbed her arms, caressing the skin I once called mine. I sat her up on my counter and touched the folds of her pussy. With my fingers inside, memories flooded my senses. Her pussy was always soft, wet walls of plush decadence. Tiny hairs covered a hole that I'd play with for fun; I remembered how her legs would twitch when I slithered my tongue in between her pussy lips, nibbling on her skin gently as she grabbed the back of my head and called me *Daddy*. My penis had never been as erect as it was for her. I stopped reminiscing, pulled my boxers down, and put it inside of her. As her head tilted back, I remembered how the skin under her neck, the brown, caramel-and-mocha complexion always gleamed when sweat would drip down the side of her neck and between her breasts. Roasted-peanut-colored nipples would stare back at me as I pushed deep inside her, rocking her body back and forth. I unhooked her bra so I could see that stare.

She gripped the edge of the counter as she chewed her lips and moaned in satisfaction. I used to hum to her moans. The sound of her satisfaction always made a tune I could hum to. Our bodies were in synch, and I loved hearing it. I hummed as I spread her thighs and listened to the backdrop of her moisture attempting to escape. Pale, white stickiness that would engulf the skin on my penis and wet the darker skin surrounding her lips, those sweet, wet pussy lips that resembled strawberries. We didn't speak. We didn't *need* to speak. There was no room for words, only the sound of her rhythmic moans and my hums. We made music that our bodies danced to.

I released the anger that I felt toward her on her body and made her body crumple, tense, shake, and scream as our sweat mixed and mingled. If she hadn't moved so close, and if I hadn't heard the drumbeat in her chest, I would've never known how badly I needed to feel her. Her sex was the narcotic I needed to make me lose control. I was intoxicated from her essence. I supported myself on my kitchen counter as I pounded into her, grabbing her left ass cheek while I went in deeper and much, much harder. She opened her mouth and moaned louder, trying not to break our rhythm or make bodies lose the beat. I watched as my desert sand-colored penis got immersed with a thickening white cream that seeped from her body and covered mine. I panted as my heart thumped to the same drumbeat. Suddenly, I stopped. I felt myself coming and stopped myself from the temptation. I pulled away from her and caught my breath. She, knowing my body, pulled me and led my dick back to its destination. I didn't want her to make me come. I didn't want her to have that hold over my body, but before I could resist, she clasped her clitoris around my shaft, and almost instantly, I came. I erupted as my penis imploded within her. I pulled away again and kept the rest outside of her. She, proud of her accomplishment, caught her breath, too, as she tied her hair up and smiled.

I helped her down. When her feet hit the floor, she leaned on my chest as she regained strength in her knees. She whispered, "I love you, Riq-ee. I want us to work again." When she kissed me again, I didn't pull away like I wanted to. I kissed her back and licked the sweat that dripped down her face. I didn't want to, but I was looking forward to round two.

Deja hunched down and grabbed her phone from her pocket. I draped my arms around her waist and kissed her shoulders. As she scrolled through her phone, she tilted her head back. She exhaled as I felt her melt in my arms. We stood there in the moment; two seconds later, I peeked over her shoulder and glanced at her phone.

She opened one of her text logs. I ain't wanna read her texts, but the name of the sender caught my attention. *Traevon*. The name looked familiar. I stopped kissing her neck as I tried to remember the emotion associated with the name Traevon. All I could think of was rage. I read the text in her inbox. "I know you're mad. I was wrong for fuckin' yo' homegirl. But I wanna kiss n' make up, fuckin' 'til the sun cum up like u know we can." Yep, rage was the fitting emotion. *Fucking* Traevon was the nigga she fucked. Her lover. Two years later, and Traevon had mistreated her like she did me, and they were still fuckin' and lovin'. I was now the man who intruded on the relationship she built with another man. I took a deep breath and let her go.

Deja looked back down at her phone and turned to face me. "Riq…"

I put up my hand to stop her. "Don't worry 'bout it." I picked up her clothes and handed them to her. After she got dressed, she put away her phone and rushed to hold my neck in her arms. I pulled her away and shook my head. "It's cool, Deja. You left me for him, and now you come here he's doin' you wrong."

Deja shook her head like she was having a seizure. "No…no, baby that's not true. It's you I wanna be with…*you*. I never left you. You kicked me out. You left me."

I walked back to my door and opened it. She stared at me and wiped her infamous tears. I turned my head and stared at the hallway. "You gotta get outta here, Deja. I can't let you keep doin' this shit to me. Run back to him."

"Riq, please. Don't do me like this." She ran up to me in an attempt to kiss me like we used to. I moved my face away and frowned.

"Deja!" I snapped. "Go. Now." I let the door go and walked into my bedroom, shuttin' the door behind me. I wasn't gonna let her stand there giving me those puppy dog eyes. I needed her out of my place, out of my face, and back to the lover that repaid her the same heartache she paid me. There was silence for a solid five minutes before I heard my front door slam shut. I took a deep breath and walked back into my living room. I was alone again and unremorseful about the experience I shared with a woman I once needed. I locked the door and stared at my empty living room. I cleared my throat and dropped my shoulders. It was clear now. I ran from love with the failure I experienced with Deja. However, more sure now than ever, I was free from her. Free to find a woman that truly did deserved my time, whenever that time was.

That was until I saw Simoné standin' at my door. Her presence at my door wasn't what took me by surprise. What really took me by surprise was the glow she had. Her big round eyes covered by her long, black bangs, like when I first met her. This time, though, when I looked into her eyes, I saw more than anger. I couldn't shoo her away as easily as I did before. I would have to stop looking at her eyes and pay more attention to her stomach, which stuck out further than when I last saw her. Her stomach was draped in a long black maxi dress like she was in mourning. I stood in my hallway with my keys in my hand as I breathed deeply. I may have wanted to walk away and never look back, but I wouldn't be the son my mother raised. Eventually, I was going to have to face the reality that there was a pregnant woman waiting for me at my door.

As I walked toward her, everything moved in slow motion while I considered numerous ways to avoid this from actually happening. In light of recent events, I felt the baby prolly wasn't even mine. But I couldn't turn her away and then find out the baby really was mine. I never really thought about fathering a baby, but when I did, I would be there to handle my business. When I reached my door, I kept my eyes on her eyes, longing eyes that prayed I wouldn't betray her like she did me. "Hey," I said.

"Hey."

Grudgingly, I asked, "You wanna come inside?"

She nodded and exhaled. When she walked in, I closed the door behind us. I couldn't help but think about the idea of running back into my G and driving off, anything but manning up to my responsibilities, especially if they were even mine to face. "How'd you find out where I stayed?"

She held her stomach and shrugged her shoulders. "Yo' mama told me. It wasn't easy gettin' it out of her. At first, I thought she gave me the wrong address."

I rubbed my eyeballs and threw my keys on the counter. "As bad as my mama cursed yo' triflin' ass out, I'm surprised she gave you the right address." I surveyed her stomach and sighed. "How you feelin'?"

"Tired, Riq. I called you."

"Been busy."

"More like been avoidin'. Why couldn't you pick up?"

"Don't play dumb, Simoné. You know why."

"It's yours."

"And how am I supposed to believe that?"

"I'm six-and-a-half months' pregnant. I wasn't wit' nobody else around that time."

"I'm supposed to believe that?"

"It's the truth."

"What the fuck is that supposed to mean comin' from yo' mouth?"

She lowered her eyes and rubbed her stomach. She sat down on one of my bar stools and exhaled. "I took a DNA test."

"The baby's not even here."

"I can still take a DNA test before the baby's born. I know I fucked up, but I knew this baby was yours. That's why I stole one of your dirty razors and told the doctors to test my unborn baby. I need you here wit' me."

"How'd you steal one of my razors?"

"After what happened between you and me, I found out I was pregnant. I knew this baby was yours, but I knew you wouldn't believe me." She stood up from my stool and walked over to me. "Before you moved here, I used my key to sneak back into your old place, and I grabbed one of your razors from the shower to take the test."

I grabbed the back of my head and blew out cold air. "Simoné, you bringin' a lot to my doorstep."

"I know." She wiped the tears that trickled down her cheekbones. "I know, and I'm sorry, but this baby is yours and I need you."

I shook my head. "Fuck," I said as I walked to my couch. I sat down and rubbed the back of my neck. "Shit…"

After taking a deep breath, she wiped her face. "I'm tired, Riq. I'm tired all the time. My body's changing. My hormones are everywhere. I'm hot all the fucking time. I'm throwing up in the morning, afternoon, and evening. Morning sickness my ass." She squeezed her hands. "And since baby has my heart rate up, I'm always tryna catch my breath. Why couldn't you pick up the damn phone, Riq? I've been doing this for the past six months by myself. If you don't wanna be with me, fine. But I need you here for your son."

I sat up. In her stomach, there was a son. Supposedly, *my* son. "How am I supposed to believe you, Simoné?"

"Believe the facts, Riq." Simoné opened her purse and pulled out some papers. Handing me the papers, she smiled. "I knew he was yours."

Grabbing the papers, I read it out loud. "Probability of Paternity, 99.999%."

I looked up at Simoné, who had a big smile on her face. "I told you."

"Still, Simoné. I can't believe half the shit that leaves your mouth. How do I even know that you really used my DNA to test that baby? Shit, you could've only tested that foul dude you had in my house that day. Because you show me some papers, I'm supposed to automatically believe this baby is mine?" I threw the papers on the couch next to me and sighed.

"What else do you want me to do? I know he's yours."

"I don't!"

"I'll take the test again. Gimme a toothbrush, another razor, a hairbrush, anything. I'll prove it to you, again."

"You ain't prove shit this time."

"You really think I would go through all this to lie to you?"

I cut my eyes at her and snarled. "Are you serious? You lied to my face so many fucking times, I can't even be sure that you're even really pregnant."

"Give me a fucking DNA sample, Tariq! I'm not gonna let you call me liar when I'm standing here carrying your damn child. If you don't believe me, take the damn test, but don't sit in my face and call me a liar."

"I will."

Simoné's chest rose and fell as her hands rattled. As I watched her body shake, I took a deep breath and turned my head. I couldn't deny that the possibility of me having a son somewhat excited me. At some point in my life, I wanted a mini-me. I wanted the opportunity to bring life into this world. The only downside to it all was that I had to share it with Simoné. I may not have wanted to be with her, but I wanted to be there for my son, if in fact he really was mine.

"If this baby really is mine, I wanna be there for you, Simoné."

"You sho' ain't acting like it."

"How'd you expect me to act? This the first time I've seen you since I put you out my house."

Simoné gritted her teeth as she placed her hand on her chest. I could tell her heart beat faster as she processed things. "Tariq, I really can't handle all this right now."

I rubbed my forehead and shrugged my shoulders. "Come sit next to me."

She sat down next to me and shuffled through her purse. She pulled out a few sonogram pictures. "I came straight here after my doctor's appointment today. They say I have high blood pressure. I been tryna keep it under control, but I can't keep doing this all by myself." Handing me the pictures, Simoné breathed deeply and relaxed her shoulders. "They confirmed the sex about a month ago, and I've been meaning to show you the pictures." Simoné pointed at a spot in the picture and said, "That's his...well, you know, that's how they know he's a boy."

"Damn." The thought of having a son was a lot to take in when two hours ago I was thinkin' 'bout orderin' a pizza and watching ESPN.

"I know this is a lot, Tariq. I would've texted you, but I wanted to tell you in person. I knew you wouldn't believe me unless I showed you proof. I'm not doing this alone, Riq." She grabbed my hand and placed it on her stomach. I rubbed her stomach and stared into her eyes, remembering the feelings I once had for her. Then, I remembered how things ended.

I pulled my hand away and shook my head. "No, Simoné. This don't mean shit about you and me. I'll be here for...my son, if he's mine, but that's it."

We sat quietly for a while. Under her breath she muttered, "I need a place to stay."

I shot up from my seat and walked toward the front door. After finding out about my son, she had the nerve to ask me for a place to stay. "Simoné, I can't do this."

She propped herself off the couch while holding her stomach and grabbing my coffee table for support. "Riq, I lost my job. I was sick all the time, showin' up late and missin' work. And soon, I couldn't keep up wit' rent. I got evicted. I have nowhere else to go."

"What about yo' mama's house?"

"My mama has a one bedroom that she shares with her boyfriend and his two kids. I can't stay there."

"I can't have you staying here. I kicked you out and I ain't lettin' you back in."

"Where the fuck am I supposed to go, Riq? You want me to live on the streets? Fine, I'll sleep in the gutter right outside yo' fuckin' building and you can see my face when you walk out the door every morning. That way, yo' son can know that his daddy ain't care about his mama enough to give her a bed to sleep on."

I laughed. It was the type of laugh I laughed whenever I was pissed and couldn't pick the best emotion to express. I was fucked. I thought I had moved on, but here was Simoné yankin' me ten steps backward. "What about yo' girls? They can't give you a couch to sleep on?"

"Riq..."

"Simoné, you gotta go somewhere else. At least fo' tonight. I can't deal wit' all this right now. We goin' have to talk about this in the mornin' o' something. My head is spinnin'." I walked into the kitchen and poured a glass of faucet water. Gulping it down, I realized that I hadn't offered a pregnant woman something to drink. I took a deep breath and said, "You thirsty?"

She shook her head and walked to the kitchen. "I'll leave, but I'm gonna call you first thing in the morning."

I didn't respond. I poured another glass and stared at the floor. Simoné walked out the door and left me alone wit' my thoughts— loud, echoing thoughts that made me wish I hadn't come home.

Fuck. We took another DNA test and surprisingly confirmed that I was the father of Simoné's baby. So, Simoné moved in. I tried every alternative I could find before finally agreeing. Simoné and I were back under the same roof, and I hated every moment of it. Even though I made it clear that she was not my girl, in her head, we were workin' things out. I would look at her and see that shower scene. I spent more time at work and less time alone with her and my weariness. The intern moved on, making it safe to spend late nights in my office workin' on excuses to stay away from home. With Simoné there, I could barely call it *home* anyway.

Tonight I had no work, and if I stayed at the job, I was technically trespassing. I begrudgingly drove to my condo, a home that I at one point happily called my own. I contemplated five different ways out before gettin' home. They all failed. I still made it home. I unlocked my door and walked in to find Simoné crying over a stack of papers at my breakfast bar. I sighed and closed the door behind me.

"What's wrong wit' you?" I asked.

She looked up at me and licked her lips. "Bills. I dunno how I'ma pay these bills. I can't…" Her words trailed off as she sighed and wiped the tears that soaked her face. "I dunno what to do, Riq."

I dropped my keys on the counter and stuck my hands in my pockets. "What bills?"

"Medical bills. I had insurance through my job. I thought I had enough saved up to pay for the doctor visits without insurance but…" She threw the papers out of her face. "Shit's rackin' up. I can't afford it, and now the doctor's tellin' me they won't see me until I make my payments. I dunno what the fuck I'm gonna do, Riq. I'm fucked."

I walked to her side and looked through the stack of bills. I was surprised to see how expensive havin' a baby was. Simoné was in debt almost five thousand. "What does this mean?"

Simoné sniffled and took a deep breath. She was preparing to lay it on thick. I wasn't goin' to like what she had to say next. "I talked to yo' mama, and we both agreed that we need to get married."

I stepped back. I untied my tie and walked into the kitchen. I shook my head and tried to avoid the conversation she had set me up for. "You are trippin', Simoné."

"I'm serious, Riq. I'm not sayin' this to make us get back together."

I pulled out a cup from my cupboard. My mouth was dry, and I needed to drink something. I filled my cup with water. "No, Simoné. This pregnancy has got you goin' crazy if you think we goin' get married, you *and* my mama."

"Riq, if we get married, I can be on your insurance. We won't be swimmin' in debt, and I don't have to worry about givin' birth in our living room or the free clinic. Riq, it's the only thing that makes sense."

"I know there are government programs out there that help women in yo' situation. You think you slick, huh?"

Simoné snatched her purse from the floor and then pulled out a set of papers. Her hands went back to rattling as her chest heaved. "Denied. Denied. Denied, Tariq. I've been denied for everything."

"How can they deny a pregnant woman with no money?"

Simoné waved the papers in her hand and snorted. "I was denied unemployment, I've been denied housing assistance. Hell, I'm pregnant and I've even been denied fuckin' Medicaid! You think

I ain't ask the same questions you asked? I ain't getting no answers, yet, this baby ain't getting any smaller. I try to appeal. I've even gone down there and got in those people's faces, but when they see me drive up there in a nice car rocking a Gucci bag, they think I'm fuckin' lying 'cause all they tell me is I simply don't qualify for benefits at this time." Simoné slammed the papers down and sighed a shaky breath. "I can't keep doing this. I can't keep making a fool out of myself. I need insurance and I need to pick my damn face up from off the floor. Marry me and put me out of my misery, Riq."

I swallowed my cup of water and poured another cup. "You talkin' insurance now, but at the end of the day, we'd still be married. I told you before we even got into this. I'm here for the baby. I don't wanna be wit' you, Simoné."

She didn't like hearing that, but I had to get her head out of the clouds. She sat up and walked into the kitchen. Pointing at her stomach, she said, "You think I have stomach mumps or somethin'? I'm pregnant! And in case you haven't figured it out, babies cost money. Do I want us to be together? Hell yea. I loved you, Riq. But I fucked up, and I take responsibility for that. The fact is, however, gettin' married is what's best for the baby. If you wanna be here for your son, fine. Be here. Marry me."

"Simoné, no. I'm not…" I walked past her and unbuttoned my shirt. I went into my bedroom and kept undressing. I couldn't stand there watching the woman carryin' my son talk about marriage. When I considered marrying, I damn sure wasn't considering marryin' a woman like Simoné. "I got a hard time believing half the shit you say. How do I know this ain't some bullshit trick?"

Simoné followed me and blocked the doorway. "You know I'm pregnant. I peed on a damn stick for you, twice! I took another damn paternity test for you. You can look at the medical bills or go through that pile of denials. You can even call yo' mama. I'll wait. Riq, I'm not tryna trick you. All I want is to have a healthy fuckin' pregnancy."

"Not like this. I ain't marryin' you. That shit ain't neva happenin'."

"We can get an annulment."

"What?"

"After the baby is born, we can get the marriage annulled. I don't wanna trick you into marriage. Why would I want to be married to a man who doesn't want me? I wanna do what's best for our son."

I didn't trust Simoné. When I looked at her, I only saw anger and betrayal. Yet, I also saw the son growin' inside of her. "You must not be hearin' me."

"Can you pay for the medical bills piling up? Riq, it's easy to get married and get it annulled. Can you afford our son if we don't get married?"

I walked back into my living room and then picked up the pile of papers from my breakfast bar. As I waded through a pile of denied government assistance letters and increasingly expensive medical bills, I chewed on my bottom lip. Huffing loudly, I threw the papers across my coffee table and stared at Simoné as she stood in my bedroom doorway. I was more prepared to go into debt than marry Simoné. Nevertheless, as she glared back at me, all I could see was my seed. A son that I fathered who I needed to protect and support, even if that meant doing what I hated most. I said, "I can't believe my mama agreed to some shit like this."

"She ain't got the cash to foot the bill either. He's your son, Riq. As much as you may hate me, you *have* to be here for him."

"What happened to your credit cards?"

"Maxed out."

"I still can't believe they denied you benefits. I can't fuckin' be married to you, Simoné. Anything but that."

Simoné stomped her foot and smacked her lips. "Riq, people do this all the time. You got the insurance. Why not put it to use?"

I sucked in my lips and huffed like the big, pissed-off wolf. I whispered, "As soon as the baby's born, we'll get it annulled?"

Simoné's face lit up. She nodded and clasped her hands together. "Yes, baby. Yes!" She rushed over to me and wrapped her arms around my neck.

I pulled away and stood up. "I'm serious, Simoné. This is only for the baby. Once he's born, we're gettin' an annulment."

She stood up beaming. "I promise, Riq. As soon as the baby's born."

CHAPTER 25

Erin

Present...

"How are you and Louis?"

I sipped my wine and pretended to enjoy answering that question. "Good."

I met up with Loraine early Saturday morning at her house, giving me an excuse not to see Louis. With me keeping my secret fantasies of Tariq from Loraine, she was good insurance that I wouldn't crack and end up knocking on Tariq's door.

"That's it?" Loraine sat on her couch with her dreads hanging off her dropped shoulders. She wore a silk maxi dress that matched her mint nail polish. I could attribute her relaxed demeanor to the fact that she was letting Lorenz fulfill the void that her pussy had been waiting on someone to fill.

I shrugged my shoulders. "We're good. What else do you want me to say?"

"You're still trippin' over that mess wit' Teona?"

"It's still on my mind. I'm tryna work past it." I didn't come over to talk about Louis. I went there to escape him. "You still sleepin' with Lorenz?"

It was apparent that my question caught Loraine off guard. But as quickly as I asked, her face lit up, and she beamed like a fat kid at a buffet. "Yes."

"I can tell it's doing you good."

"How can you tell that?"

"Look at you. You even dress differently."

Loraine blushed as she flipped her dreads off her shoulders and exhaled in satisfaction. "It feels good being with a man I know what to expect from. Since we're not trying to get remarried or anything, it feels good when he comes through, spreads my legs like pliers, and leaves."

"Are you sure you're not catching feelings?"

"That's the good thing about this whole set up. There ain't no feelings to catch. We've already done this. I already love him, and I know he already loves me. Therefore, the sex isn't meaningless; I'm satisfied, but I know I don't want a relationship with him, which means there's no guilt lingering. Only amazing sex." Loraine twirled her dreads between her fingers and grinned as she stared at nothing in particular.

"You make it sound so good."

"It *is* good. There's nothing wrong about it. And without the pressure of a relationship, the sex is that much better, wetter, and juicier."

All I thought about was Tariq pleasing my body the way it needed. The only issue was that I actually had a relationship. Louis may have been good in bed, but he was no Tariq. "When do you plan to see Lorenz again?"

"Whenever I need my fix." We laughed. "Girl, if we could bottle the feeling you get after good sex, we'd be millionaires. We'd have that real blue magic."

I laughed hard as I imagined the possibility. If I could bottle the feeling that Tariq gave me, I wouldn't need Tariq. I'd be content with Louis. "Good sex helps you think clearly; it relaxes you. You can tell which relationships aren't having enough sex. They're the ones that exude tension and frustration."

"Damn right. By eliminating the talking and adding more sex, my relationship with Lorenz has never been better."

"Maybe that's what I need to do to make my relationship with Louis work better."

When Loraine's doorbell rang, she picked her glass of wine up and headed for the door. I scrolled through Louis's apologetic and sappy text messages and missed him. I may have craved my physical connection with Tariq, but I couldn't deny my emotional connection wit' Louis. I started to text him how much I really missed him, too, but Teona walked in with her nose turned up. "Why are you always here?" she said through her throat.

I looked up at her and stood up. She wore a skin-tight, black lace dress that cut off right beneath her booty. She held her black heels in her hand and faced me while holding her flip-flops and purse. I looked back at Loraine, who was shakin' her head at the scene. I turned to Teona. "Where I spend my time is none of your concern, *lil' girl*."

She dropped her purse on Loraine's couch. "I hope you've been treatin' my man right." She roguishly grinned with her hands on her hips.

I moved away from her as I understood that I could go to jail for what I thought about doing to her. She was a child and was doing what children do. I shook my head and gathered my things. "Lemme go." I walked toward the door and left Teona to play mind games with someone who cared about her opinion.

Loraine walked me to the door. "I'll talk to you later, Erin."

I was a second from walkin' out before Teona opened her mouth again. "Tell Louis I'm pawning the ring he gave me."

I stopped and faced her. "Excuse you?"

"The engagement ring he gave me. Since he's done wit' me, I'm pawning his ring." Teona pulled out a gold, diamond ring and slid it on her finger, hand modelin' it in my face.

I looked to Loraine for an answer. She cut her eyes at Teona. "Girl, stop lying. You know that man never proposed to you."

Teona slid the ring back off her ring finger and eyed it down. She smiled and said, "Or maybe I'll keep it. There's always a chance he'll come back."

"You're full of shit," I said.

"You haven't even been down here long enough for a man like Louis to propose to you," Loraine pointed out.

Teona cut her eyes at Loraine and rolled her neck. "For your information, I met Louis when I was in college. The nigga can travel."

Teona sauntered over to us and showed us the ring. "How do we know you didn't buy the ring yo' self?" Loraine asked.

"Look what it says inside?" Teona pointed at the engraved wording on the inside. She read it out loud, "For Te, Luv Lou."

I didn't wanna be pissed, but I was fuming. Although at that point, I *could* still deny it. As many men as Teona has slept with, *Lou* could be anyone. I didn't have anything to say, but by the smirk on Teona's face, I could tell she saw the smoke whistlin' out my ears. I took a deep breath and walked out. I went to Loraine's to avoid Louis, and now I was heading straight to his place.

"Erin, I'm glad to see you." I stood at Louis's door with my arms folded. I wanted to go in nonconfrontational, but I couldn't help but believe Teona. She had tangible proof that the relationship Louis claimed to be nothing was more than what he claimed it to be.

I gave him my cheek when he went for my lips. "We need to talk."

Louis closed the door behind me as I walked in. We sat down on his sectional as he stared at me intently. "What about?"

"I saw Teona today." Louis inhaled. He held his breath as he felt the suede fabric that upholstered his sectional. I continued. "Were you two engaged?"

Louis exhaled. He licked his lips, ran his fingers through his dreads, and twirled his watch. "Why would you ask that? What did she tell you?"

"Answer the question." I expected to ask my question and get an answer. I was hoping he said no. Anyone could get something engraved to say whatever. I didn't expect Louis to answer my question with a question.

He didn't say anything for ten seconds. He kept twirling his watch as he breathed. He looked up at me. "Yeah."

I shook my head. I couldn't believe it. I stood up and tapped my foot as I stood over him. "Why didn't you tell me that? You made it seem like whatever you two had was nothing. You proposed to her, Louis. How long were you two even together?"

"I was caught up in the moment. She lied and pretended to be someone she wasn't. It wasn't anything serious."

"Asking someone to marry you…asking someone to spend the rest of her life wit' you is pretty dang serious."

"It wasn't to me."

"Do you go around proposing to every female you date?"

"Of course not."

"Then it's pretty damn serious. You weren't askin' for the time. You asked her to marry you, an' apparently she said *yes*."

"Erin, it was more spur-of-the-moment than anything else."

"How long were you two dating, Louis?"

Louis shrugged his shoulders and stared at his tile floor. "Like a couple months."

"So, after two months, you proposed to her? Damn, Louis, was the pussy that good?"

Louis rolled his eyes. "Calm down, Erin. Teona was and still means nothing to me."

"Oh really? She pawned your ring today."

He jerked his head back and froze. His face turned from apologetic to irritated. I didn't like that. "What do you mean?"

"Are you upset?"

"N-no. No, Erin. I don't care what she does with it. I'm worried about you."

"Don't worry about me." I threw up my hands. When I asked Louis about Teona before, she meant nothin', and now, she was his ex-fiancée. "I'm gonna ask you this again. Did you love her?"

"Erin…"

"Answer the dang question! And don't bullshit this time, yes or no."

"I love you, Erin."

I chuckled. "Why can't you ever answer yes or no?"

"'Cause my past feelings for that girl don't mean anything."

"The look on your face says a different story."

He took a deep breath and dropped his shoulders. He held my forearm in an effort to pull me close. He was still avoiding my question. I stepped back and surveyed his apartment. It felt like I was in a place I wasn't supposed to be. He probably shared this same space with Teona. What else wasn't he tellin' me? Did they move in together? Did *she* break things off? I saw a different person. I couldn't recognize my surroundings, and I didn't like it. There wasn't a point in talkin' anymore. When I walked to his front door, he chased after me and tried to hold me back. I yanked away. "Erin,

I'm not mad about anything. I'm frustrated that you're..." He sighed. "I'm irritated with the fact that she's puttin' you through any of this. I told you. I wanna be with you—only you."

"You have unresolved feelings for this *girl*, Louis. You keep trying to deny it, but I can see it when I look at you. When you talk about her...the way you say her name..." I ran my tongue over my teeth. Dropping my shoulders, I turned my head from the sight of him. "I don't like feeling this way. I shouldn't be feeling this way, Louis."

"Erin, it's not like that with her and me. You have to stop letting her get in your head. I'm here, trying to make this work with you. Give me that chance."

I opened his front door and stopped listening. I couldn't believe anything else he was saying. He kept things from me about a relationship that refused to go away. "I have to go, Louis."

"Erin, please stop walkin' out on me. Let's sit down and talk things through."

"Every time I talk to you, I get more frustrated than I was before. You can't answer simple questions, and that bothers me."

"Let's talk now. It's hard talking about Teona sometimes, but... let's talk. Right now."

"That's the point. It shouldn't be hard to talk about someone who meant nothing. At this point, Louis, I need to think about things and get away from you."

"You're really making this into something that it's not."

I held my hands up to prevent him from putting his hands on me. The same hands that held Teona. While I stared at him, I wondered how he proposed to her. If Louis could propose to a girl like Teona, what did that say about his standards? "She didn't pawn your ring." I disappeared. I didn't wait to see how his irritation shifted to relief. I needed air, and I needed to be away from the one man I thought I could trust.

When I knocked on the door, I paused for a second before turning to walk away. After he opened the door, I stood there not knowing what I could say next. We stared at each other for a while, and then he stepped to the side. I stared down the hall at the elevator. If I turned away now, I'd easily be forgiven. At that point, I wasn't even sure how I made it there. One minute, I was heading to the liquor store to buy a bottle of Hennessy, and the next minute, I was standing in the elevator of a familiar-looking condominium I had no business being in. My heartbeat sped up, and I had to make a decision. I did. I walked past him and let him close the door behind us. "I usually wouldn't pop up at your place, Tariq."

"It's cool. I'm glad to see you." He stood at the door shirtless with his pajama pants barely hanging off his waist. I tried not to look at him. I needed to keep my mind off his smooth skin, tight muscles, and deep crevices that made room for a six-pack I only saw in movies. When he moved closer to me, I stepped back. His presence was like a magnet, and I couldn't allow myself to be within a certain distance from him without being sucked in. "Whatchu doing here?"

"I dunno. I meant to go home, but I ended up in your parking lot. Your doorman recognized me and let me into your building. I can go." I tried to brush past him, but he held my arm and pulled me closer.

"You don't have to. I'm surprised to see you here. Where's yo' man?"

I pulled away from him and sighed. "I should go."

"Wait. What made you come by?"

"I told you. I don't know. But I know that I need to leave."

Tariq moved up close to me and put his hands around my waist. I could feel my heart beating through my chest. "Why?"

"You know why, Tariq." Even though I was on the outs wit' Louis, I still had no right being wit' Tariq, even if I simply needed someone to hold me.

When he pulled me close enough to feel his chest, it felt as if I suffered from temporary memory loss. I rested my palm on his chest while wrapping my arm around his neck. As we kissed, that same rush of heat surged through my body like a hot flash, causing my muscles to tighten. He held me tighter as I let his lips do to me what I had been dreaming of for the past three weeks. Like horny teenagers, we sucked each other's lips and tongues until we struggled to catch our breaths.

When I felt a tingle down my back, I jumped. I pulled away when I realized that it was my phone vibrating. When I saw Louis's name on my screen, I threw my head back in dismay. "I have to go."

"Why? You just got here."

"You know why." I didn't want Tariq to know that Louis and I were havin' problems; I'd only be his prey. Then again, I was there, and I was sure he knew somethin' was up. I headed toward the door and trembled as I wiped my lip. Tariq held my waist and stood in front of the door. I stepped back and shook my head. I wanted to stay, but playin' Tariq's game would only lead to disaster.

"I know you got a man, but I want you to stay."

"I can't. You're still married. And I'm still…"

Tariq yanked me closer to him. I was always turned on by his passion, but what enticed me more was how inviting he was of me.

I wanted the jerk that I first met when I dated Tariq. I wanted him to throw me out of his building for showing up unannounced. Instead, he willingly let me in and did to my body what I was hoping he wouldn't. He protested my departure as he forced me into his magnetic field, and I gravitated toward him, almost helpless to his control. He whispered, "You know my situation. You're the one I wanna be with, though."

"If I let this happen, I'll be breaking up two homes, yours and mine."

"Ain't nothin' here for you to break." I couldn't say anything else when his lips devoured mine. He pulled my purse strap off my shoulder and let it fall to the floor. He then grabbed my thighs and wrapped my legs around his waist as he carried me toward his bedroom. When he sucked the skin around my neck, I squeezed his skin and moaned in pleasure. "I've been craving you like an addict."

While he unzipped my jeans, I let him. I lay back and let him disrobe me even though I was not his to undress. My phone vibrated again. He heard it, but Tariq ignored Louis's intrusion and continued kissing my neck. I couldn't keep ignoring it. Louis was my constant reminder of what I stood to gain from a relationship with Tariq. I reluctantly pushed him away and stood up. When I caught a glimpse of Tariq's fire escape, I remembered the other woman that callously forced me out of his bedroom before. Tariq pulled me forward and grabbed the back of my thigh. As he kissed my neck, I noticed a pink thong hiding underneath his bed. I shot up and leaned back to get a better look.

There it was, a bright pink thong and a pair of high-heeled pumps. I smacked my lips toward Tariq. Either Tariq was cross-dressing or these belonged to his wife, or worse, another woman. Whoever they belonged to, they simply served as a big, bright-pink reminder that he didn't belong to me, and I couldn't be mad. This was wrong. "I have to go, Tariq."

Tariq noticed what I was staring at. He smacked his forehead and tried to pull me back. I moved away and frowned. "Erin, that ain't whatchu think." He stood up and grabbed me close.

"You don't have to explain anything to me, Tariq. I'm not yo' girl." Tariq had a hold on me that was hard to break. Still, I pushed him away and headed for his front door. Before he had the chance to stop me, I threw on my jeans, grabbed my purse from off the floor, and walked out his condo, slamming the door shut behind me. When he didn't chase after me, I caught my breath and rested my back on the wall. After catching my breath, I damn near ran back to my car and didn't look back. Taking the stairs, I ran down every step, cursing myself for letting Tariq get the best of me once again.

I wanted him so bad my fingers itched to touch his skin. By the time I reached my car, I was gasping for air. I sat in the driver's seat with my head on the headrest and my hand on my chest. Since I didn't know where Louis and I were in our relationship, I decided it would be best that Louis didn't know about this. As bad as I wanted to spread my legs and let a married man lie inside me 'til the sun came up, Louis was better believing that it was him I'd rather spread my legs for.

I had to talk to Loraine. I used my vibrator three times after the Tariq incident, and I was jonesing bad. When I walked up Loraine's doorstep, I could hear faint moans clambering through her front door. The moans were muffled at first, and then they gradually escalated as rough panting followed. Not long after, I could hear

Loraine's voice. "Shit, that feels too good. Yes, baby. Right there."
Right after, I could hear Lorenz's voice. "Right there?" Once I
realized what I was listening to, I stepped back and smirked like a
schoolgirl. Though I knew Loraine had sex, I never imagined it.
Now, I was standing outside her door hearing her love-making
noises. *"Yes! Oh, God. Please, yes!"* her voice screamed. I jumped
when I heard the sound of glass breaking. I giggled. Loraine told
me the sex was good, but dang. I didn't expect all that. I decided
to walk to my car. It would be rude of me to knock and interrupt
Loraine in the middle of her orgasm.

I sat in my car and listened to the radio for twenty minutes
before I saw Lorenz creeping out the front door. Before he could
leave, though, Loraine pulled him into her embrace as they kissed
long, lingering kisses on her doorstep. He gripped her ass underneath her robe as he held her waist close to him. She grabbed his
neck and sucked in his face as if she were tryna suck out venom.
He pushed her against the door and had begun to lead her back
inside, I presumed for round two. When he started sucking her
neck, she opened her eyes and jumped when she saw my car in her
driveway. She quickly pushed him off and pointed in my direction.
Lorenz turned and looked my way. He looked confused at first,
and then annoyed. He waved a half-hearted wave and turned back
to Loraine. After a quick kiss on the cheek, he walked toward his car.

I turned my car off and walked toward Loraine. I could see her
catching her breath as she twirled her hair and sucked on her bottom
lip. She fixated her eyes on Lorenz as he walked off, not even
noticing me standing right beside her. When he drove off, she
snapped out of her trance. "Girl, what are you doing here?"

"I came by to talk, but I see you were preoccupied."

"He was leaving anyway. Come inside." She turned on her heel and sat on the arm of her armchair. After I closed the door behind me, she asked, "What did you wanna talk about?" If she looked any more relaxed, I would've expected her to pull out a cigarette.

"I didn't know Lorenz was coming over today."

"I didn't either. He came by because he was in the area. At first, we were talkin' on the couch, drinkin' wine. Next thing I know, he was remindin' me of his magic fingers. Before I realized it, we were everywhere. He was about to leave, but when he kissed me goodbye, I dared him to make love to me standin' up. I didn't think he could, y'know, 'cause of his bad knees. He won that bet." Loraine smiled brightly as she ran her fingers through her hair.

"It looks like you were about to go another round."

"Girl, we prolly would've. I dunno what it was today. We couldn't get enough of each other."

"I'm glad he's putting it down like that."

"Erin, you don't even know." She exhaled and stared into space. I could tell she was reliving the past few minutes. After a minute, she trembled and grabbed the bottle of wine. "But really, what did you wanna talk about?"

I took a deep breath. I didn't want to bring down her high, but I had to talk to someone. "Louis."

Loraine twirled her dreads and shrugged her shoulders. "You talked to Louis about Teona."

"You know I did."

"What did he say?"

"He confirmed it. He said it didn't mean anything. I wasn't goin' for it."

"What exactly did he say? Was he in love wit' Teona?"

"I dunno. And I dunno if I care anymore. I'm tired of him and Teona. I mean, Teona and I are two completely different people.

What would make him come after a woman like me if he was interested in marrying a girl like Teona?"

"If he says it meant nothin', I believe him. Teona has a way of makin' men think she's someone else. If she could get a degree in lying, she'd have graduated by now."

Before I could continue our conversation, my phone vibrated. When I read the screen, I sighed deeply. The text read, *"Miss'n you, wish you'd call me…shit."*

"Who's texting you?"

"Louis. He calls or texts me every day, all day. He has been tryna reconcile. What irked me, though, is I told him that Teona pawned her ring, and you should've seen his face. He looked angry. When I asked him if he loved her, that fool wouldn't even answer the dang questions. He says it's hard talking about Teona. I'm so done."

"You're makin' somethin' out of nothin'. You're talkin' like you plannin' to go back to Tariq or somethin'."

"Would that be a problem?" I tried not to get wet as I remembered the night before. I regretted not finishing what I started.

"Hell yea! He's married. Louis made a few mistakes in his past, but he seems committed to you. Stay away from Tariq. Talk to Louis."

I kept my Tariq episode to myself. I wanted to dish, but I didn't want to be judged. When my phone vibrated again, I grew agitated. I was tired of Louis' apologetic texts. However, I was surprised to see a text from Tariq. *"Can't stop thinkin bout you. Wishin' you would do another dropby."* I smirked.

"What did he text you now?"

I shrugged my shoulders. "Same ol' same. Girl, I dunno what I'ma do about Louis." When I noticed Lorenz's things scattered around her living room, I asked, "Lorenz living here now?"

"Girl, no. He leaves a few things here from time to time. Sometimes it's easier if he has to sleep over."

"You better watch out. He might be trying to creep back in without you knowing."

Loraine chortled. "I doubt it. We like our arrangement. Makes things a whole lot easier. Plus, the sex is good, and I dunno if I would even mind."

"You want to get back together?"

"No, but I don't want to mess up a good thing. Lorenz doesn't either. What man wants to screw up sex with no strings attached? He doesn't have to stay and cuddle; he doesn't have to call. We're going with the flow, and I love it."

"I wish things were that easy with Louis."

"Look, if the sex is good and he makes you happy, there's no need to let him go. Don't let Teona scare you from making a love connection."

"Why can't I find a man who's not sill hung up on the woman he was with before me? Can't I make a love connection with a normal suitor?"

"Louis is normal. Teona is the one who's not normal. She's like a virus when it comes to relationships."

"And why would I wanna catch that?"

Loraine huffed. "Erin, don't be silly. Give Louis a chance. I like him for you. He seems sweet."

The only person I could think about when she spoke was Tariq. I understood where Loraine was coming from, but Tariq's toxins permeated my senses even when I had another man trying to do the same. Louis was good at times, but my body was conflicted, as was my mind. I may not have been sure about Louis, but I *was* sure that I yearned for Tariq like heroin. He was a drug that I would gladly inject into my system. Unfortunately, Loraine, as well as my mother, would frown upon my desires for a man who didn't deserve them. "You say Tariq is bad for me, but is it wrong to want something if it feels that good?"

Loraine pursed her lips and dropped her head. "Yes, Erin. Call Louis."

I could've easily addressed Loraine's double standard. Lorenz was no saint, but he pleased Loraine's body in ways that Tariq could please me. I recognized Loraine's glow from my nights with Tariq. Why couldn't I enjoy the same guiltless sex? I wanted to question Loraine's hypocrisy; instead, I accepted the seemingly safe suitor that Loraine reminded me of and pretended to be okay with it. I smiled and nodded while I pictured the man Tariq could be to me. Even though Tariq wasn't really my man, I would delight in the possibilities.

CHAPTER 26

Erin

"I have an assignment for you."

I sat at my desk and winced. Today was not the day, and Eric's voice got on my last nerves. Between clenched teeth, I said, "What?"

"Meet me in my office in five minutes."

He walked away. He didn't ask, dropped a task on my lap, and expected me to drop what I was doin' and deal wit' his mess. For all I knew, he prolly had an assignment that he didn't want to do. At the end of the day, he was my superior, and I had no choice. I locked my computer and did as I was told.

When I walked into Eric's office, he sat behind his desk with his shoulders up and his head high. He kept his eyes down and away from the woman who sat on the other side of his desk. She was a tall, statuesque woman with broad shoulders and a buzz cut. When she turned to face me, I was almost blown away by her impeccable bone structure. She had high and taut cheekbones, moon-shaped green eyes, and a pointed chin. The sunlight sneaked into Eric's office and illuminated her chestnut complexion. When she smiled a set of perfectly white teeth, her congeniality was infectious. I smiled back.

She stood up and kept eye contact as she grabbed my hand to greet me. "Hi, you must be Erin. I'm Vivian Stein. How are you?"

Her handshake was firm and to the point. Feelin' like I should do the same, I squeezed her hand firmly and shook back. "I'm fine. Thank you."

"I don't know if Eric told you, but I'm lookin' to rebrand my company." I wanted to ask which company it was, but I didn't want to sound misinformed. Eric remained quiet. He had thrown me to the wolves, and I had to figure my way out. "I've experienced a change in my life, and I'm ready to translate that change in my business. I heard Iaris Advertising was the company to do that. Can you do that for me, Erin?"

I nodded. "Yes, I can. Tell me what your vision is and we'll make it happen."

Vivian smiled brightly and cut her eyes sharply at Eric. "Can you give us the room, please?"

Eric eyed Vivian like he wanted to tell her *hell no*. But Vivian stared him back down as if to say, *Nigga, please*. Eric tapped his desk and stood up. "Sure." He gave me a crooked glare and walked out.

With the door closed, Vivian sat back down and pulled out the chair beside her for me to sit with her. "Erin, how are you doing?"

"I'm fine."

"No, I mean…" She twirled her wedding band. She stared at her ring, a platinum, solitaire diamond ring with a rock the size of a grapefruit. She pulled it off her finger and placed it on Eric's desk. She sighed and laughed. "Are you married?" She surveyed my bare wedding ring finger and handed me her ring. "You can have it."

I put her ring back down and sat confused. I wasn't sure what had been goin' on, and I was curious to know. "Excuse me? I can't take your ring. It looks really expensive."

"Erin, I don't want it. Not anymore." She picked it back up and examined it. With her eyes shimmering from the glint of her diamond, she said, "It *was* expensive, though."

"How are you?" I was genuinely concerned about her well-being.

She had a candidness about her that made me want to know her pain and hope I could offer suggestions to make things better.

"My husband was having an affair." She threw the ring on Eric's carpeted floor. "Y'know, an affair I could've forgiven. My husband and I were married for twenty-five years. We could've gone to counseling, and I would've gotten past it. Sure, he would be sleepin' on the couch for a couple months, but I loved my husband. I still love my husband, which is why it hurts this much." She looked into my eyes. She wanted me to see the pain resting in her gaze, living and breathing in her eye sockets. Her pain begged for attention. "What made me file for divorce was the pack of lies that surfaced after finding about Roxy. Roxy seemed like a stripper name. I hadn't planned to leave my man over some young stripper with a tongue ring and clear heels. What I soon discovered, though, was that Roxy was a code name." She blinked. The pain was re-surfacing, and she couldn't hold her gaze for long. She cleared her throat and continued. "Roxy was my husband's nickname for my older sister. My *sister*, Erin. Who the fuck fucks his wife's *older* sister? And I'm talkin' seven years older."

"Wow." I didn't mean to comment on her love life, but the news was shocking. I couldn't empathize, but I did sympathize.

She looked me up and down and grunted. "You look like my sister. Almond-shaped eyes, fair-skinned, dimples, long, thick re-laxed hair...beautiful, full lips. You're a younger version of her. You're very pretty."

I blushed. She frowned. She hadn't meant her last comment as a compliment. She stared at me, accusing my looks of betrayal. I shifted in my seat and tried not to show my discomfort. "That's not all, though." She stopped looking at me. She stared at Eric's empty chair. She hadn't gotten over her pain, and staring into my eyes, eyes that reminded her of the woman who betrayed her, would only make her crack. "It turns out that my nephew is also my stepson. He got her pregnant, and he has let the seed of his infidelity sleep over at our house and have sleepovers with our own children. My sister told me she got pregnant by a sperm donor. Little did I know, her sperm donor was my damn husband." She cackled, loudly doubling over in hilarity. I didn't get the joke. She wiped her dry eyes to warn her tears to stay where they were. After catchin' her breath, she looked at me again. "But...enough about my failed love life. We need to get down to business." She opened the purple folder sitting on top of Eric's desk and handed me the specifics of her business.

When I realized the business she owned, I realized the woman I had been speaking to. I didn't want my hands to start shakin' in the presence of one of my sheroes. I was embarrassed that I didn't know the face of one of the women I admired. Then again, in all her pics, she wore tons of makeup and rocked a wavy weave that reached her knees. She was the founder and CEO of Surreptitious Cosmetics. She began her company in the backseat of her car, watered it, and watched it grow into a multimillion-dollar venture. When I dreamed about meetin' her, I expected to see a Grecian goddess lined with a gold glow that shined so bright I'd need shades. Instead, she scratched her shaved head and wore a natural make-up-less glow that didn't require shades. I set her folder back on Eric's desk and grinned nonstop. "I know who you are. I don't need your specs."

She smirked and licked her lips, looking at my stilettos and up to my glossed lips. "You didn't know who I was until now." I sat quiet. I wasn't going to admit to that. "It's okay, though. I'm glad we're on the same page now."

"How did you want to rebrand your business? Why would you want to? You're extremely successful."

She picked her ring from off the carpet and sighed. "I've been safe. For the past fifteen years, I've kept my brand safe. I've even kept my life safe. Before now, I wore the same middle part in my hair; I wore colorful sundresses and bright, yet subtle makeup. Now, I'm into pantsuits. I cut off all my hair and shaved the back. I'm wearing more dramatic makeup, except for when I do business meetings. I'm tired of being safe and doing what people expect of me. It's time to do what I want. I want to be dangerous, scandalous. As crazy as my life is, it kept you on the edge of your seat wanting more details. That's how I want my customers to feel about my products. I want drama."

"But your brand is centered around subtlety, even in the name. You'll be going completely left."

"That's why I'm here, Erin. You're going to be my GPS as I go left. Change the name, change the colors, and change the brand. Obviously, what I've been doing has gotten me to where I am— hurt, abandoned, and confused. I don't want to be here." Vivian held my hand and stared back into my eyes again. "Let's go left, Erin."

Vivian was a woman scorned and she hated it. She didn't want to revel in the pain. Vivian hit a wrong turn and sought to get back on a new track, and she chose me to steer her the right way. I couldn't let her down. I wouldn't. I nodded and stood up. "Let's go."

Vivian stood up and held my hand in hers. "Thank you, Erin." Eric knocked on the door. Vivian let my hand go and walked to his door.

When I saw that she left her ring on Eric's desk, I grabbed it and put it in her hand. "I don't want your ring, but I know a pawn shop who will."

Vivian laughed and put the ring in her pocket. "Look at you, steering me right already."

"I'm glad you came by."

I gave Louis another chance. After what happened at work, I couldn't go back to Tariq. I didn't want his wife to be the next woman at my job asking me to rebrand her life. I felt sorry for Vivian even though she didn't want me to. I couldn't be the woman she saw me as *and* be the same type of woman who thought it was okay to sleep with a married man.

I showed up at Louis's apartment and chose not to discuss our previous incident. I wanted us to start fresh. Louis gave me a wet kiss as he led me into his apartment. "I missed you so much."

"I know you did. That's why I'm here."

We sat down on his sectional on opposite ends. He watched me as his eyes read his intentions. "I want you closer to me."

I hesitated until I remembered that we were starting over. I crawled over to him and rested my head on his shoulder. After ten seconds of silence, he sighed and scratched in between his dreads. "I missed you too." I could feel his heart beat faster. "Are you sure there's nothing else I need to know about your past relationship with Teona?"

"Do we need to talk about her right now?"

"Even though it was the past, your relationship with her bothers me, especially since she keeps popping back up. Whatever you two had still feels fresh, and I feel as if I'm in the middle. And when you avoid questions about her, you make me feel like there are still unresolved feelings looming over your present. If there's anything else I need to know about you two, anything else that might come back up, tell me now. I can't handle any more surprises with you two."

"Erin, it was a fling that ended as quickly as it started. I don't feel anything for Teona, and there's nothing else about our failed relationship that needs to be discussed. Trust me, boo, I'm all about you." He kissed me gently on my forehead. It was a tender embrace that made my body warm.

"Let's head to the bedroom." I wasn't horny at first, but we needed the opportunity to escape the building tension and enjoy a good round of makeup sex.

He shook his head and leaned forward to grab a bottle of oil from the drawer beneath his coffee table. "Can you oil my scalp?"

I took a deep breath and stared at the bottle of peppermint oil. I smirked when I imagined the tingling smell of peppermint that he left on my pillowcases. When he first starting sleeping over my apartment, I would sniff my sheets when he wasn't around as if I could still feel his presence. His scent played with my senses like a dirty tease. I nodded. As he sat between my legs and handed me the bottle, I sucked in my bottom lip and tried to ignore the heat that slowly built. Pouring the liquids on my fingers, I separated his dreads and tenderly massaged his scalp. I licked my lips when the skin on my inner thighs heated up. It turned me on to touch my man while he sat between my legs. His broad shoulders resting on my thighs felt good. I played in his hair as I ran the tip of my fingers up and down his scalp. When he tilted his head back to let me get his hairline, I grinned when our eyes met upside down. He smiled back. We were quiet, but he was being coy. I tilted his head forward and rubbed oil around his nape.

With oil in the palm of my hands, I brushed the ends of his dreads with oil and twirled each lock between my fingers. He wrapped his arm around my leg and pulled it closer. With his ends sealed, I went back to massaging his scalp. He moaned. An electric shock slid up my left side as he stroked my skin. Eventually, the tips of my fingers were sore, and my pussy was throbbing. Aware of my body's call, he gently kissed my inner thigh and licked circles around my knees. When my phone vibrated, a brief glance revealed Tariq's call. I sent it to voicemail as Louis's face plunged in between my legs. Once Tariq's name disappeared from my caller ID, Louis popped his head up and groaned. "Who's calling you?"

I waved my hand and shook my head. "Loraine. I'll call her back later."

"Turn your phone off for the night. I want you all to myself."

I did as I was told. I didn't want to be interrupted. I had some making up to do, and if my man wanted me all to himself, I was happy to oblige. I quickly turned off my phone before Tariq had the chance to call back. Comfortable that I wouldn't have any more interruptions, I rested my back as Louis positioned me on his sectional. He slid off my panties and placed his head between my thighs, squeezing my cheeks as he devoured me like a starving inmate. I fed him as I squeezed the couch cushions, hoping to let go of my fears of losing a good man and succumbing to the temptation of Tariq. I closed my eyes and imagined Louis. I arched my back and whispered Louis's name. "…ooh, Louis." I licked my lips as I tensed my jawline. I sucked on the oxygen tainted with lust and hunger as he spread my legs apart and went for the kill. He licked and sucked between my thighs as if his tongue had been searching for the cure to cancer lodged deep between my lips. I needed him in that.

The sound of his moans vibrating against my sensitive skin made my body shudder and my legs tense. I rested there, victim to his touch. Soon, the screams came. They bubbled at my lips and erupted like a volcano. Pouring out, reverberating off his apartment walls. At that moment, I didn't care if his neighbors heard. All I wanted was to feel that orgasm that had been longing to escape. It feened for freedom as he licked, licked and nibbled. And like that, every muscle in my body tightened as I boiled in ecstasy. He never eased up. He held on to my waist and thighs and kept his lips and tongue so close to my hole that I thought we were conjoined. I gasped for air, trying to gain composure, but my body exploded and then collapsed.

"Shit, Louis." *My* man. The man who sucked the life from my insides and breathed it back in.

"I'm glad you liked it."

"I loved it," I sang.

"I love you."

I smiled awkwardly, not knowing how to respond. I tried to break the awkwardness with my witty humor. "I need to oil your scalp more often." He bought it. He kissed my inner thigh gently and stood up. When I felt a phone vibrating, I glanced at mine but remembered that it was turned off. I looked over and noticed Louis's phone was lit up. I would've looked away had it not been for Teona's name on his caller ID. I looked up at him and handed him his phone. "Why is Teona callin' you?" I noticed the time. "It's after midnight."

Louis took his phone and sent her call to his voicemail. Throwing his phone to the couch, he said, "I told you that she keeps callin' me."

"Do you need to change your phone number? I don't like her calling you like this. I'm trying to move forward, but she's makin' it hard when she's constantly intruding."

He took a deep breath and sat down next to me. "I can understand that. I don't know why she keeps callin'."

"Are you sure things are over between you two? She doesn't seem to think so."

"We're over. After the abortion, I was done." He threw his head back and sighed. "Shit."

I jerked my head back and shot up. "Excuse me?" I didn't want him to say it again, and he wouldn't. Still, he opened Pandora's box, and I had more questions that required answers. "What do you mean *abortion?* Louis, you got that girl pregnant?"

He stood up and tried to hold my hands. I snatched my hands away and tried to shoo him away. "Erin, I…I don't know what to say."

"What *can* you say? Louis…" I squeezed the skin between my eyebrows and sighed. "I asked you if there was anything else I should know, and you lied to me. Every time I try to let things go, I find out something else."

"I know…I know. I didn't…"

"When did she get pregnant, before or after you proposed to her?"

"Does it matter?"

"If it didn't, I wouldn't be asking."

He rubbed his dreads and grunted. "Erin, what I had wit' Teona didn't mean anything. How many times do I have to say that? I thought she was something that she wasn't. She got pregnant, and at the time I wanted her to keep it, but she aborted it. After that, I found out she was sleepin' around and lying about so much bullshit."

"If she hadn't gotten the abortion, would you two still be together?"

He didn't say anything. His eyes were blank, and his mouth was open with absent words. When he realized he hadn't said much, he quickly said, "No."

I nodded and looked for my purse. "I prolly woulda believed you if you answered quicker." When I found my purse, I snatched it from Louis' sectional and walked to the door.

Louis ran after me and pleaded his case. "Erin, stop running away."

Without looking back, I waved goodbye and grabbed the door handle. "There's nothing left to discuss." Louis put his weight on the door to keep me from leaving. I turned around and folded my arms. "Open the door, Louis."

"No. Not until we discuss this. Don't you think I know how bad this looks? I love you, care about you, and I want to be with you. I don't spend my days thinkin' 'bout Teona and what we had. What Teona and I had was something at the time, but it's nothing compared to you and me."

"Oh, now it *was* something. Not too long ago, it was a fling. Then, it was an engagement; now, it was you two starting a damn family together. If it didn't mean anything, you wouldn't have kept all this from me. If I let this go, how do I know I won't find out about something else? I can't trust you. This was your third strike, Louis."

He stared at me as if he were shocked at the possibility of us being over. He held his chest and shook his dreads. I looked away from his stare. I got the same feeling I had from before, that unfamiliar feeling. I was back at Louis's place feeling like I was facing a stranger. Louis was one man to my face and someone else behind closed doors. Behind his closed doors, he shared a meaningful relationship with a woman who cared more about her makeup than her body. He shared a child with her. He contemplated the idea of sharing a last name with her. And then, not too long after, he says he's in love with me. Nothing seemed real anymore. Louis seemed too good to be true, and I finally understood why. Louis took a deep breath and moved away from the front door. "What does that mean, Erin? Are we done?"

I shrugged my shoulders. "I can't see how we wouldn't be. You made me doubt things with you. I'm a rebound from Teona. Whatever you had with Teona wasn't *nothing*. You still care about her because she's keeps finding a way back in *our* relationship. I'm tired of talkin' about it. I'm too grown for all this. I don't have to deal with this."

"Why does it even matter? Why does it have to be all or nothing? You're the one that keeps bringin' her up. I'm tryna let it go."

"Now it's my fault? Her flashing your engagement ring in my face, you showing up at Loraine's house looking for her, you two fighting over your relationship in my kitchen is all my fault, Louis?"

"Erin, can we sit down and talk? You gotta stop runnin' from all this."

"I'm not running. Louis, I don't like when you keep things from me. I keep askin' you to talk to me like an adult; instead, you keep hidin' things like a child. I'm done datin' men who act like children. We haven't even been together a year, and already your past keeps coming up like you don't want it to go away."

"Now I'm actin' like a child?"

"Imagine if the roles were reversed."

"Erin, I understand how this seems, but I don't feel my past is something important enough for us to discuss."

"It is when it keeps shoving itself back in my face."

"I can't control Teona."

"I'm not askin' you to. I asked you to be honest with me. I've given you ample time to speak up, Louis."

"What benefit would you have gotten from me tellin' you that I got her pregnant? I didn't say anything because I didn't want you to act like this."

We were going around in circles. I rubbed my eyes as our dialogue went through my mind from start to finish, and then I realized it was time to shift gears. "Did you want her to have your baby?"

"Erin..." Louis turned away from me. He was frustrated, but he was the one forcing us back into these situations. "Why would you ask me that?"

"Answer the fuckin' question, Louis! Why can't you answer simple questions? I know you still want this girl, Louis."

"I don't believe in abortion, Erin, but I don't want to be with Teona. How many times do I have to say it?"

"If I have to constantly question it, that's a problem for us, Louis."

"Tell me what I have to do, and I'll do it."

I opened my mouth and grabbed the sides of my head. We would argue, and I'd end up back where we started—nowhere. I needed to face the obvious. It was hard for me to move forward with someone I couldn't trust. I'd ask Louis questions that I needed answers to, and he'd skirt around them like they were heat-seekin' missiles. I wanted to make things work. I couldn't face the possibility that a married man was my best hope at a somewhat fulfillin' relationship. But doubt was a sneaky bastard that I couldn't leave unattended. "We need to take a break."

Louis swallowed the lump in his throat as he lowered his head and chewed his bottom lip. "I'd rather we slow things down. We can start over; I'll tell you everything you want to know."

I turned my head as I turned the doorknob. "I need time to think. I dunno if this is a relationship that I have the tolerance for anymore."

"Why do you let Teona get to you? Is she worth us not being together?"

"Teona's not the problem, Louis. You are. You can't be honest with me. Teona has a hold on you; sometimes I feel as if I can still smell her on you."

"Why do I need to tell you everything about that relationship? Should I be telling you about *all* my past relationships? You haven't even told me about your last boyfriend."

"It's not a matter of you telling me everything. Honestly, when I think about you and her, I wonder what you're doing with me. I may be wrong for judging a man for his past, but I'm human. I can see why a man would want to fuck her, but marry her, and have a child by her—she's still a child herself. When I think about the type of relationship you had with a girl like that, I question the

man I'm with, especially when it's obvious that you still have feelings for her. *Her*, Louis! Even after you found out what type of
girl she is, you still harbor feelings toward her; whether you choose
to admit it or not." I took a deep breath and rubbed between my
eyes. "I can't do this right now." I wasn't emotionally prepared to
deal with it all. I needed space. My sense of peace desired the chance
to be alone with my thoughts as I contemplated the fate of my
relationship. "I'll call you later." Louis talked a big talk, but the
reality was he didn't see the sense in lettin' me into a relationship
he knew meant more than he let on. I believed him when he said
he wanted to be with me, but he was lying when he said Teona
meant nothing. It was clear now more than ever that Teona, the
floating petri dish of venereal diseases, meant more to Louis than
a simple fling. And that revelation disgusted me.

Louis pulled me into a kiss. The kiss was apologetic and warm.
He caressed my face as he grazed the skin of his lips against mine.
I licked my lips and pulled away. He whispered, "I'll wait on that
call."

I didn't say anything. I considered the prospect of forgiving Louis,
ignoring my concerns, and allowing Louis to be the man he
begged to be for me. At the same time, I considered how it would
be when I brought along my man to the same functions where
Teona was. With Loraine as my best friend, Teona's appearances
would eventually be unavoidable. I would have to compete for
Louis's attention with a girl like Teona. The thought alone was
nothing short of irritating. I needed space, and Louis needed time
to realize why his relationship with Teona affected him the way it
clearly did. We parted ways with no more words, silenced by the
possibility that this might be too hard to fix.

CHAPTER 27

Erin

I lied. When I reached Tariq's door that warm Friday night, I lied and told him that Louis and I were completely over. Louis wanted the opportunity to start over, but I wasn't sure I wanted to. When I went home the night after Louis's confession, I stood in my shower wondering what my next move would be. My meeting with Vivian was an eye-opener. Initially, I thought it was a sign for me to give Louis another chance, but after what happened, I thought maybe it was my cue to live dangerously. I needed to stop living so earnestly and do what made me happy. The next night, I didn't call Louis. I showed up at Tariq's door and lied to ease my relationship, allowing myself to submit to him. Louis was still technically my man, as I didn't completely end things, but Tariq was callin' my body for the longest, and it was due time that I answered. Initially, when I showed up at his door again, I wanted him to tell me that I was too late and that he had reconciled with his wife when she came home to retrieve her panties and shoes, but like before, he let me in.

"We're done," I said when he shut the door behind us.

"What?"

"My man and I…well, my ex. We're over. I needed time to sort things out." I didn't mean to lie at first. In a sense, I hadn't lied. Louis and I were most likely over. But if the roles were reversed,

I'd consider Louis a cheater if he were doing the same thing I was about to do.

"Oh yeah." He smiled devilishly. "I'm glad you came by to see me then." He looked me up and down and walked over to his couch.

I expected him to rip my clothes off and lead me to the bedroom, but I followed him to his couch to have a sit down instead. When we sat, I tried not to stare at his bare chest. This time, he wore boxers that hung off his waist while his packaged peeked through the slit in the middle. I wanted to ride him at that moment. I sat quietly, not letting his glistening chest distract me. I didn't know what to say. All I wanted was an excuse to take my clothes off, but he sat there calmly.

"Why you sitting so far away?" He wrapped his arm around my waist and pulled me closer to him. My body was tense. I didn't know what game he was playing. Any other time, my pussy would've been throbbing around his dick while I screamed out in passion. Tonight, he was taking it mysteriously slow. I edged closer to him and took steady breaths. He rubbed my skin. "Damn, I really did miss you."

"That's good to hear."

Rubbing my thighs, he ran the tip of his tongue across his lips. "You look good, as always."

I peeled off my work blazer. "Thanks." I was giving him the permission to do what he begged to do for months, and he was squandering it all away with small talk. "I can't stay for long."

"Ain't like you got work in the morning." He pulled me closer to him and planted sweet and short tongue-free kisses on my lips. When he pulled away, I sat there wondering why he stopped. He was toying with me. He whispered, "I want you bad, but I'm tryna give you what you want."

"And what's that, Tariq?"

"You know, the only woman that calls me *Tariq* is my grandmother." That was the first time he had ever mentioned his family to me. For months, he had spent his time pushing me away, and now, he was awkwardly letting me in. It was discomforting. I didn't want it like this. I didn't want to build a relationship with Tariq; only sex. Then, the thought of leading two men on while I lied my way through made me feel dirty. I didn't know how men did it. I moved away from him and looked at my phone. The fact that Louis hadn't texted or called me in the past twenty minutes made me feel as if something was wrong, like he knew what I was up to. I felt wrong moving on so quickly after not giving Louis the respect to actually end things.

"I have to go."

Tariq's smile faded. "Whatchu mean? I want you to stay."

"I'm feelin' a lil' weird, like this isn't right."

"I thought you weren't with yo' man anymore."

"I'm not." I lied—again. "But it hasn't been long since we ended things, and I'm already here with you. And you're still married."

"Want me to slow it down? Erin, I know I ain't been the nicest man to be around sometimes, and my situation ain't ideal but, I'm here…you're here."

I moved away even further. I wasn't ready to be *that* girl. I was a good girl, not one of those girls who carried on like a ho, sleepin' around with two men at once. "I can't. Not right now. I dunno what I was thinking."

"I get it. I got a wife and a son. And the bullshit you saw under my bed the other night was not what you think."

"I don't care what it was. I'm not yo' woman, and it shouldn't matter to me. Not too long ago, though, I was someone else's woman, and I'm already here. How do I know yo' wife won't show up again? You goin' put me out again?"

"Erin, you're not my sidepiece. You keep saying you're not my woman, but it's gotta be clear by now that is something that we both want…that we both need."

"Tariq, sex with you…right now—"

"It ain't about sex either. If this was only about sex, I would've been gone a long time ago. And I know the same goes for you. The back and forth with us…I try to move on from you as much as you try to do the same. But like you, I end up back here with you."

I heard a ringing in my ears as I felt my palms moist. I wondered if he could hear my heart beating while I looked down at his lap and saw his package peeking through more as he grew hard to my presence. It was certain that he wanted me sexually, but I wasn't sure he could handle me emotionally. In actuality, I didn't go there for an emotional connection. But it was hard for me to be with someone in that way and not feel anything for him. I may have talked big, but at the end of the day, I'd want Tariq to hold me while we slept. I'd want him to call me the next morning and text me how much he missed me. I ran from it, but I wanted a relationship with Tariq even though he was in the same situation I chastised Louis for. He was holding on to a relationship that he claimed was over. Nevertheless, I ran to Tariq and allowed him to fill my head with colorful words that made my panties wet.

"I ain't goin' make you do anything you don't wanna do, but I ain't goin' lie. I want you more than I can even describe right now. Erin, my situation is what it is. If my wife shows up, it'll be a fucked-up situation, but I won't kick you out this time. At least not out the window." He joked but I winced. At the same time, I stared at his package that grew so big I felt the need to gift-wrap it. He held my hand, and I could feel him pulling it toward him. I wanted to pull back, but staring at him had me salivating.

Then, like clockwork, my phone vibrated. We both stopped as I checked the message. It was Louis with another reminder of my poor decision-making. In that moment, I thought about how uncomfortable I would be with Louis as I fantasized about Tariq. If I acted on my emotions, I could live out the fantasy. "I dunno what to say, Tariq."

"You can say or do whatever you feel like. If it'll make you feel better, we ain't even gotta have sex. It's gotten to the point where having you around me is enough."

"Your situation…your marriage isn't a situation. You're a married man and I'm here contemplating spending a night with you. This feels wrong."

"My marriage is a joke. It's a convenient way for me to see my son. But what it ain't is something that I can keep lettin' get in between you and me."

"Now there's a you and me?"

"If you want it. I do."

"What happened between you and your wife?"

Tariq shrugged his shoulders and turned to face his wall. Sucking his teeth, he squeezed the skin over his knees and sighed. "She cheated. She lied. She played me like a fool. And after it all, I was stupid enough to agree to marry her. Now, here I am—trying to get her to sign divorce papers that she refuses to sign while I spend my time with you."

"If she cheated on you, why did you still marry her?"

"When you have a son…" Tariq dropped his shoulders. "I hate talking about it because I feel embarrassed sometimes. When I married her, it was only for convenience, never because I loved her. That's why I call it a situation and not a marriage. That's why I don't wear a wedding ring. That's why you don't see any pictures of her up in my place. She makes my life hell and she refuses to let me go. It is what it is." Tariq took a deep breath as he clenched his fists. Licking his lips, he smiled. "I don't wanna talk about her, though."

"But I don't understand. How do two people marry for convenience?"

"It was convenient for her. I thought I was doing what was best for my son. The plan was to divorce after our son was born; well, it was my plan at least. I don't wanna get into it all, but please know, she's nobody I plan to work things out with."

When Tariq spoke about his wife, there was a ray of aggravation that often washed over his face. The corner of his lip would quiver and his jaw would tighten. Usually, his look of exasperation was often accompanied by a small vein on the side of his forehead that would rest there until he changed the subject. Interestingly enough, it was a pleasant change from the look of longing that would often wash over Louis's face whenever we discussed Teona. Nevertheless, Tariq was still Tariq, even if he was playin' nice today. I was tired of getting the Jekyll and Hyde complex with him. I wondered if I had to play hard to get him to be the man that I wanted him to be when I wanted him to be it. As I stared into his eyes and he sat there vulnerably, my pussy quaked. I was turned on by the man who was scared of me leaving and cared about my feelings. I didn't care about his wife anymore, or the past. Even though I had more questions and needed more clarity, in that moment, I wanted to do whatever I wanted to do. "Let's go to your bedroom."

Without another word, he led me to his bedroom and shut the door. When he laid me down, I wrapped my arms and legs around him like a cocoon. He kissed me in a way that made my breaths short and my insides tense. My outsides moistened in preparation for his entry. His tongue was sweet and nearly made me forget honey existed. When he stood up to remove his boxers, I sat up to watch. When I saw how erect his dick was, I literally wiped the drool from my bottom lip. He grabbed a condom from his top drawer and kept eye contact while he opened the gold wrapper. When he got back on the bed, he slowly took off my clothes as he kissed almost every inch of my skin. He started with my gray slacks. He leisurely unbuckled my belt and lifted my ass to slide my legs out from them. He kissed my toes as he played with the band around my panties. As I started to unbutton my shirt, he spread my legs and pulled my hands to the side , making sure he did the rest. He slipped my shirt off my shoulders and then kissed down my arms. Unhooking my bra, he pinned me back and climbed on top. As we lay on top of his bed naked and hot, he whispered in my ear, "I was serious about before. We don't have to do anything tonight if you don't want to. I'm still enjoying your company."

With the tip of his dick grazing my pussy lips, I grabbed his ass and pushed down. He slid in with ease. He grabbed my right leg and placed it over his shoulder while he sucked my face. He rhythmically stroked inside me as my body wiggled underneath him. I sucked on my bottom lip and put my mind at ease. When it started to rain and the droplets tapped on his window, I relaxed my muscles and held on to the covers. I moaned as I could feel myself leaking through his sheets.

He whispered, "Damn, I needed you tonight." Staring into my eyes, he pulled the ponytail holder from my hair and let my tresses fall over my shoulders.

Like the Nile river, I gushed. I spread my lips as tiny screams crept past my lips. He kindly gyrated on top of me, kissing my lips and licking my neck. I began trembling uncontrollably as I felt myself coming. Not five minutes passed, and I was already tingling from my toes to my eyelids. I squeezed my pelvic muscles as I dug my nails into his back and sucked on his earlobe, nibbling on his skin.

"I can make you come all night," he said victoriously as he kept stroking. Pushing inside of me, my pussy lips clasped around him, and I shrieked in passion.

"Damn." I could faintly hear the sound of my phone vibrating as I approached the cusp of another come. I ignored it, without remorse. I couldn't let thoughts of Louis ruin an orgasm women wrote songs about.

Tariq lifted my left leg and placed it on his shoulder while he sat on his knees. He pulled me back and forth while I arched my back. When my toes curled and heat ripped through my body, I was coming again. I didn't know I was screaming until my muscles loosened. "Feels good?" he asked right as his dick swelled inside me. He was coming, too. "Shit," he yelled out as he collapsed on top of me.

As we lay there, catching our breaths, I smirked. I enjoyed the feeling. When Tariq pulled me closer to him, I rested my head on his shoulder. We didn't say much; we relaxed in a moment that was bittersweet. Nevertheless, I lay there smiling while I focused more on the sweet part of the experience.

"Fuck you!"
"Fuck you too!"
Their voices rang through Loraine's front door like sirens blaring. I may not have wanted to hear the sounds of Loraine and her ex

making love, but I was sucker for a good domestic argument. I stood a few feet away from the door with my ear in their direction. Loraine's voice continued and said, "I didn't ask for this, Lorenz."

"Then what the fuck were we doing? Was it about dick wit' you?"

"It was always about pussy wit' you!"

"There you go wit' this bullshit again. Yeah, I cheated! I apologized. I pleaded wit' you. Hell, I even begged you to take me back. Stop bringin' that shit up!"

"Excuse me? You left me for some other woman and then came back once you realized that she couldn't hold a candle to me. You lied, snuck around, and blatantly disrespected me for a bitch that sold bus tokens. I don't care if she was your boss or not. I was your wife, Lorenz, and you betrayed me. I can bring that shit up all I want."

"I'm done hearin' it. What did you have in mind wit' all this? You honestly think I can be okay wit' you fuckin' me an' datin' otha niggas? Who the fuck do I look like, Loraine? You fuckin' them too?"

"Fuck you, Lorenz. Because you couldn't keep yo' dick in yo' pants, every man I know must be putting his dick in me?"

"I'm not playin' wit' you, Loraine. Stop tryna change the subject."

"I'm *not* playin'. I never said this was us gettin' back together. I…" She paused. I could picture her twirling her dreads through her fingers while she shook her head and bit her bottom lip. "I dunno what we were doing."

"I dunno either." Lorenz lowered his tone and sighed. "Tell me— have you been fuckin' anyone else?"

Silence. I pictured Loraine staring at her feet while Lorenz patiently waited on her answer. I didn't breathe; I wanted to hear her answer, too. "I don't have to answer that."

More silence. I didn't know what to picture then. Lorenz was boiling, though. They didn't say any more words. When I saw Loraine's doorknob turn, I ran a few steps back and pretended as if I walked up her driveway. Lorenz swung the door open and stomped past me without a hello. Loraine stood in the doorway and stared at my car. She didn't watch as Lorenz sped off without a glance back in her direction. She stood there in her robe, hair tousled, dried sweat beads around her neck. It was clear they were sexing not long before arguing. I tried to act like I didn't know what I heard. I gawkily said, "What's up, girl?" She glared at me. Turning on her heel, she disappeared into her living room and left the door open for me to follow. I walked inside and closed the door behind me. I didn't know what to say. I quickly thought up things I usually said when I didn't know she had a fight with her ex-husband. I drew a blank. I stood there with a discomfited smile.

Two seconds later, she pulled out a bottle of Grey Goose vodka. She poured a glass and gulped it down like wine. She then slammed the glass on her kitchen counter and exhaled. "Whatchu doing here?"

"Came by to chat."

"I'm not sure I'm in the mood. I know you heard."

I never had a good poker face. "What was that all about?"

Loraine poured herself another glass and guzzled it down. She wiped the excess liquid that leaked down her chin and shook her head as if I asked her a question. "Bullshit." With frustration etched about her face, she stared at her front door as if she expected Lorenz to walk back in.

"Why was he so mad?"

"'Cause he's full of shit. Why else?" Loraine didn't raise her voice. She stared at her door as she tapped the brim of her glass. "I'm so sick and tired of him."

"What did he do?" I hated the vague innuendos and ambiguous references to Lorenz's asshole tendencies. I wanted more. I needed to dish.

"I thought we were fine sexing. I thought things were…what they are. But *he* thought we were gettin' back together."

"How did this all start?"

She poured another glass. She didn't swallow it like before, though. This time, she let the alcohol sit on her tongue, allowing it to marinate on her taste buds. She sniffed the glass as if she were inhaling toxins and closed her eyes while the inebriation settled. I didn't want to stop her too soon; I wanted to get her tipsy enough to spill the beans. When she opened her eyes, she took another long sip and gently placed the glass back down. "I'm not fucking anyone else, but that doesn't mean I don't date. Either way, Lorenz is not my man anymore. He signed the fuckin' divorce papers. I have the right to see, call, or text whomever I want to. I don't answer to him."

"You're right about that."

"But when he sees another man callin' me, he's quick to start askin' me all these questions. And when I refuse to answer, he throws a fit."

"What does he want from you?"

"Apparently a relationship!" She went back to letting the alcohol flow down her throat like ripping rapids slapping against her esophagus with high tide. She threw her glass in her sink and walked toward her couch. When she sat down, she kicked her feet up on the coffee table and ran her fingers through her locks. "He drives me so crazy."

"You're not ready for a relationship with him, anyway."

"I know that. I wish he knew that. I love him. At one point, I couldn't picture myself without him, but he fucked that up when he walked out the door—twice. I learned how to fend for myself. I realized that life ain't so scary without him. I grew up. I ain't saying that there will never be a Loraine and Lorenz, but I know that there will never be the Loraine and Lorenz that existed before. I'm not accepting the shit he used to pull anymore. I'm a grown-ass woman wit' grown-ass problems." She twirled her dreads in her fingers furiously, almost ripping one from her scalp. "And dammit if I wanna fuck someone else. That's my damn prerogative. It's my pussy, not his."

"Claim yo' pussy, girl. Own it."

Loraine paused initially and burst into hysterical laughter. I wasn't tryna be funny, but my comment was enough to crack a smile and some of the unwanted tension. Loraine loosened her shoulders and let the sleeve from her oversized robe fall, revealing her come-get-me lace bra strap. She rubbed the side of her neck and pushed up her lips. "I dunno what to do, Erin. I love Lorenz. I love being with him but…I'm not ready to do this full time."

"Do you wanna date other men while you two have sex?"

"I know I don't wanna feel pressured *not* to. Whatchu think? Think I should give in? Ain't like he's tryna marry me. But he does want to keep things exclusive."

"You should do what makes you the happiest. You were always tryna make him happy. Why not make yourself happy this time? Things might turn out differently. If he can't understand what you want, forget about him."

Loraine ran the tip of her tongue slowly across her top lip. Grabbing her phone, she scrolled through it and shook her head. "We had sex. Good sex, real slow, wet and juicy lovemaking. He had me on the wall. We were clawing at each other with this animalistic rage. It felt like we were mad at each other. Fighting each other's bodies like we wanted to hurt each other for the pain we caused by staying apart. He grinded into me like a drill, and I...I came so hard it fell like the walls were coming down. We were panting on the floor, prepping ourselves for round two when my phone rang." She threw her phone down on the couch beside her. "I recognized the ring and didn't answer. Lorenz ignored it at first, but then he texted."

"Who's *he?*"

Loraine fixed her robe and folded her arms. She held her sides as if she were hugging herself. Her shoulders rose and fell as she fluttered her eyelids and pursed her lips. "I've kinda been seeing someone. Before Lorenz and I starting doin' our thing, I met someone online."

"Online? When did you start online dating?"

"I was lonely. A friend at work told me about this website called eMeet.com. I was only gonna check it out at first, but after an hour of perusing the profiles, I decided to set up my own. There were a few, well, a lot of low-lifes at first, but this one guy hit me up." She grabbed one of her red dreadlocks and caressed it between her two fingers. Staring up at the wall, she spoke slowly and softly as her lips barely spread apart and her tongue moved seductively. "Bama56 was his profile name. In his pic, he had full lips that split open to big, white teeth. His smile was perfect, and his big, round gray eyes pierced through my computer screen as if they begged me to click on his personal info. I couldn't stop staring at his mocha-skinned complexion. His profile read "*6'4", muscular/toned, loves God, plays golf, loves to read, reads/writes poetry, and enjoys watching the sunrise.*" He sounded too good to be true, and I had to know for myself. The messages started innocent before they got real passionate. Eventually, we grew tired of waiting 'til we got online to speak and decided to exchange numbers." She closed her eyes and tilted her head back. "Erin, his voice...his voice was deep. He had a Southern accent that dripped from his tone. I could almost taste it with each word he spoke. We would talk for hours about everything. I would even dream about him."

"When did this all start?"

Loraine opened her eyes and sat up straight. Her face was euphoric as she fantasized about the mocha, gray-eyed Southern gent that stole her heart through the World Wide Web. She moaned, "Four months ago."

"Why didn't you ever tell me?"

"A part of me was ashamed. I was fallin' for a man I never met in person. At first, it was really innocent, and I wanted to tell you, but then...the phone sex started. We would flirt online and make dirty comments here and there, but when I heard his voice, my thighs would stick." She grabbed a magazine from her coffee table and fanned herself. Her face turned red, and her chest rose and fell at a hurried pace. "I wanted him to use his words to make love to me like I needed. It would get hot and intense to where I'd make myself come all over my sheets as he listened. After Lorenz came over, I was horny, and he was available. Bama56 would get me hot and bothered over the phone, and Lorenz would come in and close the deal."

"Are you still talkin' to Bama56?"

"Yea, I can't stop. I still have feelings for him. The problem is I'm not the type to detach feelings from sex. Old feelings for Lorenz are resurfacing, and I'm starting to crave him. Bama56 can tell. I'm sure of it. Lorenz can tell, and when he grabbed my phone and read my text, he was sure of it."

"What'd the text say?"

"Bama56 would read his poetry to me a lot. It's really beautiful. He'd email me poems at work, and I'd lose myself in his words. He texted me part of his poem, the poem he first read to me when we first starting having phone sex." She closed her eyes and rubbed the back of her neck. She sucked in her lips and then took a long, deep breath. She whispered, "I can illustrate how the absence of you causes my world to stop. The world lacking all its presence. Time no longer having meaning. The maddening sense of uselessness. Needing you to make seconds work again. My hard exterior is but the shell of a quivering mess. Nothing but a pile of shattered promises that yearn to feel something close to you …The very appearance of you is surreal… The heavens can't shine as sweet as you…" She sat quietly with her eyes closed and her palms sweaty. After a second, she rubbed her fingers down her scalp and her skin.

"Wow," I said. "Are you in love with this man?"

"I dunno. I dunno anything anymore. Lorenz read the text and went ballistic. He feels like I'm cheating on him. I don't know if I am. I don't know if I'm cheating on Julian."

"That's Bama56's real name?"

She smiled. Her smile was warm, like fresh-baked cookies. "Yea, Julian. With Julian, things are easy. I'm afraid that if I let go of what I have with Lorenz, I'll get disappointed with Julian. He seems too perfect. And I love Lorenz. I know what to expect with Lorenz. I don't know what I'm doing, girl. I'm so confused."

"You know what you need to do. Do what makes you happy. *What* makes you happy? Talking to Julian or being with Lorenz?"

"Both. I don't find more happiness with either of them. If I could combine the two, I'd have the perfect man. I feel like if I let one of them go, I'll feel incomplete. Together, I'm happiest. Is that wrong?"

I didn't know. When dealing with my heart and mind, nothing ever made sense. I sat silently, not knowing how to answer a simply asked question. If I were in the same exact situation, I wouldn't be able to choose. Then again, wit' Tariq and Louis, I practically was in the same situation, and if I had to choose today, I couldn't pick one over the other. I shrugged my shoulders. "Only you know that."

"Do I really?"

"Girl, what I do know is that you really are claiming your pussy."

She opened her eyes and giggled. "It feels good too."

"It always does."

When I walked into my apartment building, I was surprised to see Alonzo standing at his door going through his mail. Since I'd been dealin' wit' two men, I hadn't even noticed Alonzo's brief greetings and failed attempts at small talk. Though I didn't owe him anything, I still felt obliged to stop and talk to him. I looked him up and down as he stood at his door in flannel pajama pants and an oversized NYU sweatshirt. His face was rugged from lack of shaving, and his posture slouched forward as he looked through mail that he didn't seem to want at the time. "Hi, Alonzo."

He jumped and popped his head up. When he saw me standing at my door actually interested in a *hello* in response, his face lit up and eyes widened. Excitedly, he said, "Hey, Erin. How've you been?"

"Hangin' in there? How 'bout you?"

I could tell he was even more surprised that I was interested in his well-being. He didn't say anything at first. He opened his mouth to say something, but when nothing came out, he laughed nervously and jiggled the keys in his pants pocket. "I'm okay. Could be better."

"How so?"

"Well, I…I think…" He laughed nervously again and stuffed his mail in his pockets. He leaned his shoulder against his door-frame and dug around in his pockets. "I'm a broker, and I wish the stock market was playing in my favor."

"Oh, well, I hope things work out for you."

He nodded in agreement and smiled some more. The casual moment I ensued was slowly evolving into an awkward one. I went for my keys to end our happenstance tryst. "I gotta get going. It was nice catching up."

He stood up straight as if he weren't expecting our meeting to end so quickly. He put his hand up and opened his mouth to speak. Again, nothing came out, and he stood there fumbling over his thoughts and trying desperately to force a conversation. When I got my door open and turned back to look at him, he dropped his hand and shoulders. "It was nice talking to you, too."

I smiled back and closed the door behind me. Sometimes I feared Alonzo was the type to try to kill me in my sleep. I hoped our convo was enough to ease him off the trigger. I was tired and a long hot shower would do me good. I disrobed in front of my mirror and admired the beautiful woman that had men gushing. My perky breasts, slim waist, and full hips told the story of a woman worth the gush. I only wished my body made them do more than gush; I'd rather they learned how to act right and do what I needed them to. I smiled at my reflection and slipped into my running hot shower. I let the water cascade down my skin as I sloped my head back and moaned in ecstasy. My day was long, and this shower pleased my body better than I thought water could. I rubbed and caressed my moist skin and pretended to be my own lover. Loving my curves and embracing my imperfections like the perfect lover should. It felt good holding myself and knowing that I wouldn't have to let go until I felt ready.

After stepping out of the shower, I noticed two missed calls on my cell—one from Louis and the other from Tariq. I deleted my call history and got dressed for bed. Under my covers, I heard my phone vibrating. Looking at my phone, I read the text out loud, "Can I cum see you?" A text from Tariq that I chose to ignore. I did want to see him, but I also wanted to spend the night alone instead. I rested under my covers, hugged my pillow, and tried not to stare at my blinking phone. I wanted to experience the feeling of being alone…even when the entire world wanted to lie by my side.

Present…

I was feelin' Erin. I would think about her when I tried not to. I may have been married, but it was a marriage of circumstance—one that I couldn't get out of. I didn't know what it was about Erin, but when I was around her, my palms would sweat. She had control over my emotions and I hated it. When I considered giving her more, I'd remember the situation I was in dealin' with Simoné, and I'd back out. Erin was *fine*, though. I fantasized about holding her Coke-bottle figure close to me. Her lips were plump like cornbread. She had almond-shaped eyes that reminded me of Deja, long hair that I pictured running my fingers through, and honey skin that I craved melting over mine. I'd come over her apartment with the intention to talk and end up wanting to watch her make her love faces. She had deep dimples that I wanted to stick my fingers in. When she eyed me with her coconut-skin eyes, I tried not to peer down at her full, water-balloon-shaped breasts. I'd be standing there in heat, and she would remind me of Simoné every time I came to see her. The last thing I wanted to be reminded of was the reason I couldn't claim Erin like I wanted to.

All I wanted to do was hold her close to me. But I was a man scorned by trifling women. What I felt for Erin was real, though. When she looked at me, she truly did want to be with me and be the good woman all men wanted to hold down. She didn't know that reminding me of Simoné also let in the possibility of her being the next woman to trap me in an undesirable situation. I would call and text Erin like I was her bitch. She would ignore me and disregard my attempts at reconciliation, and it turned me on. I would be on my way to the gym or on the way home, and next thing I knew, I was standing outside Erin's door hoping I could make her come by night's end. Shit, I had it bad.

Still, my situation was fucked. Simoné tricked me. She gave birth to our son, Amari, and pretended like our marriage was a sign of resolution. "We can make this work, babe," she told me. I got down on my knees and begged her to agree to the annulment. She laughed in my fuckin' face. "Why would I divorce the father of my son?" She had it good for a while. But my plans hadn't changed. Soon, I stopped caring about her feelings and only cared about mine. Simoné was not my wife. She was a bad situation I couldn't get out of.

One day, I met a dime piece. Her name was Brooklyn. She stood five feet three and had long, golden-brown hair that reached the top of her butt. Her light-brown skin always shined like gold, even in fluorescent lights. Her voice was squeaky, and I often imagined it screaming my name while I hit it from the back. She worked at the shoe department at Macy's. She helped me pick out shoes for my new suit. When I came back for the matching tie, we decided it was time to stop playing games. My son was at my mama's for the night, and I opted to bring her home. I told her about my situation. "The mother of my son lives wit' me, but it ain't nothin'. You can come home wit' me if that's cool." She was down for the cause. The rattlesnake tattoo wrapped around her upper thigh told me that she liked danger. It turned her on knowing that Simoné might catch us.

I had her on all fours. She gripped my sheets and spread her legs wide, ass up high. Burying her face in my pillow, I dug into her deep like I was lookin' for loose change. I held on to her thighs while I pulled her so close to me, almost as if I was tryna to pull her inside of me. I heard my front door slam shut. Brooklyn didn't. If she did, she sho' ain't care. I kept pounding away while she covered her screams in my pillows.

When the door swung open, Simoné stood in the entryway to my bedroom with her hands on her hips. She stared at Brooklyn's ass that rested on my lap. At first, Brooklyn kept her face down, unaware of Simoné's intrusion. When I stopped thrusting, she quickly shot up and looked back. "Why'd you stop?" she said. When she noticed Simoné, she looked back at me and smirked.

I pulled away from her and let Brooklyn cover her naked breasts with my blankets. Simoné stood holding the doorknob tightly, her nostrils flared, and her chest heaving. I got off the bed and tried to put on my boxers, but like slow motion, I could see Simoné lunging for Brooklyn. I jumped into action, holding her up to the wall. Brooklyn didn't flinch. She watched Simoné kick and scream like a madwoman, "Get the fuck off me, Riq! I'm 'bout to fuck this bitch up!"

Brooklyn sniggered as she shook her head. She turned her back as she searched for her clothes. I don't know if she felt safe knowing I was able to hold Simoné back or if she truly didn't care. When Brooklyn slid back into her body-hugging, spandex mini dress, she walked up to us and looked Simoné up and down. She laughed some more and kissed my cheek. Waving goodbye, she walked into my living room.

Simoné was stronger than I thought. She threw me to the bed and ran after her. Brooklyn didn't know what hit her as Simoné grabbed a handful of her weave and slammed her down. Brooklyn's head hit my hardwood floor like a cracked snow globe. Simoné then fell to the floor and climbed on top of Brooklyn, slappin' her face like they were having a duel. Brooklyn guarded her face before she flung Simoné off of her. Before Simoné could get in another punch, Brooklyn cocked her fist back and clocked Simoné's jaw at full speed. The blow knocked Simoné off balance, but it was the second part of Brooklyn's one-two combo that took Simoné off her feet. "Now what, bitch!" Brooklyn taunted her, begging her to get back up.

Before Simoné could, I ran to her and held her down. "You gotta go," I told Brooklyn. "I ain't tryna have all this go down." Simoné tried to break free, but my grasp was firm.

Brooklyn grimaced and walked backward to the front door. "Fine, but keep that bitch in line, 'cause I'm coming back to catch my nut."

Simoné growled as she tried desperately to break free. Brooklyn walked out laughing, confident in her victory. With the door shut and ten seconds having passed, I let Simoné go and stepped back. Apparently, not far enough. Simoné shot up and slapped me across the face. "I can't believe you, Riq!"

I put my hands up palms out and sucked in my lips. I didn't have anything to say. There was a chance that Simoné would catch us, but I had to send a message. I wanted out of our fake marriage— one way or another. However, I hadn't expected a fight to break out. Well, I realized Simoné would react, but I wasn't expecting Brooklyn to wild out like that.

Simoné wiped her bangs from her eyes and tried to stare me down. She wasn't going to intimidate me, though. I stared back at her and waited for her to tell me what I wanted to hear. "What the fuck was that, Riq? How could you do that to me?"

"We're not together, Simoné."

"I'm yo' wife, Riq. Your damn wife! Why can't you respect that?"

"'Cause it ain't shit to respect! You know why we got married. You know I ain't want all this. You chose to change shit up and stick around. I kept my end of the deal. If I wanna bring females over and fuck, I can do that."

She stared at me, tears filling her sockets, arms folded across her chest. She looked at me from head to toe and laughed. "You are so…" Simoné threw her hands up and squeezed them tight as if she were squeezing my neck. "I can't believe you, Riq. In our fucking bed, too."

"*Our* bed?" I glared at her. "Divorce me."

I wanted her to give in. She was hurt. As evil as it sounded, I wanted her hurt enough to let me go and get out of my life. She took a deep breath and wiped her face. I expected her to give in, but she laughed again. "No. You think I'ma make it that easy?"

I couldn't believe it. She was the mother of my son, but I couldn't stand to look at her. I stared into her eyes and tried to remember the feelings I thought I once had for her, but as her eyes stared back, I realized that I never should've even liked her. "I'm not goin' to stop seeing other women, Simoné."

"I'll move out tonight. I can't even imagine me sleepin' under the same roof as you." She bit her tongue and shook her head. She walked over to the kitchen and rubbed the side of her face. The blows that Brooklyn landed were finally settling in, and her jaw was sore. Taking out a bottle of gin, she grabbed a shot glass and took two to the head. Then, she threw the glass into the sink and looked over at me. "You fucked up. We're not gettin' a divorce," she said. "I wanted to work things out. I wanted us to be together. You wanna play games. Fine, we can play. But at the end of the day, I am still the mother of your son, and married or not, that will never change."

Damien and I grew close over the years, and I relied on his skewed wisdom to get me through some rough times. Sometimes he'd come over so we could watch a game. He'd also rub it in my face about how right he was about women.

Simoné moved out that night. The bad part of it was she refused to end our fake marriage. At first, it was cool. I thought I was rid of her, but she'd show up at my place unannounced and leave some of her shit around so other women could find it. She'd make it hard for me to see my son and then lambaste me for not trying to work things out with her. She was playin' all right, and she played it well.

"I tol' you. Bitches ain't shit." Damien shoved a boneless chicken wing in his mouth and chugged a beer. We sat in front of my TV watching ESPN. I never talked about my feelings for Erin with Damien because he'd speak against it. He could talk bad about Simoné all day, though. I never let Simoné know about Erin either. If Simoné knew she existed, she'd make Erin' suffer. "Next time, wrap it up."

"I did wrap it up. Condom broke."

"Double-baggy it next time."

I waved him off and chuckled. "Man, please. I ain't think she was goin' turn out like this. She's the worst type of woman."

"I'ma have to admit it, though, the shit you did having her catch you when you was fuckin'…you one cold dude."

"I'm not proud of it. I was hopin' I'd get a divorce out of it. Instead, I got the baby mama from hell."

"Shoulda played it better. I'm cool wit' both my baby mamas. I can see my kids when I want to. They both moved on, and I ain't got no drama." Takin' another sip of beer, he said, "Who marries someone for insurance? Ain't that insurance fraud? Shit, you should know."

I sipped my beer and licked my lips. "I couldn't pay them bills out of pocket. I saved much more money marrying her and lettin' the job pay for it."

"Was it worth it?"

I swallowed the rest of my beer and set it down. I stared at the TV screen and shook my head. "Hell no. I'd rather the debt."

We both stopped laughing when there was a knock at the door. I looked at my watch and back at the door. I hoped it was Erin, but then I realized, I'd rather it be nobody. I stood up and answered the door. Simoné stood in my doorway in a polka dot maxi dress and her hair pulled back. She was letting her bangs grow out. Now, she swiped her bangs to the side. "What's he doing here?"

She pointed at Damien and sneered. Damien shook his head and drank his beer. I didn't move out the way to let her in. We stood at the door, and I waited for her to tell me why she felt the need to drop by. "What do you want?"

"Are you going to let me in?"

I sighed. "Why are you here?"

She twirled her neck. "I came by to talk to you."

"I'm busy. You could've called me."

"Can you let me in so we can talk, please?"

"You see I have company."

"I'm not leaving until you let me in." She wasn't joking. She'd pull out a sleeping bag and lie outside my door until I let her in to talk. I took a deep breath and stepped aside. When I closed the door behind her, I asked, "What, Simoné?"

She walked into my kitchen and lowered her voice so Damien couldn't hear. "I want us to talk about us. This has gone on long enough."

I rubbed the top of my head and frowned. I shouldn't have let her in. "Simoné, I'm done talkin' 'bout this. Let it go."

"You're not going to hear me out?"

"What can you possibly say that would make me want to be with you? I'm still waitin' on you to sign the damn divorce papers."

"I'm not signing them."

"Then we ain't got shit to say to one another."

"It's like that, Riq?"

"It's been like that! This ain't nothin' new. You're the one who's trippin'."

Simoné looked over at Damien. He was staring at ESPN and pretending not to listen. Simoné hated having Damien in our business. In her mind, Damien was the reason why I had the *bitches ain't shit* attitude. In retrospect, she was halfway right. "Riq, we can make this work."

"No…" I shook my head and headed back for the front door. I wasn't going to stand there and listen to her talk about the same shit. "You need to go."

"Riq, I really think you need to let the past go. We can move on."

"I've moved on. You're the one who won't."

"I'm still yo' wife, Riq."

I opened the door and pointed to the hallway. "On paper."

She opened her mouth and groaned. She followed me to the door and smacked her lips. She stood outside the door with her hands on her hips. "That's it, Riq?"

"When are you gonna let me see my son, Simoné?"

She rested her tongue over her top row of teeth and sighed. "I wanted us to work things out, but since you wanna be a dick…you need to know that I'm moving to Arizona. Me *and* our son."

"Whatchu mean?"

"I got a job that pays better, and it's in Arizona. I would've stayed, but only if you agreed to work things out between us."

She was playing her game again. She probably purposely had looked for jobs out of state and had waited to put this play on the table. I was done playin'. I didn't want to work things out with Simoné; I never did, and I never would. It was time she realized that. "Fine."

Her eyes lit up and she smiled from cheek to cheek. "You agree to us workin' things out?"

"No. It's time I went for full custody."

Her smile dropped like a hot plate as she strode backward. "What?"

"I'm tired of this bullshit. I wanna see my son, and you won't let me."

"We're married. You can't do shit. You're not takin' my son, Riq."

"Keep playin' wit' me, and watch what happens." I slammed the door shut and locked it. I was through with Simoné's shit, and it was time I took back control of my life.

When I looked over at Damien, he covered his mouth, holding in his laughs. "Like I said…you one cold-ass dude."

Present…

"I'm still waiting on the copy for the new Surreptitious campaign."

Eric popped his head into my cubicle, hands rolled into fists and forearms cuddled up beneath each other. He was having a bad hair day and pretended as if no one noticed. Usually, Eric's curly salt-and-pepper hair stuck up like a fist. Today, he sported jet-black waves that sat across his forehead as if it were in the works of being a press and curl but got lost along the way. His tightly coiled naps dispersed throughout the back of his neck and loosened up as they led up to his crown. I smirked. I didn't want to smirk, but I couldn't ignore an obvious cry for help. "I'll have it by the end of today." A stifled giggle tiptoed out as he stared me down. I stopped it as soon as it started.

It didn't help much. "What's so funny?"

Is he serious? Does he truly expect me to answer honestly? If I answered honestly, there'd be a stack of work on my desk that'd keep me here 'til midnight. I didn't fear losing my job. We both knew this place would crumble without me, but I still respected my boss. If I lied, I'd be letting him win. With all the mess goin' on in my life, I wasn't sure I felt like letting him get one over on me. I ignored his question. "I've been wrapped up with my notes for the intern's first copy, but I'll have my work done ASAP."

He looked at me, arms still folded, eyes dark as darkness. Without another word, he walked out of my cubicle, daring me to say something about his hair. As he walked off, I glanced over at my coworkers, who draped their palms over their faces, trying desperately to hold back their bubbling cackles. The rookie intern we hired, who had recently earned an undergraduate degree in graphic design, greeted Eric's challenge to say something with his own pigheaded arrogance. With a sarcastic grin, he asked, "New hair today, boss?"

We couldn't hold it in after that. The entire office echoed with the giggles, chuckles, cough-laughs, and snickers that no one could contain. Eric looked around the office, embarrassed as he ran his sweaty palm over his loose waves. Clearing his throat, shoulders back, he responded, "Last one hired, first one back at unemployment. Remember that."

The rookie's grin slowly faded. Eric stomped off confidently in his victory. The rookie was confident in his own victory as my coworkers slapped him fives and patted his back. "Good job," they said. They were willingly leading the poor lamb to slaughter by gassing his head with ideas of talkin' back without the work to show for it. I shook my head and went back to working on how to sell the revamp of a product that gradually entered women's lives throughout the years with subtlety and grace, and turn it into a brand that ripped through their most intimate emotions and deliberately implored them to take notice—like the ho in the red dress sitting in the front pew at church.

Looking through my emails, I noticed a couple of emails from Louis. I sighed and scrolled past them as I cleared out my inbox. Once my inbox was clear, I sat back and stared at my computer screen. "Staring at the screen like that will make your eyes go bad." I snapped out of my train of thought when I noticed the rookie's voice.

I turned around, notes in hand. "I have your notes."

"How'd you like it?"

"It's good. My notes are suggestions on ways to make it better."

"Oh yea, like what?" He eyed me up and down. Greenish-brown eyes cascaded over me like a shadow. His fitted polo stopped short of his tattooed arms. Colorful and artistic pieces of art engraved in his muscular skin like symbolic messages told his story. Even with two men to seize my time and interest, I liked staring at the medium-height, broad-shouldered rookie with heart-shaped lips and butterscotch skin.

I tried not to stare too hard. His shiny, bald head was almost as big as his ego. As seconds went by, I almost suffocated from the air of arrogance that piled in with him. I handed him my notes and motioned him to take a gander for himself. "Read it and tell me."

"Why can't you tell me? I like hearing your advice." He wet his lips slowly and kept his eyes on mine in the process.

"Or you can *read* my advice. I have to get back to work. If you have questions about what I wrote, we can discuss it later."

"Over dinner?"

I laughed. It wasn't meant to be a laugh, but I opened my mouth, and that's all that came out. "No, during business hours."

"What's funny? We can't have dinner?"

"I don't date men without a four-oh-one K."

His stare was blank at first, like he had been trying to rack his brain to find the definition of 401K. Then, he smiled the type of million-dollar smile that Colgate commercials banked on. "I can get one."

"I'm taken, rookie." I frowned unintentionally when I remembered Louis's unread emails. I turned around to face my computer.

"Don't mean there isn't room for one more." He didn't stick around after his comment. He let his words linger, giving me the chance to mull them over. I didn't. I shook my head while my eyes circled to the ceiling.

I logged back into my computer after it timed out and opened Louis's first email. Before I read it, a text message from Louis came through. It read, *"Am I seeing you tonight? I'll cook."* I responded to it without thought. Even though I enjoyed my time with Tariq, he was my sideline action. After some thought, I realized that I was interested in taking things slow with Louis, and I wanted to give him the opportunity to win back my heart. I was tired of chasin' married men; I wanted a man who would chase me. I responded, "O…k…C…u…2…n…i…t…e."

After I put my phone away, I looked over Louis's email. *I'm at work missing you. I'm applying for the general manager position at my store. Pray for me. The promotion comes with a bigger salary and better benefits. If I get the position, I want us to take a vacation together to reconnect. I hear making love to a Hawaiian sunset is magical. I know I've put you through some things, but I'm willing to make things work if you are. I hope we see each other tonight. Love you.*

Now, I wished I hadn't responded so quickly to his text message. I wanted to take things slow, and Louis wanted us to start where we left off. I grabbed my chest 'cause all I could feel was pressure. I rubbed my temples and chewed on my bottom lip. "Shit," I mumbled under my breath.

"What?"

I turned around to notice Eric standing behind me again. I contemplated buying him a bell to put around his collar. Shaking my head, I said, "N-nothing. I'm going through my emails. Can I help you with something?"

He stood there trying to read my expression. I always gave him nothing, and he hated it. He thought I'd be as dumb as my peers that were foolish enough to let him into their personal lives, only to feel slighted when he used it against them. "I got a call from upstairs. I need that copy sooner than ASAP. Vivian is really riding me on this. She's counting on you the most. She trusts your vision over anyone else's." Saying that made him envious. "I need it more like fifteen minutes ago. How much longer?"

I sat astute and erased previous thoughts from my mind. It was time for work, and Louis's slight obsession with me was put to the side. I nodded like a good little soldier and turned back to face my computer. "I'll have it fifteen minutes ago, then."

Eric walked out my cubicle without words as I click-clacked away at my computer with the determination I was known for. I may have been unlucky at love, but I was a beast at work.

"Are you dating anyone else?"

I didn't see Louis. I made up an excuse about how stressful work had been and snuck over to Tariq's. I wanted him to relax me and give me the tranquil night of pleasure I needed. It felt weird asking a married man if he were datin' someone else, but I had to be real wit' myself.

When I asked him my question, he didn't say anything. We reposed in his bed in complete darkness. Stripped of any clothing, we only wore our sweat and bodily fluids. When we made love, he caressed my body. He thrusted inside me passionately and sensually. Tariq would rest his body on top of mine and brush my hair out of my face while he looked into my eyes. He'd kiss me softly, barely touching lips while he moved in and out, out then in. Sliding his tongue across my lips, cheeks, and neck. When we came, he slid the condom off to lie beside me, touching my skin, rubbing me back and forth in silence.

After a long pause, he broke the silence. "No." I didn't say anything. I wasn't sure if I could believe him. He'd kept things from me before, and I wondered what would stop him from doing the same now. He pulled me closer and lowered his voice as if he were tellin' me a secret. "I only wanna be wit' you."

When I rested quietly this time, it wasn't because I wanted to live peacefully in the moment; I was lost with what to say. I expected a myriad of responses but not that one. He was fallin' for me. This time, I wasn't tellin' myself what I thought I wanted to hear. It was clear. "How can you be so sure?"

"You're all I think about."

"What do you think about me?"

He didn't say anything. He ran the tips of his fingers along my skin and sighed. "Random shit."

"Random like what? I wanna know what you think about me."

"I don't know. Sometimes, I wonder…I wonder if you wit' other dudes."

"Would that matter?"

No words. Only the sound of his air conditioner blowing. "What-chu think?"

"I don't know what to think wit' you, Tariq. You confuse me sometimes."

"I know I can trip sometimes, but it don't mean I would like you to be wit' other guys. I mean, I understand if you are. Wit' my situation, I can't give you all you want. The mother of my child is crazy. I wouldn't wanna put you through all that."

"I wouldn't wanna be put through all that, either, but I wonder if you're with other women. You say you're not, but then I see women's underwear under your bed."

Breathing deeply, he said, "That's her shit. She comes over and plants stuff around in hopes that people find it. I'm not sexing anybody else."

I wanted to believe him. Then again, I wouldn't like it either way. The last thing I needed to deal wit' was a crazy wife. At the end of the day, I was sleeping wit' a woman's husband. I was the other woman. I didn't like it, but I liked Tariq. "When are you plannin' to end things wit' your wife, Tariq?"

The sound of his air conditioner seemed louder in his silence. He asked, "Why do you call me Tariq? Most women call me Riq."

"I like Tariq. You don't like it?"

"I do. I'm not used to it, that's all. Maybe that's why I like you so much."

I laughed. "'Cause I call you by your name? You barely even know me."

"I know enough." Silence. I was stumped again. I couldn't figure out what to say next. I lounged in his arms in silence. I hadn't even realized that he ignored my question. He asked, "What's your favorite color?"

"Why?"

"I'm tryna get to know you."

"By knowing what my favorite color is?"

"It's a start."

He couldn't see it, but I was smiling from ear to ear. "Red."

He didn't respond at first. He met my answer with stillness and chuckled softly. "Why red?"

"Why not red?" Silence. Two seconds later, I asked, "What's your favorite color?"

"Royal blue."

"Why *royal* blue?"

Nothing at first. No movement, no words. Only the sound of the dry air. Then with quiet words, he spoke. "My dad…before he passed, he had this royal-blue Chevy. It was beat to hell. No working engine most of the time, paint chipped, windows didn't roll down, and when you did get it to start up, you had to get past this pale-white smoke that would seep through the vents for about ten seconds before evaporatin' into thin air. That car was a wreck. My dad never knew how to fix cars, but he worked every morning tryin' to fix it."

"Why didn't he buy a new car?"

"Apparently, it was the car he met my mama in. He couldn't let it go. For my dad, that car symbolized what he felt for my mama—beat up, but nothing he wasn't willing to fix…time and time again. To me, Ol' Blue symbolized determination, drive, everything in my dad that I wanted to be. I dunno, ever since he passed, royal blue brought me back to a place of peace."

Before tonight, I barely knew much about Tariq's childhood. In actuality, I knew nothing. Let me tell it, Tariq didn't start existing until I first met him. We never invited each other into our past lives, and now he was introducing me into his. He was fallin' for me, and he wanted to make sure I was fallin' for him, too. "Where's the car now?"

"In a shop. I've been saving up to get it in working condition. It ain't cheap, though. Costin' me thousands."

"I bet." With a glimpse into his past, I kinda wanted more. I liked this gentle side of Tariq. I wanted him to feed me with more memories to the point where I was knee-deep in his past life. I asked, "How'd your dad pass?"

"He was in the marines. Died in battle."

Two seconds ago, I knew nothing about his past. Now, I wanted to be the one in his past who consoled him. The way he kept his voice low and his words steady proved he hadn't recovered fully from the loss of his father. I wrapped my body around him tighter. I snuck my leg in between his as I rubbed his chest. He welcomed my advances and the opportunity to mourn the death he already mourned years earlier. "I'm sorry to hear that," I whispered.

"You ain't kill him. Don't sweat it." He rubbed my shoulder and kissed my forehead. It was a subtle form of endearment that tempted an eruption of goose bumps all over my body. "What about you? Your parents still living?"

I was surprisingly taken back by his question. He was lettin' me into his world, but I hadn't realized that it would soon be my turn to let him in, too. Closing my eyes, I licked my lips and tried to focus on anything I could make out in a room as dark as night. "My mom's still living. My dad passed before I was born."

"What happened to him?"

"Car accident. Drunk driver took him out. Died on impact. Never found the driver. Tons of witnesses, no suspects." I never spoke in complete sentences when I discussed my late father. My relationship with my father was incomplete. I searched for his replacement in the embrace of other men and always felt the same—incomplete.

"Damn...I'm sorry to hear that."

"Don't apologize. You weren't the drunk driver."

Now, he was the one holding me tight. Pulling me close to his chest and letting me leave my troubles on him while he soothed me to sleep. I closed my eyes and relaxed. I rested my body weight on his, confident that he was strong enough to bear me. Without struggle, he held me close. I could feel his gravitational pull, tugging and pulling at me as I felt myself moving into him. I was moving into his heart, and it felt too good to stop him.

"Where were you the other night?"

Louis and I sat at my dinner table across from each other in awkward quietness. We ate leftover lasagna and avoided eye contact while I drank my wine in my T-shirt and panties. Even though my nights with Tariq were becoming more enjoyable, I needed to face Louis. The fate of our relationship was left unresolved, and I had to make a decision. Louis could lay it on strong, but I wasn't completely willin' to let him go. All the while, Tariq was slowly creepin' into my thoughts, and I learned new meaning to being conflicted. "In bed. Why?"

"*Your* bed?"

I almost choked. I slurped down the rest of my wine and cleared my throat. "Excuse me?"

He laughed mockingly and stuffed a forkful of lasagna in his mouth. I kept my eyes on him, waitin' on an explanation. After he swallowed his mouthful, he said, "I'm joking. I called you, though. You didn't answer."

"I went to bed early. Why does it matter?"

Shaking his head, he sipped his wine. "I was curious."

I didn't want to press the issue because I wasn't sleepin' in my bed. Not wanting to lie blatantly to his face about my whereabouts, I let it go. "I'm ready to go to bed."

He looked at his watch. "Want me to join you?"

"No, I wanna sleep alone tonight."

He tossed down the last of his wine and stood up from the table. Grabbing our plates, he cleaned them off and dropped them in the sink. With the wet plates lying in my sink, he stood there and stared down at them. After a few brief seconds, he wiped his face and looked over at me. "Can you oil my scalp first?"

I didn't want to; he made me feel uncomfortable. Something bothered him, and he wasn't letting me in. "Is somethin' wrong?"

He scratched his scalp and smiled. "No, my scalp is a little dry, and I miss you. Want to spend as much time with you as I can."

Louis had left a bottle of his peppermint oil under my bathroom sink. I wasn't in the mood, but I couldn't think of a valid reason not to. "Okay, lemme go get the oil."

As I walked into my bedroom, he watched me. His eyes glued on my skin. I felt his eyes on my back as I passed my bed on the way to my bathroom. When I found the peppermint oil, I walked back into the living room. Louis was sitting down on my couch staring at his hands. I cleared my throat to let him know I was back. A second passed before he looked up at me and grinned. I strolled over to him and sat with him between my legs. He let his dreads fall off his shoulders, allowing me to get my fingers in between.

As I poured the peppermint oil on the tips of my fingers, I gently pulled his head back and ran my fingers up and down his scalp. I stopped and felt his scalp with my dry hand when I realized how oily his hair felt. "Your scalp seems pretty oiled up to me."

He pushed up his lips. "It is? It felt dry to me." He rubbed the skin on my calves and exhaled. "I guess I wanted to sit between your legs before I left." I bottled up the peppermint oil and sat back. Louis kissed my inner thigh, stood up, and tied up his dreads. "Did you want to get to bed?"

I nodded. He helped me up. As I walked him to the door, I said, "I'll call you tomorrow. I'll oil your scalp then."

We reached my door, and I wrapped my arms around his neck briefly before pulling away and holding the doorknob. Before I could see him out, he stopped suddenly and pulled me into his embrace again. He clutched my waist and squeezed my skin. With his breath on my neck, he held me close and then grabbed my neck as he pushed my lips toward his. He kissed me furiously, as if to remind me of the kisses I'd be missing if I let him leave. I closed my eyes and let him remind me. It was a passion I wasn't used to with Louis, and my body hungered after more. I circled my arms around his neck and used his body to support me. Between kisses, I exhaled. I exhaled all of the conflicting emotions I felt and inhaled the one thing that made sense to me, the love that Louis did have for me. Though I could never define the emotion Tariq felt for me, Louis's emotions were always clear, no games. He wanted me desperately, and he made no attempts to hide that. He kissed me again, and I exhaled. I released the confusion I felt when Louis touched me, held me, and penetrated me. I let in the assuredness in his embrace. When he grabbed my legs and yanked me up toward his waist, my inner thighs floated up his six-foot-three stature like an elevator. I loosened his dreads and let them fall atop his shoulders. He smiled with his kisses while our tongues salsa danced with each other, letting our short, panting breaths play the music in the background. Then, right as I sucked on his bottom lip and pulled, he pressed his top lip on top of mine and used his tongue to push away. He looked in my eyes and murmured ever so tenderly, "I wish you wouldn't fight this feeling. This hot, anxious feeling that has your heart beating the same beat and the same rate as mine. *This* is what I'm feelin'. Every time you speak, every time you're near me, every time I see you…this is exactly how I feel." Kissing the millions of goose bumps scattered throughout my arms, he said, "And your heat tells me that you feel it, too." Looking into my eyes, his heavenly, deep-brown eyes that gazed into mine, he continued, "It's obvious. Stop fightin' it."

He covered my mouth with his lips and kicked the music back up, letting our tongues salsa. I gripped his shirt collar and tried to ignore the tingling feeling that slid up my thigh. The tingle was restrained but palpable. It gradually intruded my nether regions as he did a backward glide toward my bedroom. I wanted him bad, and I forgot all thoughts of the married man whose name held no relevance. All I needed was Louis's body thrusting on top of mine. When my back hit the bed, I spread my legs like eagle wings and summoned his presence inside the entrance of my body. I commanded his services and would accept nothing less than his best. "Give it to me," I demanded. I asked no questions and left no room for forethought. I quickly seized his neck and tugged him forward.

There was no foreplay. There weren't any more kisses. Certainly no more words. Upon retrieving a condom from my nightstand, Louis rested on top of me, and I welcomed him. We didn't break our gaze as he moved forward and backward, rubbing my skin with his chest. Our sweat mixed into one another, sizzling from the heat of our friction and creating a new substance. He pushed in deep, and my reflexes slid away from him. Instinctively, he grabbed my butt and ended the chase as fast as it started. He worked my body up and down like a pogo stick while my back arched.

I saw the back of my skull as my eyes rolled back. My body shook and jived as I welcomed him deeper, held on to his shoulders, and demanded he go harder, punishing me for forsaking loving as faithful as his. Opening my mouth to scream, I caught his stare. He gaped at me as if I were his goddess and he could do nothing but worship me; examining my skin, admiring my lips, adoring my dimpled cheeks. When I wanted to scream, staring into his eyes, I affirmed, "I love you." The words didn't make sense to me. I closed my mouth and clutched my jaw to keep any more words from escaping.

I thought my premature confession would break the rhythm. I tensed when I looked up at him, and the look in his eyes went from intensity to weakness, a weak passion that craved to react and respond to the words he was begging to hear. I was afraid to hear what he would say next. I closed my eyes and awaited the inevitable. Instead, he turned me over and reentered my body without breaking a step. His arm clasped across my shoulders, and his lips glued to my neck and shoulders, he steered my hips with each thrust. I leaked down my thighs as I tightened my pelvic muscles and buckled my knees. When I opened my mouth this time, only screams escaped. Loud, throat-burning screams that gnawed their way out of captivity.

Louis grunted as he pulled away and let his cum trickle down my backside, staining the sheets. As we fell on top of each other, he pulled me close to him, threw the used condom to the floor, and muttered, "I'm glad you finally realized it."

CHAPTER 30

Tariq

Present...

"You're not taking my son." I dropped the divorce papers on my coffee table. Simoné stood in front of my TV with her hands gripping her hips. The coffee table separated us as we stood across from each other. When she noticed the papers, she flipped through them and pushed them aside. "I'm not signing no damn divorce papers either."

"Simoné, I'm tired of you playing these games—"

"I'm not playin' no damn games! You started all this by fuckin' some bitch in my bed. You're the one playin' games."

Her bed? I rubbed the top of my head and sat down. "You like makin' shit hard. What happened to an annulment? What happened to you wantin' me to be there for my son? Now, you won't even let me see my son."

She smirked. "Shit changed."

"Is that right?"

She twirled her neck. "Yep, that's right. You don't get the right to walk out on me, Riq. I poured my heart into this relationship, and you betrayed me. You say you're done with me, but while we were living under the same roof, you fucked me over a dozen times. What the fuck am I supposed to think about us when you fuck me one night and fuck another bitch in our bed the next?"

"We fucked like twice, Simoné."

Simoné huffed. "If you say so, Riq. You deserve everything I'm putting you through."

I was done listening to her play the victim. I may have succumbed to temptation a few nights while living with Simoné. After passing out from a round of shots of Patrón, Simoné was all too ready to meet me on the couch and take advantage of my weak state. I enjoyed it while it happened, but come morning, she would use it against me. Nevertheless, I was done. I dropped my shoulders and tugged the skin between my fingers. "I did some research, Simoné."

"And? You're still not takin' my son."

"I know that our situation is partly my fault. I should've tried harder to divorce you, but I dunno, Simoné. What I do know is that I can't let you keep fucking my life up anymore. Simoné, we are done. We are never getting back together. I will never love you. I never loved you when we actually were together. I'm tired of this shit, Simoné. I'm tired of you. I'm tired of not seeing my son." I exhaled. "Since you won't get an annulment, I will move forward with this divorce and keep my son in the process. I've already started contacting lawyers."

"What the fuck does that mean, Riq? You think I can't fight you on this?"

I took a deep breath and pushed the divorce papers closer to her. "That means that I'm ending this. You don't have the right to keep me in this bullshit because you can't let go. I want things to be easy. I don't wanna go through all this bullshit, especially when we got Amari to deal wit'. We can either do this like two adults or I can make shit real difficult for you."

She dropped her hands and breathed. She spread her lips and whistled through her mouth as she stared at the papers. She picked them up and leafed through them. Not understanding what to say, she threw the papers back down and put her hands back on her hips. "Whatchu tryna say, Riq?"

"I tol' you, Simoné. I'm done. I'm tired of going through this. I tried to be there for my son, and you put me through hell doing it. And now, you wanna move my son away from me 'cause you can't move on. I'm done wit' it."

"I put *you* through hell?"

"Simoné, you cheated on me! Do you remember that I caught you fuckin' another nigga in my damn shower? And then you tricked me into marrying you. Why the fuck would I wanna be married to you?"

"Riq…"

"Nah…" I stood up and picked the papers back up. "We goin' get this divorce, After that, I'm coming for my son."

She snatched the papers from my hands and threw them to the floor. She kept her eyes on me intently as if she already decided where she was goin' to bury my body. Then she laughed. She looked down at the scattered papers and cackled as she walked toward my front door. "Fuck you, Riq. You're not takin' my son."

After gathering the papers from the floor, I held her arm and yanked her back. An inch away from her face, I said, "You think everything's a fuckin' game." She snatched her arm away and folded her arms over her chest. "You ain't got no job, no place to stay. You ain't got shit. You think I won't be able to take my son from you?"

"I *know* you won't."

I was the one laughing now. I looked her up and down and chuckled. When I first met Simoné, her take-no-shit attitude turned me on. At that moment, I found it amusing. She didn't realize when it was time to throw in the towel. I was serious about my son, an' Simoné was soon about to find out how much. "And what makes you so damn sure?"

Her face was expressionless. Although her nostrils were slightly flared, I couldn't accurately predict what she was about to say next. She didn't move. She stared right through me as she spoke the next six words low and slow. "'Cause he ain't *yo'* damn son."

It was as if she knocked the wind out of me. I stumbled backward. Her words packed the punch of a heavyweight champion. My ribs caved in after she knocked me out. I stared at her, searching for a tell, a smirk or a wink. Something that implied the joke. It wasn't a funny joke, but I'd take it. Her face was straight. She stared me down and silently delighted in my reaction. I wanted to punch her back and hit her wit' the same blow she'd hit me wit'. "What?"

"You heard what the fuck I said." She turned around and tried to walk out my door. I squeezed her forearm and pulled her back. She hadn't gained enough footing, and she had to grab my kitchen counter to keep from falling backward. I didn't care if she fell. I wanted answers, and I wasn't goin' let her walk out this time. She plucked her hand away from my clutch and sneered. "What the fuck is wrong wit' you? Don't put yo' damn hands on me!"

"What the fuck are you talkin' 'bout, Simoné? Whatchu mean, he ain't my son?"

"I mean what the fuck I said! He's not yours. He never was."

"Then what did you show me? What was the paternity test you showed me, Simoné? I was there when they took my DNA and tested you again. What the fuck was all that?"

"Bullshit! I faked it! You think I don't have friends in useful places? I could've had those results say our son was the president's baby. Why the fuck would I want to have a baby by a nigga wit' no fuckin' job, a lazy eye, and still lives wit' his mama? I called in a big favor to hook you, Riq." She took a deep breath. Her eyes welled with tears, but she wiped her face and shook her head. "I wanted you back."

"Simoné, are you still playin' fuckin' games?"

"Do I look like I'm playin'? Take a paternity test yo' damn self if you don't believe me. Amari's not yours, Riq. He may look like you, but trust me, he's Jamar's. Sorry."

"*Sorry?*" Did women really think that *sorry* was the cure? Women would put a knife in a man's back, turn around, and say *sorry* when blood stained his shirt. *What the fuck does* sorry *do for me in this moment?* Right then, I wanted to crack her skull against my hardwood floor, not a fuckin' sorry. "Simoné…you ain't fo' real…" I pictured Amari's face. I pictured the face of the fuckin' nigga she had in my shower. Amari had his ears and the same smug expression about his face.

"I gotta go." Simoné walked to my front door without a look back. I wanted to stop her, but if I'd moved, I wouldn't have been able to account for my hands. I closed my fists and breathed steadily. I couldn't look at her. I heard her footsteps disappear out into the hallway as the door shut behind her. I didn't move. I stood there as images of my son's face flashed through my mind. I dissected his face, his eyes, his nose, and his lips. When I used to look at him, I saw me. After hearing that, I saw a stranger. Ten minutes ago, I had a son. In that moment, I had nothing but pain and blind fury.

Damien stood in the middle of my condo eyeing the damage. He eyed the fifteen holes in my wall. Fifteen fist-wide holes that went as deep as my elbow. He watched his step as he walked over the shattered glass strewn all over my floor. Broken dishes and cups lay dead on my floor as scattered bits scratched my hardwood. Damien kept his hands in his pockets, strolling around my apartment in silent awe. I sat on my couch staring at the wall. My knuckles covered in dried blood and drywall. Dried sweat rested on my forehead, neck, and back. When he walked in, I had no words for him. I simply sat down and stared at the wall—breathing.

Simoné called. She called thirty-seven times. She blew me up with voicemails and sending text messages. I didn't react to the first ten calls. After a drink of water, she called again. I threw my water glass against the wall, then another glass, then some plates—I did that through twelve more calls. Tired of being a bitch and throwing plates, I saw Simoné's face in my walls. I punched her for each call. Then, Damien stopped by. I turned my phone off and gave my walls a rest.

"Um…is there something I need to know?"

I never knew silence made a sound. In my silence, I heard Simoné's voice constantly reminding me of the paternity of my son. I needed to drive her voice out of my head. I took a deep, much-needed breath and said, "Simoné."

Damien walked toward me. He stood in the way of my view of the wall and stared down at me. "What did she do now?"

"I tol' her I was comin' for my son." I had to remind myself to breathe to keep from getting angrier. I got lightheaded as I attempted to let the rage simmer. "She tol' me that Lil' Man ain't mine."

Damien dropped his jaw and stepped back like I hit him in the face. "Stop lying."

I stared at my feet and pressed my fists together. "Does my condo look like I'm lying?"

He chuckled nervously. His laugh was weak and shaky as he rubbed his chin and cataloged the damage. "That's fucked up."

"No, what's fucked up is that I had a bitch claimin' my last name, puttin' me through bullshit, and then lying about a son who ain't mine." I laughed. It was the first laugh I'd had since Simoné walked out my place. There wasn't anything funny, but I had to release an emotion other than anger.

"Shit, man. Whatchu goin' do?"

"I don't know, man. The only reason why my place is so fucked up is 'cause it ain't in me to knock out a female. I want to, though. I gotta stay here until it's safe for Simoné."

"I was 'bout to say we need to go out to the club."

I shook my head. "Nah, man. I can't risk it. If I get drunk enough, I'ma somehow make it to Simoné's mama house. She ain't goin' make it out alive."

Damien nodded. He understood my frustration. Damien had two kids that he knew were his. I had a son who didn't belong to me. Instantly, fury overtook me. The anger had resurfaced, and I stood back up and headed for the front door. The wall between my entryway and my kitchen had two holes in it. I clenched my fists and then punched in a third hole. The first few holes punched back. That time, my fist went through easily. That felt good. Damien stood up and walked up behind me. "Aye man, you tryna get the cops called?"

I exhaled. I wasn't breathing. I stood there staring at my three holes and holding my breath. When he spoke, I shook my head and turned my doorknob. "I'ma have to hit you up later. I can't even think straight, man."

Damien sympathized, and nodded in agreement. When I opened the door, we were both surprised to see Erin. She stood there with her hand up and ready to knock. Damien looked at me and back at her. I could sense he was undressing her out of the yellow sundress she wore. He licked his lips as he eyed her pedicured toes in beach slides and smiled when he noticed her hair pulled up into a loose bun. She stared back at him as she waited for someone to say something. When neither of us spoke, she caught a glimpse of my apartment and turned her eyes toward me. I stood there in a ripped undershirt and dirty sweatpants. With her uneasy smile, her dimples stared back at us, wanting answers. She spread her lips and looked back into my place. "Is this a bad time?"

Damien offered Erin his hand. "I was about to leave."

Erin grabbed his hand and shook it as Damien slapped my shoulder and walked out. He left us there to sort through my mess.

With Damien out of sight, Erin focused her attention on me. "I can leave."

I held her hand and pulled her inside. Without locking it, I closed the door behind us, let her hand go and walked back to the couch to stare at the wall. Erin did the same thing as Damien. She stood in the middle of my condo and tried to make sense out of the destruction. I let her take it all in before we exchanged pleasantries.

"What happened here?" She stepped over the broken glass and stood in front of me instead of standin' on the other side of the coffee table like Damien. Her body was in between my legs as she watched me sit and breathe. I didn't say anything. With her body close to me, a body that was warm and trustworthy, I glanced up at her and smiled. The smile was real. She was beautiful from every angle. She was nothing like the women I met in my past; she was simply beautiful. I wrapped my arms around her waist and pulled her close. With my head resting on her stomach, I listened to her stomach gurgle. I rubbed my hands back and forth as I soothed her back and massaged her booty. She was softer than cotton. I held her closely and listened to her heart beat through her stomach. She stood there, not moving initially, and placed her hands on my shoulders and squeezed back. "Riq…"

"Don't call me that." I inhaled and exhaled. Holding her close to me, I said, "I like when you call me *Tariq*. You're the only one that calls me that. Keep callin' me that."

"Tariq, can you tell me what's going on? What did I walk into?"

I didn't want to discuss my pain. I wanted to hold her close and delight in the fact that she felt warm and soft. I stood up and looked down into her eyes. I loosened the band that tied up her bun and watched her hair fall on her shoulders. When she stared back up at me, I pulled her even closer. I wanted our bodies to touch as I grabbed the back of her head and pressed my lips against hers. I wasn't gentle. After what I'd experienced, there was nothing gentle left inside me. I shoved my tongue in her mouth and covered her lips with mine. I wrung her ass in my palms as she held on to the back of my neck. Then, I held on to her thighs and lifted her up to my waist. She draped her legs around me as we kissed, and I slid my hands up her dress. With her pussy up against my chest, I could feel her fluids beggin' to leak from her panties.

I dropped her on my couch and snatched off her panties. I slid up her dress and pulled down my sweatpants and boxers—no time for foreplay. I spread her legs and pushed myself inside. With her legs still draped around me, she pulled me in deeper as she scratched my back and arched hers. I needed her. I needed her moisture to saturate my dick and make me feel like I was swimming inside her. I felt her come and I ignored it. I couldn't stop even when her body shook uncontrollably. She gritted her teeth as her eyes watered. Our lips met again as our eyes locked. I needed her to look at me with truthful eyes as our tongues played with each other. I stroked her pussy while I played the gimme-gimme inside her. She couldn't stop until I released. I needed to feel myself explode inside her.

She clawed at me as I craved more of her. As she licked the side of my face, I sucked her neck and left my mark on her skin. She was mine, and I wanted the world to know that her body belonged to me. Her body shook again. Her juices rained down on my dick like a tsunami, and I accepted the outpour. I dug deep inside her as she begged me to continue. I obeyed. I couldn't stop if I wanted to. Her skin was too plush, and her pussy too hot. She received every inch of me, and when I bulged, cum released from me like a volcano. I let go. I filled her with all that I could as I kissed her lips and rubbed her skin. I wanted more. I kept goin', and even though my body wanted to go limp, I stroked until I did.

I laid my body on top of her as we caught our breaths. She enclosed me in her arms as we exhaled in unison. I stopped breathing when I heard a phone vibrate. I looked up and searched for it. Erin sat up and grabbed her phone from the floor. Once she shut it off, my mind eased. I sat up and put my clothes back on. Erin sat up and stared at me. "That was…"

"I missed you," I said.

She blushed—rosy cheeks that I yearned to kiss. "I missed you too." She looked around my condo again and sighed. "Are you goin' tell me what happened here yet?"

I shook my head. "I ain't tryna get into all that."

"I thought we were gettin' to know each other."

She smiled and let those dimples shine through. I had to smile back. I didn't want to relive the pain, but I was becoming a sucker for that smile. "A bunch of bullshit wit' everythin', I guess."

"Does it involve your wife?"

I paused. I looked around, finally noticing the damage I did for the first time. I sighed and nodded. "She won't be my wife for long, though. That's fo' damn sho'."

She rubbed my back. I liked when she put her hands on me. I pulled her close to me again and kissed her. I was regaining my strength. I wanted to go for round two, hold her in my arms, and pretend that shit wasn't as bad as it seemed. Suddenly, we heard the door swing open. We both looked at the door and watched as a nigga stood in the doorway. At that moment, I remembered how my distress had caused me to forget to lock the door after Damien left. Erin and I sat on my couch with her leg between my legs and her panties on the floor. Her hair was a mess, and the smell of sex was strong. The dude stood in my doorway, shoulder-length dreads, hands balled into fists as he stared at us, not saying anything.

I stood up and protected the woman I wanted to call my own. Unsure if this was a home invasion, I wasn't goin' let a nigga stand in my spot like he owned the damn place. I tried to shake the feelin' that I saw him before. I wanted answers, and somebody was goin' give 'em to me.

"Louis."

Erin put her panties back on and tied up her hair. Taking another good look at the dark-skinned, dreaded intruder, I realized who the man I was staring at was. Louis, her old man. The man she was supposed to be separated from. For a man she was supposed to be separated from, he looked pretty damn pissed. Erin stood up but didn't move past me. They stared at each other for five seconds. I wasn't in the mood to deal with another man's drama. I stepped aside, leaving Erin vulnerable.

"I thought he was only a friend," Louis said. He showed no feeling. His hands rolled into fists as he turned his attention toward me. I wasn't the one he needed to be looking at. I had more rage built up in me than a bull, and I was looking to charge. I couldn't beat up on the woman that betrayed me time and time again, but I could rip apart the nigga trespassing on my property.

"Who the fuck do you think you are barging into my place like this?"

"What are you doing here, Louis?" Erin's voice was quiet like a whisper and scared like a child.

He didn't even acknowledge me as he stepped closer. He was the cocky zebra, and I was the king of the jungle he thought wouldn't pounce. He stormed into my territory and pranced around my spot like I would let him walk out in one piece. I took a deep breath and tried not to react, but he kept his eyes on me, challenging me. His stance was asking me to prove who the dominant being was in this matchup. He, the zebra, and I, the lion, with a score to settle. "I should be asking you that, Erin. What the fuck are you doing here?"

"Y'all goin' have to take this shit out my place. Right now, this ain't what you want." A thick vein throbbed in the middle of his forehead. He squeezed his fists tighter. He was out for blood, but I was out for guts and glory. I wanted his guts spilt across my floors and the glory of knowing that I could still triumph.

"How the fuck would you know what I want?"

"Louis, I…"

"You in here fuckin' *my* girl." He cut Erin off without a second thought. He took another step in my direction. He was pulling me into a fight, and I let him. "You think you know what the fuck I want?"

"*Your girl?*" Erin's head was down. She couldn't confirm what had already been confirmed. She was his woman, and he caught her in my living room with her panties on the floor. I shook my head and walked closer to him. "Last I checked, y'all were done. If she's your girl, why the fuck is she in my bed every other night?"

My confession stumped him. He turned his attention back to

the woman who deserved it. She rubbed her hands nervously as she cowered a few feet away from me. This wasn't the place for her to confront her wrongdoings. She stood behind me, avoiding eye contact with her and me…Louis. "That's a good fuckin' question."

"How'd you even know I was here?"

He exhaled. He waited on her to speak before he could breathe. He moved a little closer to me. I held my stance, preparing for the expected. "I saw your car."

"That still doesn't explain how you found me here. How'd you know to find me here, Louis?"

"Does it fuckin' matter? You're here, ain't you?"

"Are you following me?"

Louis squeezed his fists tighter. He turned his attention back to me, glancing me up and down. His shoulders were drooped forward, like he had no backbone. His body was tense with fear and confusion. I could use his confusion to my advantage. From his hesitation, I knew he wouldn't do anything. He wanted to attack. When he smelled his woman all over my skin, I could see his eyes play out the frustration in him. He wanted to react, but he was out of his element. Either way, I wanted it. I wanted him to do something. I moved closer to him. He instinctively stepped back, and upon realizing what he'd done, he moved a big step forward. We were but a few feet away, dancing a jig I wanted out of. "Look, bruh, you really need to get out of my living room before—"

"Before what?"

I glided in his direction. His pussyfooting demeanor called me toward him as he challenged me again. He was askin' for it. "Before I make you leave."

He laughed. Louis was in my condo, the same condo I took my rage out on. He stood two feet away from me and laughed as if my threats were empty. In his mind, he was the dominant one in this matchup, and he was doing me a favor by not reacting. He stepped back as if he wanted to walk away, but then he cocked his arm back, anchored by his balled fist. Before his punch could lock, I swung a right. He dropped the arm he cocked back to grab his jaw. Then, I swung a left. He stumbled backward, surprised by my barrage of punches. He threw his hands up to block, and I jabbed his guts. Crouching forward, I uppercut him. He fell to my floor, broken glass scratching his skin. Seeing the wounded zebra sprawled out on my floor, I stomped into his chest, stomach, legs and face. When he tried to get up, I kicked again. For a brief second, I froze when I heard someone screaming.

"Stop!" Erin ran between us and used her body as a barrier between her man and me. Louis quivered beneath her as he recovered. I kicked the back of his leg anyway. Erin threw her hands up. "Tariq, you're gonna kill him. Stop it."

Louis stared up at my ceiling, dazed. He realized that he had no chance of winning this fight. If my condo didn't stand a chance against me, how could he? He pushed Erin away from him and stood up. I lunged at him, hungry for more, but Erin held me back. "You can have this bitch!" Louis cried out. "She ain't worth this shit." Louis stormed out like a tornado.

After ten seconds, I calmed down. I pulled away from Erin. "What the fuck was that?" she asked.

I walked to the front door and looked out into the hallway to make sure I couldn't get in one last blow. I sighed when it finally registered that Louis got away. Slamming the door shut, I locked my front door and then turned to face Erin. "I should be asking you that! Why is yo' nigga following you here?"

"How should I know?"

"I thought y'all weren't together." She prepared a response, but nothing came out. She dropped her shoulders and walked back to my couch. When I stared at her, I was disappointed. She got me into the same situations I tried to avoid. She was no different than the others. "You gotta go."

"Tariq…"

"Erin, I ain't got time to deal wit' yo' bullshit. I don't need random niggas busting into my place lookin' for you. You need to get the fuck out."

"It's not what you think, Tariq."

"Why the fuck are you still here?" I opened the door that led to the other side of my life. I wanted her out of my face and back into the arms of the punk-ass nigga who thought he was the king of my jungle. "I ain't tryna hear shit you gotta say. Apparently, it's a bunch of bullshit anyway."

"That's not fair, Tariq."

"Are you deaf?"

She gave me a blank stare, twirled her neck, and snatched her things up from the floor. Without another word, she stomped her feet toward the exit, bumped past me, and turned the corner down the hallway. I slammed her out of my life and punched another hole into my defenseless wall. I was in a fucked-up situation, and I was losing it.

I went to see Louis. I stood outside his door. Tariq's stench was still embedded in my skin. I held my hand up to knock a couple times, but I couldn't work up the courage. I had to tell Louis something. He was attacked by my lover, not long after I confessed my love for him. My confession was certainly impulsive, but it was said. I owed Louis an explanation. My hair had been tousled by Tariq's loving. My face was dry from the sweat beads that dripped from Tariq's passionate sexing. It was disrespectful of me to be there after what had happened. Louis needed to calm down, as did I. I turned around right before I heard his front door unlock. I had to face my demons. Taking a deep breath, I turned around.

"What are you doing here?" Teona folded her arms over her chest and shifted her weight to her left leg. She eyed me from my open sandals to my disheveled ponytail. Staring back at me in one of Louis's old sweatshirts and no pants, she smiled. "Can I help you wit' somethin'?"

"Where's Louis?"

"Can I help you with somethin'?"

I pulled my lips in. I had words to exchange, but I held my tongue. Louis came to the door. His eye was swollen, lip split, and cheeks bruised. His face was a rainbow of colors—from his purple eye, blistered lips and pink cheeks. He moved Teona to the side and stepped outside. When he closed the door, leaving Teona inside, I was the one with my arms folded over my chest. "What is she doing here, Louis?"

"I'm not fucking her. You sneaking around fucking other guys doesn't mean I'm as trifling as you."

His words stung. I dropped my arms to my side and licked my lips. I tried to caress his disfigured face, but he moved back and grunted. "If that's the case, what is she doing here?"

"Did you come here to explain yourself?"

I stared at the hallway floor. I didn't want him to catch me staring at his bruises. "Why's Teona here? I thought you said there was nothin' goin' on wit' you and her."

"I thought Tariq was married with a family."

"Don't change the subject, Louis."

Louis cocked his head back. He strode backward, unable to be too close to me. His chest rose and fell from irritation. "Don't come here like you have the right to question me. I wasn't fuckin' anybody else but you when we were together." He was speaking in the past tense. He already had ended our relationship, and I had no say.

"You coulda fooled me. First sign of trouble, and she's already half-dressed inside your apartment."

He closed his eyes and shook his head. "I can't believe you, Erin." Opening his eyes, he stared at me as if this were his first time noticing me. He scoured my body, trying to recognize the woman that stood before him. "Teona told me about you…and him."

"Teona? How the fuck would she know about—?"

"I guess when you were leaving his condo or somethin', she saw you."

"While she was prolly screwin' another random stranger, she's out spying on me?"

"I don't give a fuck what she was doin'! She's not my woman! You were! She saw my woman leaving some man's house late at night and told me. I had to see for myself."

"It's not…"

"It's not what? It's not what it seems? You weren't the ho I caught wit' her panties off at some friend's condo."

I moved back. "Don't talk to me like that, Louis."

"Why? You disrespected me first."

"Goodbye, Louis." I turned on my heel and Louis circled around me to stop me in my tracks. "I'm not gonna stand here and let you talk to me any kind of way. I'm sorry, Louis. I'm sorry you found out about Tariq—"

"How long have you been fuckin' him?"

I glared at him. This wasn't the avenue to discuss this. I tried to walk past him, but he blocked me. I stood back and folded my arms again. "I'm not discussin' this with you."

"How long? Did you two *just* finish fuckin' when I caught you two alone in your apartment that night? Is he why you couldn't tell me that you loved me for so damn long? You were too busy fuckin' him?"

"Louis, get out of my way."

"Are you fuckin' serious? I'm standin' here tryna talk to you—"

"No, you're standin' here tryna talk down to me. I know I messed up, but I'm still a grown woman, and I won't stand here and let you talk to me like I'm your child."

Louis threw up his palms and stepped an inch back. He inhaled and exhaled deeply. "Why couldn't you tell me that there was someone else?"

I shrugged my shoulders. "To me, there was no one else. Tariq was…I can't really explain what he was to me. It all *just* happened." When men used that excuse in the past, I ignored it. Sex didn't *just* happen on its own. No man's dick magically fell into another woman's pussy; he led it there. But as I stood there searching for an explanation, I couldn't find one. Tariq *simply* happened.

Louis didn't buy it. He winced as he licked his lips while searching my eyes for an answer. "How don't you know? Last week you loved me, and now you don't know."

"I don't know what to tell you. I'm not proud of it. I understand I was stupid, and if I were sane, it would've never happened."

"Do you even love me?" I looked down at the hallway floor again, unable to come up with an answer. I shrugged my shoulders. "Why would you tell me you loved me if you didn't?"

I looked up at his swollen purple eye and hoped I'd find an answer. Nothing. I had nothing to offer him. "I don't know, Louis."

"Do you love him?"

I never considered answering that question. Even though I kept going back to Tariq, I never considered the possibility of me loving him. Tariq had a hold on me that I couldn't shake. Still, he was married, and he was a dick. I wanted to shake my head and refute any ideas of me loving a man that couldn't understand how to treat a woman right. But when I looked into Louis's eyes, I knew what my answer was. "Yes."

When Louis asked me to love him, I turned from him. I scurried off into Tariq's open arms and tried not to look back. As I stared into his eyes, squinting beneath plump, maroon skin, I was sure that the reason why I couldn't love Louis was because I already loved Tariq. He didn't flinch. He stared back at me with a frown. "Then why did you stay with me?"

"I was...conflicted."

"Don't stand in front of me tellin' me that bull; you were fuckin' him and me at the same time. You can gimme a better explanation than that."

"I can't give you a rational answer, Louis. He doesn't treat me as good as you; he doesn't respect me like you do. I would try to forget about him and love you like you deserved, but it wasn't that easy."

"If I'm so great, then why wouldn't it be easy to stay with me? Erin, I've been here whenever you needed me. Even though we went through our mess wit' Teona, I never stepped out. I loved and respected you, and all I needed from you was the same."

"It's clear that you weren't completely done with Teona, Louis. She's here in her underwear an hour after you—"

"After I got my ass whooped by your boyfriend."

I dropped my shoulders and turned my head. "I'm sorry, Louis, but it's clear that this relationship isn't what either of us wanted."

"Is he even married?" I nodded. Louis turned his scratched nose up in disgust. "Why would a woman like you be with a man like him, Erin? You could've loved me."

"I can't answer that. Nothin' made sense with either of you. When I was wit' you, I wanted to reciprocate, but I couldn't. While I was wit' him, I wanted to be with him. But while I was with you...I dunno what to tell you, Louis. I can't give you an answer that makes sense."

Teona opened Louis's front door and poked her head out. When she noticed Louis and I still talkin', she glared at us. "What is she still doin' here, Louis? Do you remember what she put you through? Tell her to get the—"

"Teona, close the door." Louis didn't raise his voice, but he spoke with conviction. He wasn't making a request. Although he didn't glance in her direction, she knew he was serious.

Stomping her feet into the ground, she slammed the door shut, snapping me out of my senses. I wiped my face and exhaled. "I'm going to go." Louis nodded and moved out of my way. I wanted to walk away before he went back to Teona without any words, but I had to say, "I'm sorry," one more time. He didn't respond. He opened his front door and left me hanging—like I did him.

There were cops everywhere. Men in blue and suited detectives were scattered throughout the front of my apartment building asking questions, taking names, and getting statements. When I walked up to the entrance, a tall, white-basketball-player-looking dude in a cop uniform put his hand up to stop me.

"Excuse me, ma'am. You can't go in here."

"I live here."

Through his thick, blond, and bushy eyebrows, he scanned me up and down as if to wonder how a woman like me could afford to live in such a nice apartment building. "Can I see some ID?"

I huffed as I rifled through my purse and looked for my wallet. When he saw my ID, he nodded and allowed me to pass. He walked to turn away other onlookers. I walked away and sarcastically mumbled, "Thanks a lot."

When I walked up to my apartment, the crowd of cops thickened. I had to squeeze through to get to my apartment door. Across from my door, Alonzo's front door was covered with yellow tape. Forensics were everywhere dusting and photographing. I wanted to stay in the hallway and watch what happened next, but I feared becoming that nosey neighbor that people shunned. After my quick peek, I grabbed my keys and contemplated how soon I'd be able to get the dish.

"Excuse me, miss." I turned around and noticed a stocky detective with pale skin and diamond-blond, balding hair toting a note pad and waving me toward Alonzo's door. I walked over and pretended not to be too eager.

"Yes," I said with a stern expression.

"I'm Detective Remy. You live here?" I pulled out my ID and flashed it in his face. "*You're* Erin?"

I didn't like how he asked that. He already knew me before I was given the courtesy to understand what was going on. I stuffed my ID back in my purse. Trying not to stare at his powdered donut lips, I asked, "What's going on?"

"Your neighbor, Alonzo Logan, did you know him?"

"In passing. Is he okay?"

He took a deep breath and unwelcomingly placed his hand on my shoulder. "He…he committed suicide a couple hours ago. One of the neighbors heard a gunshot and decided to check in on him. Apparently, the neighbor had a spare key, and…she discovered the body." He moved his hand from my shoulder and pointed over at an elderly woman, Mrs. Applebom. She was the old, rich white lady with bad joints and liver spots. I hated passing her in the hallway while she gave me those judgmental looks, as if she knew I was sleeping with men before I was married. She had her face buried in her palms as she sobbed in the arms of a consoling police officer.

"That's horrible." I stood there. He knew who I was, and I wanted him to get to the point about where I fit in to it all.

"He left a note. I can't show it to you because we have to get it processed into evidence, but he mentioned you."

That took me by surprise. The last thing I thought about was Alonzo. Yet, in his last words, he thought about me. It left a bad taste in my mouth, as if it were left from subpar sushi. Nevertheless, I was curious. "What did he say?"

"What do you think he said?"

"I don't know. That's why I'm asking you."

He looked me up and down almost as if he were a bloodhound

smelling the sex and frustration emanating from my skin. "How well did you know Alonzo?"

"I told you, I knew him in passing. We'd chat briefly as we passed each other in the hallway. That's it."

"Did you two ever have a relationship…of any kind?"

"No. What I said is all it was."

He cleared his throat into his fist. "In his note, he mentioned you and your relationship."

"What did his note say about me?" I was tired of fishing for answers. He needed to get to the details.

"I can't remember all of it, but most of it discussed how in love with you he was, and how he wished you had taken more of a liking to him. He expressed annoyance with the men you dated and wrote about how much better he would've been to you. The last thing he mentioned about you was how he'd wait for you to come home and hope he could have a conversation with you. He'd even go as far as standing at your door and listening to hear you breathe."

I was vexed by it all. As he spoke, I thought about all the conversations we'd had. I remembered how he stared at me with an eerie gaze. I realized how there were times he would be going through his mail outside his apartment at the exact same time I'd be walking up to my apartment. "Oh my goodness…"

"Don't be too alarmed. We think the main reason why he committed suicide was because of his business failings."

"From being a stock broker?"

"Stock broker?" He stifled his chuckles and cleared his throat again. "Mr. Logan wasn't a stock broker. He was an auditor who worked for the IRS. He ran a series of tax fraud dealings, cheating the federal government out of thousands of dollars in tax refunds. He was using federal dollars to pay off his debts as a result of his alleged gambling addiction. He was facing twenty years in a federal prison."

"I can't believe this."

Another cop called out and asked Detective Remy to meet him back inside Alonzo's apartment. "I have to get back inside. We wanted to make sure you were okay. We were afraid that it was a possible murder-suicide incident. You have a good night." He walked away without another word, leaving me with more questions. I shook my head toward my apartment door. After all that I'd been through, I couldn't be alone. I pulled my cell phone out and dialed Loraine's number. I was going through too much to spend a night alone.

"Your night has been crazy."

I cut my eyes at Loraine. "You think I don't know that?" We stood in the kitchen as I helped her sort through a box of coupons. She poured the wine, and I sorted the grocery coupons from the drug store clipping.

"I didn't know what to say. Everything from Tariq, to Louis, and now Alonzo. I realized that he was in love with you, but damn."

"Who are you tellin'? He'd stand at my door tryin' to hear me breathe, Loraine." I cringed. "But honestly, I don't want to think about it right now. What's going on in your life? How's the love triangle working out?"

Loraine stood still as I could see a shiver creep up her spine. She licked her lips and twirled her dreads. "I met up with Julian."

"Oh my goodness, girl. How'd that go? Was he as fine as his pictures showed, or did you find out that they were pictures from twenty years ago?"

She smiled. "He looks finer than his pictures. I didn't know what to expect when I met him, but we didn't skip a beat. We fell into a conversation like we've been together for years. It was amazing."

"Where'd you go?"

"We went out to eat at this small café in Winter Park. It was so adorable." Her eyes lit up as she stared into the ceiling. "The chemistry was still there. It all felt so good. He read me more poetry. Girl…" She exhaled and fanned her chest. "It was good, Erin."

"Did you two do more than phone sex this time?"

She giggled. "No. He wanted to. He pressed me to go back to my place, but…I still haven't told Lorenz. I can't sex Lorenz and Julian at the same time. I wanted to though. Girl, Julian wore this fitted dress shirt, open collar, and gray slacks that hugged his butt and his penis at the same time. I was wet before I had a chance to sit down. I wanted him so bad. And his poetry…" She guzzled a half-empty glass of Merlot and wiped her lips. "I dunno how I made it out of there wit' my panties still on."

We laughed. I had to stop sorting coupons. I didn't want to miss a detail. "And all you two did was eat?"

"Well, we ate at first, then we walked to this park. That's where he read me the poetry. And when we kissed, I could feel the rhymes in his poetry breathe life back into me. I wanted him desperately. We caressed each other's bodies like lovers. But…I had to turn him down when he suggested we make love for real." Her smile dropped as her giddiness faded. "I dunno what I'ma tell Lorenz. He thought we were gettin' back together."

"You're choosing Julian?"

Loraine paused, and the smile returned. She nodded. "Hell yes, Erin. I've never felt like this, not even with Lorenz. But I know when I tell Lorenz, it's gonna be crazy."

When we heard knockin' at Loraine's door, we both stopped.

Loraine took another sip of her wine, as did I. She grabbed the front of her maxi dress as she walked toward her front door. Peering into the peephole, Loraine sucked in the air around her and opened the door slowly. When Lorenz walked inside, we both shared a glance. Lorenz walked inside wearing a three-piece suit. Scratching the top of his bald head, he cleared his throat and waved to us both. "How you ladies doing?"

I raised my glass while Loraine kissed him on the cheek. Sensing that Loraine needed to handle her business, I said, "Well, I should get going."

Loraine put her hand up to stop me. She led Lorenz to her couch and sat him down. "I'm glad you're here, Lorenz."

He smiled at her, pleased by her acceptance of his arrival. Unbeknownst to him, she planned to break his heart. "We do need to talk." He looked over at me with a question mark on his face. I was curious to know why I was still there, too.

"I have something to tell you." He didn't say anything. She took a deep breath and swallowed the lump of air in her throat. "We can't do this anymore."

He squeezed his pant legs and balled his fists. "What do you mean, Loraine?"

"I've met someone else. I can't keep leadin' you on like this. You want more, and I can't give you that. Not after what you put me through."

"Loraine, I've changed. Can't you see that? I'm here tryna be the man you deserve. The man I was when we were first together. You wanna throw all this away for some dude you barely know?"

"Well, here's the thing…" She grabbed a lock of hair and crossed her legs. "Your old frat brother, Julian…he's the guy that I've been talkin' to."

"What? Talkin' to *how?*"

"We haven't had sex, but I met him online. I didn't know he was your frat brother at first, not until I saw him in person."

"How…what are you…how long?"

"A few months."

Lorenz stood up and paced the floor. He looked more irritated than angry. I tried not to watch, but with a train wreck right before my eyes, I could do nothing less. He wiped the sweat from the top of his head and then squeezed his fists. He looked down at Loraine and frowned. "What has this man told you?"

"What do you mean?"

"Did you have sex with this man?"

"No. I told you I didn't." Loraine stood up and attempted to hold a strong defense. "Lorenz, I know this is hard, but…"

"Do you know why I stopped talkin' to him? Do you remember that he was married when you first met him?"

"Vaguely, but he told me he got a divorce. I don't care why you two stopped being friends, Lorenz. What does that have to do with me?"

"His wife left him 'cause he cheated on her."

"He tol' me that, too. I know what you're trying to do, and it won't work. I want to be with him."

Rubbing his face, he shook his head and continued to pace the floor. "Did he tell you what happened after he cheated?"

"Why does that matter?" Loraine put her hands on her hips and rolled her neck.

Lorenz stopped pacing and calmed his shoulders. Staring into Loraine's eyes, he whispered, "He caught something."

Loraine jerked her head back in disbelief. "Whatever, Lorenz. Why are you doin' this? You think you can—"

"AIDS, Loraine. He contracted AIDS. That's why his wife left him."

Loraine swallowed another lump in her throat. She grabbed another lock of her hair and walked to the other side of her couch. "Is this a joke to you, Lorenz?"

"Why would I joke about this? After his wife left him, he was messed up. He loved her, and he fucked up. He couldn't find another woman who would be willin' to date a man with AIDS. After a while, he stopped tellin' them. I couldn't stay cool with a man as trifling as that."

"You're wrong, Lorenz. You're so full of shit. Julian isn't...you don't know what the fuck you're talking about!"

Lorenz shrugged his shoulders and stuffed his hands in his pockets. "Ask him yourself. If I'm lying, you don't have to ever speak to me again."

They stared at each other. My hands shook as I stood in the kitchen, a voyeur into their dialogue. Loraine chewed on her bottom lip as she stared at her floor spinning her locks. "Get out."

"Loraine..."

"Get the fuck out, Lorenz. I'm done with this conversation. You need to leave."

Lorenz put up his hands in surrender. He walked to her door and spoke softly as he said, "Ask him, Loraine. Don't take my word for it."

He walked out and closed the door behind him. Loraine stood behind her couch spinning, twirled her dreads, and began tapping her foot. I walked up behind her and patted her shoulder. She jumped as she turned to face me. "Are you okay?"

She shook her head. "He practically begged me to fuck him, Erin. Begged me. If it weren't for Lorenz, I would've, too. What if Lorenz is right?"

I found Loraine's phone from her kitchen counter and handed it to her. "Only one way to find out."

She pulled the phone out of my hand and whimpered. "What if

he's right, Erin? I remember the day Lorenz stopped talkin' to Julian. He cut him off like he was nothing. And Lorenz doesn't shun friends for nothing. He's loyal, to his friends at least. And this was his frat brother, his line brother. They were close. What if he's right?"

"Call him."

Loraine looked down at her phone, dropped it on the floor and shook her head. "No, I'm going to ask him in person. I have to know, and I have to see his face when he answers me." Loraine seized her purse and car keys from the coffee table.

"Do you want me to go with you?"

"No, I have to do this on my own." She stomped out of her front door and didn't look back. I stood in the middle of her living room with my heart racing.

CHAPTER 32

Erin

"**G**et dressed. *We're going clubbin'.*" I read Loraine's text briefly. I hadn't heard from her in a couple days. I blew her phone up wanting to make sure she was all right, but I never received a response. All the while, Louis had been blowing me up looking to rekindle what we had. He had more time to think, and he was ready to forgive; I was done, though. Tariq hadn't said a word. I wasn't in the mood to go clubbin'. My mind was an emotional dumpster, and I couldn't handle strangers asking for dances I wasn't in the mood to give. I also didn't feel like avoiding flirtatious innuendos. When Loraine wanted to go clubbin', she was lookin' for an outlet to release a frustration that liquor couldn't wash away. Still, I wanted to lie in bed and watch Lifetime movies.

Tariq texted me. After he kicked me out of his condo, I hadn't expected to ever hear from Tariq. I didn't want to. I relished in the possibility of being rid of him. My purpose in going to see Tariq was to end things. I couldn't be with a man who couldn't end a marriage he refused to address. Still, I had to read it. When his three-and-a-half-line text appeared in my inbox, I sat up and wiped the Goldfish cracker crumbs from my sweatshirt. "*She signed the divorce papers, it's done. I can't get you out of my mind. I wanna talk to you.*"

I texted back, "*I'm done with you. I thought you were done with me too.*"

The three minutes it took to receive a response were the longest three minutes of my existence. I shouldn't have been looking for a response, but I figured one was coming. When it finally came through, I hesitated. I was scared of what he had to say next. My hand shook. I had to stand up and pace my bedroom floor. There were so many thoughts going through my mind. Two nights ago, my lover and my man had it out, leaving Louis bloody and swollen. I cringed when I felt a pain creep up the left side of my skull. I took a deep breath and prepared myself for whatever was about to come next. *"I don't know if I can ever be done with you. Throwin' you out like that was fucked up on my part. My mind was gone. Can I come over?"*

My hand shook badly, I jumped when my phone banged against my carpeted bedroom floor. I finger-combed my hair and held my headboard for support when I felt the room spin. I didn't respond. I closed my eyes and stopped breathing. I refused to open my eyes until things started making sense. This morning, I was happy with the way things ended with Tariq. With Tariq married, there was no future for us, no matter how well he tried to sell it. Now, Tariq gave me options. Options that I should ignore. I didn't want to hear it anymore. I wanted peace of mind. Instead of texting back, I ran into the shower and left my phone on the floor.

As I toweled off from a quick and hot shower, I saw the red indicator on my phone blinking. I ignored it. I rummaged through my closet in search of an outfit. When I found my beige Herve Leger bandage dress, I squeezed into it and slipped into snakeskin platform pumps. I combed my hair down, pinned the front up, and let my diamond studs sparkle. Dressed to kill, I finally picked my phone up from the floor and sighed. The first text was from Loraine. *"Are you down, or not?"*

I swiftly replied back. *"On the way."*

The second text was from Tariq. *"After all I put you through, I can't blame you for wanting to be done with me. But I need to spend the night with you. Can I come over, please?"*

"I already made plans with Loraine."

I grabbed my keys and clutch purse as I rushed out the door. My haste suggested the possibility that I was fleeing from a predator. I was. I couldn't handle my love life preying on my psyche as it did. Now, I needed strange men asking me for a dance and flirtatious innuendos. I could handle *that*. Those men meant nothing to me. I could easily flip my hair in their faces as I strutted off with no remorse. I held the power as I rejected their advances and pretended not to hear their dance requests.

Once I sat in my driver's seat, I let go of my chaos and embraced a night full of tipsy slurs and overcrowded dance clubs filled with overpriced cologne and too-tight freakum dresses. Another text from Tariq came. *"Call me when you get back. Doesn't matter the hour."*

I threw my phone down in the cup holder and flew down the 408, leaving my confusion in the wind.

When I got home around three-thirty in the morning, tired and drunk, I forced Loraine to stay the night with me. I was vulnerable. She barely put up a fight. The first half-hour of the club was slow. People were gettin' their drinks, and the DJ kept playin' songs no one heard of. The dance floor was bare, and I had already dodged three dance requests, one coming from the typical eighty-year-old man who spent his nights reliving his glory days by putting on his high school Cosby sweater, snot-colored slacks, and old-man penny loafers. When he ran his fingers through his balding, gray hair and smiled a mouth full of gold teeth, I gave a quick head turn as Loraine and I laughed ourselves to another corner.

I ignored texts from Tariq all night. I needed my space, and he would not let up. I deleted his many texts. *"Don't forget about me tonight"* and *"I'm willing to put it all out on the table. You can come over here if you want."* With each text he sent, I downed another green apple martini. Eventually, I upgraded to Long Islands before stepping up to the big boy leagues and gorging shots of Patrón and Hennessy. I wouldn't have gotten so drunk had it not been for Louis's text message. *"I didn't run back to Teona. I still want to make this work. I think you were the one."* That text is what led me to the shots.

Soon, I stopped declining dance invitations and found myself gettin' low to the flo' halfway through the night. I even gave Cosby Sweater a chance. I rubbed his beer belly and pumped my fists to the music of Jessie J. Loraine stopped short of grabbing me by my ear when she dragged me out the club before I went down as one of *those* girls.

"I need you to stay with me tonight," I mumbled through slurred speech.

Loraine helped me up to my apartment and laid me down on my couch. "I might as well. You can't drive me home."

I threw my arms up and wrenched her close to me into a forced hug. "Thanks, girl. I can't be alone tonight."

"Apparently." Loraine pulled away, kicked her shoes off, and slung her jacket across my armchair. "You can barely sit upright, let alone take care of yourself."

"No, that's not what I mean." I slung myself over my couch and closed my eyes. The room spun, and I couldn't think straight while my living room ran laps around me. "I'm gonna call him if you...if you leave...me." I could barely get my words in order with all the thoughts attempting to clamber out of my dehydrated mouth at once.

"Call who? Louis?"

I grabbed the purse that fell through my fingers to my hardwood floors and searched through it. I shook my head and mumbled, "N...no." When I found my phone, I silently reread one of the texts Tariq sent me. *"U home yet? I hope you not still mad at me. I need you here wit' me."*

I let my phone fall back to the floor. Loraine watched me with perplexity as she tried to read my mind. "Who are you gonna call, Erin?"

We eyed each other with confusion. "What are you talkin' about?"

"You said you were gonna call him. Who's *him?*"

I closed my eyes and tried to remember the last thing I said to Loraine before more thoughts scurried through my brain. I unclipped the front of my hair and scratched my scalp. When I glanced at my phone, I frowned. "Oh," I shouted. "Tariq."

"Tariq?" Loraine shouted back. "Why are you gonna call Tariq? After how he treated you?"

I kicked off my shoes and turned over on the couch to where my back faced the TV. Tired of how fast the room spun, I wanted to close my eyes and prepare for the weekend. My mind wasn't in the right place to hold a rational conversation with Loraine. I kept my eyes closed and dreamt about a two-headed lion that pleasured himself on my bed. One head belonged to Tariq, and the other one belonged to Louis. Before they had the chance to beckon my inclusion in their threesome, I felt an incessant tapping on my shoulder.

I turned over to see Loraine standing over me with her hands on her hips. "What?" I grunted.

"Why are you gonna call Tariq?"

"Tariq called?" I snatched my phone from the floor and scrolled through. Another text from Tariq that came through. *"You got my mind trippin'. I keep starin' at my phone waitin' on you to call. I got some shit to get off my chest."* I shrugged my shoulders.

Loraine snatched the phone from my hand and smacked my shoulder. "Erin, answer me."

"Answer you? Answer you about what?"

"Tariq! What's going on? Are you still seeing Tariq even after he kicked you out of his place?"

I blinked a few times in hopes that I could blink away my bad dream. "I dunno what you're talkin' about. Can I go to sleep?"

Loraine stood over me for a while. Soon, the area around her faded to black. The last thing I saw was Loraine rolling her eyes as everything went dark. Suddenly, the two-headed lion reappeared in my bedroom and asked me to join in.

When I heard my shower running, I shot up from my couch. The sunlight raked through my blinds, almost blinding me. I threw the back of my wrist over my face to block the searing sunlight from burning my retinas. As I sat up, I massaged my scalp, tryna bore out the sound of chirping in my skull. The more conscious I became, the more rapidly the chirping upgraded to loud chiming. I squeezed my eyes shut as I shunned the effects of a hung-over morning. When I looked down and realized I was dressed in my Victoria's Secret pajama pants and Old Navy sweatshirt, it became clearer that my night last night was more hectic than I hoped. The sound of the shower increased as it jammed its presence into my earlobes, banging against my eardrums and compelling me to pay attention.

Finding my BlackBerry on the floor, I picked it up and hoped I could make sense of everything. As I scrolled through my text messages, my post-drunken binge evolved into a horror film. The last text I got from Tariq was, *"I'm 'bout to roll through."* The text wouldn't have freaked me out as much if the text seven minutes after it from Louis hadn't read, *"I have some things to discuss with you. I'm coming over."*

The fight scene from Tariq's condo flashed through my mind. I jumped off my couch and rushed toward the sound of my bathroom shower. There was no sign of Loraine, and I didn't know who was in my bathroom. I rushed into my bedroom, hoping I'd see the scattered clothes of the intruder showering in my bathroom. I dropped my phone on my bed and set my sights on my bathroom door. I stormed through the door and stopped when I realized who had been showering.

"What the hell!" Loraine shrieked as I stood in the bathroom door more confused than I was before I walked in there. She promptly turned the shower off and grabbed her towel from my towel rack. Having wrapped herself in my guest towel, she walked out and asked, "Are you okay?" Her question sounded more like, *"Are you crazy?"*

I felt crazy. There was no sign of Louis or Tariq, and I didn't know what happened after getting those two messages.

Tired of being confused, I sat on my toilet seat and dropped my thumping head between my thighs. "What happened last night?" My words were muddled through clenched teeth and dry lips.

Loraine took a deep breath as she finished drying off. "You were drunk last night."

"How much did I have to drink?"

"I had to pretty much carry you out the club."

I sat back up and leaned on my bathroom sink. Loraine stood in the doorway, blocking the rays of sunlight that tried to barge into our conversation. I had to know. "Did anyone come over?"

"You mean, did Louis come over?" I nodded my head and hoped that's all she knew. She smiled and asked, "Or are you wondering if Tariq came by, too?"

I put my head back between my thighs and tried not to hyperventilate. "What happened last night, Loraine? I can't remember anything."

"I didn't think you would." Loraine walked into my bedroom closet and searched for some old clothes to throw on while she let me sit literally on the edge of my seat. I sat in the steamy bathroom catching my breath until I finally followed her into my bedroom. I collapsed atop my mattress and stared at my ceiling. When she walked out of my closet, I watched as she threw on an old pair of sweats. She tied her dreads up and sat next to me. "I should've been the one drunk last night. I'm mad you stole my thunder."

"Girl, Louis and Tariq kept blowing me up last night. I needed to drown my frustrations. What happened with Louis and Tariq, though? Did they come over?"

"No. I texted them and told them you were takin' care of me 'cause I was too drunk to take care of myself. They were both pretty understanding." She lay back and sighed, rubbing her forehead.

"Why didn't I see those texts? The last text messages in my phone said they were coming over."

"I deleted the ones I sent. Wanted to scare you. I was really mad that you stole my thunder." She giggled.

"What do you mean?" I closed my eyes and gasped when I realized that I hadn't spoken to Loraine since she went to confront Julian. When I stared at her, her face was pale and lifeless, almost as if I already knew the outcome of their confrontation. "What happened when you saw Julian?"

She pulled a loc from her ponytail and pursed her lips. "He didn't say shit." She sat up and slouched her shoulders forward. "I told him I needed to see him. We met up at Chili's. I told him what Lorenz told me. He didn't even look surprised. He kept his mouth shut. Like…" She sighed. "I asked him would he have told me if I did agree to have sex with him, and the nigga shrugged his shoulders."

I raised my eyebrows in disbelief. Loraine kept playing in her hair as she spoke softly and slowly.

"The man I met before wasn't there. He was a completely different person. He was heartless and showed no regard for my well-being. He could've killed me, literally, and he didn't care."

"Why didn't you tell me this last night?"

"I didn't expect you to get so drunk." She smiled as if to tell me she didn't blame me. I still felt bad. She obviously needed a friend, and I turned last night into her taking care of me. She inhaled and wiped her cheeks as a few tears trickled down. "I dunno what to think."

"Have you spoken to Lorenz?"

"And say what? That I left him to be with a man who wanted to kill me?"

"You dodged a bullet. I know what he did was messed up, but this could've been really bad. The worst that came out of this is a broken heart."

"Somehow, I still don't feel better. I would've protected myself. I carry my own condoms in case something happens. But, I thought he was the one, or real close to it. He fooled me. How the fuck could I be so stupid that I'd fall for a man who…a man like that?"

"You're not stupid, Loraine. Men are good at their game when they need to be."

"You know what he did tell me?" Loraine dug her fingernails into her palms and tightened her jaw as she stared aimlessly at my bedroom wall. "He's not sorry. He had real feelings for me, and he knew I wouldn't have felt the way I did had I known. He said he was happy for the time we spent and was hurt by the fact that I was ending things. *He* was fucking hurt."

I felt my phone vibrating on the bed behind us. I grabbed it and frowned at Tariq's interruption. His text read, *"Good morning. Hope you slept well. Breakfast?"* I wasn't in the mood.

"Are you gonna see Lorenz?"

Loraine shook her head and sucked in her bottom lip. "I'm too embarrassed to face him."

"You know he's gonna call, asking if you spoke to Julian."

"I know." Loraine shrugged her shoulders and twisted her dreads. "Erin, what am I gonna tell this man? What if he laughs in my face?"

"He's not gonna laugh in your face."

"I would. I threw him aside. I was ready and willing to throw him to the curb for one of his oldest friends, only to find out that I was the idiot. I don't know when I'm gonna be able to face him. I know it won't be soon, though."

Another text came through. *"Is your friend still there? Can we talk?"* asked Louis. I sighed and felt it was time to turn my phone off and put on some regular clothes. "Let's go somewhere."

Loraine lay back and threw her arm over her eyes, shielding her tears from me. "Where?"

"Anywhere. You can cry on my shoulder. We can watch old movies and can contemplate spray-painting Julian's car with the word 'Murderer' in scarlet-red lettering."

Loraine smiled a quick smirk that I almost mistook for a face spasm. "If I was the one who got drunk last night, we'd be over there right now spray-painting. Hell, I considered hacking into his on-line account and plastering his sexually transmitted disease status all over his profile to ward off other unsuspecting women."

"I know a guy at work."

Loraine paused. Reluctantly, she whispered, "No. Not now at least. Talk to me after you carry my drunk butt up my driveway, and I might be more inclined."

In an effort to lighten the mood, I went back to my previous suggestion. "Let's get a hotel room and get away from the drama in our lives."

Loraine sat up and stared at her feet. After a long and hard sigh, she sniffled and dropped her shoulders. "I need somethin' like that."

"Let's go—right now. Leave your phone here and we'll get away."

Loraine picked up her phone. We both noticed the flashing red indicator. "Julian has been callin' me all night. No texts. But my phone is flooded with his empty calls every ten minutes." She shot up and headed for my bathroom. When I heard the toilet flush, I shot up, too. We both stood at my toilet as the water rose to the top, Loraine's phone stuck at the bottom.

Whenever we got back from our hotel getaway, I was gonna be pissed as I spent the next three hours on the phone with my maintenance man tryna explain why there was a phone in my toilet. But right then, I chuckled as Loraine's first smile in days finally peeked through.

"Good work on Exposé Cosmetics."

Eric's compliment caught me off-guard. We stared at each other. He was waiting on my gratitude, and I was waiting for the other shoe to drop. "Thanks."

My weekend away was a necessary luxury. Loraine and I splurged on a deluxe suite that we couldn't afford and gorged on overpriced room service. It was three days and two nights of uninterrupted girl talking, junk-food binging, and expensive wine slurping. I didn't even go home once our getaway was over.

I squeezed into Loraine's work clothes and jetted off to work in time to receive the reviews on my work from Surreptitious, now Exposé, Cosmetics. My work was good, but I hadn't expected a pat on the back from Eric. "I don't say this often, but I really value your work here."

Two compliments in a row. I had to keep myself from lookin' out the window in search of flying pigs. Takin' another look at Eric's tamed mane, I had to attribute part of his good mood to the fact that he finally met a stylist that his salt-and-pepper curls could agree with. He even dressed relaxed in his cool gray dress shirt and pleated slacks. "That's good to hear."

"When Vivian came to me with the hopes of revamping her ad campaigns, the only person I knew who could take on a project of that magnitude was you." Three compliments. He was going for a record. "I trust your work here, and that's why I recommended you for a promotion."

Eric was definitely going for a record. "What do you mean?"

"Our sister company is looking for a PR director. They asked me for a recommendation, and I recommended you. Even though you're not as experienced as many of their current candidates, you're the best for the job."

"Why didn't you recommend yourself?"

He chuckled. I'd never saw him chuckle in the four years I'd worked there. "This company wouldn't survive without me. I'm satisfied here, but I know you want more. Here's your shot." I finally smiled. He was serious. Eric wasn't tryna trick me into a forced heart-to-heart. He had genuine good news for me. "Do you need time to think about things?"

"Hell no!" I slapped my palm over my lips and swallowed the air in my throat. Eric laughed at my lack of control. It was hard containing my excitement. "I mean, I want this."

"I knew you would. Two things, though. You don't have the job yet. I could only recommend you. You still have to interview. But if you do get the job, you will have to move."

In my excitement, I forgot that our sister company was located in North Carolina. My initial zeal faded. I wasn't sure I was ready to move that far away. "If I got it, when would I have to move?"

"They'd give you two weeks to a month, and they'd also pay for your moving expenses. They need somebody as soon as possible. It's a great opportunity. I know you've been in Orlando for quite some time, but it might be time for a change."

"When's the interview?"

"Today."

The night before, I was recovering from a serious, hotel-candy sugar high and wondering how I was going to get through the messes in my life. Right then, I had an interview in tight clothes for a job that they'd ask me to uproot myself for two weeks. However, as I glanced around my cubicle, I quickly realized the opportunity my boss had put before me. "When do I go in?"

"You hidin' from me."

I stopped when I noticed Tariq outside my job in a royal-blue, two-door Chevy. It was a '75 Chevy Corvette, with shiny chrome rims that showed my reflection. It had plush, royal-blue leather interior that looked like it'd hug my skin as soon as I sat inside. It was a change from the G he threw me out of once. "I see you fixed up yo' daddy's Chevy."

A smile of accomplishment peeled across his face as he nodded and opened his passenger door. "Come take a ride wit' me."

I shook my head and waved to my coworkers as they rushed to their cars in an attempt to beat the five o'clock traffic. "I have to get home. I haven't been home in a few days."

"I know. I went by to see you a couple times."

"You stalkin' me now?"

"I gotta do what I gotta do."

"How do you even know where I work?"

"You told me you worked here on our first date. I remembered."

I nodded. "Apparently." A few guys stood around Tariq's car, eyeing the royal-blue masterpiece that sat before their eyes. I brushed past them as I walked toward my car. I could hear Tariq turning off the engine. The sound of his doors slammin' shut quickly followed.

"Erin, where are you goin'?"

I didn't turn around as I pulled out my keys to unlock my car door. When I felt Tariq's hand on my arm, I pulled away and folded my arms across my chest. "Why are you here, Tariq?"

"I been tryna talk to you for the longest."

"Ain't it obvious that I don't wanna talk to you?"

"Why? I tell you I divorced my wife, the shit you been grillin' me on since the beginnin', an' now you don't wanna talk."

"You kicked me out, remember that?"

"You threw me out yo' place many times. The one time I throw you out—"

"I'm not talking to you about this, Tariq. Especially not at my job."

Tariq glanced back at his car. A dozen people crowded around it, ogling the alloy wheels and peerin' inside, scratching their chins in amazement. He twirled around to face me again. "Well, let me take you for a ride. We can talk somewhere else."

"I don't wanna talk to you at all. I really wanna get home."

"Let me take you."

Pointing at my car, I said, "I don't need a ride home."

"Can I meet you at yo' place?"

"You're not gettin' it. I don't want to talk to you, at all. Not here and not later."

Tariq rubbed his forehead and looked back at his car. A few more people had pulled out their camera phones to take pictures. "I don't like all these people 'round my car." Suckin' his teeth, Tariq stared me up and down. "I want us to talk."

"I don't." I took a deep breath. "I'm moving."

He threw his head back and dropped his jaw. "Movin' where?"

"Out of Florida."

"When?"

"Two weeks, maybe a month."

"Two weeks!" He stepped back and scratched the back of his neck. "Whatchu mean, Erin? I left my wife—"

"I didn't ask you to. I'm tired of playin' on yo' rules. You've thrown me out of your car, your home, disrespected me, and I always come back. I'm done. I had an interview for another job, and I got it. It pays more, and it's what I want to do. There's nothin' holdin' me here."

Tariq dropped his balled fists to his sides as he looked me up and down, taking my words as salty insults. "It's like that?"

"Tariq, all we had was sex. I barely know anything about you. You barely took the time out to learn anything about me. My emotions are subject to whateva shit you're goin' through. Sometimes you treat me great, and then other times, I'm sliding down a damn fire escape to escape your wife. Did you think I was gonna keep dealin' wit' this bull forever?"

"That's why I'm here ready to talk to you."

"Yea, because you feel like it. You could've talked to me before you threw me out of your condo. I'm not doing this anymore. It really doesn't matter what you have to talk to me about, Tariq. I'm done, for good."

Tariq breathed deeply as he stepped away from me. "I'm not goin' make you give up a better job." His tone changed. It was solemn and comatose. "You know the shit I felt for you was more than the shit you're talkin', but you ain't tryna hear that shit."

I raised my shoulders. "Actions speak louder than words."

Tariq nodded and turned on his heel. He shooed the crowd of admirers away from his car and revved the engine. It was an angry sound that roared as he drove away. As I watched him disappear from the parking lot, I couldn't shake the feelin' of calm I felt. It was an unfamiliar feelin' that I wasn't used to feelin'. One of those emotions I only felt when I'd made a good decision. I was happy to drive home without the hope of good sex in the morning. For the first time in my relationship with Tariq, I chose myself.

The tattered yellow tape scattered around my apartment building left the reminder of an unspoken danger that lived across the hall from me. I stood at my door as chills ran up my spine. I hated thinkin' about Alonzo. I slid my key into my keyhole to close my door behind me, hoping to eventually forget his memories. Still, as I opened the door to my apartment, I wasn't fleeing all danger. Closing the door behind me, I turned on the lights and literally felt my heart jump up the back of my throat as I noticed the tall, black figure across from me. It was Louis on one knee, ring in tote. I couldn't stop my eyes from rolling.

My heart finally slid back into its rightful place. Louis brushed his dreads off his shoulders and stared at me. My fluorescent lights beamed off the bling from the rock in his palm and the pure white suit he'd clothed himself in. My bright lights also illuminated the purplish, blackish bruise that Tariq left on his eye. He didn't have to ask. We both knew the question. "How'd you get in here, Louis?"

"I told your maintenance man I wanted to surprise you. As a recent newlywed, he was happy to participate." I dropped my things on my kitchen counter and took a deep breath. "Are you going to answer me? I've been sitting on bended knee for hours." He smiled a smile of hope—a blinding hope that meant nothing to me at that point.

Inhaling deeply, I responded, "No." Although it was a firm and steadfast rejection that needed no explanations, one would be needed.

His smile dropped as quickly as it appeared. He didn't move. The ring still stuck out, begging me to try it on while his knee dug a dent into my floor. "...no?"

"No, Louis. Wit' all the shit we been through, why would you even wanna marry me?"

"It's my fault you cheated. I fucked up a lot. But I wanna prove to you that you're who I wanna be with."

"I don't need reassurance." It was time to stop beating around the bush. "I'm moving to North Carolina in a few weeks."

He stood up and reluctantly closed the ring box. My heart leapt a quarter of a centimeter when the box slammed shut. Every girl wants a diamond ring shoved in her face, and it's gonna hurt when it goes away, no matter what. "What?"

"I got a promotion."

"Erin, I..."

"Louis, I'm putting myself first. I've put myself in these crazy situations, and I'm too grown for this. There are a hundred reasons why I know what we had wouldn't work and—"

"So, you're runnin' back to him?"

"No. *He* is not the problem. My heart's not in this. I need to do what's best for me, and that means turning down your proposal and taking a job that I've dreamed about taking for years."

"Did you even consider how this would affect me?"

My eyes went to rolling again. "I have thought about it. I know that *this* isn't what I want. Maybe in the future we can be—"

"I'm not gonna sit around waitin' for you."

"I'm not asking you to."

"I can find someone who won't put me through this shit. You cheated on me and—"

"Look, Louis. I understand you're hurt..."

"*Hurt?* Since we first got together, I've put everything into this relationship while you've been lettin' another man put everything into you."

"Louis, we're not gettin' into this."

"Why? Because you say so? I'm not the little bitch you might think I am."

"Louis, you have to go."

He tied his dreads up. "No, we're goin' finish this shit. I put my all into you, Erin. I treated you with respect, and you dogged me out. You don't get to throw me out until you give me an explanation. Was I not man enough for you? Was I too much man for you?"

Louis was changing. In the beginning, Louis was soft and gentle. Now, due to my actions, he was someone else. I hadn't realized how my actions would affect Louis. He was hurt, but I justified my actions with his transgressions. After he kept things from me, I let Tariq do to me and be to me what Louis wanted to do and be. I never gave my all to Louis, and now he was left picking up the remains from his shattered emotions. I was guilty. He was my judge, and the anger and pain in his eyes dealt me my sentencing—the fact that my selfishness would undoubtedly be the cause for Louis's mistreatment of his next woman.

I took a deep breath and let my hair down while I threw up the white flag. I was done with the innuendos and ambiguity. Louis was my man once. At one point in my life, Louis was the man I spoke of when I rejected a number of suitors. Yet, I threw him aside without respecting him with the effort of treating him right and giving him the true benefits of a real relationship. Leaning up against my kitchen counter, I spread my feet apart and twirled a strand of hair as I channeled Loraine's frustration habits.

"One minute I'm here wanting to be with you, then next thing you know, I'm battling my feelings for someone else. I got into a relationship with you way before my feelings for him were completely resolved. I excused my actions because I shouldn't have feelings for him. I was forcing myself to be with you while searching for reasons to give up on you." I shrugged my shoulders at him. I was hoping he'd find resolve in my muddled explanations.

He stared at me with motionless irritation. His lips curled up into snarls, unsatisfied with my words. "You are so full of shit, Erin."

Regardless of how confusing or erratic my thoughts may have sounded, they were all I had to give. I opened my door and pointed my head in the direction of the hallway. "I'm not throwing you out, but I have nothing more to say to you. This isn't working. If you need to blame it all on me, do what you feel is best so long as you leave. This situation is done."

I couldn't think of any other way to explain myself. I was honest, and most importantly, I was done with our conversation. I needed him out of my life. Now more than ever, I needed to lock the door behind him, strip naked, and take a long bubble bath. Louis licked his bottom lip and chuckled. He chuckled one of those egotistical "this bitch" type of chuckles. He strolled out with a pimp-like stroll and stopped short of walking out my door.

Glaring at me, he closed his eyes and slammed his fist into the wall two inches away from my head. As I held my chest and slid back into the skin I jumped out of, I glared back at him, daring him to make another move he'd regret.

A breath away from my face, he whispered, "Well, since this shit is done, I should tell you. That email I sent you telling you that I loved you was supposed to go to Teona. Clearly, you were a mistake. I don't think I ever loved you."

Cocking my head back, I pointed at the hallway and folded my arms across my chest with that black-girl swag he was used to by dealing with a girl like Teona. After a brief pause, he stepped back and walked away with the same pimp-like stroll that was about to get the cops called on him.

Locking the door behind me, I took my finger off the call button of my BlackBerry and slid my phone out of Loraine's pants pockets, clearing out my pre-dialed nine-one-one digits. Louis's threat didn't warrant a response. However, I was prepared to call the cops had he tried me. Usually, I left my phone on my kitchen counter while I bathed; tonight, I needed my phone next to me in case Louis made his way back inside.

This day had been too crazy.

CHAPTER 34

Erin

"I missed you so much, baby...ooh, yes. Please go deeper."

I skipped my bath. I didn't feel safe at home. I disrobed, threw on a pair of flannel pajamas, and popped up at Loraine's with a bag of her work clothes in tote. Yet, as I leaned into her entrance with my ear on her wood door, I realized that it might have been best to call ahead. I thought about facing my fears and driving back home, but I was distracted by the loud thumping sound banging into her door.

"Shit! Don't stop...ooh...yes...damn, Lorenz...I want more." The thumping sped up and grew more furious as her screams escalated. "Ah! Yes! Lorenz...keep going, no, right there...yea, right there, baby...shit!"

Suddenly, the banging slowed down and Loraine's screams deescalated to moans and whimpers. "I missed you, too," I heard Lorenz's voice say.

Now was my time to knock before they started their next round. Silence, initially. I could hear her door unlocking. "Erin..."

I nodded as I held up her bag of clothes. Lorenz was nowhere in sight. Loraine's dreads were everywhere as she stood draped in a long silk robe. "I wanted to drop off your clothes."

She looked me up and down and pursed her lips. "Were you listening at my door again?"

The stench of guilt had given me up. I snickered. "Don't you guys ever have sex in a bed?"

She let me in. "You are so nasty." Two seconds later, Lorenz walked out of Loraine's bedroom dressed in a three-piece pinstriped suit; dry sweat beads tattooed his neck and forehead. "Erin's here, babe."

Lorenz waved hello and walked into Loraine's kitchen to grab a drink of water.

"Where's he going all dressed up? Does he have a different three-piece suit for every day of the week?"

Loraine giggled. "He stopped by after he got off work. What are you really doing here?"

"I have too much to tell you about my day."

We both stared at Lorenz, who stood in the kitchen gulping down his glass of tap water. He raised his hand and shook his head. "I'm on my way out now."

Walking to Loraine, he pulled her waist as they fawned over each other on their way to the door. With a sweet-as-watermelon kiss goodbye, Lorenz walked out her door and left Loraine fanning herself.

"I see you talked to Lorenz."

Loraine smirked as she fell atop her couch, the smell of sex marinating all around us. "That weekend away really helped me clear my head." She kicked the panties at her feet under her couch in an attempt to hide her dirty sex escapade. "I was gonna call him when I got home, but he was standing outside my door. We talked, and he was very understanding. He was considerate, respectful, and compassionate. He was everything I ever wanted him to be. I had to let him claim my pussy, girl; he was askin' for it."

I laughed as we slapped five. "Go 'head, woman. I'm happy. You didn't need a man like Julian in yo' life anyway."

"Thanks, but enough about me. Tell me what happened to you. I know it has something to do with your men."

I scratched the top of my head. I slightly cringed as I recalled recent events. "Tariq surprised me outside my job." Loraine's eyes bulged as she leaned in for details. "He wanted to talk."

"What happened?"

"Nothing. I was done. I can't deal wit' it. He left upset, but there's nothin' I could do. I was fed up. But…" Tariq's news wasn't as bad as the next low-life I encountered. "Louis took the cake today. Not only did I have to reject his happenstance proposal. But after I said no, he had the nerve to try to punch a hole into my wall *right* next to my head and then tell me that I was a mistake."

Loraine's mouth dropped as she struggled to process it all. "I can't believe he turned out to be such a lunatic."

I shook my head and waved it off. "Honestly, I played a major part in his behavior. I toyed with his emotions, and when men put their all into something only to find out that they've been played, they take it hard. Some men take it harder than others. Louis was one of those men."

"How do you feel about it all?"

"At peace. I mean, I was a lil' fearful of staying home alone since Louis was able to sneak into my house once before."

"Now I understand why you're here at ten at night."

I hesitated to tell her the next bit of news. "There's one more thing, though." Loraine kept her mouth closed hoping for more dish on the looney tunes that stalked me. Taking a long breath, I said, "I got a promotion."

Loraine leapt up and pulled me into a hug. "Oh my goodness! That's great, Erin. I'm so happy for you."

"It's in North Carolina."

I could see Loraine's excitement dissipate. Her chest sunk in as she sat back down and poked her bottom lip out. "You're moving?"

I nodded. "In about two weeks."

"Two weeks! Why so soon?"

"They want someone right now. It's the PR director role I've always dreamt about. Eric recommended me."

Loraine tilted her head to the side and grabbed the side of her face. "Wow, I didn't think he even liked you." We both sighed as we let the awkward pause have its moment. "I'm still happy for you. I wish you didn't have to move, but I understand."

"Well, although my new home will be in North Carolina, I'll still be here a lot with my traveling. I'm not breaking up the band."

"I know, Erin. You deserve this, though."

"Enough about me, tell me about you and Lorenz."

Loraine's glow returned as she slanted her head up to the ceiling. "We're gonna give things another shot. We're gonna date and try it over. I told him that I cheated on him with Tariq that one time. He forgave me. We're moving forward, and I'm elated."

"You should be, Loraine. Women need to be happy with themselves and with a man willing to love us for the sake of loving us."

"I know that's right."

When my phone vibrated three times, I closed my eyes and prayed it wasn't Louis. The first text read, *"I know you don't wanna talk to me, but I got some things to get off my chest."* It was Tariq, a text I knew was coming. *"The timing for what we had was off but it felt right. I been thru a lot of shit, and the last thing I need is a relationship, but I couldn't let you go. And then, my ex-wife tells me the son I claimed as mine ain't mine...being wit' you made me feel better. Then yo' nigga wanna come thru an' fuck shit up. I wasn't in the mood to deal wit' that shit. But I eventually realized that if being with you could make* me feel better after losing my son, then there was more to us than I was willing to admit."

Tariq rationalized his erratic behavior and his destructive household. He was hurting, and I'd brought my mess into the middle of his. Either way, I was at peace with my decision. I couldn't revert back to old ways like a dog that returned to its own vomit. *"I'll wait for you. I gotta let you work shit out with yo' new job, and I'm willin' to wait for this to work. I never gave this a real shot, and I need to know if this is what I think it can be. If I gotta go at yo' pace, wherever you are, I'm willin'. You're right about me puttin' you thru bullshit. But I'll wait 'til there ain't nothing left to wait for."*

I needed a break. I only had two weeks left in Florida, and I wasn't willin' to use that time working things out with Tariq. If he was willin' to wait, he'd be waiting a while. I put my phone in my purse and tried to calm the small piece of me that was doing jumping jacks of excitement about my new life.

"Who was that?" Loraine stared intently, awaiting an answer. "Louis or Tariq?"

Shakin' my head, I leaned back on her couch and smirked. "Nobody important."

ABOUT THE AUTHOR

J. Lovelace is a freelance journalist, editor and self-published author. She earned her undergraduate degree from the University of South Florida with a bachelor's in creative writing and public and organiz~~~~~~~~~ ~~~~~~~~~~~~~. She currently lives in Orlando, FL with ~~~~~~ r's degree i~~